MORE SCORCHING PRAISE FOR AWARD-WINNING

# Emma Holly

### AND HER NOVELS

"Emma Holly brings a level of sensuality to her storytelling
that may shock the uninitiated."
—*Publishers Weekly*

"Emma Holly is a name to look out for."
—Bestselling author Robin Schone

"A deliciously steamy read. This is how erotica must be written!"
—Michele Hauf, author of *Rhiana*

"Titillating, erotic, and fun."
—*The Best Reviews*

"A sensual feast."
—*Midwest Book Review*

"She creates tantalizing tales."
—*Rendezvous*

"A wonderfully passionate read."
—*Escape to Romance*

"Holly pens one hot, hot, hot story."
—*Romantic Times*

"Surprisingly erotic."
—*New York Times* bestselling author Susan Sizemore

*Books by Emma Holly*

# Heat of the Night

EMMA HOLLY

BERKLEY SENSATION, NEW YORK

**THE BERKLEY PUBLISHING GROUP**
**Published by the Penguin Group**
**Penguin Group (USA) Inc.**
**375 Hudson Street, New York, New York 10014, USA**
Penguin Group (Canada), 90 Eglinton Avenue East, Suite 700, Toronto, Ontario M4P 2Y3, Canada
(a division of Pearson Penguin Canada Inc.)
Penguin Books Ltd., 80 Strand, London WC2R 0RL, England
Penguin Group Ireland, 25 St. Stephen's Green, Dublin 2, Ireland (a division of Penguin Books Ltd.)
Penguin Group (Australia), 250 Camberwell Road, Camberwell, Victoria 3124, Australia
(a division of Pearson Australia Group Pty. Ltd.)
Penguin Books India Pvt. Ltd., 11 Community Centre, Panchsheel Park, New Delhi—110 017, India
Penguin Group (NZ), Cnr. Airborne and Rosedale Roads, Albany, Auckland 1310, New Zealand
(a division of Pearson New Zealand Ltd.)
Penguin Books (South Africa) (Pty.) Ltd., 24 Sturdee Avenue, Rosebank, Johannesburg 2196,
South Africa

Penguin Books Ltd., Registered Offices: 80 Strand, London WC2R 0RL, England

HEAT OF THE NIGHT

PRINTING HISTORY
*Hunting Midnight*: Berkley Sensation mass market edition / November 2003
"The Night Owl" from *Hot Blooded*: Berkley Sensation trade paperback edition / September 2005
Berkley Sensation trade paperback omnibus edition / January 2007

Berkley Sensation trade paperback ISBN: 978-0-425-21135-9

An application to register this book for cataloging has been submitted to the Library of Congress.

PRINTED IN THE UNITED STATES OF AMERICA

10  9  8  7  6  5  4  3  2  1

# CONTENTS

# Hunting Midnight

*This book is dedicated to the many
wonderful authors who keep my
love for vampires alive . . .
so to speak.*

# In the Beginning

*Calais, 1370*

NOT a soul saw the pair of immortal beings who hid among the wine casks piled on the quay. A wooden crane, with a chain and winch for offloading cargo, explained the barrels' presence—not that either immortal cared. Known to their own kind as *upyr*, they were beautiful male creatures, white as snow and perfectly formed in each detail: from their long black hair to their graceful limbs to the arrangement of the lashes around their jewel-bright eyes. A hint of red, like garnets glinting in shadow, shone from their locks.

It would have entranced any human who saw it.

So similar was the pair's appearance, they might have been brothers, a coincidence that had drawn Emile and Bastien together many years before. Even their wolf shapes resembled kin. Complementary natures had done the rest; to them, "friends for life" was no empty phrase.

Now there were differences between them. Emile had smudges of dirt on his raiment, in particular on his hose. Bastien was as clean as if he had been polished as well as scrubbed. His eyes mimicked the pale, clear green of a peridot. Despite their lightness, they burned with a flame of determination any priest would have called demonic.

Possible diabolic nature aside, night cloaked the fugitives as mercifully as if they were saints, helped in its task by a thick gray mist from the surrounding marshes. Both darkness and fog were welcome. Though the hour was well advanced, a number of watchmen still strolled the docks. Had their hiding place been discovered, the *upyr* could not have passed as ordinary beings. They were too drained from their long flight to hide their natural glow—dim though that was now.

Bastien, the stronger of the two—though that wasn't saying much—inhaled deeply in an attempt to marshal his flagging power. One of the ships had recently taken on a cargo of spices. In addition to human effluvia and brine, the lapping waves carried the scent of Indian cinnamon. Bastien had never been to India, nor to Spain or even the Low Countries. His branch of the immortal tree was not encouraged to roam. Maybe one day, when this was over, he would make a journey.

He promised himself he would get the chance. Freedom was too sweet a prize to give up.

"You should leave me," Emile said, his eyes a near lifeless brown. To any but his companion, his words would have been too soft to hear. "You could escape more easily alone."

Bastien offered a weary smile. "I succeeded in conveying you all the way from Burgundy, most of it over my shoulder. It would be the height of folly to leave you now."

He turned away before he could see the hopelessness in Emile's face, peering instead at the half-dozen vessels that swayed and creaked on their anchors out in the harbor. The ships were all old-fashioned, single-masted merchant's cogs: English to a one. The English had held Calais for more than a decade now, using it as a staging point for further incursions into France as well as a thriving commercial port. Normally, this would not have mattered to the *upyr*; like most of his kind, Bastien held himself aloof from human conflicts. Tonight, though, he was glad. He wanted an English ship, one that could carry him and his companion far from French soil.

If they failed, Bastien did not think much of their chances. Their enemy would do anything to drag them back. Hugo would have to, to demonstrate to the others what would happen if they rebelled.

"As soon as the docks seem quiet enough," Bastien said, "I shall steal one of those rowboats and take us out to a ship." He rubbed his jaw in regret, his skin smooth and stubble-free. "I wish these cogs were larger. I doubt any hold more than a hundred men. Thankfully, once I have fed a few times, I will be able to hide us with my glamour. God grant the crossing will be short."

"For the crew's sake, if nothing else," said the other with a crooked smile.

Bastien squeezed his wasted shoulder, thinking of the days when Emile had been robust. He wished he dared share his blood, but he would need all his remaining strength for slipping them onboard.

"We will make it," he said, reassuring himself as well. "Mortals sail with compasses these days, and far better channel maps. And there will be rats to feed upon, if preying on people seems too dangerous."

Emile shook his head over all the rules they had broken to get this far. They were not supposed to drink from humans at all, only from the natural quarry of their beast halves. Bastien did not care. He would have broken all the laws there were to keep the other safe.

Eternity was too long to face without a friend.

"We will make it," he repeated. "We will find allies among the English packs. We will petition their king and return with a force so mighty, Hugo will regret ever hearing the word *magic*. We shall cure you, Emile. Never fear."

"But if the English refuse to help . . ."

"They will agree," Bastien said, his fangs lengthening startlingly with his passion. "We will not give them a choice."

# One

*England, the town of Bridesmere, 1370*

"THOU art a sexy bastard," the woman purred, her finger trailing lightly down Ulric's jaw.

He dragged his cock from her body even though he was still hard, still vibrating with the lust his kind could never completely slake. He had spilled, but the lingering excitement kept him long and thick. With hungry eyes, the woman watched him tuck himself into his codpiece. Her cheeks bore spots of red within their English cream.

He had bitten her at the end.

That, as much as anything else, accounted for her enjoyment.

"Yes," he agreed to her accolade, "I am the sexiest bastard you shall ever meet."

They stood in the alley behind a tavern, one of seven in this human town. He had taken the woman against the wall without preliminaries: easy—nay, eager—prey.

To be fair, Ulric was no ordinary seducer. He was a member of the *upyr,* a race of shapeshifting immortal beings who lived by drinking blood. As strong as they were beautiful, they had few vulnerabilities. Most who died did so by their own hand, out of sadness or ennui. The touch of iron was a danger, but far worse was the sun. To his kind the sun was death, a slow, honeyed poison that addled their minds as surely as liquor addled a human's. If they stayed in it long enough, they would burn. At night their powers of attraction were at their height. With the superior force of their minds, they could thrall their victims into their arms, then make them forget they had ever seen them. If they chose, they could use an illusion called "glamour" to assume a human façade.

They were shadows in the mortal world, among but not of the crowd.

The line of *upyr* Ulric belonged to, the children of Auriclus, were forbidden to interact with mortals. His sire would have been shocked to know Ulric was here, much less that he was drinking human blood.

Ulric did not require it, after all. He could take his wolf form and feed as a beast. He had learned, however, in the nights during which he had haunted these winding streets, that human blood was the sweetest dram. For a while at least, it filled his heart with human passions and human joys. It strengthened him as no other creature's could.

Even if it had not, Ulric would not have cared a whit for Auriclus's rules. Not today. Not tomorrow. Not until he understood why the only woman he ever loved, the queen to his king wolf, had chosen a human lover over him. The man Gillian selected did not even have a title. He was a mere second son. Ulric was handsomer. Ulric was better in bed. Ulric could make his pack members quail with a single glare. Ulric had everything Aimery lacked. And still Gillian had left.

She had loved Ulric, but not enough.

It passed beyond understanding. Ulric could not fathom it. In fact, he positively refused to.

Sensing the loss of his attention, the woman was murmuring to him and pawing his chest, obviously greedy for more of the pleasures she could already but half recall. Her hands found the bulge between his thighs, stroking it high and hard. Her touch went no deeper than his skin.

"Leave me," he ordered, pushing her away.

When she stumbled and caught her weight against the wall, he felt a twinge of guilt. It was not her fault their coupling had left him empty. No human could give him what he needed, and no *upyr* could except for Gillian. He was broken, and cruel with it, but this female was not to blame.

"Go home," he said more gently, putting the force of his mind behind the words. "Sleep well and wake easy of mind. You did not meet me tonight. I was simply a sweet daydream."

She blinked at him with glazing eyes, far more susceptible to his thrall than one of his own kind would have been. He was strong in this human world, as powerful as a god. He might have thought that was the lure for Gillian, but she had made her lover her equal. She had made him *upyr*.

Ulric himself could not transform a human. Only the oldest and most powerful *upyr* could do that. When Gillian had discovered the ability, young as she was, that had seemed a betrayal, too. Ulric was supposed to be her protector . . . her superior, in point of fact.

"Go," he ordered the woman before his anger could rise to lash out at her.

She went, halting and reluctant, her slippers dragging in the dirt. Her head turned back over her shoulder, her veil and wimple fallen, her hair like a bird's nest straggling down. Ulric watched her gaze at him with longing, but he did not really see—no more than she had seen him.

One more night, he thought. One more night survived without Gillian. Though he knew his face remained impassive, his chest ached as if the wound were fresh. He wondered if this heartbreak would be immortal, if he would ever feel whole again. The prospect seemed intolerable, but he decided to wait and see.

"BASTARDS," said Henry Buxton. "Think they are too high and mighty to marry a son of theirs to a girl of mine."

Juliana Buxton, his daughter, tucked a blanket around him in his chair. She had already stoked the fire, just enough, and set the leather flagon next to the hearth.

Her father seldom drank, but when he did it made him fractious. He could mutter for hours about every slight anyone had ever done him. This particular rant was an old one, involving the refusal of Edmund Fitz Clare, the local baron, to affiance his eldest son to her.

"I have more money than the lot of them put together," her father said, jabbing his thumb at his sunken chest. "Was his wife's idea to turn the offer down. Too proud by far, that Claris. *She* had merchants in her family. I know for a fact her grandfather was a brigand. Stole a silver chamber pot once, from a big castle in France. Said every time he pissed in it he felt like a king."

He chuckled at this, darkly, his head pulled into the quilted velvet of his robe. Henry Buxton was a cloth merchant, and thus the material was very fine. Nonetheless, he resembled a broody owl with his heavy eyes and his feathery white hair. He was old, Juliana realized, though she could not remember him young. Her mother, God rest her soul, had been a child compared to him.

Squeezed by sudden sympathy, she knelt by his chair and pressed her cheek to his knee. Whatever his faults, he had loved Juliana's mother, and he missed her now that she was gone.

Touched by the gesture, her father's long, gnarled fingers smoothed her hair. "Look at you," he said with teary fondness. "My Juliana. Beautiful and good. Those Fitz Clares would have been blessed to have you."

Tenderness forgotten at the reminder of the slight, his hand clenched over her winding braid.

Carefully, Juliana disentangled it. "It matters not," she said, hoping to calm him. "I did not want to marry Thomas Fitz Clare."

It would have been ridiculous, for one thing. The boy was just fifteen.

"I should think not," her father huffed, "not when I have found a far better mate for my clever dove."

Though Juliana closed her eyes, she could not shut out the words. His ambitions thwarted for a noble match, her father had promised her to an associate, a rich London tradesman by the name of Gideon Drake. His financial empire—for naught else could she call it—was ten times the size of Henry Buxton's. Juliana had met Drake once and judged him no monster, only old and set in his ways—ways that were far more hidebound than her sire's.

Gideon Drake would make a trophy of her. She had seen that the moment his eyes drifted down her twenty-two-year-old curves. A smile of satisfaction had curled his lips. Her beauty pleased him. Her intelligence he deigned to ignore. Unlike her father, he had more assistants than he could use. She could easily foresee her future in his home, restricted to a suite of luxurious private rooms, her every need seen to by silent staff, her person trotted out now and then for admiring guests.

*My bride, Juliana,* Drake would say in his cool and mocking voice. *Is she not a model of wifely grace?*

Juliana doubted she would rebel once she was married. She would be who she was to her father, dutiful and quiet, without the warmth of affection to ease the burden of doing what she ought, without the sense that she had any purpose beyond her looks. A child to love was the best reward for which she could hope. Drake had two grown sons by a previous wife, and Juliana had met them as well.

Milton and Milo were . . . well, peculiar was the kindest word she could use, with pale, slightly bulging eyes and impassive faces. Drake might be cold, but his sons regarded her as if she were a bug. Certainly, no joy would come to her life from them. If Gideon Drake were capable of begetting other sons with her, she suspected the cocoon that swaddled her would become a prison.

She would be the proof that her husband was virile yet.

Admittedly, this was not the worst fate a woman could endure.

She would want for nothing, and her future would be secure. Juliana believed she was strong enough to fulfill her obligations. She merely wished the thought of it did not make her feel as if she were choking on her own heart.

Her father was so gleeful about the match he had not complained about having to find a servant to take her place. The contracts had been drawn up, and the betrothal was days away. Once formal vows were exchanged in front of a priest, backing out would be awkward, to say the least.

She had one choice, really, if she wished to escape the destiny her father had planned. She had to run away—before she put on Drake's ring. No matter that she dreaded leaving, not to mention her father's hurt, she could not delay any longer.

"I must go out," she said from the door of their dim, sparsely furnished parlor.

Startled, her father turned his eyes to the window, to the leaded glass and the faint pink light. "It is dark."

"Not quite, Father." Her voice was gentleness itself. "I want to see if the shoemaker has mended your favorite boots."

Though her father could buy new ones, he liked the old for their well-worn ease. Juliana knew she had him when he stretched his stockinged toes against the dark-brown tiles. "You will keep to the high street?"

"Yes, Father."

"No dilly-dallying at the church or old Tom the Harper's?"

"No, Father. I shall conduct my business directly."

"Well," he said, hemming a little, "take your cloak. It is cold out."

It was nearly summer, comfortably mild, but her father could not feel the warmth anymore.

"I must leave," she said, "else the light will be gone."

He waved her on, then began to nod off. To her relief, he did not suggest she take a servant. He would sleep soon over his wine. It might be hours before he noticed she had not returned.

Into the covered basket she used for shopping, she tucked her folded cloak, a sack of coin she had been saving from the household accounts by dickering over every penny, a loaf of bread, and a hunk of cheese wrapped in cloth. A good, sharp knife seemed a wise addition.

After a brief debate over frivolity, she added her prized possession: a volume of stories she had been collecting since she was a girl. They ranged from tales of high adventure in the world of knights to those of simple folk. Juliana had copied every one onto the parchment pages in her own crisp hand. The earlier ones included pictures her mother had drawn before her death five years before. Monsters, for the most part. Her dam had dearly loved tales of terror. Smiling, Juliana caressed the tooled leather binding, then snapped the basket lid shut.

Keenly aware that she might be doing this for the final time, she descended the narrow stairs, stepped over the threshold, and shut the door.

Their house rose four tall stories, with a shop on the lowest level and sturdy half-timbered eaves that overhung the street. She called a greeting to her father's apprentice, who was preparing to close for the night. As the shutters rattled together, top and bottom, she drew her first deep breath. Within her plain blue gown, her shoulders relaxed.

Juliana did not mind being good. There was a kind of contentment in knowing precisely what was expected, in knowing she was able to do her duty well. But she also needed moments like this, incandescent bubbles in the regimen of her life. Tonight she was neither daughter nor future bride, just a woman whose thoughts and feelings were her own.

Turning from her home with the faintest of palpitations, she headed for Bridesmere's high street. Her final promise she would keep. After that, she would guide her life for herself.

---

"YOU have taken leave of your senses," Bridesmere's single tanner sputtered to Juliana.

Behind her tall and sweating form, two muscular females scraped hair from a pair of skins that were draped on a wooden beam. The tannery yard emitted an unearthly reek, a product of the concoctions in which the hides were cured. Many of the women—because all who labored for Mistress Melisent were of that sex—had tied linen cloths across their noses and mouths.

If Juliana had been employed here, she would have covered her eyes as well. Blinking against the heavy fumes, she tried to look strong and stout.

Mistress Melisent's own travails had taught her to value stoutness. Her husband had beat her daily when he was alive, but now that he was dead and she had taken control of his business, she was acclaimed the stubbornest woman in town.

"I assure you, Mistress Melisent," Juliana said, "I am in full possession of my wits. Your tannery transports leather all over this part of England. No one would think of searching your carts for hidden passengers."

"That is hardly the point. What would you do if I helped you run away? How would you live?"

"I could work in the fields or as a laundress. I have a skill for it, you know. No one's linen is as white as mine. If I am careful, I will have money enough to open a shop."

The tanner snorted. "If you had asked me for a position, I might have agreed, even if you are a scrawny piece of work. But you will never survive on your own."

"I will," Juliana insisted. "I am not afraid of hardship, only of being trapped."

Mistress Melisent sighed. "I almost believe you, but I would not like your 'hardship' to be on my hands. The men of this town rail at me enough as it is. Your father would have me in the pillory if you came to grief."

"He need never know!"

"I cannot help you," said Mistress Melisent, going back to stirring her steaming vat with a long, wood pole. "Go home, Juliana. Live the life you were born to."

It was a dismissal Juliana lacked the nerve to ignore, despite the fact that Mistress Melisent was her only remaining hope. Out of caution, she had compiled a limited list of prospects to approach: people who, while fond of her, were not overly indebted to her father. Mistress Melisent had been the last of the three. The first two had refused her out of hand, no matter what she offered to pay. They did this not from fear of her father, but because they felt too much care for her. Incapable of believing she could succeed, they did not want to see her hurt.

She had thought it to her advantage that most of Bridesmere liked her. Plainly, it was not.

She contemplated accepting the tanner's lukewarm offer of a job. Sadly, if she remained within her father's reach, he would be certain to drag her home. Worse, she would have destroyed his trust. Once his faith was squandered, Henry Buxton did not give it again. Chances were, neither would Juliana's intended. She would end up more a prisoner than she was now.

She plodded from the tannery, scarcely noticing where she went. She should have been heading home in the hope that she could slip inside before her father woke. She should have been praying no one she had spoken to tonight would give him word of what she had done. While she had put no gossips on her list, prayers like that seemed unlikely to be answered. Clearly, she could have used more practice at rebellion. If only she had tried subterfuge, rather than seeking aid . . .

I have cast the die already, she thought. It is too late to turn back.

Overwhelmed by the realization, she stopped dead in the street and dropped her basket. She stared at the patterns in the dirt, cloven hoofmarks from a herd of pigs who had been driven back to their stable after a day of foraging. She might never see sights like this again. She might be locked in her room for good.

She laughed at the idea of getting misty-eyed over pig-prints, then covered her face and sobbed.

She allowed herself one tearing rasp. When it was done, she lowered her hands to fist them at her sides. She had tried and she had failed, but she would live with whatever consequences came. She was Juliana Buxton. If nothing else, she had fortitude.

Retrieving her belongings, she started walking toward the light and noise of the Dancing Cat. Maybe she would find someone she knew at the tavern. Maybe they would see her home. Shaky as she was, she would not have minded the company.

This decided, she pulled herself from her thoughts.

She saw a minstrel had gathered a group of watchers outside the tavern, most of them female. The clink of their coins as they tossed them caught her ear. A pile of them lay at the minstrel's feet.

"No stinting now," he said in a teasing voice. "It will take more than a few farthings to prime my pipes."

Juliana suspected something other than his pipes had drawn this crowd. He was taller than average, by at least half a head, and his rich gold hair hung to his shoulders in a shining mane. From his jaunty chaperon to his pointed shoes, he was dressed in crimson velvet, product no doubt of the famous *Arte*—or guilds—of Tuscany. Even more eye-catching, his tunic was scarcely long enough to obscure his loins. From the well-packed appearance of his codpiece, he had a great deal to hide.

"I would be happy to prime your pipe," offered one of the women, no doubt as sharp-eyed as Juliana. "I would not even demand you sing!"

Her companions laughed bawdily, while Juliana restricted herself to a smile. Their enthusiasm might be unseemly, but the minstrel was worth admiring—and not merely for the obvious. The belt that cinched his tunic's pleats showed off a narrow waist. His thighs were solid, and his calves quite nicely curved. He held no instrument to accompany his song, but his hands were music in and of themselves. White as snow and seemingly as light, their tapered fingers held a fascination Juliana could not explain.

"Very well," he said, spreading them in surrender. "I shall let you have me cheaply just this once."

From the first note he uttered she was lost.

To call his voice a pleasant tenor was to be cruel. Each note was clear but mysteriously complex, hinting at barely heard harmonies, like a howl forced to obey the laws of time and tune. Her hair stood up as if her skin were being brushed all over by butterflies. What he sang did not matter: some romantic nonsense such as high-born ladies liked to hear. It was the sound itself that nailed her to the earth with bliss. She closed her eyes and let his voice roll through her, the troubles of the evening melting away.

So powerful was the effect, she found herself swaying. When she opened her eyes, she was actually walking toward the man. To her surprise, the street was empty but for her and him. She had not heard the other women leave.

Even more surprisingly, he was staring directly at her. His gaze was gold and fiery, as penetrating as his voice. A tingle centered between her legs. She would have been embarrassed except that what was happening seemed like a dream. She felt tugged by the intensity of his expression, chosen for something she could not name.

What are you doing? she demanded of herself. You do not know this stranger.

Her feet did not listen. She came to a halt a foot away from him. He smelled delicious, like a wild thing from the woods. When she inhaled a second time, he smiled at her, a lazy upcurve of perfect lips. Amazingly, she had not noticed when his singing stopped.

"You need a player," she blurted out before she could guard her tongue. "A voice like yours deserves accompaniment."

"Does it?" His hand was in her hair, pulling the pins from her braid and spreading it across her shoulders. A wave of heat coursed through her limbs.

"Yes," she gasped, striving not to tremble. "I play the harp, as it happens, passably well. If you wished, I could come with you when you leave town."

Mistress Melisent was right, she thought, astonished by her own boldness. Juliana must have gone mad. On the other hand, what did she have to lose? Everyone else had refused her. And she still had her knife if it came to that.

The stranger continued to smile at her like a teacher humoring a child. His face was so beautiful it seemed unreal. Flawless as a pearl, his skin glowed in the darkness, even brighter than the torches of the Dancing Cat. His lashes looked as if a jeweler had attached them to the lids—pure gold spread out in multi-layered fans.

He is alone, she thought out of the blue. Magnificent though he was, he had been abandoned.

She swayed again, dizzy, knowing her musings made little sense. The man caught her elbows with cool, firm hands.

"Why not come with me now?" he said. "I would adore your accompaniment."

She did not agree so much as not know how to resist. He half-carried, half-led her to a nearby alley, past people who suddenly seemed to find them invisible. The shadows of the buildings covered everything but his face.

She gasped as his body crowded hers into the wall. She was small and helpless, trapped beyond breaking free. Her basket, and the knife she had tucked inside, fell with a thunk from her nerveless fingers. She could not remember why she should care. Her heart beat like a cornered rabbit, but fear was not what drove it.

*Oh, yes,* said something she had not known she had inside her. *Oh, yes, keep me right here.*

The bulge of his codpiece pressed her mound as fiercely as if her desires had instructed it where to go.

"Yes," she might have whispered out loud. "Yes, please, keep doing that."

He rolled the hardness against her, his head dropping to her neck. Slowly, savoringly, he dragged his tongue up one tendon to her ear. She would not have thought this could arouse her, but it did. Him, as well, apparently. His breathing came shallower.

"What are you doing?" she forced herself to ask.

"I am getting ready to swive you," he said, "unless you have some objection."

He said this as if he knew she would not, as if seducing a perfect stranger were the most natural thing in the world. She felt his shaft pulse eagerly against her mound.

"I—" she said, surprised it was so difficult to turn him down.

"You?" he teasingly responded.

Before she could speak, he covered her mouth with his.

Oh, that kiss—! His lips were silk, his arms a wonderful pressure around her back. They tightened the moment she wished they would and lifted her off the ground. Juliana was not such a goose that she had not been wooed a time or two, but this kiss was a different beast, not merely skilled but enchanting. Her head spun with pleasure as she kissed him back, clutching his shoulders and opening to his forays.

He drew on her as if she were a piece of honeyed fruit.

"Like that, do you?" he chuckled against her lips, but *like* was not the word. This was what she had been missing all her life, this marvelous freedom.

When he kissed her again, his tongue stabbed inside. His aggression affected her even more strongly than being pressed to the wall, making her quiver and go weak. She could not hold back a moan, but he seemed to like the reaction. One of his hands was lifting her skirt and chemise, freeing her legs to move. She raised her thighs to his narrow hips without thinking twice. The warm spring air swirled around her bareness. Behind the cloth of his codpiece, against her most private parts, his erection throbbed.

"The people from the tavern . . ." she murmured, still hearing them in the distance.

He kissed her hard enough to bruise. "They cannot hear," he said. "And they cannot see. In all the world, you and I are alone."

She did not know why she believed him. What he said made no sense. But when his hand slipped between them to free his member, she could not protest. Completely unashamed, he stroked it leisurely with his fist.

*For you,* his gesture seemed to say. *Look at what I have for you.*

With each manipulation, his knuckles brushed her woman's hair. She gasped for air and he let go, using the selfsame hand to cup her quim. His prick pressed her belly beside his forearm. He had stretched even more with his own caress. Liquid heat flooded her body. She tried to tighten the place it filled, but the moisture trickled onto his palm.

"You need this," he growled against her mouth. "You cannot live without it."

Surprise widened her eyes. "You are right," she said. "I feel as if I shall die unless you take me soon."

He pulled back to peer at her. "I almost believe you know what you are saying."

She reached for his mouth and kissed him of her own free will. The hand that supported her bottom clenched painfully.

"Now," he said. "No more waiting."

He shifted her until her folds met his thrusting hardness. The tip of his penis was broad and smooth. For one moment, as he eased it inward, its skin felt cool. A heartbeat later, it blazed.

*No pain,* said a voice that seemed to come from within her head. *It is easy for you to take me.*

He pushed, determined, steady. The sense of being stretched would have alarmed her had she not been eager to have him inside. With a brief and painless flash of heat, her barrier rent.

He swore, at himself perhaps, then murmured praise: how tight she was, how wonderfully warm and wet, how he loved the feel of her around him. Reluctant to disappoint him, Juliana did her best to hold on.

He seemed immense as he worked his shaft incrementally in and out, reaching a little deeper with each effort. The push and pull was delicious, tugging every inch of her sexual flesh. She widened her hips and received a grunt of thanks. His hair spilled over her arms where they twined behind his neck. Unable to resist, she ran her fingers through its silken thickness, her head falling helplessly back.

"Do not tempt me," he panted against her throat. "I am close enough to losing control."

She neither knew nor cared what he meant. With a final shove, he achieved full penetration, his weapon contained but not conquered.

"Hold tight," he warned. "I am about to give you the ride of your life."

She would have laughed, but he did not lie. Nothing she had ever done for herself prepared her for this. The first slamming thrust made her cry out with excitement, impossible to think of as anything but an assault—on her body, on her nerves, on her understanding of what coupling was supposed to be. And this was only the beginning. Pulling her arms from behind his neck, he trapped them against the wall and stretched them out by the wrist. The stone was hard, but not as hard as his fingers. His body coiled, drew out, and then he began to drive in a swift and steady rhythm.

"Open to me," he demanded. "Take it all."

She was taking it all, every inch of his length and girth. She shook like she had a fever. She groaned like she wanted more.

"You need this," he rasped, sweat dripping down his beautiful face. "You were born to be ravished."

She moaned because her mouth would not work well enough to say yes. Waves of red-hot sensation spread out from her pummeled loins. The pleasure suffused her thighs, her breasts, the tips of her tingling fingers. She was almost there, almost over the edge.

As if he knew, he switched angles, pounding some unsuspected sweet spot. One hand released her wrist to grip her hip, to position her just so, to hold her where he could slide his bulbous tip against that aching place.

"Yes," he said, "I can feel how much you want it."

She gasped for air, the ecstasy so intense it approached pain.

Desperate to touch him, she wrapped her free hand behind his neck. He was trembling, tight in every muscle. She could feel him shake even as he drove inside her with all his might.

"Come," he snarled in her ear, his lips pulled back, his teeth gleaming strangely sharp. "Die . . . with . . . me."

When he sucked in a breath of shock, she knew his crisis was upon him. She had a moment to feel him drive to his deepest limit and then her body convulsed, a head-to-toe squeeze of genuinely startling bliss. Her flesh could barely comprehend such pleasure. It sparked and flared like pinecones thrown in a fire.

A glow followed the conflagration, wonderfully warm and sweet. The sigh she released seemed to belong to a different woman.

But she was a different woman. Maid no more, she had seen the carnal world.

She smiled into the stranger's hair. She had both arms wrapped around him—and both legs. Despite their mutual accomplishment of delight, his hold on her was tight. Barely diminished, his member remained inside her. Occasionally it jerked, small, unpredictable surges that reminded her just how much she had enjoyed its more energetic activity.

At the memory, a fresh rush of moisture slid from inside her.

Feeling it, he ground himself a little closer. "I must get you somewhere more private. I cannot swive you like this and keep up my glamour."

How lovely, she thought, indifferent to the mystery of his words. He was going to ravish her again.

# Two

ULRIC had just begun to sing when he noticed the woman watching dumbstruck from behind the crowd. Women often did this, but rarely without him first turning his attention to them. Left to themselves, they were circumspect.

She was pretty enough to catch his jaded eye: slim, a bit above average height, with a pair of breasts that cried out to be cupped—more than a handful but not by much. A braid of perfectly ordinary brown hair was coiled up neatly and pinned to her head. Her gown, while plain, seemed to fit her better than the others'. Or perhaps she stood inside it differently. With her shoulders straight and her head erect, she seemed capable and unafraid. He suspected she had been born in Bridesmere and knew her surroundings well. The roses in her cheeks and the sweetness of her scent spoke of good health.

She looked a doughty daughter of England, with a roof over her head and an unshaken faith in her next meal—same as he had seen a hundred times before.

Only her eyes told a different story. Huge and sable dark, they held the emotions the rest of her hid. Vulnerability. Imagination.

A hunger for more from life than Fate seemed likely to offer. Something in those eyes set Ulric's heart beating harder in his chest. He was not the strongest reader of minds. Emotions he could sense, but seldom specific thoughts. He was more adept at putting thoughts *into* other people's heads.

He had not, however, put that lust for experience into hers.

Intrigued, he dispersed the crowd and called her to him. She obeyed the silent order without resistance, seeming as drawn by his voice as by his power. When she spoke, he barely listened to what she said, something about playing the harp and wanting to leave town. Her words could not have mattered less. What mattered was that she interested him more than anything had since Gillian left, more than blood, more than rest, certainly more than the woman he had coupled with earlier.

He did not know why this should be, nor did he care. He wanted her, and he would have her without delay.

When she kissed him, apparently of her own volition, he was surprised—not because no woman would wish to, but because he had thought her more deeply under his thrall.

Whatever the cause for her initiative, the pleasure of touching her, of knowing he would have her frayed his concentration. He barely managed to hide the two of them with his glamour as he took her that first time.

Her maiden state surprised him; she had not seemed that young. It pleased him, too, though he could not have said why. That it did he could not doubt. His climax was all-consuming, as if for one mindless moment he knew the pleasure of completely being his wolf. He wanted, he took, he got—until he should have been incapable of wanting more.

But he desired her again as soon as it ended. More kisses. More sighs. More gentle touches from her human hands.

Maybe, he thought, I should seek a virgin every time.

"I must get you somewhere more private," he said half to himself. "I cannot swive you like this and keep up my glamour."

Completely pliant, she put her head on his shoulder. He carried her, her little basket over his elbow, into the stable for a hostelry. Her hair was a cape of silk hanging down his back. Up the wooden ladder, he hefted her to the loft. Then, behind a wall of bundled hay, he laid her down.

She smiled up at him from the blanket of his crimson cloak, sprawled but somehow still innocent. Her hand reached out to caress the side of his knee. "Thank you for bringing my things. They might not have been safe left in the alley."

He set the basket down. He had picked it up without thinking. He hoped she did not interpret this as implying he would take her away from Bridesmere. He vaguely recalled her asking him to do that. Judging it best not to speak, he knelt beside her and cupped her gown against her mound.

He had held back with her earlier, as he had learned to do with human women. All the same, he knew he had been rough.

"Are you sore?" he asked.

"Yes," she answered, then smiled quite blindingly. "I loved it: the feel of you inside me, the way you went so fast and hard I could barely move."

She seemed clearheaded, virtually unthralled apart from the lessening of inhibitions. Hardening furiously at her words, Ulric cleared his throat. His body was eager for hers again.

With an eye toward seeing if she was, too, he tightened his hold until the fine wool of her gown pushed between her folds. She was damp there, and she dampened more as he massaged her, despite the layer of linen beneath her gown. Her hips squirmed up at him in a small, involuntary motion. When he looked at her face, her teeth had caught her lower lip, red now from his kisses. At the sight, his fangs shot out against his will. He wanted to put his teeth where hers were; he craved it as if he were starved.

He was not certain what held him back. Maybe fear of losing what control he had, or perhaps of liking her taste too much. It was rare to kill a human simply by feeding. His kind required no more blood than a healthy mortal could spare. On the other hand, he did not want this woman to be his first mishap.

He knew it was possible. Nim Wei, his sire's rival, had few rules for her children beyond not getting caught. Before Ulric had agreed to oversee the packs, he had met a few of her broods. They cared even less for humans than he did, less than his wolf did for a rabbit. His wolf never made the rabbit fall in love.

Uncomfortable with his thoughts, he rubbed his thumb along her labia. "I could kiss you here," he offered. "It might help to ease your soreness."

She pushed up at him, this time deliberately. "Is that what you really want?"

He thought of her secret parts, of how hot they would be and how tender against his skin. All *upyr* had some ability to heal injuries in human beings. Ulric had no doubt he could soothe hers. But then her hand slid up his thigh to his tarse, exploring it with a boldness he did not expect.

"Is that what you really want?" she repeated.

Something flickered through him that felt like fear. Women never asked him this. They did not have to. What he wanted, he took. Rather than answer, he bent to drag his cheek along her breast.

"Shall I guess?" she whispered. "Is that what I am supposed to do?"

He groaned as her fingers worked inside his codpiece to find bare skin. The touch of mortal hands, so warm compared to their own, was especially pleasurable to *upyr,* a magic as potent as a thrall. Her fingers skated up his length, delicate yet strong. His swollen rim fit the curve formed by her palm and thumb. She looked at what she held, then up at him, wonder clear in her eyes. When her fingers tightened around him, his last scrap of consideration fled.

"I want you," he growled, crawling over her and caging her in his arms.

Her breath caught with excitement. She pulled up her skirt and urged him in.

The first sultry, slippery contact set his instincts free. He took her as wildly as before, plunging instantly to the hilt, completely selfish in his quest for satisfaction. He was aware that she was with him, and grateful for it, though he was not certain he could have stopped. He lost count of her orgasmic cries, knowing only that every peak had him shuddering with shared echoes.

"How do you do that?" she asked after a particularly pleasant spasm, breathing hard and stroking his face. Beneath his thrusts, her body gave with delicious ease, a cushion fit for a king.

"How do I pleasure you?" he asked, "or how do I keep wanting more?"

"How do you know exactly what I want?"

He could only answer her with a kiss. He had not known what she wanted. He had been taking what he desired. That she wanted it as well was simply luck.

Fisting his hands in her hair, he began to stroke for a final peak, a sweet to top what had been a sensual feast. His thrusts were slower but still deep. *Upyr* nerves were more sensitive than humans' and recovered almost immediately from surfeit. Now her every fold and quiver registered against his shaft. If this had been their first coupling, he might have embarrassed himself by finishing too fast. Instead, he relaxed into his pleasure, relishing the dreamy sensation of peace.

His urgency was sated. He could take his time.

When the woman stretched her back and hummed, he knew she felt it, too.

"Last one," he warned softly.

"You need not rush," she answered back.

He laughed, delighted with her understanding, as euphoric as if he were drunk. The gods had been smiling on him tonight. This whole encounter had been an unexpected gift.

The woman's scent, warmer now and rich, mingled with that of the hay and the horses stamping in their stalls below. The wolf in him enjoyed all the smells immensely. The man in him sent his senses out to survey the sleeping town. Their dreams were quiet, even complacent. The people of Bridesmere did not care that they were not lords, or that their lives were the merest blink. Their little dramas were more than big enough for them.

For once, that did not annoy him.

Instead, he was endeared. These people, these humans, lived with a courage they were unaware they had. They struggled for achievement, knowing it would not last. Ulric could almost understand why Gillian admired them.

Not that he wanted to think of her. He felt too good, too comfortable in his skin. He smiled at the woman and she smiled back, her eyes shining in his glow like stars. In his enthusiasm for coupling with her, he had dropped his glamour. But what matter? He could thrall her later. She would forget everything. For now, she had caught his rhythm and was lifting her hips in perfect synchrony with his thrusts, her enchanting human hands smoothing lazily along his back. When she cupped the rounds of his buttocks, her grip made his penis jolt.

Amazingly, he was almost too tired to spend. She sent him over with a broken sigh.

"Oh," she said, pulsing around him. "Oh, that feels so sweet."

Savoring the last burst of pleasure, Ulric felt almost fond as he gazed at her love-flushed face. The woman looked as relaxed as he. Her lashes fanned against her cheeks and her breasts gently rose and fell in her gown. With a start, he realized she was asleep. She had dozed off with him still inside her.

Taken aback but also amused, he rolled onto his back and pulled her atop him, wrapping them both in the half of his cloak that they were not lying on. He could do with a nap himself, a short one, with plenty of time to slip away before she woke.

Yawning hugely, he closed his eyes and gave in.

It did not occur to him to check if the hayloft had a window.

Even if it had, he might not have bothered. Ulric had never, in all his life, failed to secure himself for the dawn.

⎯⎯⎯⎯⎯⎯

LYING on her back in perfect comfort, Juliana stretched beneath the soft velvet cloak, curling her toes and cracking her spine. The bed of hay rustled at her movements, crisp and fragrant in the morning warmth. Her body felt wonderful, every ache mysteriously turned pleasurable. Best of all, she was free. No fires to rekindle. No breakfast to prepare. No floors to sweep or linens to wash. All because the stranger had agreed to take her away.

The stranger. Her smile curled deeper into her cheeks. Obviously, traveling with him would have benefits.

She opened her eyes a slit to check the height of the sun. Alive with dust, beams shot through the chinks in the stable walls, as well as through the single window near the peaking roof. The workers in this hostelry must be lazy. Well past dawn, she heard no grooms moving below.

She did hear a long, weak moan. To her confusion, the stranger lay on his face a short distance away, as if he had been trying to crawl somewhere but had not made it. His hands, which moved feebly in the hay, were marked by angry welts. His beautiful golden hair, spilled across his heaving back, seemed to be issuing a wisp of smoke.

Had someone attacked him? Was he hurt? Juliana rushed to him, looking for the source of whatever had burned his hands. As she reached him, a tiny flame sprang to life in his hair.

"Dark," he pleaded weakly as she beat it out. "Drag me into the dark."

Juliana's mind instantly shut out everything but action. Grabbing the stranger beneath his arms and digging in with her heels, she dragged his heavy body into a cul de sac of bales. He was able to sit up then, but he lifted his hand to shield his face from a ray of sun. As he did, his palm turned pink. Juliana ran back for his cloak, tossing it over the hay bales to form a tent. The door she blocked with her body.

Then she let herself think.

She knew what he was. The knowledge snapped into place like one of the counters on her father's abacus. Merchants and their employees journeyed around the world. Along with silk and spices, they brought back tales, some witnessed for themselves, others merely gossip, and many very strange indeed. Juliana had heard them all as she played hostess to her father's friends. This tale would have been too strange to credit had she not seen it for herself, had she not experienced the stranger's thrall. No wonder she had acceded to his demands. He was *upyr,* an impossibly handsome, impossibly powerful drinker of blood.

Oh, how mortifying it was! Everything considered, she supposed she could live without her maidenhead. Drake would have expected her to possess it, but the chance that she would end up with another man of his station seemed remote. What troubled her were the things she had said and done . . . Why, she practically begged this creature to bed her. In fact, if you put a fine enough point on it, she had.

Her cheeks flamed hot as coal beneath her hands. Yes, she distinctly remembered urging him on.

"You are *upyr,*" she accused, furious with herself for having been gulled. "One of those French monsters."

"French!" His laugh was hoarse. "No doubt in France they claim we are English."

"Fine. You are not French. You are still a monster."

"You did not think I was a monster last night."

Juliana ignored the reminder. "I suppose you never had any intention of helping me run away."

"No," he admitted without remorse. "You convinced yourself I had promised."

Juliana ground her teeth. Because of him, she had delayed her departure beyond any chance of success. By now her father had surely raised the alarm. Soon every soul in Bridesmere would join the search. She did not ride well enough to steal a horse, even if she had been willing to turn to crime. Certainly, no townsman in his right mind would let her buy one.

It was hopeless. She had no choice but to throw herself on her father's mercy.

But how could she bear to do that when she had tasted how sweet freedom could be? When turning back meant living under the cold, old thumb of Gideon Drake?

"Now, now," crooned the *upyr*. "What could be so bad that you believe you must run away?"

"Would *you* want to live in a cage?"

When he flinched, she felt a flash of satisfaction that she could make him react. How could he understand what it was to live without what you truly wanted, to not even dare admit to yourself what that was? She felt a monster herself in her frustration, wanting to roar to the heavens in impotent rage.

Then, as if it had been in her mind all along, the idea came. She was not powerless. She had something to bargain with. While she might be biddable at home, if anyone knew how to ruthlessly press an advantage, it was the daughter of Henry Buxton. She must think of this as no different than haggling over a roast.

Girding herself, she crossed her arms beneath her breasts. "I will expose you," she said, "if you do not agree to help. One moment in the sun and everyone will believe. What is more, I shall tell the townspeople you abducted me and that is why I did not go home."

The *upyr* gaped at her. "You would not dare."

"But I would."

To prove it, she stepped aside from the door to his makeshift shelter. His breath hissed through his teeth as a beam of light struck the side of his face. Juliana felt sick to watch the burn that was there begin to blister. Nonetheless, she held her ground.

"All right," the *upyr* surrendered, fruitlessly shrinking back. "I will help you."

"I want you to make me what you are," she added. "I want to have your powers."

The demand astounded her even as she spoke it, though it made a kind of sense. Whatever skills she might have to sell, as a woman alone she was vulnerable. Only with an *upyr*'s strength could she be positive of thriving. The need to drink blood did not appeal, but she had faced unpleasant necessities in the past.

If her stomach clenched with anxiety, that was because she had no experience in making decisions of this scope. She had never had the liberty before. But better to bite someone than to live with Gideon Drake and his fish-eyed sons.

Assuming, of course, that she was not shoved off in disgrace on someone worse.

"You know," said the *upyr* as he tried to pull his tunic over his face, "most people run from monsters. They do not attempt blackmail."

"You are the one who is about to go up in smoke."

"I take your point. Could you—?" As hunched as he could get, he gestured toward the entering light. "I will agree to escort you to safety."

"That is not all I asked."

"And I will agree to see that you share my powers if you still want them by summer's end."

Juliana wished her response to this delay did not include so much relief. She would have preferred to trod her path with unswerving courage. That aside, his suggestion seemed reasonable. Being a monster was not a choice one should rush.

"Done," she said and stepped in front of the sun. Exhilaration swept her from scalp to boot. Unswerving or not, she had outbargained a powerful immortal being. Surely that bode well for her destiny.

"Glad to have made you happy," said the *upyr,* noting her bounce. "Do you think you could stack a few more hay bales across that door?"

"Your word is good?" she asked, suddenly unsure.

The *upyr* sighed. "Yes. Sadly. Monster though I am, my word is good."

Elated once more, Juliana hurried to find the necessary bales. She heaved the last one into place with an undeniably common grunt.

"You are lucky I am strong," she panted, plunking down to sit beside him.

"I assure you, I feel positively blessed."

Pricked by his sarcasm, Juliana bit the side of her thumb. "I am sorry I had to threaten you."

He snorted. "That 'had to' undercuts your apology just a bit."

"My father wanted me to marry an old man. I saw no other way to escape."

"You could not have told your father you did not like his choice?"

"No," she said. "He loves me, but he believes he always knows what is best. He would not have heard."

The *upyr* held her eyes as if measuring hers for sureness. Being looked at that way felt strange, as if she were a person whose judgment might be worthwhile.

After a moment, he blew out a breath. "Ah, well. No doubt, in your shoes, I would have done the same." She could barely see him in the dimness, but she heard him shift on the straw. "If we are to travel together, I suppose I should know your name."

Juliana laughed, the outrageousness of their situation striking her all at once. "My name is Juliana," she said, "and I am very pleased to make your acquaintance."

---

HE winced at the similarity of the names. Gillian. Juliana. But it did not matter. This woman was nothing like the woman he loved. In any event, he doubted he would have her on his hands for long. As soon as she saw what *upyr* life entailed, this pampered town girl would beg him to let her go.

He would never have to admit he lacked the power to make her *upyr*.

"My name is Ulric," he said. With no room to bow, he settled for inclining his head. "It means 'wolf king.' I am a shapechanger."

"A shapechanger?"

"The wolf is my animal. Because I took one as my familiar, his soul exists within my own. If I wish, I can assume his form. But I am not surprised you have not heard of my kind. Shapechangers are different from the line of *upyr* who most often cross paths with humans. We live apart from the mortal realm."

She took this in, turning on her hip to face him. "Do you look like a real wolf when you change, or are you in between beast and man?"

"I resemble a wolf—a very large, very dangerous wolf."

"Good," she said.

Amusement lifted his brows. This woman was the most audacious mortal he had ever met. "Good?"

"I meant no offense . . . Ulric, but the other option sounds rather—"

Exhaustion overwhelmed him without warning. His head nodded down before she finished, bumping her shoulder as it fell.

"Oh!" she exclaimed as he jerked back. "You are weary. You should sleep."

The concern in her voice was strangely touching, but he knew better than to succumb. "I need to keep my glamour in place, to ensure our hiding place is not discovered."

Juliana glanced upward. "I was thinking your cloak is bright enough to call attention, but I can slip out, get my basket, and put my own up there instead. Mine is gray. I can scatter some hay atop it like a hunter's blind."

Before he could stop her, she put her words into action. Such was his fatigue that she woke him again when she returned. He had not even noticed her make the change.

"You rest," she said firmly. "I will keep watch and alert you if anyone approaches."

"You need sleep yourself," he objected, thinking of their long amorous discourse.

A smile ghosted around her lips. "I feel as if I have been sleeping all my life."

The smile told him she, too, was speaking of last night. To have her first experience be that exciting must have shocked her. However much she might have heard older matrons talk, their stories would not have prepared her for him. Under other circumstances, he would have teased her into saying more. Regrettably, at the moment, he could barely keep his eyes open.

"Sleep," she said, her hand curling firmly behind his neck. He listed irresistibly at the pressure, then found his cheek lying on her thigh. The contact stung where he had been burned, but more compelling than pain was his need to rest.

"I will watch," she promised, her fingers combing through his hair, making him feel even heavier.

"Th—" was all the thank you he could get out.

<hr/>

A change came over Ulric as he slept, one that fascinated Juliana even as it unsettled her. His breathing slowed, then appeared to stop. His skin grew cooler, and his pulse was too weak to count. If she had not known a bit about his kind, she would have worried. As it was, he lay against her leg like a corpse. The gradual fading of his burns was all that told her he was alive.

He is helpless, she thought. Without me to protect him he could be slain.

The recognition that she had almost murdered him made her break into a sweat. Part of her thought maybe she should have. She had no sensible reason to trust him. The fact that he had not hurt her, that he had—truth be told—shown her nothing but pleasure, guaranteed nothing at all. All the traders she had spoken to claimed *upyr* were ravening demons. Just because Ulric seemed more rational than ravening did not mean he would not kill if it became convenient.

But was Juliana any better? She had nearly killed him to get her way. She stroked his thick golden hair behind his ear. The strands had a marvelous texture beneath her hands, a cross between human hair and a pelt. Truly, to kill such a handsome beast without better reason than some vague fear would be a shame. She would judge him for herself, she decided, as she had done all her life.

Men's tales could be unreliable. Well traveled they might be, but sometimes they made monsters of things that threatened their sense of mastery. Juliana could hardly imagine anything more threatening to the average human male than a paragon like Ulric.

Smiling to herself, she rubbed his back through his tunic. She was glad it was in her interest to give him a chance.

# Three

YOU are not going home to get your harp," Ulric said as though he begrudged the time it took to contradict her. "You have already almost killed me once."

"But I can help you earn money with it," Juliana said, "when we are traveling. You can hide me with your glamour while I sneak in."

They were having this argument, or Juliana was, in the shadows beside the public bathhouse. With night's arrival, Ulric's vitality—and his arrogance—had returned. He cupped her cheek in his big, cool palm. Despite its strength, his hand was smooth as satin. Every sign of his burns was gone.

She was glad for that, though she would not say so. He seemed unimpressed enough with her supposed murderous tendencies. If he concluded she had been bluffing, he might leave her behind.

"First," he said. "My glamour can only hide you if we are touching. Second, God only knows how many men your father might have gathered to search for you. If they are at your house, there is no guarantee I could thrall them all. Finally, never have I sung because I needed coin. That is simply a part of passing as human. Half the time I do not even pick it up." When she opened her mouth to ask why, he pressed his finger to her lips. "Think, Juliana. Does a man like me have to pay for what he wants?"

The smugness of his smile underscored his meaning. Of course he did not sing for money. He sang to draw women to him, so he could feed from them or whatever else struck his fancy. That, after all, was what he had done to her.

Embarrassment smoldered in her cheeks. Naturally, Ulric saw it.

"Do not worry," he teased, bending to kiss the warmth, to touch it with the very tip of his tongue. "I have other ways you can *contribute* to our trip."

Juliana wanted to say something barbed; she truly did. Unfortunately, when he spoke to her in that fashion, his voice gone husky, her insides began to melt.

She knew she would betray herself if she spoke. Wiping his lick mark from her cheek was all the riposte she could afford.

Ulric's knowing chuckle rumbled in her ear. "Ah, Juliana, if you knew how good you smell to me at this moment, you would run screaming into the night. I cannot decide whether to bite you or lift your skirts."

"Neither," she huffed, ignoring her breathless tone. "I refuse to spend another day inside Bridesmere's walls."

"Then you will not balk if I insist we leave immediately."

He did not wait for an answer—most likely he did not care if she had one—but took her hand and led her to the empty street. A candle or two burned in the windows of the buildings along the way, casting a gentle, domestic glow. At this hour, most residents were at home. Juliana did not need to fear many eyes—though there was little enough to see. If she squinted, she could just make out Ulric's glamour around them both, like a ripple of heat on a summer day. The illusion dimmed his glow but not his beauty. Now and then an admiring head turned their way.

"They cannot recognize you," he assured her in an undertone. "With my glamour to shield your looks, you are too plain to merit a second glance."

"I notice you have not made yourself look plain."

He laughed at that. "You are not plain to me, my dear. You are a feast for mouth and eyes."

"Wonderful. Now I feel like a fresh-baked pie."

Though the friendly way he squeezed her fingers eased the offense, her nervousness remained. Her heart beat harder as Bridesmere's two-towered gate rose up ahead. Every night at sunset the great wooden doors were barred. Getting the guards to let them out would be a true test of Ulric's power.

To her dismay, a knot of armored men stood in the street before the gate. They were dressed for riding and had swords buckled at their hips. When Juliana saw whose colors covered their mail, she pulled up short and spat a curse no well-mannered female should have known.

"Do you recognize them?" Ulric asked.

"No, but that is Gideon Drake's livery, the man I am supposed to marry. He must have had men in town."

"He does not live in Bridesmere?"

"His firm is based in London, but my father and he have frequent dealings. Drake has been looking into establishing a local branch." She clutched Ulric's arm in a sudden panic. "Please, they must not find out who I am."

Ulric patted her hand, but the muscles of his face were tight. "Leave this to me," he said distractedly.

Juliana bit her lip and tried to let him think in peace. She knew he was handsome and had who-knew-what exotic powers, but was he clever enough to get them through this? She was considered clever and, at the moment, she could barely recall her name.

"Maybe we could climb the wall somewhere else," she said. "You could toss me over with your *upyr* strength or, um, maybe we could rig a ladder so I would not break every bone in my body when I came down."

He grinned at her, the first full-out amusement she had seen him wear. He looked wonderfully boyish with those lines crinkling his eyes.

"I have a better idea," he said. "Sometimes a glamour needs a bit of help."

He took off his cloak and handed it to her.

"What?" she said, wondering confusedly if he meant for her to put it over her head.

"Ball it up and stick it under your gown. You are my pregnant wife and you have been having early labor pains. You insist on seeing your mother, who lives in a cottage outside the walls. I tried to stop you, but you are scared and determined."

He stood in front of her while she hurriedly obeyed. The effect was not terribly convincing. Juliana had to hold the lump of cloth in place to keep it from falling. Looking scared was not going to be hard.

"Leave the talking to me," Ulric said as he once again took her hand. "The more they hear my voice and meet my gaze, the deeper I can thrall them. Whatever you do, keep your hold on my hand. The contact will help me make your condition look genuine."

The gatekeeper, whose watch post was a chamber built into the wide stone arch, had come down to speak to Drake's soldiers. Ulric approached him sheepishly.

"Sorry to put you out," he said, his cap to his breast. "My wife here has been having early pains. Wants to see her mother in case the babe is on the way."

He shrugged as if to say *what can you do when a woman makes up her mind?*

The gatekeeper peered at Juliana, then back at him. "Her mother works at the castle?"

"Nay," said Ulric. "She is a shepherd's wife."

" 'Tis a bad night to be roaming out," one of Drake's men put in. Beneath his bright mail coif, he had the same cold gaze Juliana had noticed on Drake's sons. His stance was wide, as if he were prepared to fight. Perhaps by chance or perhaps not, he gripped the pommel of his sword.

"Really?" Ulric turned his face to the sky. "The weather looks clear enough."

"Wolves," said the soldier, and even Ulric flinched at that.

"Wolves?" he said once he recovered.

"Or things that act like wolves but are not. A woman was attacked outside a tavern the other night. Said a wolf seduced her and drank her blood."

Ulric laughed, but Juliana could feel the sweat on his palm. "Sounds like she might have got a bad batch of ale."

"Maybe," said the soldier. He seemed neither amused nor convinced. He barely blinked as he faced Ulric. Hopefully, this meant Ulric's thrall would succeed. Juliana prayed the soldier could not hear her heart thumping in her breast. If he turned to her, she knew she would wear a look of guilty terror.

"Well, I have my dagger," Ulric said, patting his belt. Juliana saw a flash as if an old baselard hung there, but then it disappeared. For whatever reason, Ulric's illusion did not work perfectly on her. "To tell the truth, gentlemen, I would rather face a wolf than my wife's mother when her back is up. You would think a child had never been born before this one."

"I remember that," said the gatekeeper with a laugh. "That first one is always the end of the world."

Ulric shifted his gaze to him, a natural enough thing to do, though she felt him tense in preparation. *Control your fear,* he said to her in her head. *Otherwise, you will distract me.* Juliana blew out a breath and silently said a prayer. As soon as she calmed, she felt a prickling whoosh. Ulric was exerting the fullest potency of his thrall. The gatekeeper blinked at the assault.

"Thank you," Ulric said. "It is kind of you to let us out."

To Juliana's ears, his voice sounded strange, as if another, darker voice were layered beneath it. The gatekeeper's eyes went a little crossed. A heartbeat later, he shook his head. "It is no trouble," he said. "Just take care if you leave the road."

Juliana expected Gideon Drake's men to stop them, but they remained where they were, silent and watchful, as the guard unbarred the heavy doors.

"Godspeed," he called as they exited the outer arch.

Ulric returned the hail by touching his forelock.

By silent agreement, neither of them spoke until they had crossed the open fields and reached Bridesmere's woods. Juliana returned his cloak. Even as he put it on, she could not bring herself to drop her comforting hold on his hand.

She thought it rather nice of him not to complain.

"They knew you had been in Bridesmere," she said, "even if they did not know you were you. They knew an *upyr* had been in town."

"It appears that way," Ulric said. "I suppose I owe you my life for bullying me to leave."

"This is serious. Did you— Were you in your wolf form when you seduced those other women?"

"Of course not." Clearly, he found the suggestion humorous. "I did as I always do. I told them the encounter was a pleasant dream and that nothing unusual had happened. One of them must have sensed the wolf inside me and spun that into her fantasy."

"But she remembered you had drunk her blood."

"I cannot dictate what women dream."

His nonchalance spurred her temper. "That is precisely what you do. I would not put it past you to leave them a bit of a memory out of pride, to allow them to compare every other lover with you."

"Why, Juliana, are you suggesting that I am vain?" When he grinned, his eyeteeth were sharp as knives. Brief experience had taught her what this meant. Their brush with danger must have aroused him. A sound broke in her throat that was not fear.

Hearing it, he pulled her to him with a single tug, his mouth dropping ruthlessly to cover hers. His chest was hard, his hands locking her to him at head and waist. His body warmed as he rubbed against her like a cat. Being close to her seemed to raise his temperature. Warm or not, the ridge of his loins was firm. His tongue slid between her lips, slowly this time, stroking and sucking hers, making the kiss a true persuasion.

"Hold me," he said. "Wrap me in your human arms."

She held him because she could not help it. She did not sense him trying to thrall her, but his lure without it was just as strong.

"Yes," he urged, lifting her off the ground. "Yes, I need your hands."

She put them on whatever skin she could reach: the hollows of his cheeks, his jaw, behind his neck where his hair fell free. Every inch of him was perfect, every plane and curve a tactile delight. Her hands were humming, her own skin hot. Obviously craving more, he ripped off his belt and coaxed her arms beneath his shirt. The muscles of his back felt like silk-wrapped granite, rippling everywhere she touched.

When she traced the furrow of his spine, he quivered like a horse.

"Juliana," he gasped as if she had hurt him.

She knew she had not. He kissed her over and over, each penetration hungrier than the last. Pulling down the bodice of her gown, he bared her breasts and caressed them, then buried his face between. She shivered to feel his teeth scrape gently across her skin, especially her hardened peaks. She expected him to bite her. She feared it a little, but was prepared. To her surprise, he only teased her. Or perhaps he teased them both.

"Just a kiss," he whispered before he took one reddened nipple into his mouth. When he pulled it deeper, her pleasure swelled.

He must have heard her groan of longing, but all he did was move to the other breast.

The act of holding his desires in check seemed to excite him. By the time he lowered her onto a bed of crackling leaves, he was half-crazed. Wrenching her thighs up and apart, he rocked forward on his knees and took her quickly—deep, smooth strokes that drove her to moans of enjoyment almost at once. When he slid his hand between their bodies to touch her, she could not contain a sob.

He came as she did, a gasping, jerking peak that looked just as hard as hers. He rolled off her immediately after.

"There," he said, slightly breathless. "Now I can think straight enough to hunt."

His words raised a knot of hurt she told herself to disregard; they were, after all, hardly sweethearts. She wondered, though: If he intended their coupling to be a matter of mere convenience—as his words implied—why care that she was pleasured? Why refrain from biting her as he wished? Did he think she would not taste good?

Juliana shook her head, bemused by her own concerns. What a thing to worry about! Apparently, this business of taking lovers was more complicated than she guessed.

ULRIC stood above her, offering his hand, feeling stupid and hoping she could not see. To have stopped this close to pursuit, and for such a reason, was insane.

"Did I hurt you?" he asked as she gripped his fingers and pulled to her feet.

"No," she said. "You just surprised me."

Unconvinced, he watched her closely as she tried to smooth her hair. She seemed flustered, withdrawn into herself. That he did not like. Admittedly, his apology came a little late, but he had no wish to cause her harm.

"I am all right," she insisted, then: "Will you hunt as your wolf?"

"Yes," he said, letting her change the subject. "But not here."

If those soldiers were on the watch for *upyr,* every wolf they spotted would be suspect.

He regretted bringing the danger. Juliana had called his behavior pride. In principle, she was right. In his anger and grief over

Gillian's betrayal, he might not have been as careful as he should. If any real wolves had to pay for that, their deaths would be on his hands.

"We must walk," he said, chafing Juliana's fingers between his own. "There is better hunting farther on."

She nodded as if she could guess the reasons for herself. To his relief, she did not argue or ask why he had taken her as he did. Ulric was not sure he could answer that. He only knew, when he heard her moan of arousal, he had been unable to wait another instant to pull her close.

That being the case, he appreciated her restraint. Human women could be contentious, even though—unlike female *upyr*—most could not hope to best their mates in a fight. Of course, in talking a thing to death, he had observed that human females could hold their own.

Happily, Juliana was showing better sense—apart from running away. That could only be viewed as reckless, though he understood the impulse behind it. Freedom was the heart of who *upyr* were.

He swept his thumb across the back of her hand. "You handled yourself well," he said, judging she deserved the praise. "You did not panic back at the gate."

"I felt like I was panicking."

When her eyes met his, twinkling wryly, something warm and unexpected slid through his chest. At that moment, they were so attuned she could have been pack.

"What you do," he said, "is more important than what you feel."

She smiled to herself as if she knew a secret he did not. But that was to be expected. She was a woman. Pack or human, women thought their feelings mattered most of all.

"Ulric," she said, "have you decided where we are going?"

His step faltered as he realized how thoroughly she had put her fate in his hands. "To my home," he said, "across the border— unless you see a settlement you like better along the way. I have a cave in the Highlands where we will be safe."

She thought about this for a dozen steps. "You live with others of your kind?"

"Yes. I am leader to a pack of *upyr,* to all this realm's packs, though we rarely gather."

"Meeting your pack would probably help me decide if I want to become like you."

Unless I scare you off before then, he thought but did not say.

They walked in silence until they neared the northern edge of the woods. The open land beyond, where their progress would be exposed, would take hours to cover. Juliana was growing weary and, unlike some of his kind, Ulric was unable to share much of his vitality without first biting its recipient. Only a blood-bond could forge a strong enough link. Given his recent loss of control, he was loathe to form one. For all he knew, a single taste might be dangerous.

He had not intended to take her under his protection, but now that he had, he could not do it halfway. Their safety depended on him keeping his head.

Given his thoughts, he was happy to spy a hollow beneath the roots of a large oak tree. The space looked big enough to shelter them both.

"You wait here while I hunt," he said. "I will bring something back for you."

Juliana wrinkled her nose at the shadowed hole. "Can I not come with you?"

"No," he said. "You would only get in the way."

"But what if there are bugs?"

"There are bugs in town, Juliana, and those bugs have no fear of humans." Once again he handed her his cloak. "Spread this beneath you. The cloth has absorbed my power. It will keep vermin away, at least for a couple hours."

"Will it?" Juliana examined the garment with new interest. "How convenient!"

Ulric left her pressing the velvet curiously to her face. Let her try to sniff out its secrets. He was glad to have her distracted.

Then again, if he wanted to discourage her ambition to become *upyr,* he ought to let her watch him hunt, ought to rub her nose in the gore. He knew why he did not. He was enjoying the trust with which she accepted almost everything he did. He did not have to fight or thrall her. She wanted what he did. When they made love, he did not gaze into her eyes as the last sigh faded and know he had made her sad. When she looked at him, she did not see a jailer.

That, he thought, had been the worst thing Gillian did.

If he revealed the beast who lived inside him, Juliana's acceptance might be destroyed.

He decided he could show her later, once he had burned this attraction out. Human that she was, surely it would not take long. With luck, he would have many nights to dissuade her from her goal.

The matter settled, at least in his mind, he stripped off his clothes before he changed. Though this was a more natural state for him than being dressed, he felt odd preparing by himself. If he had been with his pack, they would have had a communal howl. Sharing their excitement helped them work as a team. He shrugged off a homesick twinge. His wolf was strong enough to hunt alone.

Shaking his arms, he cleared his mind to summon his familiar. His beast was too much a part of him to need a name, their thoughts woven together like a single being. After centuries of exchanging forms, a simple wish was enough to pull the other out.

He pictured the forest rushing by him as he ran, the scent of prey, the feel of soft, spring earth under pounding paws.

Come, he thought, and his world broke into glittering pieces. It hurt, but only for an instant. As his edges shattered, the wind of the nothing-place filled his soul. There, where no one could hear, his wolf howled to the brothers it could not join.

*Now,* thought Ulric and fell onto four strong limbs.

---

JULIANA willingly followed orders when they made sense, or even when they did not if she had no choice. She failed to see, however, why she should follow orders now. Clearly she was safer in Ulric's presence than huddling under a tree. She had a right to see him in his wolf form. How else could she decide if his existence would suit her?

So thinking, she wrapped his cloak around her shoulders, retrieved her knife from her basket, and trailed him to a clearing, being as careful as she could to make no noise. Perhaps the power that clung to his cloak helped her achieve this. When he began to pull off his clothes, he showed no sign he knew she was near.

Heavens, Juliana thought, her breath catching in her throat as she watched the various parts of him appear. He had been garbed in all their encounters thus far. Now she saw him as God—or perhaps His opposite—had made him. Whoever his maker had been, he was exceedingly well put together. Lean without being thin. Muscular but not big. His arms were lovely, his hind parts quite the nicest she had ever seen. Biteable, she thought, her mouth watering unexpectedly. When he shook out his limbs and rolled his head around his shoulders, he looked the way she pictured Adam in the Garden.

This was where he belonged, in the wild places and the woods, getting ready to seek his prey.

Her hands had steepled before her mouth in a kind of prayer when he broke into a million sparks. She cried out, but it did not matter. He had no ears to hear, only a whirl of power and light. A heartbeat later, he hit the ground as a wolf, the biggest she had ever heard of. Long of leg and sleek of pelt, his shoulders came to her waist. He lifted his muzzle to scent the air. She expected him to smell her then, but he did not. Perhaps his cloak shielded that as well. Chills swept her skin as he took off with a silent, four-footed leap.

Oh, she thought. Oh, my, he is marvelous.

She hesitated a moment too long to follow. By the time she recovered, he was gone. To her relief, the ground was soft enough to take tracks. Each print was huge and amazingly far apart. Fortunately for her human sight, the depressions glowed like fireflies around their edges—at least until they dissolved. She had to be quick to catch them before they vanished. They moved in as straight a line as the trees allowed. Whatever Ulric smelled, he was heading directly for it.

A crashing noise alerted her to activity up ahead. She shrank behind a tree in time for a large gray hare to burst through the undergrowth. It quartered from side to side, but Ulric was right behind it. With a final pounce, he caught its long hind leg. The hare barely had time to squeal before Ulric tossed it up in the air. When it fell, he broke its neck with his jaws.

It was a clean kill; merciful, she supposed. He ate every bit of it, down to its final, furry foot. As he did, his eyes glowed gold and his throat vibrated with muffled growls, growls that sounded very much like enjoyment. When the hare was gone, his tongue swept out to clean his bloodied teeth. Juliana could hardly breathe. It was the single, rawest act she had ever seen.

Evidently, it was not over. As soon as he finished panting, the wolf-Ulric turned, his nose lowered to snuffle back along the hare's zigzagging tracks.

Juliana could not have put a word to her feelings as she trailed behind him. Dread mingled with excitement, while pity and horror formed a turmoil behind her ribs. She could not do what he had done. She knew that with all her heart . . . or wanted to believe she knew. Maybe what he had done was no different from wringing a chicken's neck. And maybe it was better. For all the wolf-Ulric's swiftness, that hare *did* have a chance to escape.

The wolf-Ulric stopped at a snarl of bracken, then nosed at the soil beneath. He must have found the mother hare's burrow, because three small leverets tumbled out of the ground. Two escaped in different directions. The third ran straight at him.

Juliana covered her mouth. "No," she said, the tiniest whisper of sound.

This was too much for his cloak's magic to conceal.

Ulric whirled around with the baby squirming in his teeth. His gaze was bright, intent, and terribly familiar. Whatever his shape, this was the man she had slept with. The same intelligence filled those golden eyes.

She could not begin to guess what was passing through his mind. He padded toward her, paw by paw, his tail high but not wagging. His ears pointed slightly toward her, and the hair on his neck looked puffed. His wolf eyes watched her as he laid the leveret at her feet, gently, like a dog leaving a gift. Juliana had never wanted a present less. The leveret did not move except to tremble.

*I told you,* his husky voice said in her head. *I told you I would catch something for you to cook.*

She was shaking her head before she realized she had done it. That helpless bundle . . . That quivering baby thing . . .

*It will not live without its mother. If you do not eat it, some other animal will.*

Like a woman in a dream, Juliana bent to pick up the baby, cuddling it against her chest as she rose. Its fur was soft and warm.

This is food, she thought, trying to convince herself. Like a lamb or a side of beef. Just because someone else kills those creatures does not mean I take no part in their end.

The wolf-Ulric cocked his head at her as if trying to hear her thoughts.

*Kill it with respect,* he said. *Quickly, so it does not feel pain or fear.*

She was already holding the knife. She set the leveret down again and slit its throat in a single stroke.

The wolf's eyes flashed at the blood, a hint of green touching the gold. It licked the side of its mouth. *Take it,* he said, sounding angry. *Take it away.*

She retreated a step with her burden, but farther than that she would not go. Nor would she look away from Ulric's wolfish glower. She sensed he was waiting for her to flee, that part of him wished she would.

"It *is* food," she said defiantly. "I was not happy to kill it, but I understood."

He must have changed when she blinked. Suddenly he stood before her in his own form. His hands, warm now from feeding, brushed away the tears she had not known she shed.

"I am sorry," he said. "I did not want you to see that."

"Why not?" She sniffed and tossed her head. "This is who you are."

"Who *you* will be if you hold me to my promise."

"Do you think this is worse than what humans do to eat? You were not cruel, Ulric. I saw you. You enjoyed the chase, but you were not cruel." She wiped the back of her hand across her cheek. Ulric's gaze lingered on her bloodied fingers. She forced herself not to hide them. "You should find the other two and catch them. They should not go to waste."

With a muffled laugh, he kissed her forehead. "Now you are pretending to be harder than you are. Let the foxes catch them if they can. You have faced enough for one night."

She did not argue, more relieved than she wanted him to suspect. "I will dress this one," she said briskly, "when we get back to your tree."

---

USUALLY, after a hunt, Ulric liked nothing better than a good, hard tumble with a willing lass. Tonight he felt as if his body belonged to someone else, as if it were more foreign to him than his wolf's. He could not fall on Juliana as he had before. His mind was too busy making sense of the night's events.

Juliana claimed to have found him by following his glowing tracks, but they should have been impossible for her to see. Most *upyr* did not have the skill to trace energy. Juliana was human, and unbitten. Ulric could imagine no reason for the two of them to be manifesting that strong a bond. Good or not, two nights of carnal acquaintance was insufficient cause.

But perhaps she had a bit of the Sight and did not know it. Perhaps that accounted for her resistance to his thrall.

Not that Ulric had been trying very hard to thrall her recently.

He could have expunged her memory of his hunt, could have spared her the horror before it sank in. Instead, he had dropped that leveret at her feet, knowing it would appall her tender woman's heart. Every female he knew got teary over baby creatures. Hares, squirrels, even baby turtles could make them coo. And he had dared her to kill one.

He did not understand his own intent. Had he wished to shock her? Or did he want to see if she could accept his most brutal self? Neither answer made much sense. This human's opinion ought to have meant nothing to him.

Unable to sort it out, he curled around her in the space beneath the old oak's roots. In spite of his confusion, the closeness was comforting. The hollow was tall enough for her to sit but not him. Her cloak and a heap of branches blocked the door. With the exit shielded, the sound of her breathing filled the earthen walls, a soothing music he did not know if he had heard before. He had been young when he fell in battle, no more than seventeen. He could not remember if he had bedded a woman before that. Being saved by Auriclus and learning to live as an immortal had dimmed those memories.

Juliana called him back by wriggling slightly in his arms.

"Ulric?" she said into the intimacy of the dark. "When you changed out of your wolf form, how did you finish digesting that hare?"

He nosed a lock of her hair from his face. "Even in my wolf form, I am *upyr*. We process sustenance very quickly. By the time I changed, it was gone."

"Even the bones?"

He smiled against her ear. Her tone was barely squeamish. He should have known her horror would fade. If nothing else, the neat efficiency with which she had prepared her own meal told him that.

"Even the bones," he confirmed. "All the substance of its life became mine."

She hesitated, a tiny inhalation before she spoke. "Is drinking from humans more exciting?"

Abruptly, her scent was everywhere in his head, his body stirring with telltale force. All too easily could he imagine her on his tongue.

"Yes," he said and no more after that.

---

HE would not bite her. He wanted to. She had known that from the start. But every time he came close to it, he pulled back. He would kiss her throat as he drove inside her, would caress it with his mouth and hands and groan as if he were dying. He would drag his fangs across her breasts and lick the bending of her arm. When he came, he sometimes sucked her skin so hard bruises would bloom.

He kissed them later and made them heal, but now and then she would hide one for the pleasure of touching it privately. The marks told her the hold she had on him was real, more real than he might have cared to admit. Sometimes she caught him staring at her veins as if he were transfixed. A simple flash of her wrist could make him stumble. He would swallow then, and lick his sharpening teeth, but he never pierced her skin and drank.

She knew he could not make her *upyr* simply by feeding. On that the merchants' tales agreed—though the actual secret of the transformation was a mystery.

No, the significance of being bitten was that it made *upyr* coupling complete. Reputedly, humans liked it as well, but—from what she had seen—it was the thing Ulric's kind most wanted when they reached climax. Unfortunately for her, the more he refrained from claiming this pleasure, the more she desired to give it.

She feared she was dangerously close to falling in love. It seemed impossible, briefly as she had known him, but Juliana was not in the habit of hiding from her heart.

He was all she thought about, all she wanted to think about. His praise, his amusement were prizes she wished to win. When he looked sad, she wanted to soothe him. When he was kind, he seemed to her a knight. Even his flaws, which she was not blind to, seemed charming.

If these were not love's warning signs, she wished someone would tell her what were.

"Why?" she asked the third night in succession that he had torn his lips from her throat. "Why will you not bite me?"

His pupils dilated at the word. "It is too enjoyable," he said, turning away as he dragged his hand across his mouth. "Biting you would not be safe."

"It did not harm those women in Bridesmere."

"That was different."

She laid her cheek against the tension of his shoulder. "Because I am different?"

He slipped from her hold so swiftly her arms tingled at the loss. He stood over her, feet spread wide on the forest floor. His muscles bunched as he crossed his arms. "Biting you would give me more power to control you. Is that really what you want?"

"You have the power to control me now. You have not used it since we left."

The reminder seemed to incense him. "You should not trust me," he said, his features gone faintly pink. "I could kill you!"

"I could kill you as well, every day when the sun comes up. Instead, I lie between you and the light."

"Because you want something from me. You are glamoured by the idea of being *upyr*." He dropped his arms, his anger faded to peevishness.

"That is not all I am glamoured by," she said with a suggestive smile.

Her teasing did not amuse him. "I will not bite you," he said, "and that is that."

She inclined her head, implying agreement without offering a promise. Life had taught Juliana there was more than one way to get around a stubborn man.

# Four

~~~~

"YOU are getting better at that," Ulric said as she polished off a piece of roasted ptarmigan. Juliana had stuffed the bird with wild garlic, and the smell was heavenly—not too burned and not too raw, but crackling with juice and fat. At home she mostly sent their meat to a cookshop. Happily, along with many other things, her cooking skills had improved since joining Ulric.

Well into Scotland now, they lazed beside a campfire in a hollow between two hills, open but empty country. Her gown and chemise, newly washed in a stream, were drying on a rock. She had scrubbed herself as well, with Ulric's cloak to warm her when she got out.

Ulric had simply peeled off his clothes and set them aside. Like his person, they required no cleaning. His sigh of relief told her how much he preferred wearing naught but skin.

More modest than he, she could still appreciate the sense of freedom. Her existence could not have been more different than her life back home. No bed of feathers awaited her rest, no brazier or heated wine. A pit Ulric had dug in a nearby copse would serve as tomorrow's shelter. For tonight they lounged at ease beneath a star-filled sky. If she closed her eyes, Juliana could imagine the world was theirs.

For a week they had been traveling, making steady progress north—through forest when they could, but also unsettled land. Forced to do everything for themselves, Juliana had grown fitter and Ulric more relaxed. He seemed to take her presence for granted, as if bringing her with him had been his idea. She wondered if this was the effect of his wolf soul, to accept life as it came.

In other ways, he was very much like any man. His moods she could not predict. Sometimes he told her what he knew of the country around them. Sometimes he did not speak for hours. Luckily, since the incident with the hare, he had shown her whatever she wished to see. Sometimes he gave her orders, but for the most part, he left her to her own good sense.

They fell into a pattern, each choosing whichever chores suited them.

In all their travels, they had seen no sign of pursuit.

Juliana had a feeling she was seeing Ulric as he ruled his pack, a leader who was at his most benevolent when he got his way, but also one who kept his inner nature to himself. Even at their most intimate, she never breached his reserve.

Most likely, Ulric would have said there was nothing to breach.

This night, her full stomach made her feel expansive. On the chance that Ulric's recent hunt might have had the same effect, she licked her greasy thumb and gestured to the dripping spit. "Would you like some?" she offered. "There is plenty."

Ulric leaned back on his elbows and shook his head, one leg lolling out to touch hers. "I would have to change to consume it, and I am too comfortable as I am. I like the smell, though. It reminds me of when I was a boy. My mother used to spoil me terribly."

"My mother treated me like a partner, as if I were important to our house."

"You probably were, from what I have observed. I, on the other hand, was a wastrel. I might not remember much of my mortal life, but I remember that. We raised goats, I believe. I liked to lie on my back in the pasture and dream as I watched the clouds. I was the youngest. Everyone protected me."

She could see his eyes reaching for the memories, wistful, unable to catch what he had lost. She put her cheek on her bent knee, doubting she would ever tire of watching him. "Now you are the protector."

"Yes," he said with a glimmer of a smile. "Auriclus made me that. In some ways, my sire was more unreliable than I was. He needed someone to keep order among his children, once he had taught them what secrets he had the patience to impart. I found I liked being responsible when I learned how."

"You said he changed you after you fell in battle?"

"My fellow foot soldiers left me for dead on the field at Hastings. I never got to see William conquer the day, though I doubt I would have enjoyed it, as I was fighting for King Harold. Auriclus found me round about my last breath. He claimed the way I fought to live made him decide to save me. I remember . . . I remember lying there in the dark on the cold and broken ground, squeezing the dirt between my fingers because that was all I could move. I was cursing in my head, I think, and crying with anger at the unfairness of dying young."

She touched the leg that bumped hers, picturing the boy he had been. "Are you glad he made you *upyr*?"

Ulric tweaked a lock of her hair. "I should lie to you, but no, I was never sorry. He found a boy that night and turned him into a man. I never would have been what I am now if I had remained a mortal. You, however, could make a good life. I could find you a husband, you know, in any village along the way. A bit of a thrall to hook him and the rest would be up to you. I am sure you could handle anyone you chose."

She stared at him, taken aback. Could he really hand her over that easily? But perhaps she should not have been surprised. When he could have any woman he wanted, it must have been difficult to esteem any one more than the rest. Especially when he had only known her a week.

Hurt, but wishing to hide it, she turned her gaze to the fire. "I do not want to marry. I like living free like this."

"It is true you have proved more adaptable than I expected, but surely—in time—you will miss the luxuries you left behind."

He sounded like her father. *I know what is best for you and the devil take what you want for yourself.*

"You promised me," she said, struggling not to grind her teeth. "I have the summer to make up my mind."

She could hear her own defensiveness and feared he knew what lay behind it—not so much a love for freedom as a growing tenderness for him.

"There is more to life," she said, "than luxuries."

His shrug was cool. "As you please. Your decision makes no difference to me."

It was difficult to convince herself he was lying. She might think of herself as special, but that did not mean he would.

He rose then and stretched, his beautiful, naked body limned by the flames. She ached inside to see him, and even more when he turned to face her. His shaft was thickening and rising, as if he could will it upward with his mind. His thatch was honey-gold, the same bright color that furred his muscular thighs. The evidence of his maleness struck something deep inside her, something beyond her control. Her body tightened and grew wet. She knew when he caught her scent, for his nostrils flared. He smiled at her with hooded eyes, not speaking, merely letting her watch him grow.

He did not have to thrall her. Without a single instruction, she found herself on her knees. His cloak dropped to the ground behind her and the cool night air caressed her breasts. When he gripped her hair in a single fist, she uttered a longing cry. With a force she could not resist, he pushed her mouth toward the reddened crown.

"I do not know how to do this," she said, even as her body shook with excitement.

He brushed her lips with the silken skin, with the tiny, dampening slit. "It does not matter," he said. "It is impossible for you to hurt me."

Something in his voice made her look up.

"Did someone hurt you, Ulric? Is that why you hold a part of yourself aloof?"

"Do it," he said in his harshest growl. "Take me in your mouth."

She took him, as gentle as he was rough. He trembled when her lips enclosed his swollen crest.

"Ah," he sighed, rich and throaty, "you burn like fire."

She had learned, in the nights since they had met, that her touch had power. He tried not to betray how much he loved it, but she knew. To him, her human warmth was as magical as his thrall. With it, she could make him almost as weak as he made her.

"I burn because I want you," she whispered against his tip. "I burn because my desire for you fills my blood."

"I will not—"

She drew him in before he could repeat his vow to leave her unbitten. He used his words to guide her then, and his hands, surprisingly careful not to overwhelm her. She loved the feel of him, the way he pulsed when her lips tightened around him, the way he shivered and grew hot.

"Do not come," she whispered, knowing it would make him wild. Though their first lovemaking of the night pushed him the hardest to release, if he put his will to it, he could hold off his peak. She wanted him to be desperate by the time he drove inside her, wanted him to forget everything but taking what he wished. She stroked his scrotum as he groaned, then ran her palms up and down the back of his legs. His buttocks clenched as she moved her caresses there. He swore at her but did not order her to stop. In fact, he widened his stance to better brace his weight.

"Squeeze me again," he said, the order hushed. "I like it when you cup my stones."

His toes curled strongly into the grass as she not only obeyed him but also pulled him deeper into her mouth. She took him at his word that she could not hurt him, using both force and the barest edge of her teeth. He began to pant and lengthen even more, until his swollen size was too much to take. Holding the base of him in one fist, she sucked strongly at the rest.

"Lord," he cursed, his fingers clenching in her hair. "Juliana, yes."

He was fast approaching his edge, but he held on. His hips began to push at her: tight forward jerks he seemed unable to restrain. She teased the tip of her tongue into the little slit and kneaded his drawn up sack. This he tolerated for a heartbeat, then thrust greedily past her lips again.

"Harder," he growled, his thickness pulsing against her tongue. "Wetter."

When he could stand the torment no longer, he pulled free and dropped to his knees. With hands like heated steel, he swung her splay-legged onto his lap.

His anxiously throbbing crown homed immediately on her gate.

"Now," he said, breathing hard around the words, "let us see if you can handle what you have wrought."

———

THE answer was not in doubt. Ulric knew she had been ready since he turned and let her watch him rise. Whatever the differences between them, their bodies were in harmony.

He entered her clinging warmth as if he were buttered, barely needing to push until the final inch. Her growl as she accepted it could have been his own. At his coaxing, she rose on her knees to ride. His hands on her bottom guided her untutored movements, adding to the pleasure of touching her the undeniably stronger one of telling her what to do.

He urged her as fast as he could bear without going over the crest of climax. For once, he intended to take his fill of anticipation.

There was, after all, so much of it to enjoy. He loved seeing Juliana naked, loved watching the light play over her human flesh. No *upyr* could jiggle this delightfully, nor give so readily before his thrust. How many levels of melting softness could there be? How many shades of pink and cream?

Her nipples were a blend of plum and rose, swollen at their base and hard at their tips. The threads of blue that ran beneath the silken surface of her breasts called irresistibly to his hands. He palmed one soft weight and lifted it, watching the peak grow dark. Brushing his fingertip back and forth made it even sharper.

*Kiss it,* he imagined he heard her say, though he was not trying to read her thoughts. Real or not, the exhortation spurred him. He bent her backward over his arm, then fastened his mouth to the peak. She trembled as he drew on her, her hair swinging to the grass. While its brown might be ordinary, its satiny sheen was not. Its shining length no longer bore the ripples of her braids. It was as free as the rest of her.

"Ulric," she sighed as he played on her with his tongue.

His fangs were fully extended, and he had to draw carefully. It would have been all too easy to cut her, to take a sweet, accidental taste. His body burned with frustration, despite the movement of her hips. As if she wanted to soothe him, her fingers stroked the knotted tendons behind his neck, then slid apart to massage his shoulders.

"You are a cat," she teased. "You would let me pet you all night."

He groaned as her nails dragged up and down his spine, fearing the words were true. The way she touched him, the way she sighed his name and melted beneath his kiss, was different from any woman in his past. Her tenderness reached inside him to twist and tug the strings of his heart. As it did, the bruises Gillian had left there ached.

He knew Juliana believed she loved him.

The irony should have made him laugh. Part of him welcomed her feelings, if only to salve his pride. How long had he chased Gillian, only to end up rebuffed? In one week, this woman had shown him more true attraction, more faith in his good intentions, than Gillian had in years. He felt taller when he held Juliana, the king he was supposed to be.

But all of it, every scrap, was based on an illusion. His outward perfection had tricked Juliana into thinking his insides were perfect, too. Any *upyr,* whether he thralled her or not, might have had the same effect. Juliana was dazzled, and that meant he could trust her emotions no more than she should have been trusting his.

Pleasure was no substitute for love.

He steeled himself as he felt his orgasm rise, always the lowest ebb of control. It was like trying to stop a flood. The siren song of release had him in its spell. His hips took over from her rhythm, driving faster, growing more frenzied with his desire. His fangs were like stakes driven in his gums.

But he would not bite her. He would not bind them in that way, even if every fiber of his being urged him on.

Wrenching his mouth from her breast, he hid his face in her shoulder, but that flesh was tempting, too: salty and smooth, with a good, firm muscle to take his teeth. Her hands seemed to coax him to it, combing through his hair to press his scalp. She found the spot behind his ears that always made him shiver. Groaning, he tipped his head to the stars.

Juliana clasped his jaw.

"Ulric," she said, exasperation mixing with pity. "For God's sake, take what you want."

Her eagerness was too much. Crying out, he tore himself from her body, sprawling backward, so close to spending and so in need of it that he could not keep from finishing with his hand—hard, fisting pumps that had him spitting against her belly like a callow boy. The fluid came in spurting arcs, as if his body meant to spill everything at once.

Juliana gaped at him as he finished, her palm covering the mess.

Angry and embarrassed, Ulric did not know what to say. What could he say? He would not let himself be sorry. He had done what he knew was right for them both. If she was unsatisfied with their exchange, she could damn well follow his example.

The thought of her doing so made his member twitch.

"I am going to the stream," he announced, rising stiffly to his feet. "I feel in need of cooling off."

"You feel in need," she said, the most sarcastic he had ever heard her. She shook her head and turned away, leaving him to his hollow victory.

<hr>

EVEN though she was furious—with herself as well as with him—Juliana spread her body on top of his when they squirmed into their carefully camouflaged pit. If anything knocked off the woven branches that formed the roof, she did not want to see him burn.

"You do not have to do that," he said, already sounding drowsy.

"Of course I do. What if you accidentally set fire to me?"

He snorted into the darkness, but it was no carefree laugh. Beneath his tunic, his muscles felt like boards. His arms lay at his sides rather than hold her.

Juliana sighed. More than anything in the world, she hated having to apologize. She minded it especially when she was in the wrong. She, after all, was the one who almost always did what was right.

"Ulric," she said against his velvet-covered chest. "I am sorry for pushing you to bite me earlier. Even though I know you wanted to, and even though I fail to understand your reasons, I should have respected your wishes."

"Yes," he agreed. "You should have."

She coughed in disbelief. This was how he accepted her apology?

"You should have," he repeated. "Or do you think your words will have more meaning if I say you did nothing wrong?"

"You could apologize back."

"I do not feel the need."

"Of all the—"

"Juliana." His hand came up to cover her mouth. "There is something you should know. Seven days before I met you, the woman I loved for the last two decades left me for another man. These feelings you have are wasted on me. From the first time I saw Gillian, when my sire abandoned her on my doorstep, I knew she would be important to my life. I spent years coaxing her to trust me, watching her grow into her powers. I taught her the pleasures of flesh and hunt. I could never love anyone after her."

Juliana's skin felt as if he had plunged her into an icy stream. He loved someone else. Ulric loved someone else. She could hear the depth of his devotion in the gentleness of his tone. What was worse, she could tell he knew that she possibly loved him. As swiftly as it had chilled, her face blazed hot. The clenching of her jaw made it hard to speak.

"I shall keep that in mind," she said with all the dignity she could muster.

"Good," he said. "That will make everything easier."

Then he fell asleep, effectively giving himself the final word.

Juliana, naturally, lay awake most of the day. A mist had settled over the surrounding wood shortly after dawn. Damp and cool, it collected around the needles of the pines to roll off in intermittent drops. Though Ulric's gift kept their refuge dry, the unpredictable *plip plop plip* of water to the forest floor formed a background to her circling thoughts.

Who was this Gillian? A human? Another wolf-*upyr*? That seemed likeliest if, as he said, his sire had abandoned her on his doorstep. Twenty years was a long time to be pining after a woman, but why was Ulric so certain he could never love again? And why was he so insistent that Juliana know? Maybe his telling her meant he was afraid he *could* love her, and to avoid the risk he pushed her away.

Though that idea was appealing, it reeked of self-flattery. Most likely the thought of Juliana wanting him for anything but bed play was just annoying.

And he might have wished to be kind by warning her. He did seem to like her at least a bit.

Her cape and the pine-bough roof screened out most but not all the light. Pushing up on her arms, Juliana stared at Ulric's sleeping face. He looked an enchanted prince as she curtained him with her hair. His brow was noble, his feature white and pure. Sadly, his still, marble visage told her nothing of his secret thoughts.

You have fallen for a statue, she thought, but she could not make herself believe it. He was arrogant and controlling and probably too powerful for his own good, but under that handsome immortal exterior, he was definitely flesh and blood. She flounced back on his chest with a sigh. For one tempting moment, she thought of beating him with her fist. Either he would wake and argue with her, or he would not feel it at all. Neither outcome seemed very useful.

"It must be love," she grumbled to herself. No other man had ever made her act like a child.

# Five

S HE was still angry at him when she awoke. Ulric knew this because she was making little faces to herself as she helped erase
the signs of their camp. Despite her pique, he noticed she wore his
cloak to walk to the stream.

"Yours is warmer," she said, spying his raised eyebrows.

"Be my guest, Juliana. Just remember if you do not let me don
it now and then, the good of it will wear off."

"You slept on top of it all day," she said, caught between annoyance and interest.

"True, but I have more power for it to soak up after dark."

Even with that, she did not return his garment. As Ulric suspected, its magical properties were not its greatest attraction—and
probably not its warmth, either. Grimacing, he shook Juliana's cloak
free of leaves and tucked it into her basket. He knew he had been
right to tell her about Gillian. Unlike some *upyr,* he found no enter-
tainment in breaking hearts.

"There is a town just east of here," he said when she returned
from washing. "As we have seen no pursuit, I think it is safe to purchase supplies. I expect you are weary of eating meat."

She had been untangling her hair with her fingers. Now she glared at him through the strands. "I am not picking out a husband."

"No one said you were."

"You did not have to say it. I can guess what is in your thoughts. I am not a puppy to be left on the first convenient doorstep. If you wish to break your promise, you will have to do it without my co-operation."

She cursed as her fingers refused to go through a knot, her brown eyes glittering ominously close to tears. Ulric put his hand over hers. "I will help you if you promise you will not cry."

At that, she dropped her hands and said something truly nasty.

Ulric grinned and worked through the snarl, using a pulse of power to encourage the locks to lie straight.

"There." He smoothed the silken mass over her shoulders. "That should stay mannerly for a while."

She did not smile or thank him, but removed his cloak and handed it back. "I am warm enough. You can put your power inside the cloth again."

He had wanted her to distance herself from him. That being so, he could not account for the sting of insult he felt.

---

THE "town" Ulric spoke of was more of a crofter's village, an assemblage of crooked stone buildings built low to the ground. Moss grew up the sides of the houses and over the weathered thatch, which was secured by nets of rope. A square, four-storied tower—also crumbling but somewhat repaired—overlooked the village from the north. Juliana surmised this was the dwelling of the local laird.

The still-thick mist lent the humble scene an air of romance—at least until they got close. As she and Ulric entered the single, rutted street, they found a litter of piglets rooting in the dirt.

Before she could worry that they might look tasty to her companion, a boy in a ragged linen shift came running out of a cottage,

calling what she assumed was the Scottish version of "Here, piggy."
It being Gaelic, Juliana understood not a word.

"Hm," said Ulric as the boy shooed his charges back inside. "I
am not sure these people can spare what I could charm out of
them."

Juliana handed him her sack of coin. "You can pay them with
this if they will take money."

"Oh, people have use for coin even out here. We are not that far
from the markets of Dundee."

"I thought your kind of *upyr* stayed away from humans."

"We have to know which places to avoid, do we not? In any
case, I thought you"—he jingled the sack—"had no money but
what you were going to earn with your harp."

"I was saving that to open a little shop."

"Very practical," he said, beginning to walk toward what looked
like the busier end of the village, where lanterns hung outside doors.
"Even I, however, would not suggest you try to start a business
here."

If she had not known he was teasing, she would have bristled.
Unfortunately, it was hard to stay angry when he assumed that af-
fable expression, as if he were delighted with all the world. He had
spun just a touch of glamour, enough to dim his glow and color his
complexion. When a dog began to bark wildly at their approach
and Ulric growled it to silence, the pleasant set of his features did
not change. He looked a too-handsome human, a rake to be reck-
oned with. A housewife stared as she came outside to empty a bucket
of slops. Ulric tipped his cap at her, and her hand fluttered to her
breast.

Juliana rolled her eyes. If he was not vain, she was the queen of
England.

She had to admit his manner got them what they wanted. Before
much time had passed, he had coaxed a few blushing wives out of a
round of cheese, two loaves of bread, a crock of dried figs, an ivory
comb, and, best of all, a tiny collection of spices. Ulric had insisted

on smelling each packet before she decided which ones to buy. The price was dear, of course, but she had not been able to resist the pleasure on his face.

"We should get you a little cauldron," he said, taking her loaded basket over his arm. "Then you will have a choice as to how you cook."

Turning back, he spoke to the woman who had just parted with her larder's prize. She answered shyly and pointed in the direction from whence they came.

"Blacksmith," Ulric explained to Juliana. "She thinks he might still be working at his forge."

As if there were no reason for him to refrain, he hooked his elbow around hers. Juliana's arm tingled strongly at the contact, but if he could be casual, so could she.

"How is it that you speak Gaelic?" she asked. "I thought you came from England."

"Most *upyr* have a knack for picking up what they need, and we travel occasionally amongst ourselves. Lucius came to us that way." A single crease appeared on his forehead. "Lucius was . . . is a member of my pack. I never did learn where he came from originally. He simply showed up one night and asked permission to join a hunt. But as I was saying, there are five packs in Scotland. One in Skye, one in Orkney, and two in the Grampian Mountains. My pack lives a day or so west of Inverness. Because there is only one English group, had I not learned the Scottish tongue, it would have been difficult to rule them all."

Juliana smiled to herself. *Difficult,* he said, but not impossible.

Despite her averted head, Ulric caught her amusement. "Come, Juliana. Do you really doubt I could have prevailed?"

"No, no," she began to laughingly deny. He cut her off by pulling her without warning into a building's lee. If he had been in his wolf form, she would have said his ears were pricked. She began to ask what was wrong.

"Hush," he said, touching her cheek. "I hear English voices."

Juliana heard nothing, but could not doubt his wolf-*upyr* ears. With Ulric holding her hand, they crept to the window of what had to be the village forge. A glow like hell itself filled the single room. Crouched beneath the unglazed window, Ulric set her basket silently on the dirt. Glad it had not occurred to him to leave her behind, she tried to stick her nose over the ledge.

Before she made it, Ulric put his hand on her head and shoved her down.

She would have argued had she not suspected one was easier than two to cloak with a glamour. He, of course, could look all he pleased.

Whoever the other Englishmen were, their reception was not as warm as Ulric's.

"Nay," said a rumbling Scottish baritone, thankfully speaking English. "I am not interested in yer coin."

"How about our swords? Are you interested in them?"

The cool, drawling tones turned her blood to icicles. This voice belonged to Milo Drake, Gideon's younger son. Ulric covered her mouth as soon as she drew breath to warn him. For once, she cursed his lack of skill in reading her actual thoughts.

The blacksmith made a sound that said Milo's sword was prodding a sensitive body part.

"We only want to know," Milo went on, "if you have seen the woman in this locket. Her name is Juliana Buxton. She is English just like us. She might be traveling with a man, a very handsome, very pale, gold-haired man. We think they are pretending to be man and wife."

"Oh, give it up," said a voice Juliana recognized as Milo's older brother, Milton. "We have ridden to every chicken-scratch bung-hole on the map. Good riddance, I say. Father can find himself another broodmare to disrupt our home. No one has seen them. They have not come this way."

"They would go north," insisted another man. "His kind live in the wilderness."

" 'His kind,' " Milton sneered. "What a steaming heap of twaddle. Did you ever think they might have had the good sense to avoid stopping in towns?"

"He has partaken of human blood," said the voice she could not place. "Once they get a taste of the prime elixir, they lose their appetite for beasts."

"Christ on a pitchfork," Milton swore. "I am weary to death of this nonsense."

The smith cried out as someone scuffled through the dirt. Juliana guessed the someone was Milton and that he had poked the smith with his sword.

"If you know anything," Milton snapped, "tell us now, or you can watch your favorite member roast in your fire."

"I ken nothing," said the smith and loudly spat.

Juliana winced. The Milton she knew would kill the blacksmith out of pride alone. Gideon's heir would not care that he was innocent. She straightened beside the window, out of sight but trembling in every limb. "I must stop him," she whispered to Ulric.

He opened his mouth, but to her astonishment did not protest. She had to admit, a shameful part of her wished he would.

*Give me your wrist,* he said instead. *I am going to drink from you and loan you my power to thrall. They will not expect you to have it, and that will give you an advantage, but the transfer will not last long. You must lure them out here, all of them if you can, where I can bite them. Once I do that, I will be able to change their beliefs in a lasting way. I can make them forget they ever wanted to find us—at least long enough for us to disappear. Nod to me now if you understand.*

She nodded, her teeth beginning to chatter.

*Shh,* he hushed her. *This will not hurt at all.*

He kissed her wrist, then the center of her sweating palm. The unexpected tenderness closed her throat. Despite the situation, his breathing sped up. She felt his fangs start to lengthen against her skin. The sensation was peculiar in the extreme.

"I am sorry," she mouthed, the barest brush of sound. "I know you did not want to do this."

His lashes rose, his gaze reluctantly leaving the veins that marked the base of her arm. He was paler than she had ever seen him, a pure blue-white. His glow was so bright it was leaking out from beneath his glamour. With his pupils nearly swallowing his golden eyes, his tongue curled between his teeth.

Juliana's body tightened deep inside.

*I will enjoy this,* he admitted, *no matter what we might regret afterward.*

He lowered his head, licking her wrist as he closed his eyes. His mind-voice murmured her name as reverently as a prayer. Her heart hammered as he set his teeth. Then he bit down.

His tiny moan of pleasure, soft but eloquent, drowned out the quick stab of pain. For a heartbeat, she was in his head, sucking hungrily at her wrist, feeling the sweet, hot fluid run down her throat. Her body resonated with his delight, a languorous orgasm of the mouth.

Lost in his pleasure, in his longing, she had the most astonishing urge to surrender everything she was. *Here I am,* she thought. *Take what you wish.* She tasted spice and wildness. Smelled a forest after a rain. Time folded back on itself and spun. A memory swallowed her in light.

It could have been happening that very moment. She was small, only four or five, and she was sitting on her mother's lap in their home in Bridesmere. They were at the battered kitchen table, the scent of flour heavy in the air. Her mother's long, work-hardened hands covered her short ones. Under both lay a ball of dough.

"Here is how we knead the bread," sing-songed her mother, kissing her wispy hair. "Knead it up, knead it down, knead it all around the town. Yes, Juliana, look how clever you are!"

She was young enough to take her mother's love for granted, but she sensed it all around her like a wonderful, soothing hum, her favorite music in the world. Her mother's voice, her smell, the touch of her gentle hands had faded in the five years since her death, but now Juliana had them back.

She would not let the chance slip away.

"I love you," she said, squirming around to see her mother's face.

"I love you, too, sweetheart," said her mother.

No time would have been enough to savor her smile, and no time was what she had. With a snap like a fresh-washed shirt flapping on a line, Juliana was in the street again, behind the smithy, with Ulric kneeling at her feet. His forehead rested on her hip as if he were too weak to hold it up.

His fingers pressed the place he had bitten. The wound tingled and itched, and she thought it must be healing. Whether it was hardly signified. Ulric had given her a gift greater than his power. Her cheeks were wet with tears she did not trouble to wipe away.

"Thank you," she mouthed when his head came up.

He looked away as if he were embarrassed. *Be careful,* he said, his mind-voice much clearer than it had been before. *Try to catch their eyes, but do not be obvious. You want to convince them just as you would if you had no power. The thrall is merely to help you be more persuasive.*

She could not feel where inside her his thrall might be, but she was calmer now, her shakiness nearly gone. She squeezed his hand and he squeezed back, the grip comfortingly firm. If he believed she could do this, she imagined she had a chance.

She bent to retrieve her knife from her basket, feeling slightly woozy as she changed position. Then she walked around the building to the door. The smoke from the furnace, or some of it, fed through a hole in the roof. The room was hot. Even standing on the threshold, she broke into a sweat.

To her dismay, six men—rather than the three she had expected—ranged around the fire-lit room. She discovered she knew them all.

The four soldiers who accompanied Milton and Milo were the same who had gathered at Bridesmere's gate the night she and Ulric escaped. The captain, the only one who had spoken then, wore a silver cross on a chain around his neck. She did not recall seeing it before. Holding it in one hand, he rubbed it absently with his thumb as he watched the burly, soot-streaked man who had fallen to one knee on the bare dirt floor.

Juliana knew this man must be the smith. His arm and chest bore bloody slashes, and the top of his leather apron hung in strips. So far Drake's sons seemed to have administered nothing but shallow cuts. As she watched, the smith clutched the large stone block on which his anvil sat, trying to regain his feet. Seeing his opponent had no intention of giving up, Milton laughed and caressed his sword.

"You must stop this," Juliana said, turning all eyes to her. "I am the one you want."

This was not the wisest statement to utter when in possession of a borrowed thrall. Every man but the smith took a step toward her.

"Well, well," said Milo, "look who turns up at our heels when we least expect her." He leered at her, his face for once showing an expression, though that particular expression was small improvement. He rubbed his hand up and down his mail-covered thigh. "You cannot imagine how happy I am to get this chance to put you in your place."

Juliana did not think she wanted to know what this meant. "I am sorry," she said, resisting her inclination to bow her head. Ulric had told her she must hold their eyes. "I panicked at the thought of marrying your father, but I am over it. I am ready to go home. Running away was harder than I thought."

Her beaten tone was precisely what Milo expected. Still smirking, he closed the distance between them and clamped his hand on her jaw. At the instant of contact, a glaze entered his eyes. For the first time, Juliana was sure the thrall was at work.

"You do not want to hurt this man," she said softly. "He has nothing to do with me."

Milo's eyes narrowed, but he jerked his head toward his brother. "Release him, Milton. We have what we want."

"Ask her where the *upyr* is," the captain of the men insisted. "We want him as well."

Juliana considered denying Ulric's presence, but feared that lie was too big to sell. "He is outside," she said, careful to meet the captain's gaze. "I wounded him when I got away—rather badly, I believe."

She held up the knife to show them how. To her amazement, the blade was redder than could be accounted for by the fire.

"I will handle him," Milo sneered, but the captain grabbed his arm.

"Do not repeat the mistake I made in Bridesmere. We must take this beast seriously. The *upyr* will heal quickly. We need to catch him before he runs."

"You must all go," Juliana said, trying to look at each face in turn. Even Milton shivered when she did. "I fear his power is too great for any less."

As the six men piled through the door, she prayed she was making the right decision. Strong though Ulric was, she was not certain he could overcome them all. But he had peered in the window. He must have known how many there were.

She directed them around the building where Ulric, bless his quickness, lay in the dirt with his feigned wound. His pretense was so lifelike, she could see blood.

"Do not kill him," Milo said. "He has secrets we might be able to use."

The captain rushed ahead. "Stay back," he ordered. "Whatever you do, do not meet his eyes. I will stun him with my crucifix."

For an instant, the cross did seem to flare with holy fire, but when Juliana blinked, the effect was gone. Maybe the silver had caught a reflection. Whatever the source of the flash, the captain would have been better off leading with his sword. As soon as he was close enough, Ulric's hand shot out to grab the chain, which he used to yank the soldier to his mouth. Thrusting back the aventails of his coif, Ulric bit his neck.

He swallowed once before shoving the man away.

"Be still," he said with a wolflike growl.

The captain collapsed to his knees, two lines of red trickling down his throat. He did not even lift his hand to check the wounds.

Ulric had not lied about a bite giving him more power.

At the sight of their companion, empty-eyed and openmouthed, the others cried out and ran.

"Stop," Ulric ordered, but only two of them did.

Juliana managed to stick her leg in Milo's way, but not to rob him of breath when he tripped. He grabbed her ankle and pulled her down beside him, immediately climbing on top of her and shaking her by the neck. As she struggled to wrench off his choking hold, she saw the blacksmith clout the other two with a pan. Milo's brother, Milton, dropped with a broken moan.

He was lucky the smith had not grabbed his hammer. His skull would have been split.

Not that her own was in such good shape.

"Release me," she ordered, but Milo ignored her, her power to thrall plainly spent. Milo was grinning like a wolf himself. If he did not mean to kill her, he certainly meant to make her swoon—and who knew what he would do then?

To her dismay, she barely had strength to fight. Ulric's feeding had sapped her. Unable to knee her attacker with any force, she attempted to rake his eyes. More annoyed than hurt, he buffeted her ear hard enough to ring. Both hands, apparently, were not required to hold down her neck.

"Help," she gasped, not knowing what else to do.

Milo was swinging his fist again when Ulric grabbed his hauberk from the back and half-yanked, half-hoisted him away. In case she could be of aid, Juliana fought off a fit of coughing. She might as well have indulged. In a blur of motion, and with one hand, Ulric drew Milo's sword from its scabbard and tossed it into the dark. Milo fumbled for his dagger, but Ulric already had it. He threw it hard enough to whistle as it whirled end over end. Juliana heard it stick in the ground with a distant thunk.

Her heart pounded with more than relief. The sight of Ulric coming to the rescue was really quite wonderful—a thrill she would have sworn she was too practical to appreciate. He seemed ten feet tall as he spun Milo around and lifted him by the neck.

If she had not been in love already, this would have sealed her fate.

"You dare," Ulric said in the fiercest voice she had ever heard, his features twisted with rage. "You dare to touch my mate?"

"Ack," said Milo, his feet dangling a foot off the ground. Ulric's left fist held him firmly beneath the jaw, a more impressive echo of what Milo had done to her. Juliana understood Milo's fear. The *upyr*'s eyes were practically spitting fire.

"Please, your worthiness," Milo pleaded, "I meant no harm. I did not know she was yours."

The groveling won him no quarter. Ulric tossed him against the wall with rattling force. "You are almost too disgusting to bite."

He did bite him, though, then yanked the portrait locket Gideon Drake had commissioned off Milo's sword belt. That taken care of, Milo sank under Ulric's thrall as easily as the captain had.

Ulric moved to the others one by one. Even the unconscious men felt his teeth. The instructions Ulric gave them were mind to mind and, whatever they were, they struck each man like physical blows. After the twitch of reaction, their eyes went glassy, the muscles of their faces slack. The effect was eerie, as if they were losing part of themselves. Finally, only the smith remained.

The Scotsman lifted his work-scarred hands to show he was harmless but did not back away. Breathing hard, he looked as if he had thought the brawl good fun. Perhaps a big man like him refused to fear anyone.

"I helped ye fight," he said. "Ye doona have to mess with me."

"I must erase your memory," Ulric said.

The blacksmith grinned and shook his head. "Ye canna," he said. "We follow the old ways here." He pulled aside what Milton had left of his leather apron to bare a blue tattoo in the center of his hairy chest. The simple figure was a warrior with a shield and spear. His feet stood on a spiral, and above his head shone the sun. "Ye see. The wolf-men are no enemies to me and mine. Leave us be, and our races can live in peace." He chuckled as if he were remembering a good joke. "Always thought me granddad was lying when he told those tales."

"No," said Ulric. "He did not lie."

The blacksmith slapped his knee. "Nearly laughed meself silly when that fellow ran at ye with his cross."

Juliana wondered if she were the only one who had seen it flash.

"That is human nature," Ulric said with a shrug. "People like to think their God wipes out the ones who came before."

"Not here." The smith gestured to the cross carved roughly above his door. "In Dunburn we honor them all."

Though Ulric's expression was serene, Juliana sensed his discomfort with this exchange. She stepped forward to catch the Scotsman's eye.

"Master smith," she addressed him politely, "now that these men pose no danger, do you suppose you could sell us a small cauldron?"

This, to her, did not seem a humorous request, but the smith roared out a laugh. "Aye," he said. "Never lose sight of business and ye'll go far."

He fetched what she wanted from his sweltering workroom, then accepted Juliana's coin with an approving nod. Juliana took the cauldron herself, knowing Ulric could not touch the iron.

"Ye're a smart, braw lass," the blacksmith said, adding to Ulric, "Ye take care of her."

They were dismissed, it seemed, a treatment Ulric took in unexpected stride. Once again collecting her basket, he left the smith to deal with the fallen Englishmen as he pleased.

As soon as the village was well behind their backs, Juliana spoke. "What was that picture on his chest?"

"Honestly, I do not know. A Pictish spell drawing is my best guess. The packs use similar designs to mark their territory, but my sire never said much about their origin."

From tales her mother told her as a girl, Juliana knew the Picts were early inhabitants of Scotland. They lived in tribes at first, later uniting under a king. Hunters and warriors, they liked to run around naked except for their blue tattoos. It was said they were small of stature but as swift as their fighting steeds. Good seamen, they worshiped the sun, and their priests were called Druids. Their successors, the Scots, adopted many Pictish practices as their own, later blending them with Christian rite.

This was the sum of Juliana's knowledge and yet, from what Ulric was saying, she knew more than he.

"Could the smith's tattoo have prevented you from thralling him?"

"Possibly. He did seem to have strong guards."

"But why would a Pictish spell work and not a cross?"

"Because, supposedly, Pictish magic was inspired by the magic of the first *upyr*. Whatever essence makes us immortal understands and does homage to those symbols."

"Are you certain a cross has no power? I thought I saw a flash when the captain first held it up."

"I see no reason for Christian objects to work on us, but, as I said, I cannot tell you more than that."

"Forgive me for being blunt, Ulric, but had I been in your shoes, I would have insisted my sire explain."

"You and Gillian both," Ulric said dryly. "She always wanted to know the reason for everything."

The reminder of her rival—if Juliana did not flatter herself with the term—quashed any thought of further conversation. How fortunate she was to possess none of his previous lover's good points, yet still have room for the bad!

But bitterness would gain her nothing. She comforted herself that he had called her his mate and had reclaimed her locket. Ulric might not have meant much by these deeds, but both suggested attachment.

Assuming, of course, that she was not grasping at straws.

She began to shiver as the night's events caught up with her nerves. Seeing Milton and Milo again, witnessing the violence she had not known they were capable of, made her aware of how fragile her freedom was. Certainly, she need no longer feel a shred of remorse for running away. Her decision had been wiser than she suspected.

Seeing her shudder in earnest, Ulric swung off his cloak and wrapped it around her. "Take it," he ordered, though she had not thought to resist.

That his arm would have been more welcome she kept to herself.

In silence, they labored up a slope on which the grass had been cropped by cattle. When she glanced over her shoulder to see if she could spot the herd, the village had been engulfed by the mist. She wondered if the smith would tell his children of the encounter, and if they, too, would roll their eyes.

However far-fetched, the tale would make a perfect addition to her collection, just the sort her mother had preferred. Nothing pleased her more than drawing scenes of fantastic combat. Demons with lots of teeth had been her favorite, followed closely by dragons.

And maybe, Juliana thought, that preference went a way toward explaining her daughter's affinity for Ulric. She had cut her teeth, so to speak, on tales of monsters.

She had this revelation as they reached the top of the hill. Beyond it lay another even higher, dotted with clumps of trees and cut in two by a silvery stream, the same that she had washed in earlier. As if they stood within the edges of a cloud, here the mist thinned to a veil. She could just make out a line of mountains behind the hills. Their bulk stretched like a wall across the horizon, remnants of the winter's snow snaking at their peaks.

For a moment, she was frightened. This country was too big, too remote. It would swallow her like an ogre in a tale. But then the shiver of fear was chased away by exhilaration. Juliana broke into a grin. The wild, strange beauty of the land sang to some newly awakened corner of her soul. She wanted to paint it, or perhaps hold it in her arms.

To her surprise, Ulric did not pause.

"I want to thank you," she said, knowing she owed him that.

"I need no thanks. You are the one who risked the most rescuing that smith."

"I meant for the memory of my mother. I had almost forgotten what she was like. When you bit me, you gave her back."

Ulric stopped and rubbed his face with both hands. When he dropped them, he met her eyes. His held an emotion she could not read, though it might have been wariness.

"That was your doing," he said. "Your heart called her up. And I am the one who should be thanking you."

He strode ahead of her, almost too quickly for her to keep up—not what she considered the actions of a grateful man. She drew breath to question him, then let it out. In his current mood, she was not certain she wanted him to explain.

He might start in again about how he could never love her.

"We will reach the Grampians tonight," he said, nodding toward the mountains' spectacular silhouette. "It will not be much longer till we are home."

Till *you* are home, she thought, biting her lower lip. Where she would find hers seemed much less clear.

—————

SHE wanted to thank him. *She* wanted to thank *him.*

Ulric watched the early summer grasses flatten beneath his boots, his mind refusing to stop reeling. He had barely been able to control his thoughts since he bit her, shoving back his shock from necessity. Now that the danger had passed, his extremely unwise feelings whirled to the fore.

She had opened her soul without hesitation. Never had he connected with anyone so deeply, not even Gillian. He had been there with Juliana, held in her mother's arms, the love they shared jabbing his heart as if he, too, were cherished. This memory was the key to who she was. Her bravery, her warmth, her confidence in herself, even her natural sensuality, all grew out of her mother's love.

Juliana was real to him now, as real as he was to himself. Because of this, he was forced to admit the very last thing he wanted to. Less than a fortnight after meeting her, less than a month after Gillian broke his heart, he had fallen in love with this human girl.

His stupidity would have been comical had it involved anyone but him. Only hours before, he had been congratulating himself on driving her to arm's length—an accomplishment that now seemed especially idiotic. Even worse, Juliana was more like Gillian than he had guessed, with the same curiosity, the same craving for independence, the same attachment to the creations of the human world. Never would she be content living with his pack, taking his orders, isolated in a cave.

He would lose her, just as he had lost Gillian.

Unless he changed.

The thought pulled him up short. Could he change? He had been who and what he was for two hundred years. But maybe, if he put his heart into the effort . . . He rubbed the ball of his chin and finally noticed Juliana panting in his wake.

"Phew," she said, drawing her sleeve across her forehead. "That is a little too fast for me."

"Forgive me, Juliana. I should have kept to your normal pace."

"No matter." She waved her hand in dismissal. "Now that we have left the danger behind us, I feel more vigorous than usual. All that excitement must have done me good."

Her grin caused his chest to tighten in the most ludicrous way. What spirit she had! What a wonderful *upyr* she would be! And, oh, what nonsense men in love could spout.

"That is the effect of my bite," he said gruffly. "After a brief period of weakness, it endows a human with extra strength."

"I see. Maybe if you keep biting me, we can reach your home in record time."

*Your* home as well, he thought but did not presume to say.

"We can rest if you require it," he offered, determined to make a start on his reformation.

"No, no." She drew a bracing breath of sweet Highland air. "I am ready to push on."

Despite her declaration, he proceeded more moderately. He felt awkward, unable to think of what he ought to say. She was quiet, too, matching him stride for stride. Because they often walked without speaking, the atmosphere should have been more comfortable than it was.

Without the distraction of conversation, his mind returned to what she had said. The thought of biting her again caused him to fist his hands and swallow hard.

He could keep biting her. The damage was already done.

He wanted to that very instant, wanted to push her over the nearest boulder, facedown, skirts shoved to her waist, to take her in every way an *upyr* could. He did not want to ask permission or be polite. He just wanted to do it—hard, fast, deep—until she cried out in complete surrender.

He shook his head in disgust. He was a beast, an unrepentant marauder of maidens. The mere thought of changing his ways made him want to ravish her even more.

"Ulric?" Juliana said, reduced to trotting again to keep up.

He cursed himself under his breath.

"I was wondering," she said, seeming more hesitant than upset. "I am not doubting you, only asking. Are you certain Gideon Drake's men will not trouble us again?"

"Yes," he said, then debated whether to explain. Gillian would have wanted him to. Most likely, so would Juliana. "I was not . . . delicate with them. When they return to normal awareness, they might not recall their names. Most of the effect should wear off within a season, but a full memory of what happened might never come back. Hopefully, the people of Dunburn will point them back toward England."

Juliana's eyes were wide. "You have that much power?"

"Actually, the extent of the damage is evidence that my power is not as practiced as it might be. Greater skill than mine is required to remove precisely what is desired. With my victims in Bridesmere, I was careful to do no harm. That might be why they were left with vague memories."

Concern flickered across Juliana's face an instant before she hid it.

With a fair idea of what she was thinking, Ulric clasped her shoulder to make her stop. "Juliana, I shall never thrall you against your will."

He felt better as soon as he said it, as if the promise lifted a burden of doubt. Whatever his faults, Ulric never broke his word.

She stared at him for a moment and then blinked. "Thank you, Ulric. I would appreciate that very much."

"It is nothing," he said, beginning to walk again. "Besides, I am not certain I could coerce you as I did those men. I suspect you have a partial resistance."

"I do?" Her voice was as pleased as if he had given her a gift. "I thought I might but I was not sure. Of course, I have no idea why that would be. Until I met you I never had the least bit of sensitivity to otherworldly things. Never saw a ghost or had a vision—though I knew some who did. Maybe I understand human nature better than others, but that is only because I listen to what people say."

Her words burbled over him, a definite spring entering her step. He wished she were not this elated. More than anything, her reaction convinced him that she wanted to rule herself. He could not conceive how that would work when his nature drove him to conquer everything he saw.

Hell, he thought as she lifted her skirts to scramble over a fallen pine. Keeping Juliana happy would be the biggest challenge of his life.

# Six

APPROPRIATELY enough, they took shelter for the day in the weedy ruins of an ancient Pict's tower. Built as two concentric shells of dry stone, the broch's thick walls still held between them a few sound rooms. In one of these Ulric and Juliana curled up together, front to back, truly safe for once from entry by the sun. They did not build a fire, but Ulric's closeness and his cloak were enough to keep Juliana cozy in the chamber of cool, damp stone.

She had never been anywhere this quiet. No bird sound penetrated the massive walls, no wind, no rustle and snap of squirrels through leaves. The only noises were those she and Ulric made themselves. From the manner in which he held her, with his fingers idly fanning her hip, she could tell he was still awake.

She would not have minded making love, but his mood had been so strange since they left Dunburn, she lacked the nerve to suggest it. Instead, she squirmed a little deeper into his hold. Lifting his arm to let her move, he grunted as the front of his knee hit the back of hers. Happily, the grunt did not seem annoyed.

"I wonder how your kind first crossed paths with the Picts," she mused aloud. "Do you suppose some of the early Druid priests were *upyr*? Maybe their position as kings' advisors ensured that the people of this region would view you in a friendly light. Perhaps it was considered an honor to give a blood sacrifice."

She blushed to remember how she had enjoyed it, but Ulric's response was another noncommittal noise. The arm he resettled around her waist seemed tense. Maybe she should not have mentioned blood. Just because he had finally bitten her did not mean he was reconciled to the idea. Obviously, it was a very personal act.

"Do you suppose the Picts hid in these towers when they were attacked?" she asked, trying to choose a safer topic. "I think they must have had other dwellings for day to day. Living without windows would get dreary."

Ulric released his breath, a wearier sound than she expected. "I cannot answer these questions. I was not here."

"You really are not curious?"

"I do not think about the past. The present has interest enough." He shifted behind her as if he could not get comfortable, despite Juliana having fit them together perfectly. "Possibly I could learn to be curious."

He sounded like a child offering to eat a turnip as the price of some better treat. Juliana did not try to hide her amusement. "Do not strain yourself," she laughed. "I think people are either born curious or they are not. Of course, you might be saving your curiosity for things like wolves and deer."

"I like wine," he said, oddly defensive. "When I was in Bridesmere, I enjoyed it—though it did not make me drunk. And velvet. If one has to wear clothes, velvet is acceptable. It is almost as soft as skin."

"Silk velvet," she said with a merchant's daughter's sigh. "The Italians make the best. And their brocades! Though they cost the moon, they are worth every penny. Of course, much can be said for English wool. If it is well woven and fulled, you could drag it behind a donkey and it would not shred—as I am proving on this trip.

Then again, the survival of my gown might be due to you lending your magic to preserve it."

"I would happily preserve whatever you wish."

His arm tightened around her, his chest moving close enough to support her back. She suspected she felt more comforted than was wise.

Never mind, she told herself stubbornly. I will enjoy this for as long as it lasts. Bodily, at least, she was safe. If he had ever wanted to hurt her, he would have done so by now.

As if he also enjoyed their closeness, Ulric nuzzled closer to her neck. The growing heaviness of his hold told her he would soon rest.

"Ulric?" she said, determined to overcome her earlier cowardice.

"Mm?"

"The woman you loved—was she an *upyr*?"

"Yes." The acknowledgment sighed out against her ear. "Gillian was *upyr*."

"And the man she . . . left you for?"

"He was human. She made him immortal after she fell in love."

"I cannot imagine any woman turning away from you."

She meant the words to reassure him, but his answer was strangely dour. "It is true we *upyr* possess a powerful draw."

"You are irresistible," she said, trying to tease.

All she got for her efforts was a grunt. Behind her, Ulric's chest felt more rocklike than usual.

"You do not want to talk about her."

"No, but if you insist, I will."

This response was quite enough to shut her up.

<hr />

ULRIC roused before Juliana, the arrival of dusk bringing him fully awake. Not so for his companion. Either Juliana was growing accustomed to days turned on their heads, or she needed to see the sun to know the hour. Ulric could feel its departure, a cool and quiet tingling beneath his skin. His eyes snapped open, the world once again safe for his kind.

In the distance a fox yipped to her kits—a scold, he thought, for wandering from the den.

Ulric was tempted to answer with a howl. He and Juliana lay on their sides as before, but she had turned in her sleep until her face was buried in his tunic. One arm hugged him to her, while the other was caught between their bellies. Her upper leg was slung over his, completely lax, the roundness of her calf pressed softly behind his own.

Observing how deeply she slept made him realize she was usually on guard, watching over him when he could not.

Would she really do this for any *upyr,* or was a portion of her protectiveness just for him?

At a loss to answer, Ulric eased away from her and straightened his clothes, ignoring the nagging heaviness of his loins. He knew how to test his theory easily enough. As soon as they joined up with his pack, she would be confronted with one of the most flirtatious immortals ever created. Though Ulric would stop him if he went too far, Stephen could be relied upon to try to seduce her. For that matter, Lucius had been known to attract female eyes. By the time they returned, his most senior pack member should have gotten back from his self-appointed mission as Gillian's mentor.

The memory of Lucius's defection further darkened Ulric's mood. Lucius had supported Gillian's efforts to run away, then helped her learn how to change her human lover into *upyr*. Ulric would have disciplined any other subordinate, but Lucius followed him strictly by choice. Had he ever challenged Ulric, Ulric could not say who would have won. In the end, Lucius turned out to have more power than anyone suspected—including Lucius himself. He was, so he claimed, one of their kind's few elders. Until Gillian prodded his memories with her endless questions, Lucius had forgotten how much he knew.

The discovery had startled them all, but no one more than Ulric.

The man he had known for ages, the man he had considered a sort of friend despite his reserve, had turned out to be an utter stranger. Ulric had to wonder if it were possible to know anyone. What he would say to Lucius when they met again he could not conceive.

Ulric shook his head. He would cross that bridge when he got home.

To that, he was looking forward. Once he returned to familiar surroundings, once he had people to lead, he was certain he would feel more himself, more able to lay siege to Juliana's heart. He would be glad to see even Gytha, who never missed an opportunity to be a thorn in his side.

He doubted she would be pleased to meet Juliana. As the pack's dominant female, Gytha had hoped to replace Gillian as his queen. That he had not invited her to do so stuck in her craw. If he showed up with a human . . . Well, he would have to move swiftly to put Gytha in her place—before she chewed Juliana to pieces and spit her out.

Juliana drew him from the thought of that daunting prospect by mumbling in her sleep. His gaze drifted to the pulse beating in her throat. If he were sensible, he would feed from her when she woke. By the time she finished her ablutions, her lassitude would have faded. She would be ready for hard travel.

Or maybe it would be better to abstain. If he bit her now, with his nature urging him to claim her, they might not end up traveling at all.

She was strong for a human. They could manage as they had before.

JULIANA heard the river before she saw it, neither roar nor splash, but a ceaseless ripple where waves met air.

"The Spey," Ulric said, tipping his head toward the sound. "We have reached the crossing."

They had been tramping up and down forested slopes most of

the night. Now they emerged from a final line of trees onto a gravel shingle. As they did, a twisted pine branch, silvered by the crescent moon, swept down the current. The speed of its passage stopped her breath. To her horror, by "crossing" Ulric did not mean over a bridge.

"Er," she said, "would now be a good time to mention I cannot swim?"

Ulric's laugh rumbled in his chest. This, of all things, restored his mood. "We can wade much of the way. The bed is shallow along the banks. Where it is too deep, I will carry you on my back. My wolf is an excellent swimmer."

"Your wolf! Ulric, I do not think—"

He hooked his arm behind her neck and kissed her, a cheery smacking of lips. "We will tie you on if you like. Believe me, your head is likelier to stay above water that way than if I took you in my human form."

She swallowed back further protest. Bridges meant humans, and she would not soon forget the pursuit they had faced in Dunburn. One memory in particular haunted her thoughts. While trying to prevent his men-at-arms from killing Ulric, Milo had claimed Ulric had secrets they might be able to use. To her, that suggested they were as interested as she was in Ulric's power. Many humans wanted to cheat death or gain advantages over their peers. Could a desire that seductive be erased from their minds? Until she was certain, she did not want to risk meeting Milo and Milton again—or anyone else who might share their aims.

She began to see why Ulric's sire wanted his children to live apart from her kind. Juliana herself could not claim her desire to become *upyr* had brought out her best.

Ulric had been chosen. Juliana tried to demand.

Ulric read the consternation on her face, if not its cause. "I will not let the river have you," he assured her, gently stroking her cheek. "You are in my care."

After tucking his clothes into her basket, he changed into his wolf form at the river's edge. For once, she was too distracted to enjoy the show. Though the water was icy and the gravel slick with moss, she forged ahead until the current rose to her hips. At that point she could not keep her footing except by clinging to his ruff. Her skirts felt ten times as heavy wet.

Her hands were shaking far too badly to tie herself to his back.

*Give me the basket,* he instructed, his eyes dancing as if this were a game of fetch. *I will carry it in my teeth. If you lock your hands around my ribs, you will not interfere with my stroke.*

His back was broad, thank goodness, and a far less slippery platform than the riverbed. Gritting her teeth, Juliana wrapped her arms around him and gripped each of her wrists with the opposite hand. His fur did not smell the least bit doggy even wet, but more like the forest they had just left. In the hope that the danger she could not see would not upset her, she screwed her eyes shut and buried her face behind his ear.

*Here we go,* he said, his voice laughing in her head.

She would have cursed him if she had not wanted to keep her mouth firmly shut.

As soon as he began to swim, they started lurching up and down. Waves broke over her shoulders, soaking even her hair. Sputtering, she opened her eyes.

"You are not going straight!" she exclaimed, to which Ulric's wolf gave a wet snort.

*Even I cannot fight a current this strong. We will land downstream at that other spit where the river bends.*

She kept quiet after that because he actually seemed to be laboring. Beneath her chest, his heart was beating as fast as hers. The farther shore seemed leagues away.

Oh, God, she thought. I should have insisted he feed from me when we woke. That pine marten he caught could not have been satisfying. Maybe he is too weak.

He was puffing through his nose by the time his paws hit gravel again. Completely numb, Juliana rolled off his back. Had he not changed quickly enough to grab her, the current would have washed her away.

"Only knee-high here," he panted. "We can walk the rest."

Stumble was more like it. No longer able to feel her feet, Juliana fell face-first onto the bank.

"I cannot move," she mumbled into the flattened reeds.

"Fine," he said. "You wait here."

To her surprise, she heard a whoosh of air as he changed into his wolf form and then, even more amazingly, a splash.

Juliana was so stunned she managed to sit up. If she had not seen it for herself, she would not have believed it. He had gone back into the river and was performing a peculiar dance, pouncing left, then right, then disappearing altogether beneath the waves. Though the logical part of her knew he would be all right, the part that had just been dragged across an icy deluge began to cry.

When she saw what he had dived under the water for, her tears turned into sobs. He had no consideration—none!—risking that river a second time for a stupid fish.

He, naturally, had no idea she was angry. Ears erect and tail waving proudly, he was prancing as he trotted toward her. He dropped the fish, a fat Scottish salmon, at her feet. He was laughing already as he whirled into his human form.

"There," he said. "Something for dinner. I thought I would give my wolf the chance to sample your cookery."

At that moment, she regretted she was too well brought up to slap him.

"Hey," he said, kneeling down as he saw her tears. "Did something happen while I was gone?"

"What happened was that you left!" she spat. "You went back into that terrible river."

"No, no." He dried her cheeks with his palms. "It is a good river, Juliana. See, it gave us a fish."

"I suppose you expect me to gut it."

His faint, pink flush gave her a satisfaction she was almost ashamed to feel. "It *is* your knife. And you do have more practice at that than I."

"I am all wet," she said. "And I am freezing. And you frightened me very much!"

"Very well." He pulled her into his naked chest. He, she noticed, was completely dry. "I suppose you are entitled to have a cry. God knows, you have been through enough in the last few days."

"Do not humor me. I am not being childish!"

"No, no," he agreed against her hair. "The thought never crossed my mind."

She knew it had and, what is more, she knew it might be justified. He had, to be fair, carried her across that river at some effort to himself. Indeed, he had been a good sport for this whole journey, considering she had forced him to bring her along. Most likely she did owe his wolf a meal.

Pulling her dignity together, she stuck out her hand. "I will take the fish now."

"No," he said more firmly. "Sit for a bit and get warm."

Without waiting for permission, he lifted her into his lap, running his hands over her clothes and skin. His *upyr* magic dried her quickly, but then she did not want to move. She could not say which was more mortifying: her earlier loss of control or this boneless compliancy. She supposed it did not matter. She intended to remain as she was either way.

She could not be blamed if Ulric put her humors out of sort.

"We should have stripped you," he said. "That English wool weighs a ton."

Another woman might have been insulted. Juliana sighed and pressed her nose to his neck. She knew it must be cold if his skin felt warm.

Ulric squeezed her upper arm. "Better get up," he warned, "before you fall asleep. We would not want the fish that struck such terror to go to waste."

She had recovered enough to smile.

He pressed his own smile lightly onto her lips.

He cares for me, she thought, whatever he may tell himself. For now, that was enough to get her on her feet.

"Ulric?" she said, glancing at her sodden and increasingly battered basket. "Do you think you could dry my spices, too?"

"I live to serve," he said with a grin.

Watching him turn on his knees to rescue her belongings, she wished he would as easily agree to serve her in bed. As he propped himself on one arm, the muscles of his back fanned out from his spine in lovely patterns. The single dimple at the top of his narrow buttocks put her in mind of his waving tail. Beneath that flawless skin, his wolf still dwelled, a creature of impulse and dark hungers. If nothing else, she thought she could count on those traits to drive him back to her arms.

She needed every chance she could get to win him from the memory of Gillian.

———————

AS it turned out, Juliana's cooking tasted as good as it smelled. Ulric's enjoyment was marred only by his efforts to eat it delicately. Though he had to change form to consume it, it seemed inconsiderate to wolf her creation down.

"Ulric?" she said as he swallowed the last smoky pink bite.

The sound of her voice saying his name made a shiver run through his pelt. It felt odd that she was beginning to treat his beast and him as one—not bad, but slightly unnerving.

He wagged his tail in answer, wondering if he should change.

"Could I pet you a bit?" she asked. "If that would not be impolite?"

A whine slipped from his throat over which he had no control, the sound of a puppy pleading for a cuddle. He snapped his teeth on the noise, hoping she could not guess what it meant.

He had not known his wolf could fall in love, as well.

Aware that she was waiting, he rose from the place where he

had laid down to eat, stretched his legs, and padded to her side. As soon as he sat, she buried both face and hands in his fur.

"You are so soft!" she exclaimed, then fought a laugh. "I am sorry, Ulric. I will try not to coo again."

He was not certain he would have cared. Her gently thorough scratching sent him straight into wolfish bliss.

*Behind the ears,* he said, giving in to his longing to lay his muzzle on her feet.

Tomorrow night would be soon enough to put her wishes first.

⚬

JULIANA did not know why, but Ulric was politeness itself during the next stretch of their journey, consulting her on more decisions than she felt any need to be consulted on. She had no idea if it was easier to hike down a valley or over a pass, nor if hunting geese was better than hunting deer.

"Do as you wish," she said. "You know these lands and, I trust, the preferences of your stomach."

"But I want to do what you would most like."

"Do I have some strange transforming substance in my blood? You have not been yourself since you bit me."

His chest inflated with offense. "I am myself. Who else would I be? This is precisely who I am. I treat my companions as equals."

Juliana paused to shake a pebble out of her shoe. "Maybe it was biting Milo that caused the problem. If anyone's blood contained something sickening, it would be his."

"There is nothing sick about my wanting you to enjoy this trip!"

Juliana stared at him, taken aback by his display of temper. She could actually hear him grinding his teeth. "I am enjoying this trip. This country is beautiful. But because I know nothing of what you are asking me to choose between, I cannot predict which I would like more. Truly, I did not mean to upset you."

"I . . . am . . . not . . . upset."

The words were so close to a growl, she had to grin.

"Go ahead," he said, throwing up his hands. "Laugh at the foolish wolf king. God knows, I would laugh if I could."

Still confused as to what was bothering him, she slipped her hand under his hair to cup the back of his neck. The smoothness and strength of the tendons that lay beneath gave her pleasure all by themselves. She tried to encourage them to relax by kneading them with her fingers.

"Devil take it," he surrendered, rolling his head around with a sigh. "We will follow the route that leads by Loch Ness. Maybe we will get lucky and see the monster."

"Good," she said, lowering her hand to lightly scratch his back. "Monsters are my favorite things."

Even a week ago, he would have preened at this obvious compliment. Now, he pulled a face and pressed on. Her only consolation was that he did not avoid her touch.

---

LOCH Ness was huge and deep and long, its waters black from the peat-soaked rivers that flowed in from the surrounding hills. Though Ulric and Juliana watched for some time, they were not fortunate enough to encounter the famous monster, merely a herd of tall red deer. Ulric's wolf self was just as pleased with that, nearly driving him to change before he noticed what was happening and forced a stop. The slip filled him with unease. The more Ulric suppressed his hungers, the stronger his wolf's became.

Juliana could claim to love monsters all she liked; if Ulric was not careful, he would never convince her he could be more.

And he did, after all, prefer that she love one monster above the rest.

"Go," she said, misreading his hesitation. "I will be fine right here."

Their camp being nowhere near habitation, Ulric expected she was right. Eager to be off, his wolf gave him just enough time to remove his clothes.

More control than he had ever exerted was required to keep from gutting the first deer he brought down. The scent of the creature's fear, the excitement of the chase, and the warmth of its russet hide went to his head, leaving him with urges and instincts and precious little rational thought. The merest shred remained to remind him Juliana watched. If a hare had shocked her, she would faint at the sight of him tearing into a deer's viscera.

With a whimpering growl, he wrenched his muzzle away, changing into his man form so he could drink from the young stag's neck. His instincts calmed at the first few swallows. He was able to leave the animal alive.

Two more deer succumbed to his chase before he was sated, the hunt leading him far from Juliana's camp. He returned near dawn, weary, but at peace. He waded into the loch to cool the last of his hunter's heat.

When he emerged, temporarily dripping and raking his hair back with his hands, the way her eyes slid over his body made him break into a sweat again.

"You did not kill that first deer," she said, looking away too soon to see his member swell.

For some reason, Ulric was embarrassed to admit he had refrained from killing because of her. "It would have been wasteful," he said. "Without the pack to help me, I could not have eaten all that meat."

"Ah," she said, her hands smoothing her skirt.

She sat on a boulder near the shallow cave where they would sleep, their doorstep further sheltered by the drooping branches of a pine. Needles carpeted the ground around the circle of stones in which she had built her cook fire. Only embers remained, but they lit her face enough for an *upyr* like him to see.

When she tucked her hair behind her ears, her downturned profile entranced his eyes. Her nose was straight, her cheeks childishly soft, her lips both wide and full. The slight squareness of her jaw was all that intimated stubbornness. Ulric tried to imagine her as an *upyr* but could pick no feature in need of improvement. Even the tiny pock that marked one temple had won a place in his heart. She was Juliana. She was perfect just as she was.

"I suppose you are weary after your hunt," she said, her eyes sliding to his.

Through the heavy perfume of pine he thought he caught a hint of arousal, suggesting that she, too, was tired of him holding back. The possibility made his body throb hard and hot.

Say the words, he thought, without pushing into her mind. Ask me to take you, and I will have proved that I can wait, that I can put a woman's desires above my own.

But perhaps she was remembering his earlier rebuffs. She pointed toward the outcropping of rock behind her. "I have woven some branches together as a barrier for the opening."

"Good," he said. "Thank you."

Despite his recent feeding, his mouth went dry at the graceful turn of her neck. He wanted to kiss that firelit column, wanted to drag his teeth and lips over every inch of her skin.

Then he wanted to repeat the process with his cock.

"I will—" He stopped to clear the roughness from his voice. "I will come in with you in a moment. I think I would like to take one last swim."

She did not offer to join him. He had a feeling she guessed why he needed to cool off and was—to judge by the pursing of her lips—insulted by his restraint. Ulric cursed himself in his head.

He had backed them into a corner he could not fathom how to escape.

# Seven

ALMOST lost among the oak and ash, two upright slabs of granite marked the southern edge of Ulric's territory. Like winter frost, the moon reflected off the tiny crystals that made up the stones. As if uncertain what she was seeing, Juliana squinted and rubbed her eyes.

"What are those things?" she asked in a stymied voice.

"Menhirs," he said. "Standing stones." He laid his hand on her shoulder, the urge to touch her too strong to defy. She belonged beside him when he crossed this final barrier to his home.

"Why do they look so blurry?"

Ulric glanced back at the stones. To him, the menhirs seemed bright and clear, almost white under the rising moon. "Perhaps they carry a touch of glamour, to hide them from human eyes. Take my hand and I will lead you through them."

The bracken was thick here, the path the merest shadow of clearer ground. Juliana shivered as they passed between the sentinels, but her fingers remained warm. By unspoken accord, they turned once they were through. The stones were twice Ulric's height and wider than his arms could reach. Unlike the roughness of their backs, their fronts were clearly worked. Chisels had planed them flat and marked them with carvings.

"Those are the symbols you spoke of," Juliana said, her voice hushed with respect. "The ones that guard the boundaries of your lands."

"Yes." He carried her knuckles upward for a kiss that she was too caught up to notice. "These glyphs have probably been here for thousands of years. I am sorry I cannot translate them, but at least you are seeing them for yourself."

"They are amazing. And so simple! I feel as if I ought to know what they mean, as if all I needed was the patience to stare at them long enough and they would speak."

Ulric smiled at her fancy. "I cannot promise that method would lead to success, but if you like, you can come back some time and try."

"There is a fish," she said, pointing at the obvious. "And, look, that must be the sun!"

Ulric tried to see the marks as she did. They were spirals for the most part, crudely drawn and interspersed with signs for the sun and moon. Seemingly at random, they grouped themselves around a centaurlike version of a wolf, half-person and half-beast. On the right stone, the wolf had a man's torso, and on the left it bore a woman's, both worn to faintness by wind and rain.

They did not strike him as particularly interesting depictions, but when Juliana tentatively traced the outline of the female wolf, hairs bristled on his arms. Dimly, perhaps only visible to Ulric's eyes, the lines bore a tinge of rust.

"I should feed them," he said, remembering a long-ago lesson from his sire.

"Feed them?"

"My sire, Auriclus, once told me that a blood offering is supposed to renew their magic. They must still have some if they are hiding themselves from you."

"And maybe humans who had not been traveling in your

company would see nothing at all. Maybe they would walk right past this place and keep going."

"Maybe," he agreed. They met each other's gaze and smiled, the moon-bright stones reflected small in Juliana's eyes.

"I will leave if the ritual is too private," she said, but Ulric shook his head. Whatever magic lived in the stones, he sensed it had accepted her.

Not one to fuss, he cut his wrist with a quick slash of his teeth, dabbed his fingertip in the blood, and dragged it around the man-wolf's outline. The cut had healed by the time he moved to the second stone.

"Wait." Juliana stopped him as he lifted his wrist to his mouth again. Her manner was hesitant. "I would like to make an offering—if you think the stone would not mind." She nodded toward the drawing in front of her. "I know I am not *upyr,* but this one *is* a girl."

"So she is."

He did not suggest she prick herself with her knife—even he did not have that much self-denial—but brought her hand slowly to his lips. She could have stopped him any time she wished. As he had behind the forge in Dunburn, he kissed her palm, then drew her middle finger into his mouth. Rather than bite her wrist, he nipped her finger's pad. She gasped in surprise, her gaze widening on his own. He sucked at the wound, once, to start the flow. Even at this small taste, his body thrummed. She was as sweet and potent as he recalled.

The bite affected her as well. He felt the change in her vibration like a caress.

With obvious reluctance, she pulled her finger free. She stared at the welling crimson as if entranced. When he tried to speak, his voice was hoarse.

"Less blood from a finger," he explained. "You bleed more easily than I."

She shook herself, then turned to press the cut to the stone.

The instant she touched it the air seemed to quake, as if the stone were shaking itself, too. If Juliana felt it, she gave no sign. Biting her lip and careful not to miss a spot, she drew her blood around the glyph. He would have laughed at her concentration if he had been able to keep his lungs filled with breath. His veins were throbbing, his skin itchy and warm.

He desired her, but more than that, he wanted her to complete the rite. Her act fed something deep inside him, as much as it fed the stone. It was a gift a queen would give, a gift a queen should have been giving for centuries.

*Guide me,* he thought, a spontaneous prayer to the old gods. *Help me make her mine. I know she will always treat you with respect.*

Light flared as she closed the outline, not flame but hot blue glow. Abruptly, every spell-picture on the menhirs sprang to life— suns, moons, spirals, as well as carvings that had been invisible before. Ulric spotted a serpent and a tree and an odd, pointy cylinder, which two stick figures rode like witches on a broom. He could not imagine what they represented. No *upyr* he knew had the power to fly. Without warning, the desire to solve the mystery swelled inside him. This was what Juliana experienced every day. This was curiosity.

He turned to her, watching her hands draw back to cover her mouth.

"Oh," she breathed. "Look how marvelous."

Ulric could not look. Ulric only had eyes for her.

She was glowing in the reflection of the stones, flushed with wonder and delight, the biggest mystery of all. What did she feel, truly? What did love and loyalty mean to her? What drove her to embrace the world so completely? He had seen a hint of the answer in her mother's memory, but it was not nearly enough.

He wanted to spend his life discovering her secrets.

"Juliana," he said, his voice more wolf than man.

When she turned to him, joy thumped in his chest.

"Did you see?" she said with a gasping laugh. "I did a little bit of magic."

"Not just a little." Throat tight, he tugged her into his arms. "You used your magic to steal my heart."

Her lips moved on his name. He could see the war in her: to believe or to guard her heart. His tone had been deliberately light. Was he teasing, she must wonder, or did he mean what he said?

The words she needed for reassurance were too big, too soon; he could not admit to them yet. Instead, he lowered his head to kiss her. It seemed an eternity since he had held her without restraint. In truth, he was not certain he ever had.

"I missed you," she said when he finally let her break for air. She cradled his face between her hands, her beautiful, dark eyes on the edge of tears. Seeing them shimmer, his own felt hot.

The depth of her emotion was humbling. One wrong step, one wrong sigh, seemed as if it would shatter all.

*I cannot do this,* cried the part of him that remembered being devastated by Gillian. *I cannot fall from this height.*

"Juliana," he murmured helplessly. "Oh, Juliana."

She gathered her hair and pulled the mass of it to one side, the invitation obvious. Less clear was whether she knew the symbolism of her act. His wolf knew and exulted in victory. To bare the vulnerability of one's throat was to admit who was one's king.

Unable to check his reaction, Ulric's breathing turned rough.

"I offer you what you want," she said, her breast rising and falling in time with his. "How long do you intend to wait to accept?"

Her challenge snapped the last thin thread of his control. Desire blazed through his body, blinding him to everything but her blood. Gripping her upper arms, he lifted her neck to his mouth until her feet dangled off the ground. Her skin was smooth and warm, her pulse an unbearably exciting patter. He licked the salt from her, felt the throbbing ache of his teeth.

When he clamped down on her skin, the taste sent him to his knees.

Their moans tangled together, her arms wrapping his back, his cinched beneath her bottom and behind her neck. His body was almost more aroused than he could bear. He rubbed his hardness against her belly as she rode his thigh. His prick sang at the friction, his ballocks aching for release. He wanted more than to feed from her but could not tear himself from her throat.

This was the elixir of which the fables spoke, not simply blood, but the blood of a woman loved.

Slowly he drew on her, taking her essence in tiny pulls to make it last. Sparks of color danced in the air around them. Lemon. Rose. The blue of the autumn sky. Each color had a scent, each a unique sensation against his skin. Like gentle fingers they plucked his loins, tugging and teasing until, without him realizing it was near, the pleasure grew so intense his climax broke. He spilled before he could stop it, a gasp the only remnant of his lost control. When she shuddered against him, he knew the release was shared.

At her sigh, he drew his teeth from her skin.

"Lick it," she whispered, her head fallen languidly back.

Neither order nor plea, the words caused him to shudder with renewing lust. He curled his tongue across the wounds, healing them even as he drew one final shiver of ecstasy.

Like a woman waking from a dream, Juliana lifted her head. "I saw lights," she slurred drunkenly, "and colors like dancing flowers."

He coaxed her forward until her cheek rested on his chest. He was aware of the two menhirs behind them, still glowing faintly, still exuding a sense of presence—as if they held something alive. If they did, Juliana had woken it. He had never seen them burn like that before.

He suspected they did not mind this impromptu erotic rite.

Beginning to come down from it, he stroked her hair. "I saw the colors, too," he said. "They are not usual, but feeding is our closest connection. Even those who cannot normally share thoughts can do so then."

"Mm," she hummed. "A woman could get used to that."

A woman could grow addicted, he thought as he rubbed the small of her back.

The possibility should not have troubled him. It would have bound her to him as nothing else. But he was too proud. He wanted her to love him for him, rather than for something any *upyr* worth his salt could do.

"Jus' lemme rest for a bit," she mumbled against his neck. "Then I shall be ready to go."

But he did not intend them to go any farther. He wanted to slide inside her and join their bodies in the human way. He wanted to make the act they had shared complete.

For one last night, they would savor their privacy.

# Emile

I promise," Bastien said to his friend Emile, "once I am certain I have Ulric's pack under my thumb, I will get you out of this hole. Without their leader, they are ripe for plucking. In no time, we shall have them battling for our cause."

The hole Bastien spoke of was a burrow, previously home to badgers, and now Emile's hiding place. Emile should have been accustomed to his confinement, but every night his fears gained ground, driving his heart a little faster, draining his small reserves of energy. Buttressed by a net of roots, the actual hollow of the den gave him room enough to sit up. Thankfully, he still possessed the strength to do so. Thus far, the weakness that crept like ice from his feet had only reached mid-thigh. In the beginning his toes had tingled. Tonight they were empty space, as if they had been not just paralyzed but erased.

Emile did not share this new development with Bastien. He had worries enough.

"It shall be soon," Bastien insisted, helping him lie down. "I promise. No more than another sennight."

Though Emile nodded as if he believed, he had grown to dread

the words. Doubt dwelled like a canker beneath the forced cheer of
Bastien's gaze; fear, too, that the lengths to which he went to protect his pack mate would damn his soul. If Emile had been braver,
he would have insisted he be let go.

Sadly, he was not brave. As the days and weeks drew out with
nothing to do but lie here fighting panic, he had discovered in himself a terrible wish: that he and Bastien had never stood against their
pack leader, that they had let Hugo's villainy stand. Shamed, Emile
turned his face to the earthen wall.

Bastien gave his elbow one last squeeze. "I shall return tomorrow to share my blood," he said. "Right before dawn just as always. Trust me, Emile. I know it is hard, but we shall prevail."

As his friend squirmed out of the burrow, Emile swallowed back
his pleas for more assurances. Even if Bastien's chances were better
on his own, even if Emile had become no better than a leech, he
knew his friend could be counted on.

"Tomorrow," he rasped, but Bastien was already heading for
the absent pack leader's cave in his need to outrace the sun.

Without him there, the whispers were impossible to drown out.
What if some disaster prevented Bastien's reappearance? What if
Emile were left in this hole alone?

He would starve, without even the strength to drag himself into
the sun. He did not know how long his kind were capable of living
without sustenance. Conceivably, he might languish here for years.

When he closed his eyes, a tear trickled out one corner.

The tear disgusted him enough to stop. Wallowing in misery
would accomplish nothing.

Forcing his breath to slow, he let his senses reach beyond the
burrow. The forest surrounded his little hill, sweet and spacious
and quiet, sinking its roots deep into the earth. The wind blew, the
streams clattered over stones, and the land hummed with the magic
of the growing things.

Without warning, fear grabbed his heart and shook it. More

than earth magic hummed outside. The magic of the *upyr* rode the midnight air.

Hugo must have come for him after all.

Except . . . the magic did not feel like Hugo's, not built from fury and theft. No, this was a gift given for a gift, a wall of warm safety. Feeling it, the *upyr*'s eyes welled with hope. Up from the soil the good magic rose, stretching through the woods like two golden, embracing arms until the ends met and closed.

As they did, his hackles rippled in alarm.

*No*, he thought, the cry locked in his throat.

Whoever had raised that sheltering wall had shut him outside.

# Eight

THE next night's wind gave Ulric no warning. The pack was almost on them before he sensed their energy in the air: not wolf, not human, but a dangerous mingling of both.

He stood, helping Juliana to her feet as well.

"They come," he said as she laid one hand inquiringly on his arm.

Knowing her reception might be ticklish, he was already on guard. His nostrils flared as he caught an unfamiliar scent, a male he did not recognize. Immediately, every muscle in his body coiled. What *upyr* would dare intrude upon his lands when he was not here to give leave?

"What is wrong?" Juliana asked.

"Hush," he said, the sound coming out a growl. "I shall handle this."

He was glad he could trust her to be quiet. She stilled as the others galloped in wolf form through the trees, her hold thankfully calm. He felt her stand even straighter as he frowned at his approaching pack.

They should have been howling a welcome, should have been groveling on their forelegs and waving their tails. Instead, only

Stephen gave an uncertain yip. His tail was curled between his legs. As if afraid to come closer, he sat a body length away. The two subordinate females, Ingrith and Helewis, came to a quivering halt on either side of him, but whether to protect or be protected Ulric could not say. They did not sit, but leaned their shoulders into Stephen's flanks.

Gytha and the stranger were the first to shimmer into human form. Her usual defiant self, Gytha slung her arm around the male *upyr*'s shoulders and tossed her head.

She was a handsome woman, tall and taut, with flashing eyes and blue-black hair as rough as a horse's tail. Helewis was larger, but what Gytha lacked in bulk she made up for in combativeness. She never walked but strutted, never stood except with feet planted wide. She did not merely meet others' eyes, she dared them to take her down. The thrust of her nose was an insult to lesser beings, the swing of her hips a mockery. No man took Gytha without invitation, and no man had refused her before Ulric.

Ulric knew the stranger's presence was meant to challenge him.

*I welcomed him,* said Gytha's stance. *To my bed and to this pack. Make of it what you will.*

Ulric lifted his brows and was pleased to see her bravado falter, though not for long. "I see we have a guest."

"A new pack member," Gytha contradicted.

"That," Ulric said mildly, "remains to be seen."

The stranger stepped forward at the cue. He was as tall as Gytha, and as strongly built. His hair was berry-black, not coarse, but satiny smooth. It fell over his shoulders in shining waves, nearly reaching his waist. His eyes, a pale, clear green, were tilted with an amusement that invited Ulric to smile along. What lay beneath the amusement Ulric suspected the stranger did not wish him to see.

Behind the façade of sardonic humor, this man walked a desperate, knife-sharp edge. Wherever he had lived before, Ulric did not think he had left of his own accord. This, far more than Gytha's backing, made him dangerous. An *upyr* without a home, who felt his survival in question, would fight tooth and nail to be safe.

Ulric was grateful for the handspan of height being made *upyr* had added to his human frame. He had inches on this man and likely a couple stone. The stranger's power Ulric could not judge without more study. He thought it less than his own but not by much. This was no follower wolf. A second perhaps, one with the potential to be first. Though it did not show, Ulric sensed that he was weary to his bones, the sort of weariness that has nothing to do with lack of sleep.

"My name is Bastien," said the stranger with a hooded smile and a French accent. "Gytha was kind enough to offer the hospitality of your pack."

He extended his hand in the human way, the picture of bonhomie. Ulric stared at the pale appendage, then into Bastien's green eyes.

"Offer your throat," he said just as pleasantly, "and perhaps I shall extend Gytha's kindness."

The stranger flinched, obviously not expecting the demand. Before he could speak, Gytha lost her control.

"Have your whore offer her throat!" she cried. "No one invited her!"

"No one but me," Ulric responded with a coolness that should have warned her to hold her tongue.

"She is *human*," Gytha hissed. "And you have bitten her. I can smell her stench on your breath."

Ulric moved before Gytha could blink, twisting her arm behind her back so that she had to go on her toes to prevent him from popping it out of its socket. With his second hand, he yanked her head back by the hair. Her throat was bared to him then, her pulse beating with a wildness *upyr* seldom showed. Though she snarled her defiance, a bead of fear-sweat rolled down her neck.

"I do not answer to you," he said, putting his power into the words until the air pulsed with his will and the leaves shivered delicately on the trees. "And though it is not your concern, I will tell you this: You should be so fortunate to know a fount as sweet as my Juliana."

"I imagine she is sweet," Gytha scoffed. "You could not master Gillian and thus you try again with this paltry human."

"Human now," Ulric said, "but not for long, and perhaps not as paltry as you think. Juliana woke the old menhirs. Their power protects us because she gave her blood."

"We felt them wake while we were hunting," Helewis put in. He had not noticed her change, but she wore human form, as sturdy and diffident as ever. As befitted the lowest member of the pack, she spoke through the fox-red curtain of her hair. "We wondered what had happened."

"Idiot," Gytha snapped, ignoring the fact that Ulric held her. "You are too stupid to speak. Bastien will put you in your place when he leads the pack."

Using her bent arm for leverage, Ulric forced Gytha down until her nose touched the ground. Though she tried to evade the humiliation and cursed him most passionately, she could not counteract his strength.

"Do you not think," he said, "that you are being premature?"

Through the whole exchange, the newcomer, her supposed ally, simply watched. Ulric did not assume this meant Gytha's dreams of grandeur were all her own. He had no doubt the stranger hoped to take his pack. He had sense enough, however, to wait until he judged the moment ripe.

Wait as long as you please, Ulric thought. This pack will always be mine.

Because Gytha was crying now—angrily, he presumed—he let her up. Wisely, Juliana stepped to his side, but Gytha's fit of temper had run its course. He squeezed Juliana's hand. To his surprise, she was only shaking a little.

"We will discuss this back at the cave," he said to his pack in a tone that demanded obedience. He was careful to hide his relief when they complied. For Juliana's sake if not his own, this was altercation enough for one night. By the same reasoning, he did not ask why Ingrith and Stephen still walked as wolves. Whatever their justification, he would handle them in good time.

⸻ ⁂ ⸻

OF all the ways Juliana had imagined meeting Ulric's pack, none had come close to this.

Being greeted by beautiful naked people was disconcerting enough—as was Gytha's immediate hostility. The way she said "human" made it sound like a pestilence. The Frenchman, Bastien, seemed to want Ulric's place, the two who remained in wolf form cowered like beaten dogs, and the solidly built redhead refused to meet anybody's eye.

What really troubled her, though, was watching Ulric make a woman cry.

She could see Gytha was rebellious, but using violence to subdue her seemed as natural to her lover as catching hares. Though he did not appear to act out of anger, he also did not turn a hair at her tears. Was this how he led his pack? Was this how he would lead her?

Gytha had accused him of not being able to "master" Gillian. Was he hoping to master her?

Juliana's legs felt numb as she plodded through the trees beside him, her fingers stiff and chilly within his hand. Ulric was too distracted to notice, or perhaps too watchful for more trouble.

She was surprised when the big redhead, the one who had seemed so shy, fell back from the others to keep pace with her.

"I am Helewis," she said softly, as if she did not wish to disturb Ulric. Her gaze slid briefly toward him before returning to Juliana.

Apparently, humans were lowly enough that staring at them was allowed. Juliana felt her shoulders stiffen, then told herself to be tolerant. She was a stranger here. Neither of them knew each other's ways.

"I am Juliana," she responded, equally soft.

Helewis smiled and nodded. "A pretty name for a pretty woman. I can see why Ulric brought you back."

Even as she bristled at the assumption that she was some sort of souvenir, Juliana thought how odd it was to be called pretty by this glowing creature. Helewis might be big, but her muscles were fluid, her movements graceful and strong. Watching her made Juliana feel too scrawny by far. Whatever her inadequacy, however, she would not be taken for a toy.

"I tricked him into bringing me," she said.

Helewis's smile widened to a grin. "He would not have let you trick him unless he liked the idea."

"I am right here," Ulric reminded them, "and have not gone deaf."

Despite the treatment her sister wolf had received at his hands, Helewis dared to laugh. Skipping ahead of them backward, she took Ulric's hand—with Juliana's still in it—and pressed its back to her cheek. It was a gesture Juliana might have made to her father.

"I am happy you have returned," she said, "and glad you have found a mate."

Juliana's eyes went round. *This* was what Helewis assumed?

"Helewis," Ulric said, but if he meant to contradict her, he got no chance. Quick as a wink, Helewis changed and bounded away in wolf form, curving off into the trees to give Gytha and the Frenchman a nice, wide berth.

They did not see her again until they arrived at the cliff.

In Juliana's horrified opinion, the path that led up the sheer granite wall would not support a goat. Indeed, the few saplings that had taken root on its ledges looked in danger of toppling off.

Apparently, *upyr* had no trouble with steep ascents. The other four had gone up already. Only Helewis awaited them.

"I can carry her," she offered. "You know I am the best at climbing."

Unsure what she thought of this, Juliana was relieved when

Ulric turned to her. "You are probably strong enough to manage by yourself, unless the height bothers you too much."

Juliana squinted at the towering rock, noting how the moon made long, jagged shadows of even small projections in the stone. She was not aware if she were afraid of heights, though it struck her any reasonable person would be. "Your cave is up there?"

Ulric put his hands on her shoulders, his thumbs stroking her neck. "It is two-thirds up the face. You need not attempt it unless you wish, but you will have more freedom if you can scale it on your own—at least until you decide what you want to do at summer's end."

This was the first time in a while that he had mentioned the deadline to their agreement. She wondered what it meant that he was bringing it up now.

"I will try," she said, "if you stay close."

He patted her cheeks as if he approved, but also as if he thought her a child. "We will tie you to my waist as a precaution. I did not bring you this far just to let you fall."

Without waiting to be asked, Helewis scurried up the cliff to find a rope. Juliana grew dizzy watching her clamber quickly up and down. The *upyr* jumped the last few meters when she returned, landing lightly on broad bare feet. The rope was coiled around her shoulder.

"Shall I help?" she asked, handing Ulric the twisted hemp. "I could follow behind her."

Ulric thanked her but refused. As unquestioning as before, Helewis disappeared the way she had come. Fortunately, the climb was within Juliana's power, at least with the added strength Ulric's bite had lent her. After she had tucked up her skirts, she followed his instructions, putting her feet where he stepped, trusting her fingers to the crevices that held his. The only order she disobeyed was his injunction against looking down. That did make her head swim, but she thought she ought to face it once.

"Good," he said when she reached the midpoint. "You are doing better than I hoped."

She took more pleasure than annoyance in his surprise.

Despite the shocks she was facing, she reveled in her success, a tiny taste of what life would be as an *upyr*. *Is it really so bad?* a voice whispered in her head. *Can you not forgive him his rough-ness against Gytha? Look what you would get in return.*

Finally, they reached the entry to the cave, a low, vine-shrouded opening lipped by a solid ledge. Ulric made no complaint when she tottered to the nearest wall and collapsed. Lowering himself beside her, he laid his palm atop her now banged-up knee.

"Very well," she admitted, "that was really hard."

Ulric laughed and kissed her bruises. A tingle of sensation told her he was working to make them heal.

She found it difficult to reconcile his care with the man who had rubbed his inferior's nose in the dirt.

"We do not always fight," he said as if he had read her mind. "We hunt, we sleep, we play. Our life is simple. Once this . . . situation with Gytha and Bastien is settled, you are more likely to be bored than afraid." He wrinkled his brows as if he disliked the thought. "Maybe we will begin to do new things. Times seem to be changing whether I wish it or not."

He sounded lost when he said this, and Juliana did not know how to comfort him. From what she had seen, a change or two might be just the thing.

───────

ULRIC could not say when being with Juliana had become his idea of peace. He only knew he did not want to face his pack. He wanted to sit here with his shoulder pressed to hers, with his hand on her bruised knee and his power flowing gently out.

Instead, he released his breath and stood. Nothing would be gained by avoiding what lay ahead.

Juliana reached up for the hand he was holding out, groaning with human tiredness as he pulled her up.

"Let me settle you in my room," he said. "I am sure you would like to rest."

"Where will you be?"

He wondered if any *upyr* had ever had eyes that wide. "Speaking with my pack. I must decide if it is safe to let the stranger stay, and I must make clear how everyone is to treat you."

"Are you going to hurt them?" Her voice was low.

"Only if they force my hand."

She opened her mouth, then closed it and shook her head. Without a word, she gestured him to lead the way.

The cave was a warren of tunnels and chambers honeycombed into the rock. Some were in use, and some were neglected to the point of filling up with rubble. Though many stretches were rough—whatever wind and water had carved—elsewhere the hand of man was obvious. Walls would be finished to glassy smoothness, or passages marble-tiled. One room boasted a temple's worth of columns, while another was decorated in mosaics so intricate they resembled paint.

Someone—Helewis, no doubt—had hung their path with small oil lamps. Without them, a human like Juliana would have been blind.

"How old is this place?" Juliana breathed.

"No one knows. My sire once told me it was a home other elders built, elders who walked into the sun before he was born."

"But why would they—"

Her voice stopped as he halted before his chamber. He did not mean to hesitate, but suddenly he felt odd. The last time he had shut these heavy planks behind him, he had expected to be returning with Gillian. He had vowed he would, had promised himself she only needed to be reminded of what she had been missing and she would come back.

How can I trust my judgment, he thought, when I have given my heart again?

Gritting his teeth, he forced his hand to the door.

To his shock, his chamber was occupied.

# Nine

*UPYR* hands, or perhaps unknown *upyr* devices, had hollowed Ulric's chamber from the rock. Square in shape, its only structural adornments were the marks left by the chisel and the natural striations in the hard gray stone. A sleeping niche, large enough for two, had been carved into the rightward wall. Two wooden stools, a tapestry of men hunting stags, and a strange glass lamp in which the oil never burned away—all collected by Gillian from forgotten caches and given to Ulric as gifts—comprised its furnishings. No window brightened the gloom, no hearth, no shelf on which to display prized possessions.

It seemed very plain when Ulric pictured Juliana stepping inside.

At the moment, he barely had room to step inside himself. Everyone was there except Lucius, whom Ulric had not yet seen. He was uneasy to think that the pack's third male, the one with the steadiest nature, might not have come back. Of course, he had known it was a possibility—maybe even a likelihood. If Ulric had discovered he were an elder, he would not have wanted to bow to anyone else. The admission did not make Lucius's absence palatable. Changes enough had come into Ulric's life since Gillian left.

To judge by Gytha's smug expression, this invasion of his chamber had been her idea.

Making themselves at home, the pack had dragged Ulric's furs from his sleeping niche to the floor, where they spread them for sitting in comfort. Bastien was the sole exception. He lounged on the first of Ulric's stools with his feet propped on the second. His hands were folded across the muscles of his belly, and his shoulders rested on the wall. His hair hung over them like a cape. Interestingly, he had not invited Gytha to sit on his level. Gillian's rescued lamp he also kept to himself. It stood on the floor beside him, bathing his lean and perfect body in a golden glow.

The pose presented quite the image of a king.

"Would you prefer I moved?" he asked with the same faint smile he had shown before.

Ulric shook off his annoyance. He would look weak if he argued over a stool. "Sit where you please," he said and turned to the rest.

To his amazement, Stephen and Ingrith still held wolf form.

"Enough," he said, losing patience. "You know better to stay in beast form during a discussion. Both of you change at once."

Stephen whimpered a wordless plea.

"Now," Ulric insisted.

Stephen heaved a human-sounding sigh before he obeyed, coming into man form on his knees. His soft brown curls hung around his beautiful face. His neck was bowed and his fists opened and closed on his thighs. A moment later Ingrith appeared. Ulric stiffened in shock. Though she buried her face behind Stephen's shoulder almost at once, she had too many bruises to hide, bruises no *upyr* should have been able to inflict. They covered her from head to toe, blotching her skin in shades of brown and green.

"Ingrith," he gasped and immediately crouched beside her. She was trembling violently. Gingerly, he tilted her face away from Stephen. Her lower lip was split and scabbed, and one of her eyes was swollen shut. Between the blackened lids it was leaking tears.

"Who did this to you?" he asked, torn between the need to be gentle and mindless rage. "Was it Gytha's friend?"

Ingrith choked out something too garbled to understand.

"I did it," Gytha said, bringing him around and to his feet. Her arms were crossed beneath her breasts, her expression a mix of stubbornness and shame.

The shame he suspected she would rather die than admit.

"You did this?" he repeated. "You beat a sister wolf?"

"She did not want Bastien to stay. She said he 'frightened' her."

Gytha's scorn was obvious in her mimicry. She had never had much use for Ingrith. The pretty blonde was too docile to earn Gytha's respect: a rival for males' attentions without being a true match. Nor was Ingrith as useful as Helewis, who at least had a stout arm. This, however, was beyond what Ulric would have guessed she would do.

He turned back to Stephen. "Why did you not fight?"

"You left us!" he said, a cry of accusing pain. "We did not know when you would be back from chasing after Gillian. Gytha was too strong. Especially with Bastien helping her."

"But there are three of you," Ulric protested. "Together you could have held them off."

Even as he said the words, he knew the solution was not that simple. Without Lucius to bolster their nerve, none of them had the aggressiveness to be lead wolf. When Gytha pushed her will on them, their instincts would have driven them to submit. The effect was subtler than a thrall, but it was strong.

Though he must have known this, Stephen's head sank even lower, his chin nudging his chest. "Helewis tried to fight," he admitted, "but Ingrith and I were scared."

Ulric looked at Helewis, mildly surprised. Of them all, she was the most submissive.

"They were stronger than us," she said in defense of Stephen, her eyes briefly meeting his. "And the Frenchman was using magic."

That is how he made Ingrith's bruises stay." She pointed to a glyph painted in blood on Ingrith's arm, almost lost among the discoloration. Ulric did not know many letters, but it looked like a curving M with an arrow on the final tail.

He licked his thumb and tried to remove it to no avail. The glyph would not come off. He felt nothing when he touched it—which did not mean no magic was there. Clearly, Ingrith was not recovering as she should.

"I assume you tried to heal her," he said to Helewis.

She nodded emphatically. "Nothing we could think of helped. Gytha told Stephen if he even thought of standing against them, Bastien would never erase the mark. We feared Ingrith would end up scarred."

"She would not let us bow, though," Stephen said, touching his lover's averted cheek. "You are still our king."

"Yes," Helewis agreed. "Our vows still belong to you."

Ulric supposed he should be grateful for this favor. Indeed, Ingrith's stubbornness surprised him a bit.

Gytha had chosen her victim well. Stephen and Helewis could each bear pain on their own, but Ingrith was a gentler soul, made for loveplay not fighting. She was, without question, the most innocent of them all. Even among *upyr*, her angelic loveliness was rare. Ingrith was not overly vain herself, but Ulric understood why the prospect of seeing her beauty ruined would disturb the others. Her looks were a matter of pride for the pack.

He closed his eyes to fight a surge of fury. Justice, he had always thought, was best meted out cold.

Before he could calm, Gytha's temper exploded.

"Interfering bitch," she snarled, leaping forward to claw her accuser. Luckily for Gytha, the Frenchman held her back by the arms. A more trusting soul might have concluded he was less violent than she. Ulric thought Bastien had simply realized the tide was shifting against them.

"Bastien," he said, calling his gaze.

The stranger's eyes showed none of Gytha's awareness of guilt. Instead, they looked so resigned they were almost dead. His humor of before might have been a dream.

"I needed shelter," he explained without inflection. "Gytha offered it in return for my cooperation. For the price of a home, I would have done anything short of letting her kill Ingrith."

It was a stupefying admission, and one Ulric hardly knew how to address. But whatever sympathy he might feel for Bastien's situation, whatever his understanding of Gytha's desire to seize her chance to rule, he could not let their behavior stand. In the end, the decision came swifter than thought. Long before the stranger could read his intention, long before Gytha could move to help, Ulric changed and leapt for Bastien's throat.

He knocked both conspirators over when he hit. A stool splintered beneath them and a female shrieked. Gytha's head struck the wall with a solid crack. Bastien tried to wrestle Ulric off but was too slow—stunned perhaps by his fall. Even as his hands grabbed Ulric's ruff, Ulric's fangs sank home. He tore the flesh they held, determinedly overcoming the resistance of *upyr* skin. Cool red blood flew into his face. More screams. More hands. He shook them off and backed away from Bastien.

The Frenchman lay on his side, his eyes white all around, his muscles twitching as his blood pooled beneath his head. Even to Ulric, who had made it, the gash in his neck came as a shock. For any other creature, this would have been a mortal wound. In truth, his wolf believed it should be. Battling back the urge to finish the kill was no small feat. Breathing hard, Ulric returned to his human form.

"No," he barked as Gytha tried to crawl to her lover.

He knelt beside Bastien himself, his hand closing on Bastien's wounded throat. Beneath his palm, the muscle and cartilage squirmed like living things, already trying to knit. Ulric's power could help or hinder that process as he desired. The stranger's eyes said he knew this, but weakened by loss of blood, he could not escape.

"Please," he rasped. "Please let me live. I will do anything you want."

The agony in his voice sounded utterly sincere, taking Ulric aback. Defiance he expected, not a plea.

"I do not intend to kill you," he said, "only make you understand that in my pack we are more than our wolves. Perhaps matters are different in France, but here we protect those who need protecting. We do not maim them with magic."

The stranger closed his eyes. "If that is true, I will serve you with all my heart."

At a loss for words, Ulric turned to Gytha. She had shrunk back against the wall, her arms straight at her sides, her fingers digging into the stone. Her reaction he understood. She knew she was in trouble, and he had shown just how easily he could defeat her sole ally.

"This wound should have been yours," he said to her, "for yours was the greater sin. You betrayed your pack to an outsider, choosing to fight not the strongest, but to harm the weak by unfair means. I would be within my rights to do far worse to you than I did to him."

"Then do it," she snapped, one last burst of rebellion.

"Go to your chamber," he said. "I will give you my decision before sunrise."

"Go," Bastien seconded from the floor. "He is justified in what he says."

Though Ulric resented the implication that he needed help controlling Gytha, he held his tongue. After all, she was glaring at Bastien as furiously as she glared at him.

"I will go," she huffed, "but I am not in the wrong. No matter what you try to tell yourself, I deserve to be queen."

As she stumped from the room, everyone heaved a sigh—everyone, that is, except Juliana.

Gripped by a sudden panic, Ulric searched the shadows of the passage outside the door. He could not see her, could not smell her, could not feel her essence in the air.

She was gone.

He cursed but could not blame her. If she had seen even a portion of what he had done, she must think him worse than a monster.

"I must find Juliana," he said, knowing where his first duty lay but for once unable to do it. "I want that mark removed from Ingrith before I return."

Thus saying, he left the others with their mouths agape.

———

JULIANA swore she was not going to weep or scream or flee in terror. Never mind that her pulse beat so hard in her throat she feared she might be sick. Never mind that her knees had turned to water and she had to steady her wrist with her second hand to keep the lamp she had grabbed from spilling its oil.

She was calm. She merely needed to walk and think.

Her strides were jerky, taking her deeper into the cliff. She knew this because the air grew cooler and more quiet, until the silence seemed to have weight. She passed smooth tunnels and rough ones, cluttered ones and clean. They smelled of the pack, like rain-soaked earth and ferns, like mossy rocks and leaves slowly turning brown while wildflowers poked between.

You will be lost, she thought, but did not slow. She had no doubt Ulric could track her anywhere she went.

The image of her lover ripping the Frenchman's throat came bright as day. Bastien's blood was as red as the doublet and hose Ulric's change had left on the floor. When Ulric appeared again as a man, the red still painted his face and chest. She was reasonably certain he could have thrown off the stain. Instead, she watched him lick it from sharpened teeth, watched him pant with the same excitement he showed on his hunts.

His body had been aroused.

Everything inside her had rebelled at the evidence of his blood-lust, but there was no thought in her reaction, no judgment she could put in words. She only knew she had to get away.

She came to the end of the passage she was in, not blank rock but a small octagonal room with carved stone benches ringing its walls. It had the look of an abandoned chapel, dusty and lost in time.

A flutter of warm, night-scented air made her lift the lamp. Above her, a natural chimney pierced the cavernous ceiling, wide enough to admit a glimmer of stars.

She sat beneath the opening, legs crossed, neck tilted back. The smoothness of the floor told her countless others had done this before.

I am out of my depth, she thought. This *upyr* life is much stranger than I could foresee.

She had to laugh, ruefully, at Ulric's claim that she would be bored.

---

**WITH** a surge of relief strong enough to leave him weak, Ulric found her in the solar. She had not run. He had a chance to win her back. Aware she had not yet seen him, he watched her as he waited for his hammering pulse to slow. She sat with her plain blue gown spread around her, her head hanging back until her hair pooled on the floor. As if to hold herself together, her hands clutched white-knuckled at her knees.

Despite his fears, he wanted her with an intensity that stole his breath.

"I see you have found our drunkard's chamber," he said, striving for flippancy.

Her head jerked up and her eyes widened. He waved at the star-filled opening in the roof. "We come here when we wish to forget our troubles or celebrate. Just enough sun comes through to blur our thoughts."

She said nothing, her expression wary, seemingly waiting for something more. Ulric hoped he could provide it.

He took a few steps closer and hunkered down. She flinched when he reached out to touch her knee. Not knowing what else to do, he spoke from the heart. "We are not just people, Juliana. We are wolves. What you saw me do to Bastien, that is the language we understand."

"The language of violence? Of might makes right?"

"Unless I seriously misspent my time in the human world, your kind speaks that language, too."

Though his response was gentle, she looked away, fussing with a crease in her skirt. "What will happen to Gytha?"

He began to answer, then stopped, some intuition checking his response. "What do you think should happen to her?"

"Me?"

He had her eyes again, round and shining. "Yes, you."

"I . . . I do not know. You could . . . banish her."

"Gytha has been a part of this pack from the beginning. It is true she has more will than wisdom, but will is part of what allows our kind to survive. If I banish her, the other packs might refuse to take her in. I think she would be unhappy on her own."

"She deserves to be unhappy. She beat Ingrith black and blue!"

He stroked her shining hair around her shoulder. This time she was too caught up in anger to pull away. "Perhaps I should banish Stephen as well. He failed to defend her. True, expecting a subordinate wolf to do battle against a superior might be unfair. Perhaps I should banish myself for leaving them without a responsible leader."

"There must be consequences for her actions!"

"I agree. I am asking you what they should be."

She frowned at him. "You are trying to show me it is easier to criticize a choice than to make one."

He was, but he knew enough not to admit it. "Make a suggestion, Juliana. Maybe it will be one I could not devise on my own."

"If I thought you really believed that . . ." She shook her head. "All right. Reward Helewis. Move her up in the pack."

He was unprepared for her decisiveness. "I cannot do that. Helewis has to earn her rank. She cannot move up unless she fights the female wolves above her: either Ingrith, which she will not do, or Gytha, whom she cannot defeat."

"Those rules are for wolves. You said yourself that you are more. If you treat Helewis with extra respect, the others will as well. And," she added, warming up, "I think no one in the pack should speak to Gytha until Ingrith ceases to be afraid of her. Because you can smell fear, I assume you will know when that occurs. For as long as Gytha terrorizes Ingrith, she should be shunned."

Ulric rubbed his chin, then released an ironic laugh. "I suspect Gytha would rather I beat her senseless."

"Which is precisely why you should not." Her hand almost touched his arm. He felt the heat shadow it left. "Just consider my idea. If it does not change Gytha's behavior, you can do whatever you would have before."

Ulric mulled over her words. He had asked her opinion on impulse, not realizing she might expect him to take it. He was king here, after all. His way had worked for centuries.

"And another thing," she went on with an earnestness that made his shoulders tense. "You must ask more questions."

"Questions?"

"Yes. You should demand to know what that magic symbol was and how it kept Ingrith from healing."

"I demanded that Bastien take it off."

"Well, yes, that was the most important thing, but you need to know how it worked in case he tries to do it again."

"I will order him not to."

To his amazement, she looked dubious, as if she doubted his orders would suffice. "Oh, never mind. I can ask him myself."

"You shall do nothing of the kind!" he exclaimed. The thought of her nosing around the Frenchman made him want to gnash his teeth. The men of Bastien's country had a reputation for seducing women. Unlike Stephen, Bastien was not an *upyr* Ulric could govern with a look. "I do not want you near him!"

"If you think he is dangerous, why let him stay?"

Her tone was challenging enough to make his hands ball into

fists. With an effort, he forced them to relax. "We are all dangerous, Juliana. I let him stay, for now, because our kind are few. He deserves a chance to earn a home. And, in case you had any doubt, I shall judge his worthiness by observing what he does, not by peppering him with intrusive questions."

"I should have known you did not really want my opinion."

"I did," he said, stung by her bitter tone. "I do. But you cannot be with my pack for an evening and think you know how to run it."

"You are right," she said, letting her shoulders slump. "I do not know anything."

Her surrender should have made him happy, but it did not. Filled with a vague unease, he stroked her arm. "It is not safe for you to be alone here. You should return to my room."

She shook her head. "I need to think. I need to make sense of what I am doing."

He did not like the sound of that any more than he liked the thought of leaving her on her own. If nothing else, tonight had proved his pack was unpredictable. If one of them slipped his control, she would have no defense. The desire to order her—nay, to compel her—to be sensible burned in his throat. His promise not to thrall her against her will chafed like a chain.

"As you wish," he said, his reluctance roughening his voice. "Return when you are ready. Just promise it shall be soon."

"Soon," she agreed, without sharing her understanding of what that meant.

<hr />

HE ran into Helewis at the tunnel's end.

"Stephen is still with Ingrith," she reported before he could ask. "Bastien is removing the mark and Ingrith was nervous to be alone with him. Did you find Juliana?"

"Yes." He glanced back over his shoulder. "She is fine, just . . . sorting her feelings out."

Helewis nodded as if she could not imagine this posing a problem, then scuffed her feet. "Ulric, where is Lucius? We thought he would return with you."

Ulric blew out his breath. "I do not think he is coming back."

"Not coming back! But—"

"He discovered he is an elder."

Helewis's brows shot up in surprise. "An elder! You mean he can—"

"Yes, he can make a mortal one of us. He taught Gillian how to change the man with whom she fell in love."

"I did not know that secret could be taught. And Gillian is so young. But I upset you. Forgive me for treading on painful ground."

Ulric waved his hand, knowing his frustration showed on his face. He was not certain why Lucius's absence bothered him this much. What was Lucius to him? A friend? A brother? Someone whose presence he had taken for granted but apparently never understood? Though the pack was more than a comforting huddle of bodies, that was part of its appeal. Take one member away, and its very fabric came in to doubt.

"I am not angry at you," he said to reassure Helewis. "You did well. You stood against the danger."

"I knew you would have wanted me to," she said shyly. "I am only sorry I did not succeed." Without warning she touched his wrist. "Ulric, you should forget Gillian. You have this Juliana now. Maybe she—"

He cut her off. "I do not 'have' her any more than I had Gillian. After tonight, I suspect my hold on her is even shakier." He rubbed Helewis's hand to take the bite from his tone. As usual, she ventured only a glance at his eyes. He remembered what Juliana had said about her rank. "Helewis, you could help me now if you would. I would like you to guard Juliana when I cannot, or when she would rather I stay away."

"You would trust me to do that?"

"No one more."

As if his words held a spell, she pulled her shoulders back. "I will do it," she declared, immediately moving to position herself before the tunnel where Juliana had flown. It was the only entrance to the solar. No one would get past her without a fight.

In spite of his worries, Ulric had to suppress a smile. He had done what Juliana advised; he had shown Helewis more respect. Now they would see how Juliana liked the results.

———

A hand shook Juliana from her doze on the solar floor. It was Helewis, the big *upyr* who had spoken to her before.

"It is nearly sunrise," she said. "Ulric will worry if you do not join him."

Juliana pushed herself stiffly up, knowing there was little point in proclaiming she did not care what Ulric felt. She did care after all; she simply did not know what she ought to do.

Just as muddled as before, she shoved her hair back from her face. "Is Ingrith all right?"

Helewis seemed happy to speak to someone she did not have to be afraid of. "Oh, yes. As soon as Bastien's throat closed up, he said a chant to take off the mark. It was Latin, which I do not speak, but Stephen told me he was saying something like 'remove the force of my stars.' After a few minutes, the symbol disappeared."

" 'Remove the force of my stars'? As in, the stars he was born under?"

"I do not know," Helewis answered. "I have never seen anyone use that kind of magic. I am sure it is not allowed."

"I would like to know where he learned it," Juliana mused, allowing Helewis to help her up. Sadly, Helewis did not have the same effect on her clothes as Ulric. Juliana supposed she had less magical force to share. As a result, her skirts stayed dusty.

"I could never dare to ask," the *upyr* declared. "Such things are dangerous to know."

"Or not to know, in this case."

Helewis pursed her lips in disapproval, but Juliana had no intention of giving up. If no one would help her, she would find a way to ask the Frenchman herself.

They walked in silence to Ulric's door, with Juliana doing her best to memorize the landmarks along the way, especially the bathing chamber with the hot spring. From the looks of the room's appointments, humans had been guests in this cave before. She knew the facilities would make her residence more comfortable.

"Well," she said, turning to thank Helewis.

"Do not fight him," Helewis blurted in an undertone. "Gillian always had to get her way, but it is good to have a strong leader. When the leader is strong, everyone feels safe."

Juliana thought it was more important to be safe than to feel safe but did not say this aloud. Rather, she dipped her head in a bow. "Thank you," she said. "I am grateful for the escort."

Her thanks seemed to put Helewis off balance. The *upyr* nearly tripped as she backed away.

With a sigh for all the dilemmas she had not solved, Juliana opened the door.

Inside, Ulric perched on the edge of his sleeping niche, his hands braced beside his hips as if deciding whether to leap up. His nakedness seemed different here, both more natural and more erotic—perhaps because this was the place where his beast ran free.

Ill-at-ease with the change, she turned her glance from the curves and shadows of his sex. The lamp she had noticed before sat on the floor beside his feet. It was a strange creation, an opaque, gold-white glass tube that did not smoke or flicker or have an opening for oil. She meant to greet Ulric, to say something to assure him that she had calmed, but the conundrum of the lamp distracted her completely.

"I do not know how it works," he said even as she opened her mouth to ask. "I do not know where it came from or what it burns. Someone found it in one of the older tunnels and gave it to me. We think the elders lived here in ancient times and they are the ones who made it."

"Oh," she said and rubbed her finger across the tip of her nose.

His lips twitched with a smile that was half grimace. "If I knew, believe me I would tell you."

"I have no doubt you would," she answered politely.

"Juliana," he said with a little laugh, then patted his furs. "Lie down, Juliana, where I know you will not come to harm."

She felt awkward, but did not remotely want to leave. She climbed into the bed behind him, guessing he would want to lie between her and the door, to protect her from whatever threat might come in. The niche was cozy, the furs cloud-soft. She settled into them with a shiver of pure enjoyment. When Ulric stretched out in front of her, she curled herself around his back. She did not try to distance herself but snuggled close. The other distance, the one in her head and heart, he needed no reminder of. His movements were too cautious to be unaware.

He held her arm against his chest as if he had missed its warmth.

"I am sorry I worried you," she said.

"And I am sorry I frightened you. It was my fault you had to see me discipline the Frenchman. I left my pack alone too long. I was too angry, too proud to return from Bridesmere without her."

Juliana knew very well who he meant by "her." She strove not to let her tone grow terse. "Your pack members are not children, Ulric. They should have been able to behave themselves."

"They are unused to being on their own. I should have prepared them."

"Maybe, but even if you had, you cannot control their every thought and deed. If you could, they would be puppets. I suspect you would take no pleasure in ruling that."

He was quiet while he considered what she had said. Though he did not agree in words, she sensed a slight unwinding of the tension in his back. His hip and shoulder shifted into more relaxed positions. "I only left them once before," he said. "If we met with other packs, we traveled together."

"Where did you go the other time?" she asked, more to keep him talking than anything else. His answer made her sit up.

"I went to visit my mother before she died. She never had a body to bury after the battle. I wanted her to know that I had survived."

He rolled onto his back while Juliana blinked down at his face. His hair gleamed like spun gold in the strange lamplight. He seemed to relish having surprised her.

"Were you afraid?" she asked once she had found her voice.

His laugh was a rush of air. "Terrified. I worried that she would think I was a demon, that she would wonder why I only came to talk to her at night. I even feared she would not know me. Instead, I almost did not recognize her. She had aged—and I had forgotten much of my human life."

"But she remembered you?"

"Yes. She said she always knew I would return. She prattled at me for a week, cooked meals I could not eat, and never once asked why I looked half the age I should."

"I imagine she was happy to see her son alive."

He shrugged as Juliana laid her hand on the golden hair that dusted his chest. "Maybe. But she did not argue when I told her I had to leave. I sometimes wonder if she suspected what I was and did not want to know for sure."

Juliana thought of her father. She could not imagine Henry Buxton being that tolerant. His merchant's view of the world had no room for mysteries.

No doubt he was thoroughly annoyed with her by now, having lost not just her services but the right to crow about her match. Oh, he would miss her, but fury was more likely to be the emotion he would acknowledge. She pitied whoever he hired to replace her. Their ears would be ringing constantly with his plaints.

"What makes you frown?" Ulric asked, reaching up to run his finger along her cheek.

"I was thinking my father would not believe what has happened to me if I told him. He would insist I had lost my mind. Probably lock me in my room."

"What about your mother? What would she have thought?"

Juliana's eyes pricked as she laughed. "She would have loved this. Even the gory bits. *Especially* the gory bits."

"Then we must pray more of her blood runs in your veins." His smile was wistful as he ran his palm down her now-clean sleeve. "You are the first person I have told about visiting my mother. I never shared that story before."

"Not even with—" She stopped and bit back the name.

"No," he said, even graver. "Not even with Gillian."

# Ten

GIVEN the ordeal his beloved had been through, Ulric knew he ought to leave her alone. His need to be close, to reassert his sensual supremacy, overrode his good sense. And perhaps if he proved he could love her gently as well as rough, that he was in truth more than his wolf, she would forget her horror. For her, he was willing to change his ways. For her, he would risk heartache.

She was leaning over him in his sleeping niche, her hair falling forward in shining waves. Hoping for the best, he reached to cup the side of her neck. She must have sensed what he meant the caress to lead to. Her body went very still.

"Tell me," he said, watching his thumb slide up and down the front of her throat. "Could you bear to let me touch you, or have I grown too hideous?"

"Never," she said and covered his hand.

He knew the gesture was meant to comfort, but the warmth of contact sluiced straight through his body to his loins, bringing him swiftly to readiness. "I wish I had the fortitude to let you rest," he said, "instead of wanting to tear you out of these clothes."

She smiled at his admission. "I want that, too—no matter what else I feel."

That "else" was the problem, but the part of him that yearned to touch her could not care. His skin thrummed with anticipation, his fangs beginning to lengthen despite his wish to conceal his inhuman side. He had no hope of turning back the response. He was *upyr* and wolf, and she aroused every desire he had: for sex, for blood, and most of all for control.

Clenching his jaw so firmly its muscles ached, he tugged her to the furs and shifted position until he straddled her hips. He could see his actions had amused her.

"You cannot reach my laces from there," she pointed out. "I think you will have to let me up."

"Clothes are evil," he growled. "Humans never should have invented them."

"Humans get cold," she said reasonably.

He backed off just enough to let her sit up. Though his cock felt as heavy as iron, he was careful not to tear the material when he loosened the snugging laces behind her gown. Easing off her bodice and sleeves, he left her breasts to rise and fall beneath her chemise.

"You see," she said, her eyes sparkling, "it is like unwrapping a present. The delay increases the delight."

"You think I cannot do this. You think I am going to lose control."

"Oh, no, Ulric, I have faith you can do whatever you set your mind to." Still laughing silently, she wriggled onto her back. Her curves were lush, her nipples pushing tight and dark against the linen of her undergown. The temptation to rip and plunder pounded inside him like an extra heart.

"I can," he said, but he had forgotten what they were debating. The fact that she was here, in his chamber, in his home, in a place where other wolves might approach her, pushed him to claim her as never before. A slave collar would not have been too extreme a measure for his wolf. She could not have stopped him. As a human, she was totally vulnerable.

"I want to touch you," he confessed, his throat almost too thick for sound. "I want to rub you with my penis, to feel every inch of you through my skin."

Her hands feathered across his chest and down his belly, making his skin twitch like a horse. Oh, yes, he thought, touch me all you wish. He sucked in a breath as she reached his erection, caressing it shyly from root to crown, pulling it subtly longer, increasing its heat and girth. His tension mounted at her gentleness until he could have howled.

Instead, he dragged her clothes down her legs.

They were beautiful legs, long and shapely and even stronger now than when they first met. The lamplight brought out a hint of red in the triangle of curls at her abdomen, sign of the fire he knew awaited inside.

"You are going to touch every inch," she reminded. "I am holding you to your word."

His smile barely supplanted his need to moan. "You may hold me to anything you like." He shifted down the length of his bed, sat back on his heels, and lifted her ankle. Despite their wordplay, this surprised her.

He pressed the sole of her foot against his hardness. "You mean it," she said, curling her toes.

"Yes, Juliana. Your wish is my command."

More cat than wolf, he rubbed his shaft against her. The arches of her feet, the roundness of her calves, even her knees felt his swollen length. He propped his weight on his arms to stroke along the silken softness of her inner thighs. She seemed to like the intimacy of the touch. Wriggling with pleasure, she stretched her arms high above her head, her fingertips brushing the niche's wall.

His teeth pulsed to full length.

Her posture was that of a slave waiting to be bound.

With a fierceness that stole his breath, he wanted to shackle her wrists and hold them captive. In Bridesmere he had done that when he took her against the tavern wall. Then, the only limits he had accepted were those of human tolerance. Regretting his good intentions more than he could express, he ran his cock across her belly instead. The curve trembled beneath him, his reward for restraint.

She lifted her knee to caress his hip. "I love the way your skin goes from cool to hot."

"You make me hot." He swallowed hard at the flush that had risen to stain her skin. "Take me in your hand again. Put the tip of me against your breast."

Without his meaning to, his request came out as an order.

"Please," he added and saw her smile knowingly.

"Like this?" She curled her slender fingers around his shaft, then scooted down between his straddled legs, stopping when his crown bumped the underside of one breast. Her flesh was warm and soft, but not precisely what he wished. Even as he told himself to hold his tongue, his preference came bursting out.

"Higher," he gasped.

She pressed the very tip of him against the bead of her nipple. "There?"

"Yes."

"Rub it?"

"Oh, yes." He shivered at the feel of her hard little peak brushing his member, at the sight of her ruddy color against his pink. A tiny bead of moisture welled from his slit. His nerves were practically shooting stars. "All around," he rasped. "Rub the head . . . all around."

She obeyed with the faintest curving of her lips. Her gaze dropped admiringly to his cock.

"You are still pale," she murmured, "but very hard." One of her fingers circled his rim, then tapped the sensitive dome. The touch made him lurch a fraction longer. "I can feel your pulse beating fast right here."

He was struggling not to gasp for air. His eyes slid closed as the nails of her second hand combed up the hair on his thigh. She shifted between his legs again, holding him, turning her face back and forth across his shaft. Her cheeks were soft, her mouth mobile and damp. She kissed the throbbing river of a vein.

"Ulric," she whispered. "I think I would like you inside me."

He groaned because, no matter what he intended, he knew he could not resist.

He dragged her upward along the bed, his hands planting in her outspread hair, his mouth sinking onto hers. Her tongue met his in slow, wet turns. Greedily, he sucked it into his mouth.

Though he longed to nip her lower lip, he did not dare. If he drew blood, he would be lost.

"Now," she said. "Take me now."

He clasped his shaft to guide himself inside her, then felt her hand settle over his to help.

His arousal was almost too much to bear. Everything about her seemed to accept him. Her thighs were spread, her entrance sleek and wet. He pressed easily inward, smooth, hot, holding at the furthest reach, then pulling carefully out. His stroke was steady: not too fast, not too forceful, gliding all the way in and almost all the way out. She pushed upward with a little moan each time he sank home. Her knees rose higher along his sides, and her hands slid down his back. They clenched his buttocks, but her nails did not prick his skin.

Clasped in living silk, he groaned her name and hid his face in her hair. He could do this. He could stay this gentle. It was good. It was heaven. But, Lord, it was killing him to hold back.

He tried pushing one of her legs over his shoulder, tried kissing her deep and hard. She grew warmer, wetter, while his cock screamed at him to pound in.

When he turned his head to kiss her ankle, he found himself sucking it against his teeth. His fingers dug into her haunches, his hipbones grinding hers hard enough to bruise.

"Ul-ric," she said, a catch in the middle of his name.

To his lust-addled mind, she sounded as though she wanted him
to be rough.

Cursing the need to rein his urges, he eased free of her body's
hold, hushing her when she whimpered, murmuring soothing
sounds.

This was as much for him as it was for her. His cock throbbed
with impatience as he coaxed her onto her belly and then up on her
knees. Her bottom bumped his loins with unerring aim. The position was nearly perfect but not quite. He lifted her arms until her
weight was propped on the niche's wall.

"Knees apart," he said, nudging them with his own, trying not
to grow too aroused from telling her what to do. He did not want
to spill before he satisfied her. "Brace your palms on the stone."

A shiver ran down her spine. Unable to stop himself, he dragged
his tongue up the knobs of her vertebrae. Her shoulders shook
again.

"Bottom up," he whispered, fighting shivers himself. "I want to
take you from behind."

He spread his hand on her belly to support her, to tilt her mount
of Venus just as he liked. Her scent was heady, her secret places glistening wet. He let his tip find its own way into her sweetness, pulsing wildly as he eased in. When she moaned, he withdrew and did
it again.

He could tell she was happy to have him back. Her body rippled
around him as hot as fire. A sound far too close to a snarl issued
from his throat. He had misjudged how enjoyable this would be.

He had thought it would be easier if he could not watch her
heat-flushed face. Instead, he found the new position almost too
exciting, just what his wolf most craved. Even as he thrust, he
could run his hands over her breasts, could tease her nipples,
could let his lips curl back over aching fangs without fear of being
frightening. Though he kept his movements slow, the pressure hit
him exactly right, under the head where he felt it most. Considering his *upyr* sensitivity, that meant he felt it quite a bit. Wanting

her to experience their lovemaking as intensely, he cupped her pubis and used his fingers to press the bud of her pleasure against his shaft.

She arched to him, opening her body to each intrusion, pushing back against it cooperatively.

Her eagerness was too much. Already frayed, the remains of his discipline fell in tatters. The only thing that saved him was knowing they both would be spending soon. Juliana's breath was coming harder, her movements losing their grace. His stones felt full enough to explode.

Her head dropped as she braced herself on the wall. Though he longed to cuff her wrists, he merely spread one of his hands beside hers. Seeing it, she gripped his forearm with surprising strength.

"That," she panted as the head of him glided over something she liked, something at the front of her tight passage. "Oh, *there.*"

"Harder?" he suggested, or maybe pleaded, already increasing his speed.

Her answer was lost in a pleasured moan. His member swelled at the sudden clutching of her sheath. He mouthed her nape, her shoulder, his instincts urging him to bite, if only to hold her in place for his final drive. He moaned at the longing he could not fulfill. He had a feeling he was pressing her far too hard.

"Ulric," she said. "Yes."

He did not know what she was saying yes to, but he bit and drank as his ecstasy began to peak, half blind with pleasure, clamping down on her neck to suck. As he felt her shudder around him, an unexpected tingle swept his scalp.

The sun was breaching the horizon.

He was so close to complete release, so desperate for it, he could have cried. To his supreme relief, dawn slowed his orgasm but did not dim it. The vessels of his sex contracted, ripples of bliss so singular and so lengthy they felt like tight, oiled hands squeezing down his cock. His spine bowed hard as he groaned against her neck, wrapping her in his arms, emptying himself in languorous, heated spurts, filling her with the *upyr*'s infertile ejaculate.

He was barely aware of falling into the softness of his furs, of tumbling weakly to the side. Opening heavy eyes, he found her leaning over him as before, as if their loveplay had been a dream. Her expression held a shadow that he misliked.

"Sorry," he mumbled, trying to stroke her cheek with his hand but succeeding only in batting her hip. "Forgot . . . sunrise."

She combed his hair out of his face. "Sleep," she said. "You gave me everything I needed."

He sensed this was not the truth, or not completely, but had neither the wakefulness nor the nerve to ask. When he fumbled to pull her beside him, she slipped away.

<hr />

KNOWING how leaden his arm could get when he fell asleep, Juliana eased away before it could trap her. She was too restless to lie with him all day, even more restless than before. Feeling the need for a shield, she drew on her chemise.

For all her horror at Ulric's violence, she had no objection to roughness in bed. She had discovered already that she enjoyed it, but to find that she *needed* it, that the experience was not complete unless he took her forcefully, disturbed her more than a bit.

His verbal orders had been a tease. The control she longed for was physical. For her, being left a little too tender was as necessary for satisfaction as a drink of blood was to him.

Helewis said when the leader was strong, everyone felt safe. Outwardly dutiful, Juliana had always prided herself on her independence. Could it be that, in her heart, she agreed with Helewis?

Halfway to the door, she hugged herself, shivering in her linen shift. As if of its own will, her hand slid up to find the place Ulric's fangs had pierced, where the muscle of her shoulder met her neck. The bite was healing, a mark a tomcat might have left. She wondered what it said about her that she found this exciting. Certainly, she could not deny she did. Tiny flickers of arousal moved deep inside her as she probed the spot. If Ulric had been awake, she would have climbed on him then and there.

But she could not solve the riddle now. Shaking it off, she pulled Ulric's door open.

Her heart jumped as her foot almost struck a body. For some reason, Helewis was sleeping on the threshold. Juliana wondered if Ulric knew: surely this was taking subservience too far! Holding her breath for silence, she stepped over the slumbering woman and into the corridor. Though the darkness was not as thick as before, she lifted a small bronze lantern from its hook.

She would have to learn to move through these tunnels blind, at least until she decided if she was going to be *upyr*. That she had not ruled this out troubled her anew. Maybe the difference between her and Ulric—and never mind between her and Helewis—was not so great.

She padded barefoot down the passage, this time toward the entry ledge. She had a longing to see the sun. Even if she was sleeping with a creature of darkness, she did not have to live like a mole.

To her relief, she recalled the route. As she walked, she began to see shadows without the lamp. The sound of ravens cawing in the trees was humorously sweet.

The cave faced west—better for viewing sunset than sunrise, though there were signs of the dawning day. A thin line of clouds, their edges fired with reflected pink, flew like feathers above the trees. Last night, Juliana had not realized how high Ulric's cave was, or how isolated. The forest was immense, a sea of pine and oak that followed the rise and dip of the land in every direction she could see. An eagle circled to the north, riding the warming air.

No wonder Ulric acted like the king of the world. This was quite a holding. Here, surrounded by this forest, one could forget the human realm existed, much less that it posed a threat.

It is up to me to remember, Juliana thought, touched by an unexpected sense of guardianship.

She was testing the weight of this new emotion when she noticed something moving along the base of the cliff. Startled, she drew back behind the opening and peered out. One of the male *upyr,* cloaked and gloved and booted in black, was scaling the rock. The clothes foiled her for a moment, but the height and an errant wisp of black hair told her the climber was Bastien.

Before she could decide whether to leave, he was there, his hair smoking faintly as he heaved himself over the edge. When he threw back his hood, she saw a half-healed bite mark on his neck. The edges were bruised, as if someone had drawn on it very hard. Gytha, she supposed, and blushed at the other activities the bruise implied. The mark had to be recent. Evidently, the failure of Gytha's coup had not quenched their mutual attraction.

Knowing he might spot her at any moment, and not wanting him to take her for a spy, Juliana cleared her throat.

Bastien spun around, as startled to see her as she had been to see him. His eyes bore circles as purple as his bruise. His alarm shored up her confidence.

"Step into the shadow," she suggested. "You will blister if you stand and gape."

He shuffled back to the wall, comfortingly out of reach. She hoped the strip of light between them would be as good as a wall.

"I was taking the sun," he explained, then laughed sheepishly. "Getting drunk, you would say. I am afraid it is a personal vice."

"A discreet vice, as few will ever be awake to see you indulge."

"Yes," he agreed, and ran his tongue along his lower lip.

Her father had taught her such nervous gestures were giveaways, signs that it was time to call a rival's bluff. Bastien had lied about his reason for being out. When he spoke again, she was even surer her guess was right.

"If you would keep this to yourself, I would be grateful. The others would think less of me if they knew."

"Tell me what stars were rising when you were born and I shall consider remaining quiet."

He hesitated, though he seemed more interested than angry. "The sign of the scorpion," he said, then: "You are curious about the mark I put on Ingrith."

"It gave you power over her." She made it a statement rather than a query. "I was under the impression that you had to be very strong to have that much influence on each other."

"We do." His smile was filled with genuine amusement. "Mortals, of course, are easier to thrall."

"They are unless they have been bitten by another *upyr* first. Then they have protection."

"Know about that, do you?"

She said nothing of the merchant's stories that held this lore, trusting in silence to serve her ends. The more he thought she knew, the less secretive he would be. Bending one leg, he braced his weight against the rock. Unlike Ulric, who preferred going naked, Bastien seemed comfortable in his clothes. Perhaps he had grown used to them while traveling from France. He was different from Ulric in other ways as well: not as still as the pack leader, nor as self-assured.

She met Bastien's half-smile with one of her own. He might be immortal, but if he thought she was going to run out of patience and speak first, he was deceived. Finally, with a grimace to cede the victory, he answered the question she had been hinting at all along.

"The mark I put on Ingrith is called a *point de convergence*. It draws on the power of my personal stars to concentrate my will, thus allowing me to thrall my fellow *upyr*."

"So you convinced her she could not heal."

"Yes," he said and pushed his long, wine-black hair back from his face.

His answer hinted at a host of possibilities. The power of astrology she was not qualified to judge. A thrall she had seen in action for herself. From what she had witnessed, that was the same as persuasion with an extra boost. She wondered if Ingrith failed to heal because she believed Bastien's claims. If this was the case, was his power responsible or her own? Had Ingrith, in essence, thralled herself? Could another *upyr* have removed the mark if they were as charismatic? Finally, was this the same mechanism by which the blacksmith's tattoo worked?

For the time being, she felt more comfortable keeping these questions to herself. She turned her gaze back to Bastien. Beneath his sardonic smirk, and despite his story of getting sundrunk, she judged him quite sober. He was wary of her, she concluded, not only because she was Ulric's lover, but because she had the kind of mind that loved a mystery.

"I hear using magic is forbidden," she said, hoping to coax him to reveal who had taught him what he knew. "At least among the children of Auriclus."

This time her feint did not bear fruit. With one gloved hand, Bastien reached out from his pool of shadow to touch her neck. The tip of his index finger traced a vein. "Feeding from humans is forbidden, too, and nonetheless there are those among us who cannot resist."

When she shivered and flinched away, his smile lifted the weariness from his face. She could not help noting that his fangs had partially emerged.

"If Ulric tires of you," he said so softly it was barely speech, "I would be happy to taste you myself."

---

DECIDING it was unsafe to wander the cave until the sun was higher, Juliana returned to Ulric's chamber, once again clambering carefully over Helewis. Ulric mumbled something as she slipped back in. He, apparently, was a lighter sleeper than his junior wolf, though he was not disturbed enough to rouse.

She lay awake on her back, her fingers laced beneath her breasts as she stared at the niche's ceiling, thinking about magic and the things it might be used for now that she knew it was real.

If her experience with the standing stones was any indication, magic was not a power for *upyr* alone. Not only could renegades like Bastien wield it to their advantage, but so could humans—maybe even humans like the soldier who had rushed at Ulric with his cross.

Ulric said he saw no reason why a Christian symbol should have power over *upyr*. Juliana was not as sure, but if he was right, the soldiers believing a lie could be providential. The less truth humans knew, the safer *upyr* would be. It might even be worthwhile to spread a few misleading stories: say, that silver weakened them instead of iron, or that immortals had a dread of scallions. Juliana smiled to imagine villagers running around with long green stalks strung on their necks. She knew precisely how such falsehoods could be spread through the merchant network. If she drew on her familiarity with the biggest gossips, fooling them would not even take much time.

Abruptly shocked by her ruminations, Juliana's hands flew up to her cheeks. She was thinking of humans as "them." In her mind, she had begun to side with *upyr*.

I have not yet made my choice, she insisted to herself as she rolled toward the wall to sleep. Regardless of her conflict, rest came easily.

She was not as bothered by her disloyalty as she should have been.

# Eleven

ULRIC woke later than usual, at least an hour past dusk. Juliana was gone, as was Helewis. Disconcerted but not alarmed, he raked his fingers through his hair, smoothing it absently as he turned in a circle to check the room.

Metal flashed in his pile of clothes, folded and left in the corner since his return. He bent to see what the gleam belonged to and found Juliana's portrait locket, the one he had rescued from the sons of Gideon Drake. No more than half aware of what he was doing, he bounced the chain in his hand.

Juliana would not have run again, not without telling him. He had, so far as he knew, done nothing to upset her. More to the point, if Helewis was gone as well, she had a guard.

Knowing Helewis's strict adherence to duty, Juliana might welcome a change of company.

Decision made, he dropped the locket over his head and began his search. Luckily, she and Helewis had moved slowly enough to track. Ulric rolled his shoulders and shook his arms as he followed them deeper into the cliff. Already, Juliana's scent was twining with his pack's. That pleased him, even if Bastien's contribution to the perfume made his hackles rise.

His nose informed him that Juliana had washed in the chamber of the hot spring, with Helewis standing outside. The chamber of the cold spring, where the old mosaics ringed the walls, provided her a drink. Then she and Helewis took the opposite turning from the one that led to the solar. The hall of columns held her attention long enough that Stephen and Ingrith had a chance to join her. From there, the group proceeded down a tiled corridor. This was a seldom-traveled tunnel, low of ceiling and awkwardly round. Ulric moved through it slightly crouched, easily following their footprints in the dust. Because his power tended to repel any kind of soil, he had to be careful not to scatter the trail.

He caught up with their voices in a square storeroom. With a tightening behind his neck, he realized it was the room where Gillian stashed her best finds. Many was the night Ulric had pulled her from her treasures, urging her to join the pack. *Time to hunt,* he would say. *You will learn nothing from this rubbish.*

Four sets of eyes turned to his entry as he stepped inside. Covered in dust and cobwebs, Juliana lit up like the sun. Against her breasts, she cradled a leather volume as carefully as if it were a child.

"Look!" She bounded to her feet. "We found all these beautiful things!"

"I see," he said, happy for her enjoyment but unable to imitate her smile.

"I tried to stop her," Helewis said, her arms hugging her waist. "I told her reading was forbidden."

Stephen clucked in the manner of one who has uttered a rebuke before. "The rules are changing," he said. "Surely this one can, too."

He turned to Ulric, a plea in his eyes. To Ulric's amazement, the pack's least inhibited member, the one who loved to show off his masculine charms, was wearing what looked like a blanket wrapped around his shoulder and waist.

"It is a plaid," Stephen informed him. "We found it in a chest. I grew tired of her"—he tipped his head at Juliana—"refusing to stare."

"I did not ask him to wear it," Juliana said. "It was entirely his idea. He claimed a woman not looking at him seemed wrong."

"I th-think it is sexy," Ingrith put in so softly Ulric had to strain to hear. "You have to imagine the dangly bits."

Overwhelmed by the chorus, Ulric rubbed the center of his forehead. Of them all, Ingrith seemed the safest to address. He noticed she had a length of sea-green silk bundled to her chest. "Your bruises are nearly gone," he observed. "Do you feel better as well?"

Her head was bowed too low for him to see her eyes. "Yes," she whispered through the flaxen curtain of her hair. "Thank you for asking."

Stephen put his arm around her shoulder, as she was clearly uncomfortable with Ulric. Before Ulric could demand to know why, Juliana spoke.

"Ingrith was wondering," she began cautiously, "would you take it amiss if she wore the dress we found?"

"Because I remembered," Ingrith explained. "When I was human, I liked to wear pretty things."

"She would not wear it all the time," Stephen assured him. "Just now and then."

"Mary in heaven," Ulric swore, "why are you all acting as if I were an ogre? Ingrith can wear whatever she pleases. Gillian—" He caught his breath at the name. "Gillian used to dress all the time."

A silence fell that none save Helewis tried to break. "I do not care what they do. *I* am not wearing clothes."

"Good." Ulric rubbed his brow again. "I would hate to think we were turning into Eden after the fall."

"I know that story!" Ingrith exclaimed with a little gasp. "The nuns taught me about that."

"Nuns." Stephen wagged his brows. "I remember nuns."

Ulric closed his eyes and struggled to keep his temper under control. Juliana had been here one blessed day and she was well on her way to infecting them all with her human habits. Stephen wearing clothes . . . Ingrith recalling her mortal life . . . Ulric dared not contemplate what she might accomplish by summer's end.

Seeing his reaction, Juliana set down the book and came to his side. Like magic, his frustration faded. One of her hands nestled in his while the other stroked the length of his arm.

"It might be useful," she said, "to know your history. You would not want to be caught unawares a second time."

"But how can this help?" He waved at the jumble of chests and furniture. In one corner, a golden throne with wings for arms rested upside down on a bronze table. In the opposite corner, marble statues tumbled together like fallen knights. A collection of red and black pottery lay strewn across the floor, fighting for space with a chess set, a silver harp, and a long, rolled tapestry. This was not history; this was a mess. "These are just the belongings of dead *upyr*."

"Maybe," Juliana conceded. "But maybe they are clues. I found books underneath the piles. Nothing terribly useful as yet: a *Book of Hours,* a few of philosophy, and something that looks like a medical treatise in French. Alas"—she shook her head mournfully—"I cannot read that tongue."

When her lashes rose again, her big, brown eyes were a little too innocent.

"No," he said firmly before she could ask. "You may dress everyone in feathers and explore to your heart's content but, by all that is holy, you are going to stay away from that Frenchman."

"But—" said Juliana, then shut her mouth. The stubborn set of her jaw told him her silence did not mean she was giving up. She must not have realized how big his concession was.

He put his hand on her shoulder and dropped his voice. "Juliana, if you will not do this out of respect for my authority, then do it for Ingrith. She feels comfortable with you now. Could that continue if you cozied up to the man who helped Gytha attack her?"

"I have no intention of cozying up to him." She jabbed her

finger at his chest. "You are not fighting fair to bring Ingrith into this."

Though he knew she had the right of it, he felt no remorse. She was too apt to get herself into trouble, poking her nose where it did not belong. "Promise you will keep your distance from Bastien."

A flush he found distractingly attractive washed her cheeks. "I will not make a promise I am not positive I can keep."

"Damn it—"

"You do not give your word lightly. Why should I?"

"I never asked you to give it lightly. I simply want you to give it."

His voice had risen sharply enough that he knew the others could hear. Of course, with ears such as his kind possessed, they had probably heard it all. When Juliana splayed her hand gently across his chest, he tried to resist its soothing allure. In just this manner, he imagined her trying to get around her father.

"I am not flirting with him," she said calmly. "I am trying to ferret out his secrets."

"You are trying?" he spluttered. "As in, you already have begun?"

She was toe to toe with him, her conciliatory pose forgotten. He noticed she did not deny his claim.

"You will not do what needs to be done," she said. "You think all you have to do is issue a decree, and everyone will comply."

Her defiance sent a flash of blinding red across his vision. She dared to take him to task. In front of his pack. As if she were a fishwife and he her child. All the days of holding back dissolved in one instant. He clenched his hands and felt the hair on his body prick up with rage.

To hell with his promise. He could not allow this. For her own good, he would make her behave. The air thickened and his face grew unnaturally hot. He was dimly aware of the others drawing back at his swelling power.

Let them, he thought. Let them remember who is their king.

"I will show you an order," he said with a warning growl.

"As you please," Juliana snapped back, "but if you thrall me against my will, you will prove your word is worthless."

She was trembling hard, but she was not backing down. He damned the fact that he could not hit her, a human and a female. Then he damned the fact that she was counting on his restraint. His arm muscle was so cramped, he almost could not relax it.

He blew out a long, slow breath before hearing Ingrith whimper. He turned to find her curled into a ball at Stephen's feet. Stephen looked as if he longed to join her. By the skin of his teeth, the younger wolf managed to crouch beside his lover and pat her back. Ulric cursed the picture they made. Was everyone convinced he had lost all control?

With an effort, he swallowed back his vexation.

"I am not angry at you," he said, kneeling down to put his hand behind Ingrith's neck. To his relief, she did not flinch.

"You m-must not hurt Juliana," Ingrith said through chattering teeth. "She is only a human."

Ulric's brows rose at this response, but he found himself oddly touched. He rubbed the knots in Ingrith's back. "I shall not hurt her," he said, then added dryly, "as Juliana knows very well."

"It is true." Juliana stepped to his side. "Ulric would never hurt anyone who could not fight back."

Ingrith lifted her beautiful, tearstained face. The tinge of pink to her whiteness made her look even more lovely. With one slender hand she dashed a last tear away. "I am sorry, Ulric. I did not mean to be a goose. It is just, I am not used to seeing you as you were last night. Oh, I know you had to do it. Violence was the only way B-Bastien would back down. If you had not acted swiftly, there would have been more bloodshed."

"I am glad someone knows that," Ulric said.

"We all know it." Stephen met his eyes head-on, the gratitude in them raw. "Your coming back put things right."

Ulric wished he believed that. Too tired to argue, he rose and put out his arms.

"Give me the books," he said to Juliana, who responded by biting her lip. "I am not going to destroy them, merely carry them to my room. If you are going to read these texts, at least you will not have to sneak away."

She piled them reluctantly into his hold, as if afraid he would change his mind. In truth, Ulric was tempted. This, after all, was how matters first went awry with Gillian. In the end, she had chosen her love of learning over her love of him.

I must not make the same mistakes, he told himself. I must not make Juliana choose. He had to have faith that if he let her sate her curiosity, she would not run away.

———————

THE sight of Gytha blocking the tunnel up ahead stopped Juliana in her tracks.

"Well, well," the haughty *upyr* said. "Look who has turned packhorse."

The others had stopped when Juliana did, but Gytha's scorn was directed toward Helewis. Deeply offended by the sight of her pack leader carrying Juliana's books, she had begged him to let her take them, thus earning Gytha's contempt. With her hands on her hips and her lip curled in a sneer, Gytha's wolf nature shone bright. Even in human form, her rough black hair and lean physique were those of a huntress. From the arrogance of her pose, Juliana inferred that Ulric had not imposed her punishment yet.

Gytha seemed to have no idea that her present behavior might be deciding how it was announced.

"I am glad you are here," Ulric said in his coolest manner. "You have saved me a trip to inform you of your penance."

"We should leave," said Stephen, edging away nervously.

Ulric stopped him by lifting a finger. "Stay where you are, Stephen. This concerns everyone." He circled Gytha until he stood behind her, a position that must have made her feel vulnerable.

Though she refused to turn, she grew noticeably tense. Ulric waited until a muscle ticked in her neck.

"Gytha is to be shunned," he said to the others. "For a fortnight, none of us shall speak to her or communicate in any way. When the fortnight ends, so does her punishment—on one condition. Ingrith must have gotten over her fear. If she has not, the sentence will continue. So you see, Gytha, you should endeavor not to intimidate your sister wolf."

"Oh!" said Ingrith, a soft, involuntary sound.

When she heard it, Gytha's gape of astonishment turned to mockery. "Poor wittle Ingrith. Is she afraid?"

As threats went, it was not much to speak of, but Ingrith shrank back against Stephen.

"Leave her alone," said Bastien, coming up the tunnel behind Ulric. "Nothing can be gained by terrorizing Ingrith."

"Fine," said Gytha, lashing out to grab Helewis by the hair. "Maybe I should terrorize this idiot instead."

The books Helewis had fought to carry tumbled to the floor just as Ulric caught her attacker around the neck. Gytha screamed with fury and kicked backward at Ulric's shins. They fell and wrestled with Gytha still clutching Helewis's thick red hair. Back and forth the two of them rolled with Helewis trying fruitlessly to escape.

*Fight,* Juliana mouthed, but for her own sake Helewis would not.

"Hey!" was all she said as Ulric smashed Gytha against the wall.

Gytha swung Helewis between her and Ulric's next rush. He snarled and checked and turned into a blur of motion. Juliana presumed he was changing, but he was simply moving too fast for her human eyes. He grabbed Gytha's ankles, yanked both out from under her, then pinned her neck to the floor.

Gytha's face filled with the faint rose-pink that served the *upyr* as flush. Ulric's forearm and weight were cutting off her air.

"Ow," said Helewis, her head having hit the stone.

Realizing Gytha would rather choke to death than let go of

Helewis's hair, Bastien forcibly unclenched her fingers to set the other female free. This defection drove Gytha so wild she thrashed and wailed like one possessed. Finally, Ulric slapped her to silence.

The imprint of his hand remained on her cheek.

"I will beat you if I must," he said, "but it will not exempt you from my decree."

"I believe I will save the pleasure of being beaten for another day," Gytha rasped from her breathless sprawl. "I know how much you like it rough."

Ulric pushed away in disgust, but Juliana perceived her barb had struck home. "Take your punishment like a wolf," he said, looking down at her where she lay, "not like a coward."

He walked by her without a word, and Juliana knew the shunning had begun. They all filed past her one by one, with Bastien standing as a shield between his lover and the line. Ingrith followed Juliana closely enough that she risked trodding on her heels.

"Traitor," Gytha hissed when Bastien turned to go.

Juliana's ears must have been sharper than she thought because she heard his apology.

"I am sorry," he said under his breath. "I need this haven more than you know."

Gytha's reaction posed no challenge to anyone's ears. Her curses followed them down the passageway. "Take heed, king," she shouted to Ulric. "Bastien is more than ready to rule through a queen. If you choose another, he will steal yours!"

Ulric's jaw was tight, his golden brows glowering. They did not lighten when Juliana reached for his hand.

———◦◦◦———

"THERE must be a desk you can read on," Ulric said, "somewhere in that pile of castaways."

Having little furniture had obliged him to set her books on his one unbroken stool. They looked odd there, like a tower about to fall.

"You need a wall hanging, too," he added, "one you select

yourself. Humans like those, do they not? It will give you something to rest your eyes upon when they are tired."

Juliana came up behind him, sliding her arms around his waist
and kissing his nape above her locket's chain. Ulric closed his eyes,
his fingers resting lightly on the leather binding of the topmost
book. Jewels were set into its cover, as smooth as river stones.

"I am not interested in Bastien," she said, her mouth brushing
his skin through his hair, "except as an object of inquiry. You are
the one I care about."

For now, he thought, dismayed that his jealousy was this trans-
parent. But any *upyr* might attract her with time. If that were true,
he needed to know—little though he would enjoy it.

"What about you?" she said, her breath finding a ticklish spot
beneath his ear.

"Me?"

"And Gytha."

"There is no me and Gytha. She has never shared my bed."

Juliana snorted softly in disbelief.

"It is true. I know she is beautiful and wild, but she is far too
troublesome."

"Well." Juliana's chuckle warmed his back. "It is good to know
I am less trouble than someone."

Ulric turned and took her in his arms. "You are good trouble,
the kind of trouble I desire."

"I am glad. I like your kind of trouble, too."

Ulric did not think he was trouble but held his tongue. He enjoyed the way she leaned back trustingly in his hold, the way her
eyes caught the light as she clasped his neck. For one sweet moment, they simply smiled in accord.

"Will you hunt tonight?" she asked.

"We should. Working together will help heal what happened
in my absence. Gytha will have to be excluded. Hunting without
being able to communicate would not work."

"You can watch how Bastien behaves."

"Yes." Ulric scratched the side of his jaw. "That had occurred to me. It is difficult to hide one's nature when in wolf form. Cowards show, and bullies, and those who have no patience."

"You have patience," she said, "even if you lose it now and then."

He did not know what to make of her compliment. It pleased him, but also caused him to feel exposed. She had seen something inside him he had not expected. Unable to answer, he spread his hands behind her shoulder blades.

"Bar the door while I am gone. I do not expect problems, but just in case."

"I will," she promised and kissed his chin where Gytha's elbow had left a bruise. "Ulric?"

"Yes, Juliana?"

"I was wondering . . . Do you read at all?"

He sighed. "I can pick out a few letters, but no more. I do not believe I learned as a mortal."

"But if I showed you a word, you would remember it. *Upyr* are quick-witted, yes? You could learn to read that way."

"I suppose I could—if it means that much to you."

"I was thinking it would be useful if all of you could read a prayer or two. In a pinch, it might convince a human you are not ungodly."

Her suggestion took him by surprise. He opened his mouth to explain that they did not mingle with mortal kind, but that was not as true as it had once been. He had found a reason to break Auriclus's rules, and up till then he had been more dutiful than most. He could not guarantee no other *upyr* would disobey.

As to that, if Ulric had known more of mortals and their ways, perhaps he would not have left signs of himself in Bridesmere.

Mulling this over, he rubbed a lock of Juliana's hair between his finger and thumb. She had recognized what he was without being told, proof that stories of his kind were circulating. If she had taught him anything, it was that humans loved unearthing secrets.

Even if every *upyr* in the isles stayed where they were, mortals like those sons of Gideon Drake might decide to pursue them. Capable though Ulric was, he could not subdue them all.

Maybe what she proposed was wise.

"I will think on it," he said finally.

"Good," she answered with a brilliant smile. "I want you and your pack to stay safe."

She seemed to believe his promise to consider her request was the same as him saying "yes."

# Twelve

O VER the course of the next sennight, Juliana found many books hidden in the cave. Fascinating though they were, none contained what she was seeking. Without exception, they were about and by humans, from religious texts to pagan philosophers she would never have been exposed to as a respectable merchant's daughter—even if she had been able to read Greek. Juliana had been taught only those languages that were useful: the Latin and English required to help her father in his trade. The scholars of her world would have given their eyeteeth to peruse these pages for a single day. Sadly, Juliana mainly felt irked.

She wanted to know the origins of the *upyr* or, failing that, the secret of their power.

"There is nothing there," Helewis sighed gustily as Juliana opened yet another text.

Along with Stephen and Ingrith, Juliana's usual companions, they sat in a cavernous hall of red porphyry columns. The scale of the construction dwarfed them, as if this room had been designed for giants—the how and why of it another mystery for her list.

In the murky shadows of the coffered ceiling, gold and crystal

chandeliers glinted like leviathans. The two near the dais still func-
tioned, operating—apparently—on the same principles as Ulric's
lamp. No candles were needed to create the soft golden glow. One
simply palmed the crystal sphere that perched in the sconce beside
the doorway and they sprang to life.

They did not, however, provide enough light for reading. For
that, Juliana relied on a collection of ordinary oil lamps. Though
rendered easier to keep lit by the *upyr*'s influence, their illumination
stretched no more than halfway up the forest of smooth red stone.

She was not certain what she would do when the oil they had
found ran out. Regardless of Ulric's concessions, she could not
imagine him granting permission to purchase more.

Untroubled by such concerns, Stephen, who had gallantly provided the women with cushions, was looking smug because he had
found a cache of books in a hollow beneath a floor tile.

Prying it up had allowed him to show off his muscles.

As always, Ingrith snuggled beside him, dressed like a Roman
maiden in her reclaimed gown. She was laboriously puzzling through
the prayers in a *Book of Hours*. Ever since Ulric had given his con-
sent, she had thrown herself into trying to read. She, it seemed, had
learned the skill as a mortal, taught by the nuns with whom she had
resided as a young widow.

Less enthused by the lifting of Auriclus's ban, Stephen entertained himself by playing with Ingrith's hair. Helewis refused to
consider reading at all, devoting herself instead to her new position
as Juliana's guard. Though Juliana could scarcely wash her hands
without Helewis's attendance, she did not object. In his own devi-
ous way, Ulric had done what she asked.

"What I want to know," Juliana said into the echoing space, "is
who collected these books in the first place."

Ingrith's lips stopped sounding out words. "That is easy. They
were brought here by Lucius."

Her fellow *upyr* stared at her, causing her to shrink back.

"Well, it stands to reason," she said defensively. "Lucius was always going off without warning, whether Ulric approved or not. Plus, these books smell like him."

"Lucius does not have a smell," Stephen declared with great assurance.

"Yes, he does. He smells like snow, or something like snow, but I am certain he has a scent."

Ingrith was so offended by her lover's contradiction that she forgot to hide behind her hair. Juliana smiled to see it. Ingrith was getting stronger.

"Maybe Stephen's nose is only good for sniffing women," Helewis said in a rare jest.

"Did *you* smell him?" Stephen demanded.

Helewis shrugged her strong shoulders. "I am willing to admit Ingrith's nose is better than mine."

Before the pair could get into a scuffle, Juliana spoke. "Lucius is the *upyr* who turned out to be an elder?"

"Yes," Ingrith confirmed, "though I would not have guessed it. While he was living with us, he never did anything elder-ly."

"He was a good tracker," Stephen put in, scratching his chest where it was draped by the woollen plaid.

"Yes," Ingrith said, "but he did not have special powers. We never saw him turn into a mist, or order an *upyr* to stop breathing with just his mind. If he were old enough to be an elder, he ought to have had those gifts or others like them. Most of all, he did not know the secret of the change."

"You have no proof of that," said Helewis.

"But he never made any children."

"Maybe he made them and forgot, just like you forgot how to read." Helewis nodded to herself as if she liked this theory. It was the first time Juliana could remember hearing her think for herself.

"What I cannot believe," Stephen said, stretching out his legs the better to let the women admire them, "is that Gillian was an elder. She definitely was a young *upyr*."

Ingrith gave her partner a jab.

"What?" said Stephen, looking at her stupidly.

"It is all right," Juliana said. "I know Ulric was in love with her."

"Crazy in love." Stephen nodded emphatically. "Obsessed. Besotted. From the moment she joined the pack. Sometimes I thought if she did not return his feelings, he would go mad."

"Stephen!" Ingrith hissed under her breath.

"The pack leader is much calmer with you," Stephen said to Juliana as if that would undo the harm. "Barely crazy at all."

This time Ingrith responded by whacking him behind the head. Though Juliana laughed, her eyes were dangerously hot. She dared not blink for fear they would spill over. Knowing the man she loved had once loved another was different from hearing he had been "crazier" about Gillian.

As luck would have it, Ulric chose that moment to appear. Juliana pretended the text she held in her lap was infinitely engrossing. Better that than to have him know how close she was to tears.

He wears my locket, she told herself. That has to mean something.

"So," said Ulric, rubbing his hands together, "the deer are grazing at Loch Monar. Who is ready for a hunt?"

"Not tonight," Stephen groaned. "It was raining when we woke and Juliana promised us a story."

"A real one," Ingrith said, "with fighting and blood."

Juliana could not help herself. She looked up to see Ulric's reaction.

"A story," he repeated, dragging his thick gold hair back along his head. Though the gesture did lovely things to his chest, she could tell the pack's reluctance took him aback.

As usual, Helewis disapproved of anything their leader misliked.

"You can hear a story *after* you hunt," she said to Stephen repressively.

"Oh," said Stephen, abruptly realizing how he had just behaved. "After we hunt. Of course that would be best. We would not want to hear about blood until we have had some."

"No," Ulric wryly agreed. "That would be most distracting." His humor mended if not restored, he bent to kiss Juliana's cheek. "Will you be all right on your own? I thought we would try taking Gytha with us tonight. She is getting a little too malcontent for my taste."

Juliana concurred with that. Ever since the pack had stopped talking to her, Gytha had been stumping around like a baited bear. Given her surly mood, Juliana was virtually certain she and Bastien no longer shared a bed—though, come to think of it, she had spotted more bite marks on his neck.

But what the pair were or were not doing was their concern. She merely hoped the punishment she had suggested was not ill-conceived. Maybe Ulric did know his people best. Maybe she had blundered. The only promising sign was that Gytha had not attacked anyone in days.

"I will be fine," she said to Ulric. "I shall take these new books to your room."

"Meet us later," he suggested, his voice gentle and warm. "If the rain lets up, you can cook your own meal outside."

"I would like that," she said and received a second kiss as reward.

"Woo-woo," Stephen hooted, making her blush.

It was after the foursome left that something Ingrith said finally sank in. According to her, only elders could change humans into *upyr*. Because Ulric was not an elder, that meant he could not change her. Juliana thought back to his original oath. *I will see that you share my powers,* was what he said: misleading, but not a lie. A matter of pride, she suspected, especially if his precious Gillian had mastered that gift.

What mattered to her was not his dissembling. Ulric had more than enough strength for her. What bothered Juliana was that, if she became *upyr*, she would have to trust her transformation to a stranger.

Possibly even a stranger like Gillian.

---

JULIANA should have guessed none of the pack would carry clothes to a hunt—whatever their recent habits. Once again, she was surrounded by stunning, naked *upyr*. Obviously pleased by their successful chase, the six immortals sprawled about the fire Ulric had built in a clearing not too far from the foot of the cliff. The light the *upyr* gave off was brighter than both fire and moon, the result—she assumed—of being well fed. Childish though it might be, she took pride in the fact that Ulric was the most luminous. Even Bastien's shine could not compare.

Still being shunned, Gytha lay on her back, staring at the stars with her head pillowed on her hands, slightly outside the others' circle. She had given up on talking, no doubt tired of being ignored, though being included in the hunt had clearly calmed her. To her left, but not close, was Bastien. He had positioned himself among the rest, a move the others undercut by leaving extra space between him and them. Ulric and Helewis sat on either side of Juliana, after which came Stephen and Ingrith. They lay on their bellies, their chins on their forearms, their fingers playing idly—and identically—with the grass. Because Gytha and Bastien were present, Ingrith occasionally hid her face on Stephen's smoothly muscled back. Aside from this, she seemed well.

Stephen, Juliana noticed, had taken to wearing the front of his long curly hair in braids, like a Celtic warrior of old. She wondered if a beaver sporran was likely to be next.

Smiling to herself, she leaned back against a tree, her stomach full, her mood content. An enclosure of pines rose around them, as majestic in their way as the columns in Ulric's hall. Despite the varied tensions in the pack, despite their very foreign appearance, she experienced an unexpected and unfamiliar sense of family. In her home, they had never been more than three.

The emotion was a delicate bubble. How miraculous that she sat among these strange and wondrous people, a race so mysterious that they had barely entered into myth! With her, they shared their natural selves. With her, they shared their squabbles.

She could not deny that felt like a privilege.

"You are an excellent cook," Bastien said, his back resting on a rock, his tongue dragging savoringly across his teeth. Like the rest— excepting Gytha—he had changed into his beast form to taste her roast venison. Though his fellow wolves had snapped back the treat with apparent enjoyment, Bastien was the only one to compliment her skill.

Something about his tone, or mayhap his accent, made the words sound more like a seduction than a compliment.

Lounging there in the firelight, with his sly green eyes and his half-curled smile, Juliana could believe Gytha's accusations. Bastien's nakedness seemed different, too, as if it were a challenge rather than a lack of clothes. Though one upbent knee covered what Ingrith had called his dangly bits, Juliana found it impossible to look directly his way.

Sensitive to her discomfort, Ulric laid his palm on her leg. His hand was pale and strong, his fingers curled protectively around her thigh. The warmth they sent sliding through her put her even less at ease. How could it do otherwise, when every nose in the place would know the instant she grew aroused?

At the very thought of it, her ears turned hot.

"That deer you caught was fat and tender," she said in hope of furnishing a distraction. "A child could not have ruined it."

"Not true," Helewis protested. "My . . . my father was cook to a Norman lord. I never saw him serve a better roast—fancier, but not better."

Juliana suspected this was an exaggeration. Even with the spices she and Ulric had acquired in Dunburn, her skills were only average. Apparently, Helewis felt compelled to defend her charge even from herself.

Bastien found a different significance in Helewis's words. "Interesting," he said, switching the leg he had raised. "A human comes among you and you all begin recalling your mortal past."

"Unl-like you," Ingrith stammered, her face tucked close to Stephen's back, "who do not speak of your past at all."

"Ha!" barked Gytha, but everyone had grown so used to paying her no mind, they did not jump.

Equally unmoved, Bastien leaned forward to rest his chin on his knee. His fingers fanned up and down his shin. "If you asked me, sweet Ingrith, I would bare all."

This time there could be no doubt of the Frenchman's suggestive intent. Juliana wondered if he hoped to sway the pack one female at a time. Possibly thinking along the same lines, Stephen bristled and bared his teeth. Oddly enough, Ingrith seemed unruffled.

"No fighting," Juliana ordered, "or I will not tell my story."

"He is frightening her," Stephen accused in a rumble considerably lower than his normal tone.

"Not as much as you would like," Helewis muttered beneath her breath.

Bastien laughed and lifted his hands. "Forgive me," he said with a beguiling smile. "Your Ingrith is so charming I could not resist. But, please, Mistress Juliana, do commence your tale. I confess I await it with bated breath."

At this, Ulric moved his hand from Juliana's leg to drape her back. The hold pulled her gently against his side.

She was both flattered and bemused. Meeting other *upyr,* the plainest of whom were impossibly lovely, made her realize her appeal for Ulric could not be her looks. *I taste better than they do,* she mused with a mental eye roll. Even as she had the thought, she knew the reasons ran deeper. Ulric might not love her the way he loved Gillian, but he cared for her very much.

Possessiveness aside, the pack leader seemed content to leave his supposed rival in one piece. "Yes," he said somewhat grimly, "we all are panting to hear."

---

ULRIC'S words were not a lie. Though the changes his pack had been going through strained his patience, he, too, enjoyed a sensation of shrugging off rusty chains. Gillian and Lucius's discovery of their gifts had disrupted more than his existence. With four elders instead of two, the balance of power among the *upyr* was turned on its head. No one of them could dictate to his or her inferiors as before. Few might know it yet, but tonight the elders' children had a choice of allegiances.

If the world was ripe for changes, Ulric saw no reason why some of them could not be pleasurable.

Pushing off a lingering scrap of guilt for ignoring the edicts of his sire, he stroked Juliana's softly waving hair. She was pulling her much-treasured volume of stories into her lap, opening its parchment pages to a green ribbon. As if reaching through the ink to touch her mother, her fingertips stroked a picture of a huge green giant on a huge green horse, every fearsome detail lovingly drawn. Ulric wished he could kiss away the yearning he saw in her face.

Juliana's mother had indeed liked monsters.

Looking at her daughter, he was struck by what a dear and serious person his love could be, studying his pack with her wide, brown eyes, adding up their foibles like a merchant with a sack of coin. Apart from a moment or two of shock, she had never once turned away, requiting what must have seemed like eccentricities with fondness.

Ulric's sole regret was that fondness would never be enough for him.

But Juliana was ready to begin. He knew that when she cleared the wistfulness from her throat.

"This story," she said, "which I heard from a wandering bard, is

the tale of Sir Gawain and the dread Green Knight, the most ferocious, most underhanded, most deathly foe King Arthur's court had
ever seen."

This was enough to make Ingrith gasp.

"No, no," she said when Juliana paused. "Please go on. I can
tell it will be exciting."

"Yes," Stephen insisted. "Ingrith is fine."

"Goodness," Juliana laughed. "I see I shall not have cause to
complain about my audience."

In truth she did not. For good or ill, the pack had been deprived
of human stories for centuries. Hunting and eating, fighting and
making love had comprised their lives. As a result, not a one of
them could resist drawing closer. Bastien's sophistication, Gytha's
resentment, even Helewis's love of rules were swept away. Like children, they listened with open mouths and shining eyes as Juliana
described the giant's uninvited entrance into King Arthur's New
Year's feast.

"The knight who rode into the hall was green," she said, "from
head to toe, as was his charger. Together they were so much larger
than normal beings that the knight had to duck his head to keep his
helm from bumping the roof beams. The axe he carried stretched
the length of a tall man's arm along its hairsplitting blade. Arthur's
famous knights, who had gathered for the celebration, knew at once
that the stranger was magical. Though they had fought enchanted
creatures before, I would be lying if I claimed none of them quailed.

" 'Good eve, stranger,' said Arthur, for the king was gracious no
matter what. 'How may we serve you this blessed day?'

" 'I have heard tales of your court,' said the big green knight,
'that those who follow you are the bravest men in the land. I admit
I cannot credit it myself, but because I love nothing better than a
knock-down, bloody fight, I thought I would come to you to issue
my challenge. Perhaps, for once, I shall meet my match.'

" 'What challenge would that be?' Arthur politely asked, clenching his teeth just a bit at the Green Knight's cheek. Giant or not, the knights at his table were all heroes!

" 'The challenge is this,' said the Green Knight. 'Whichever of your men has the stones to accept shall take this axe I carry and strike a single blow to my neck. Should I survive, one year from hence I will smite him once, and only once, in return.'

"Arthur's men exchanged glances across the remnants of the feast. One blow from this giant would mean their deaths. Ashamed of his followers' silence, Arthur leapt up from his seat beside Guenevere.

" 'I accept your challenge,' he declared, though he was not a young and beardless champion anymore.

"With a mocking smile, the giant handed him the axe. The haft alone was so weighty, Arthur could barely lift the blade from the floor. To make matters worse, the Green Knight refused to bend. In his attempts to reach the spot prescribed for the blow, Arthur was forced to jump and huff and swing himself clear off his feet.

"Sad as I am to say it, the great King Arthur appeared a fool.

" 'My liege!' exclaimed Gawain, who was Arthur's favorite nephew. 'You must not risk yourself in this manner. Allow me, who will not be as sorely missed, to accept the challenge in your stead.'

"To everyone's surprise, the Green Knight agreed to the substitution. Indeed, there were those who said he seemed secretly pleased. Still tottering, the winded Arthur handed the giant's axe to Gawain."

"And could he lift it?" Stephen asked breathlessly.

"He could," Juliana said, "though the effort did make sweat spring out on his noble brow. Even more astounding, the Green Knight, after shamelessly teasing Arthur, went down on one knee so Gawain could strike his neck without leaping up."

"He did not kill the giant!" protested Helewis.

Ulric feared her outburst might nettle Juliana; Gawain was obviously the hero of this human tale. To his relief, Juliana broke into a wolfish grin.

"Gawain struck off his hideous head!" she crowed, then lifted her hands as Helewis groaned. "Mind you, the Green Knight did not die. Instead, gushing gouts of grass-green blood, his decapitated torso stood, walked across the hall to where his head had rolled beneath a bench, and picked it up by the hair. When he mounted his huge green warhorse, he tucked the gory trophy beneath his arm—presumably face forward, in order to see where he was going."

"Yay," said Helewis.

"Yay, indeed," said Juliana, clearly amused. "But not such happy tidings for Gawain. According to the bargain he had struck, one twelvemonth from that day, Gawain would have to let the giant smite him in return. Everyone in the hall knew such a blow would spell the young man's doom. 'For honor's sake,' the giant reminded as he spurred his horse around with a clatter, 'you must not fail to seek me out.'"

"Gawain had to go to him?" Bastien shook his head in disbelief. In Gawain's place, Ulric suspected Bastien would have stayed home.

"Yes," Juliana said, "and it would not be easy to find the Green Knight again. It was proof of Gawain's courage that he would overcome many perils just to face his demise."

"Ooh, perils," Ingrith said with a shiver of pure enjoyment. "Tell us about those."

Juliana bent confidingly across her book. "The year was drawing to a close," she said, "when Gawain at last departed on his quest. The dangerous wilderness of Wirral was in his path and many monsters opposed him—not to mention the hardships of a harsh winter."

As she described these obstacles, Ulric found himself caught up in the adventure, his blood quickening in his veins just as it did when he stalked prey. Gawain's terrors and triumphs became his own. When Gawain stabbed a dragon or wrestled a raging troll, Ulric's muscles tightened in sympathy.

"Finally," Juliana continued, "on Christmas Eve, exhausted by his journey, Gawain reached a fabulous castle perched on a lonely rock. The lord of this residence was nearly as gracious as Arthur.

Inviting Gawain to stay, he assured the doughty knight that the Green Chapel, where he had promised to meet his foe, was very near. His lady wife seconded her husband's suit. Gladly, Gawain agreed to accept their hospitality until the appointed day.

"Little did Gawain suspect that this seeming stroke of luck would prove his greatest trial. The lady of the castle, though married in the eyes of God, had her eye upon Gawain. His reputation as a man of matchless vigor with the ladies went before him. Consequently, she vowed to try him for herself. No ploy was too bold for this wandering wife. Even into his private bedchamber she crept, then had the nerve to berate him for allowing her to steal in. He was, she claimed, too sound a sleeper to be a famous warrior."

"He had to give in then," Stephen said waggishly.

"He did not," answered Juliana, "for that would have stained both the lady's honor and his own. Instead, he put her off with flattering, golden words, claiming he did not deserve to touch one inch of her glorious person and that his dearest desire was only to be her knight."

"Huh," said Stephen, frowning in disappointment.

Soon, though, he was chuckling at Gawain's ingeniousness. The lord of the castle made a bargain with his guest. Each would spend the day hunting on their own, then trade each other for their best prize.

"Imagine the lord's amazement when he handed Gawain a stag and received but a kiss from his guest in return."

"His lady's kiss," Ingrith guessed, her eyes shining with amusement.

"None other's," Juliana said, and described how the lady—frustrated in her attempts to seduce the great Gawain—insisted that he accept a magic girdle, cleverly fashioned of green silk, which would prevent its wearer from being slain.

"That is cheating," Helewis huffed, obviously looking ahead to Gawain's battle with the Green Knight.

"Perhaps," said Juliana. "It certainly was not honorable of Sir

Gawain to withhold the girdle when he and the castle's lord traded prizes at day's end."

"Withholding the prize was smart," Bastien objected. "Gawain knew the Green Knight had special powers. If that giant lopped off his head, Gawain could not walk away."

"That is true," said Juliana. "If Gawain resorted to magic tricks, one could argue he was only leveling the field."

From the way Bastien's mouth dropped open and then snapped shut, Ulric knew the Frenchman had betrayed himself in some way. One look at Juliana's small, satisfied smile made him glad she was not spying on him.

"The fight," Stephen demanded. "Surely it is time for that!"

"Ah, yes," said Juliana, turning the page and grinning all around, "the long-anticipated date with destiny. As you might imagine, Arthur's nephew awoke on the awful day with a heavy heart. Could the girdle save him, or was this to be the end of his short life? The Green Knight was magical himself. Perhaps the girdle would have no effect. Despite his fears, Gawain pulled on his armor, called for his horse, and rode to the Green Chapel.

"The giant awaited with his terrible four-foot axe, whose edge he teasingly tested with his big green thumb. 'You have come after all then,' he said derisively. 'On your knees, knight, and accept your just desserts, as I accepted mine in your uncle's court.'

" 'As God wills,' said Gawain, and humbly obeyed. Alas, the giant had not tired of playing games. He pretended to swing at the good knight's neck, then mocked him when he flinched. 'You are not the Gawain whose fame all men admire. That Gawain would not have shrunk from my blow.' Gawain swore he would not do so again and set himself even more determinedly to meet his end.

"The Green Knight gathered his strength and swung, this time aiming true. For all his power, the blade merely nicked Gawain's neck and bounced away. Amazed, the giant tried to strike him again. Seeing his blood sprinkling the chapel floor, Gawain leapt up and sprang away. 'Enough!' he cried, 'I have kept the terms of our agreement, which was only for a single blow. You may not assault me more!'

" 'May I not?' said the giant. 'What of the assault I owe you for accepting kisses from my wife? What of the magic garter you took from her and failed to give back to me? Yes, Gawain'—the giant nodded at his growing horror—'I know about your deception. In addition to this monstrous form you see me wear, I am also lord of yon castle. I sent my wife to woo you as a test.'

"Mortified, Gawain covered his face, cursing his own cowardice and deceit. 'I confess,' he bemoaned to the giant lord. 'Requite my sins as you see fit.'

"At this the Green Knight laughed kindly. 'You have repaid your folly with your fear,' he said, 'and acted more honorably than most men. Most important, I can see your remorse is true. Accept my girdle as a reminder of our contest and go in peace to be wiser from now on.'

"This Gawain did, thereafter wearing the belt as a baldric across his chest, and confessing to whomever asked what faults it was meant to remind him of. So admired was he for this meekness that all Arthur's knights took to donning green sashes as a sign of their respect for him."

Thus saying, Juliana closed her book. For a moment, the pack was quiet. Ingrith was the first to release her breath. "That was wonderful," she sighed.

"Wonderful?" Stephen exclaimed, sitting up to stare. "How can it be wonderful when Gawain is wallowing in guilt and the giant was twice as dishonest as he? Plus, I refuse to believe that lady tried to seduce Gawain just because her husband told her to. If Gawain had given in, you can bet your sweet arse she would have enjoyed herself."

Helewis and Ingrith both snorted at this. Ignoring them, Stephen turned to Juliana and addressed her sternly. "Please admit you told the story wrong."

Juliana pursed her lips to hide her amusement and innocently spread her hands. "I read the words that were on the page, which I wrote down as the bard told them."

"Are you certain?" Stephen pressed. "Maybe you got some of them confused."

"Of course she did not," said Helewis. "Juliana reads very well."

"If you knew how to read," said Juliana, "you could confirm the words for yourself. In fact"—she paused to let her grin break free—"if you learned your letters, you could rewrite the story as you pleased."

Stephen narrowed his eyes, abruptly aware that he had stepped into a trap. "I will do it," he declared. "You can start teaching me tomorrow."

"Say 'please,'" Ingrith reminded laughingly.

"Please," Stephen said, then added a wolfish whine.

"You are a silly man," said Juliana, beaming as if she thought him quite wonderful. "But it would be my honor to help you learn."

She seemed so pleased with his brother wolf that Ulric felt compelled to squeeze her hand. The brilliant smile she turned on him did much toward easing his jealousy—though it could not erase it completely. That undertaking he would have to handle on his own.

# Thirteen

I wish to speak with you," Ulric said, nodding for Stephen to walk beside him. The ground was damp from the earlier rain, the pine needles matted beneath their feet. Above them, beadlike drops of water plopped from the boughs.

Beyond these tiny noises, the life of the forest pulsed: things that flew and things that crawled, things that slept and things that hunted the dark like them. Ulric could even sense, like a distant ribbon of force, the protective barrier around his land, brought to life by Juliana's blood. *This is home,* said his heart. *This is safety.* For the first time, he really felt as if he were back. He did not worry that Gytha and Bastien had slipped away. For now, his world was in balance.

Ingrith, Helewis, and Juliana walked ahead of them on the path, their shoulders bumping as they whispered to one another and laughed as women have since the world was made. From Stephen's wistful expression, he would far rather be with them.

His gaze remained on Ingrith, whose steps were almost a prance. The only sign of her lingering trepidation was how close she stayed to the two females.

"It is funny how she trusts them to protect her," Stephen mused, "particularly Juliana. I am not sure what Ingrith expects a human to do if she is attacked."

"Talk her way around the threat," Ulric suggested humorously. "Or else convince Helewis she really is fierce enough to fight."

"I would not put either past her. Your Juliana has an odd assortment of gifts." With a smile as fond as Ulric's, Stephen shoved his side braids behind his ears. "Her presence makes me wonder who we all used to be when we were human. My guess for Gytha is that she was the wife of a marauding Viking warrior."

"Not a warrior herself?" Ulric said, supposing there must have been a few among the fairer sex.

"Nay. No woman gets that snappish except as a wife." Stephen grinned, baring teeth still sharp from the excitement of Juliana's story. Then he sobered. "Her husband probably beat her, come to think of it. Taught her only bullies were safe from harm."

"Or maybe she beat him," Ulric said, surprised to discover how easy it was to speculate. "Maybe her Viking spouse never rose to the heights her ambition craved."

"Mm," said Stephen, silent for a few more strides. "What was it you wanted to speak to me about?"

Now that they had come to it, Ulric found himself unable to answer as he had meant, shamed from it by Stephen's trust. How could he admit he wanted Stephen to try to seduce his lover, for no better reason than to prove she could not be glamoured by other *upyr*? How could he explain he wanted Stephen to do it because Bastien, who was already making the attempt, did not so easily obey his rule? Scorn would be the least of the responses to which Stephen would be entitled.

Were Ulric in his position, he would have been outraged. The mere thought of the plan was childish, no better than that giant pandering his wife. Worse, given the timing, it was cruel. True, Ingrith had seen Stephen cast his lures at other women, but Ingrith needed to feel more secure now, not less.

Stephen's next words pulled him from his thoughts. "If you are concerned about my taking lessons from Juliana . . ."

"No," Ulric said. "That is perfectly fine."

"But if you wanted to take them first . . ."

The suggestion made him blink. He had said he would learn to read if it was important to Juliana, but he had not thought the promise through. Could he learn? Should he? He shook his head to clear it. "Do not worry," he said to Stephen. "I am certain she would make time for me if I asked."

Stephen nodded and scuffed his feet. Startled by the noise, a small, brown snake arced across their path.

"She cares about you," Stephen said as if uncertain the assurance was appropriate for him to make. "I have never seen a woman look at a man the way Juliana looks at you—except for Ingrith, of course."

"Of course," Ulric said, feigning seriousness. Stephen need not have worried his words would be unwelcome. Indeed, Ulric had to struggle not to ask for more.

"If that is not the problem," Stephen said, "why did you want to speak to me?"

Ulric took one last look at Juliana laughing up ahead and cast away his plan, though not without a silent sigh. "I wanted to ask if you think Ingrith will be over her fear by the time Gytha's fortnight is up."

Stephen fingered the end of one braid in thought. "She might be, though Gytha would probably prefer that she would not. A quick recovery seems a mite insulting."

"Maybe you can convince Ingrith to counterfeit some timidity. Out of kindness."

Stephen laughed outright, causing Ingrith to turn back and wave. "That truly would drive Gytha up a tree." He wiped at his eyes, then turned. "I should thank you," he said, "for asking my opinion."

Considering what Ulric had intended to ask, he could only shrug. "You are the one who knows Ingrith best."

"Many pack leaders would not care. *You* would not have cared before you came back. I simply want to say that it feels good to be consulted." His words must have required more courage than he was used to. Stephen blew out a breath. "There. Enough womanish talk of feelings! You should tell your Juliana that even Gytha enjoyed her tale. When she thought no one was looking, I saw her mimicking the fights with her fists."

"I shall," Ulric said.

For the second time that night, he did not object to Juliana being called "his."

---

HE was tenderness itself as he slid inside her, his eyes like molten gold in the dark. The muscles in his chest and belly shifted rhythmically as he thrust, causing her locket to swing from his neck. His palms pressed hers beside her head, trapping them gently against the furs with their fingers twined.

"You shine when you make love to me," Juliana whispered, tilting her hips up to take him deep. "It is the most beautiful sight I have ever seen."

"Is it?" His smile was oddly melancholy. Colors fluttered like butterflies through his glow. She wondered if they were the colors of sadness, and why she could see them now. On a whim, she rolled him beneath her.

"There," she said, straddling him in his bed, copying his drawn-out strokes. "Now I shall ride you."

His neck arched as she slowly sank, his lips pulling back over sharp, white teeth. "Is that what you like? Being in control?"

She bent to lick the side of his throat. "I like everything I do with you."

"Wait." His hands smoothed around her bottom to hold her in place.

"Wait?" Her body quivered at the pause. She thought he had some game in mind, but he did not.

"I need to ask you something," he said, "before dawn makes me forget. Why were you so interested in Bastien's reaction to your story?"

Juliana shoved her hair back from her face. He was hard inside her, throbbing, but he wanted to ask her about Bastien. She wondered if she would ever understand this man.

"He defended Gawain's decision to keep the magic girdle to himself," she said. "He put himself in Gawain's shoes, rather than the giant's."

"But why is that important?"

"Because Bastien used magic on Ingrith, something your branch of the *upyr* forbids. Maybe the reason he left his pack was because someone else used magic to injure him. Maybe he learned it in self-defense."

Ulric struggled up on his elbows, his hardness shifting inside her. "That is a bit of a leap."

"Is it? He said he would follow you with all his heart if you were as honorable as you claimed. Apart from flirting a little, has he caused any trouble since?"

Ulric could not say he had. "If you ask me, he has been too virtuous. The only complaint I could make is that he eats more than anyone else on hunts. But that could be because he is French. Everyone says they enjoy their meals."

"Very well. Apart from being a flirt and a glutton, you have no complaints."

"No," he admitted reluctantly.

"I do not think he lays with Gytha anymore."

"It is true they no longer carry each others' scents, but that only proves he is willing to forsake his friends."

"Maybe," she said.

He covered her hands where they were playing idly with his chest hair. "Maybe you seek excuses for him on account of his silver tongue."

"Nonsense. Your clay tongue is the only one that interests me."

The hurt that flashed across his face caught her off-guard. She expected him to have more of a sense of humor. "I speak in jest," she said, lifting of his knuckles for a kiss. "Truly, Ulric, I am flattered you are jealous, but there is no need."

"I am not jealous," he denied, then frowned at her raised eyebrows. "All right then, I am. What of it? I want you to belong only to me."

His expression held more grumpiness than romance, but her heart stumbled nonetheless. When she spoke, her voice was rough. "As far as any woman can belong to any man, I belong to you."

"Do you?"

Again, his manner held a challenge, choler struggling with anxiety. She stroked his face between her palms, waiting until the crease in the center of his forehead eased.

"Yes, Ulric. You have my word."

His response was a grunt of satisfaction.

How like a man, she thought with a private smile, to demand a promise and offer none in return.

Then he surprised her, his hand smoothing down the curve of her spine. "You have *my* word," he said, "that you are the only woman I want." He rolled them onto their sides and arched her backward to kiss her breast, his hand shaping it closer, his incisors compressing either side of the swollen tip. His lips tugged it arousingly. "The . . . only . . . one."

The only one in his reach, she could not help but think as the flicking of his tongue made her shudder down to her toes.

"I do wonder about one thing," she said with her final scrap of rational thought. "If Gytha and Bastien no longer lie together, who is biting his neck? Certainly not Ingrith, and Helewis does not seem interested."

Ulric shut her up by nipping her skin. "Bastien's neck," he growled, "is not my concern."

Juliana's hand flew to her breast. She could not say whether her shock came from the fact that he would bite her there, or the way her body melted in response. Ulric's gaze slipped to the bead of red his teeth had set free. Fascination locked it there helplessly.

"I am sorry," he said even as his tongue curled over his upper lip. "I only meant to nip you, not break the skin. I have no wish to cause you pain."

As if to contradict his words, his ribs rose and fell like a bellows. His cock was only partially inside her, but suddenly it felt twice as thick. With his eyes still on her breast, her nipple was blazing hot.

"Never mind," she said huskily, reaching for the back of his neck. "Now that you have done it, there is no reason to turn back."

He fastened onto her with a moan, pulling deeply at the tiny cut, curving his back to thrust himself inside her at the same time. As he did, Juliana clutched his shoulder with so much force, her nails drew blood.

"It is all right," he said, moving his head to nuzzle the other breast. "It is all right."

His mouth was cool, wet fire, licking her, flicking her, suckling so strongly she gasped for air. His mouth fell away when he shifted her atop him and slid his hands up her sides. As he licked the last of her from his lips, fire gleamed in the depths of his golden eyes. She felt his fingers tighten on her ribs and then release, as if he were unable to decide what he ought to do.

Juliana knew she had to move on him or scream.

"Shall I ride you again?" she whispered.

He closed his eyes, seeming wracked by exquisite pain. "Yes. You do it. Take your desire."

She placed the heels of her hands directly over his tightened nipples, then pushed up her weight. She hesitated before she let it fall. She was not certain how to take charge.

"You cannot harm me," he said. "No matter what you do, it will not hurt."

She took him at his word, putting all the strength she could stand into every motion, driving her body against him just where she wished. His hands, now warm, smoothed and caressed her breasts before sliding down to put more pressure on her pubis. Beneath his fingers, her soft flesh squeezed against his hardness, her nerves keen enough to feel every ridge and vein.

The added provocation made her bite her lip, a gesture Ulric watched hungrily. Steadied by his hold, she dared to go faster. Her thighs seemed to hum as they rose and fell. She felt as if she were flying—that powerful and free. His expression tightened and his head rolled from side to side. With a grimace, he pushed his upper body up to meet hers. His mouth nuzzled yearningly at her neck.

"I will not trap you," he murmured, which she did not understand.

She had no time to. With this much stimulation, neither took long to reach their peak, both gasping sharply as the crisis came. Ulric's arms were wonderfully tight. Knowing she had driven him to pleasure was almost, but not quite, as nice as being overpowered by him.

Only when she snuggled down against him, when she felt sleep begin to claim her as it claimed him, did she remember she had not yet told him about Bastien's morning jaunts. She knew the confession was overdue.

Bastien was too cunning to leave to his own devices. They had to discover what he was hiding.

--------

ULRIC roused, reluctantly, to the feel of someone shaking his shoulder hard.

"Get up," Juliana urged, grabbing his wrists and hauling him to the side of his sleeping niche. "It is just about the time Bastien usually comes back. I want you to see for yourself."

She handed him a long hooded cloak and a pair of boots. Then, failing to inspire motion, she began to stuff his feet into them herself.

Too confused to resist, Ulric rubbed his palms over his face. "Juliana, I am certain the sun is up."

"If Bastien can be awake now, so can you."

"Bastien?"

"Yes." She tugged at his hand. "If you do not hurry we will miss him."

More than half asleep, he let her pull him past a blissfully slumbering Helewis and down the passage to the entry ledge. The light was misty and indirect, a haze across the shadowy impressions of the pack's footsteps. No part of Ulric wanted to go near it.

"He comes," she whispered, pulling him behind a curve of the wall. "Be sure to look at his neck."

Ulric heard nothing, smelled nothing, his senses dulled by the risen sun. Sliding into a crouch beside Juliana, he pulled his hood over his head and began to doze. A sharp pinch on his arm jerked him awake.

"Watch," she hissed. "This is important."

He watched as Bastien stepped onto the rocky lip, his body muffled from head to toe in black. Ulric's eyes widened at his appearance. Even with the protection of his clothes, the *upyr* moved more vigorously than Ulric expected, seeming drained rather than sleepy. Clearly, this was not the first time he had been out during the day. He had built up a tolerance.

As he entered the cave, Ulric threw up a hasty glamour, but Bastien did not look around. Instead, he strode swiftly down the tunnel and out of sight.

"Damn," said Juliana. "That cloak covered his neck."

"His neck?"

"Where I told you I have been seeing bite marks."

Ulric could not contain a yawn. Vaguely, he remembered her mentioning this the night before. "Maybe he *is* meeting Gytha, only in secret. Maybe they are throwing off the mingling of their scents with power."

"I do not think that can be true. For one thing, Gytha is not acting like a woman who is being met. For another, I do not believe she is a good enough liar to pretend." Frowning with concentration,

Juliana squeezed her lower lip. "I am afraid there is nothing for it. We will have to go out and retrace his trail. I would leave you here, but I need your nose to sniff out where he has been."

In spite of her earnestness, Ulric laughed. "Even if I were willing, at this time of day, I doubt I could track a skunk."

"Really? You cannot smell during the day?"

She seemed intrigued by this new fact. Ulric rubbed one hand across his smile. "No better than you."

"That is unfortunate. I have noticed Bastien's feet do not leave lasting prints. He must be almost as strong as you." Her brows drew together and went up as a new idea occurred to her. "You could change into your wolf form and smell him that way."

"I could," he agreed, "but I would rather not."

"I suppose you would look silly as a wolf wearing a cloak."

"I would not require a cloak," Ulric said. "As long as I had enough strength to change, the sun could not harm my other form."

"Then why not investigate?"

Ulric cupped her astonished face. "Juliana, I know you have taken it into your head that I simply order people to do things and assume they will obey. I cannot deny I never think that way, but being a leader requires more than that. My pack members have to trust me."

"But why would Bastien not trust you? Considering what he helped Gytha do to Ingrith, you have treated him more than fairly."

"I have tolerated him. Bastien knows he is being watched for mistakes. If I do as you say, I will probably find one, but I would rather give him a chance to undo it first, of his own free will. For that to happen, he must believe I will show him not merely justice but mercy."

"You have shown him mercy!" she exclaimed with a staunchness that made him smile.

"He holds himself aloof, Juliana. He hunts without joy and flirts without friendliness. He does not move against me, and yet I sense him seeking out weaknesses. As I watch him, thus he watches me.

Maybe you are correct and he was abused by his former pack. If that is true, he will be slower to trust than most—and quicker to find causes for suspicion. Until he gives me a reason that I should not, I will show the same respect for his privacy that I would for Stephen or Ingrith. A pack lives cheek by jowl. We must give each other what room we can."

"But what if his secret is dangerous?"

Ulric stroked her sleeve down her arm. "I would know if there was malice in Bastien's heart. I would smell it."

"But—"

He hugged her to him until her frustration eased. "Trust me," he soothed, privately amazed that he did not resent the need to explain. "I have been through this process with every pack member I have. Loyalty cannot be forced."

"But I want to know," she murmured plaintively against his chest.

Ulric chuckled and kissed her hair. "I see that, love. You will simply have to be patient."

"Not patient," she mumbled.

Despite her denial, the way she held him spoke of acceptance. He knew she respected his position, even if she disagreed, an awareness that brought a curious mixture of peace and longing. We were made for each other, he thought. We are different but we fit.

She sighed as he rocked her from side to side, her body soft in his arms. The gentle weight of her was sweet and warm. In a moment, when he did not feel this sleepy, he would lead her back to his room.

"Ulric?" she said, her head tilting back from his chest. "I do not think I need until summer's end."

"Mm," he said, his thoughts hazy and relaxed.

"I know there are still things I need to learn and to get used to, but my life was never this interesting before. I want to be part of what is happening here. I want to be a member of your pack."

His lids flew open as if on strings. "Juliana! You want to become *upyr*?"

She laughed softly at his reaction. "Yes, if you do not think it is a bad idea."

"I think it is a wonderful idea! I will contact my sire and ask him to, er . . ." Ulric's voice trailed off as he remembered his previous omission.

"I know," she said, her fingers brushing his embarrassed wince. "Ingrith let it slip that you could not change me."

"I did not mean to mislead you, exactly. It seemed a lot to explain when I barely knew you."

"Quite a lot," she agreed with an indulgent grin. "And me a blackmailer to boot."

"I was reluctant to admit that I could not do it. It was flattering to have you think me that powerful. But are you certain of what you want? Being made *upyr* is a big decision."

She drew a short, broken breath as if she did indeed have reservations, then thankfully shook her head. "I would prefer that it was you who changed me, but if you think your sire will agree to help, I am certain that will be fine."

"He will agree. He has only to meet you to know what a perfect pack member you will be."

As she hugged him, he felt her smiling against his heart. "Perfect I do not hope for, only to be a useful part of your pack."

"They love you already," he said. "Most of them. And perhaps Gytha will, too, someday—though I would not hold my breath."

Juliana laughed, a wonderful sound.

If she had expressed an equal interest in being his queen, his happiness would have been complete.

SOON after sunset, Ulric ordered his pack to meet him in the hall of columns.

For his own taste, he would have chosen another room. Surely, there was something ridiculous in a space this grand being in a cave. The white-veined pink marble tiles were bigger than he was, the red porphyry columns too large to encircle in his arms. Their flowery capitals—which had been gilded and which loomed over them in the distance like titans' heads—were no possible use at all. What function this room had served in previous ages he could not guess. Did sufficient numbers of *upyr* exist to fill it? Even if they did, a ballroom for wolves struck him as nonsensical in the extreme. No doubt, it was due to Juliana's influence that the question even crossed his mind.

He was beginning to wonder why just like her.

For all its senseless grandeur, there were advantages to making his announcement here. The hall was a place Juliana felt comfortable. She had stamped it with her human slippers and her dusty books, with the friendships she had forged among his lesser wolves.

His pack watched him take Juliana's hand, their expressions open and interested—with the inevitable exception of Gytha. She stood behind the others, one shoulder propped on a column, her arms crossed sullenly. Ulric met her eye, both to warn and reassure. She might be under penance, but she was still a part of his pack.

"Tell us," Stephen said while bouncing on his toes. "What is your news?"

"My news," said Ulric, his own smile broad, "is that Juliana has decided to become *upyr*."

"Oh!" Ingrith cried, turning to Juliana, her hands clasped in excitement before her breast. "I am so glad. Just think of the fun we shall have!"

"Huh," said Gytha from the background. "I notice he does not mention making her his queen."

Leave it to Gytha to poke the sorest spot. Ulric could conceive of no good response, even if her punishment had allowed it. Juliana had ducked her head in an attempt to ignore the jibe, but a rosy flush swept up her neck. Strangely, when Ulric's glance fell on Bastien, he thought he saw the Frenchman looking at her with envy. If this was what he felt, he hid it quickly. A heartbeat later, his face was blank.

Stephen filled the awkward pause by folding Juliana into a hug. "Welcome to our pack," he said, clasping her tight. The full press of his naked body heightened the color in her face. Presumably feeling this, Stephen pulled back and teasingly tapped her cheek. "You will have to get over this human modesty if you are going to be one of us."

"I am not one of you yet," she said, smiling through her blush. "Auriclus must agree to change me. From what I hear, he can be choosey."

"He will agree," Stephen assured her. "And if he does not, maybe Gill—Well, I am sure Auriclus will see you as we do, even if you have turned a few of the rules on their heads."

"There is that," said Juliana, rubbing her nose and trying not to look worried.

"It shall be well," Ulric promised, vowing to himself that it would. For many years he had kept his sire's children safe. Auriclus owed him a boon or two.

"We should have a howl," Stephen suggested, "to celebrate."

Helewis and Ingrith jumped at this. "Yes, yes," Helewis enthused. "Maybe we can coax the real wolves to join in."

"Stephen can teach you," Ingrith said to Juliana. "His howls are the best."

"Can that really be true?" Juliana asked with a secret smile. "I have, after all, heard your pack leader sing."

"Now that," said Ingrith, "is a tale I would like to hear."

They departed from the hall, leaving Ulric with Bastien.

"It is kind of them to welcome her," the Frenchman said to his fingernails.

"They enjoy her company. And she has earned their trust."

Bastien could not miss this implication. His gaze met Ulric's directly. "If I swear fealty to you . . ."

"You fear I will let you down."

"I fear that all this"—Bastien spread his hands to indicate what he had just witnessed—"cannot be as pretty as it seems."

"Your fear is of your own making."

Bastien closed his eyes and clenched his fists, his emotions obviously at war. "I cannot afford to guess wrong. If you knew what we . . . what I have come from . . . If I swore to you, I would be under your power. I would owe you allegiance."

"And I would owe you protection."

"Protection." Bastien wagged his head as if that were a joke.

"I will not press you," Ulric said. "This is a decision you must come to on your own, a decision you must be prepared to stand by once it is made."

Bastien nodded but did not speak. Ulric knew he was thinking hard.

⚜

ULRIC and Bastien joined the others, shifting into wolf form with plenty of time to spare. Ulric had forgotten how much fun a howl could be. To Juliana's evident delight, they managed to get the true pack who lived in the neighboring valley to answer back. After a few laughing attempts, however, she gave up trying to imitate their song.

"I can almost see them," she said, her expression dreamy, her fingers buried in Ulric's ruff, "as if I were a pup listening from the den."

Glad she was enjoying this, Ulric leaned into her leg, mutely inviting her to scratch him behind the ears.

She did this as if it were natural.

When they tired of howling, Stephen and Ingrith reenacted the battle between Gawain and the Green Knight, after which Helewis and Bastien made a game of wrestling while changing forms. The two were evenly matched in strength, though Bastien had the advantage in aggressiveness. Ulric could tell he was holding back so as not to hurt Helewis, going as far as allowing her to pin him at the end.

"Cheater!" Helewis accused, pretending to bite his muzzle.

Bastien was laughing silently when he returned to his human

shape. It was the first time Ulric could remember seeing him happy. He sobered soon after, almost guiltily, turning his head and frowning into the trees.

"Rabbit hunt!" Stephen shouted, possibly inspired by the direction of Bastien's gaze. He and the women tore off immediately. Bastien hesitated, then flashed into wolf form to catch up. His pelt was darker than the others, his stride a smooth gallop. Ulric could see how he might have caught Gytha's eye.

"You can join them," Juliana said.

Ulric smiled. "I was thinking you and I might enjoy having the rest of the night to ourselves."

Her slow, sweet smile told him she agreed.

He carried her to the chamber of the hot spring, making love to her in the steaming, mineral-laden water. For once he did not mind being gentle. This was precisely how he wanted to show his care. Their bodies were buoyant, their hair soon sleeking wetly around their heads. Pleasure rolled through them in slow motion.

"I love you," she said when it was over, her head nestled shyly against his neck.

He let her declaration ease him like the heat, not questioning what it meant or how long it would last. Instead, he pressed his lips to her damp temple.

*I love you, too*, he said, reaching for her mind. This alone could convey the truth of what he felt. A weight left him with the words—or maybe it was a ghost. Tomorrow would be soon enough for worries. Tonight he reveled in her answering sigh.

# Emile

E MILE had plenty of time to lie in his hole and listen—and
think, of course, but as listening provoked less worry, he
did that. He memorized the nightly routines of squirrels and spi-
ders, of swooping owls and scurrying mice. Sometimes, beyond
the golden barrier, he heard the others hunt. Bastien hunted
with them. When they brought down prey, Emile sensed his old
friend's joy.

The only pleasure Emile looked forward to was sleep, and lately
that had been slow to come. Bastien's morning visits had trained
him to stay awake.

Despite his misery, he knew Bastien had a right to those moments of exultation. Forswearing them would not change Emile's
fate. Regardless of whether Bastien swayed this pack in the end,
Emile was almost certainly doomed.

The disappearance of all feeling in his feet had been followed
by that in his calves. Below his hips, everything was blurred. The
numbing effect seemed likely to progress, but he could hardly bring
himself to mind.

This is my destiny, he thought, one weary arm flung across his eyes. Who was he to question God's plan? Not a chosen creation, he did not think. More like an uninvited guest.

His mouth was twisting crookedly at his own black wit when he heard a crashing in the undergrowth—sounds too heavy, too deliberate to be made by any but mortal men. Back and forth the humans tramped near the spot where the golden wall had been brought to life. Snuffling noises accompanied the stamp of boots, along with the yip and whimper of hounds.

Emile welcomed his surge of fear as a sign of life, until he realized the searchers were not looking for him.

"The trail leads here," said the voice of an older male, "but I see no way through these thorns. Could the dogs be confused?"

A second human answered. "Perhaps they have been magicked to lead us the wrong way."

"Bollocks," said the first. "Perhaps you chose the wrong scent to track from Dunburn. Perhaps you were no more immune to that creature's thrall than my idiot sons."

"I assure you, master, my cross protected me—may God be blessed. Most of my memories have come back."

"Most but maybe not enough." Disgusted, the older human ground out a curse. "That thing stole not only my heirs' good sense but my future bride. I will have its secrets or the Almighty Himself will answer why not."

"Master . . ."

"Cease your puling, Captain. You are pious enough for us both. Let us go farther north. Maybe we can find a spot where this wall of thorns is thin enough to hack through."

Emile knew of no thorns that they might mean. He and Bastien had encountered none. But maybe they were a glamour generated by the barrier.

As he pondered this, the tramping and snuffling got louder. He estimated a dozen men at the least—all coming his way.

"We should wait until full light," cautioned the second man.

"Nonsense," said the first. "Everyone knows these creatures become insensible at dawn."

Emile wished he were insensible. Then he would not be choking on his fear. He braced his hands against the earthen walls, bloodsweat prickling along his scalp. He could only hope the dogs would not smell it.

Dreading their approach, he squinted past his useless feet to the open end of his burrow. Bastien had blocked it with branches, but the barrier seemed horribly flimsy now.

They will find me, he thought, sureness tolling through him. Today is the day I die.

He was shocked to discover how much he wanted to live.

The discovery came too late. Better to grit his teeth and prepare. Despite his resolve, his heart seized as a hound barked once and began to dig. Branches were nosed away. Dirt was hitting his feet. He must have smelled like whatever *upyr* they were seeking, because he was also Auriclus's child. His lips moved in a long-forgotten prayer.

"Badger hole," someone scoffed, but the dismissal was no reprieve.

"Let her dig," said the older man when someone grabbed the dog's collar. "Something is here."

Two more dogs joined the first in throwing soil from the opening. The hole widened. Voices cried out in discovery.

Emile did not feel the hands that reached in to grab his ankles, only the drag and bump of his upper body along the dirt. Roots tore from his fingers as he clutched them to no avail. Smoke drifted thinly into the burrow, telling him his belly must be exposed.

A second later, he had to shield his face from the light.

"Christ," someone said, tight with fear. "They *are* more than a tale."

The thin, morning sun sapped what remained of Emile's strength. He was helpless to fight as the soldiers heaved him to his feet. His knees immediately collapsed. They had to grip his arms to keep him upright.

"Pull his hood forward," ordered the older man. "I do not want him going up in flames."

Emile's eyes streamed from their brief exposure as the man who led the others stepped forward. Frantically, he blinked to clear his sight. When he did, he was almost sorry. The human who confronted him wore the chilliest expression he had ever seen on a mortal man. Age might have robbed him of his vigor, but the willful set of his jaw seemed determined to deny the loss. Despite the seams of living in his skin, his eyes held no more life than stones.

*All right, Bastien,* Emile thought, though he doubted the words could reach his friend. *If you want to save me, now would be good.*

"Do not look into its eyes," the captain warned, a caution Emile wished was needed. At the moment, he could not have thralled a flea.

The cold-eyed human simply smiled. "I think this one is weak enough. Else, he would have prevented his being found. At any rate, with this many men he cannot bespell us all." A cool, gnarled hand slipped inside Emile's hood to trail caressingly along his cheek. Emile flinched but could not escape. The touch made him feel more like an object than a living being.

The older man did not react when his captain stepped to his side.

"This is not the creature who stole Buxton's daughter."

The old man snorted, his oddly bloodless finger sliding down Emile's jaw. "Juliana Buxton can go hang for the whore she is. She could never give me more than the illusion of restored youth. This one is going to give me its truth."

Emile doubted that declaring this was impossible would help his cause.

"Never," he said instead and felt an unexpected triumph at the angry narrowing of his captor's eyes.

# Fourteen

BASTIEN must have been more closely linked with the pack than Ulric guessed. Daytime sleep was a kind of stupor, thrown off only with great will. In spite of this, the mental echo of Bastien's distress cut through Ulric's slumber. He sat up before his mind sorted out what it had heard.

The motion woke Juliana.

"What is it?" she asked, going up on one elbow.

Ulric could not immediately answer. He swung his legs over the edge of his bed and tried to breathe alertness into his mind. "Bastien is in trouble," he said. "You stay here."

Juliana reached for her gown. "I cannot stay here. It is light. If something is wrong, you might need a helper who keeps her wits about her after dawn."

His head was too muddled for debate. Rather than try, he pushed through his door and stepped heavily over Helewis. An inadvertent jostling from his heel failed to make her twitch. If she was going to sleep this soundly, he probably ought to tell her not to bother to guard their room.

He was scratching his head over this quandary when Bastien

staggered down the corridor. Though he wore his black cloak and clothes, his hood must have fallen back because his cheeks and nose were burned. Ulric marveled at the panic that could cause such heedlessness.

"Pack leader," the Frenchman gasped. "I need . . . your aid."

Still trying to marshal his thoughts, Ulric's eyes grew round as the other *upyr* fell to his knees. "I will swear to you," he said, clutching Ulric's hand to his reddened face. "Only promise not to let them kill Emile."

When Ulric blinked at him in confusion, Bastien threw himself to the floor. "I will be your wolf," he cried desperately. "No matter what you ask, I shall obey."

Ulric could see this was a terrible oath for the other man. "Bastien . . ." he said, hardly knowing what he was cautioning him against. He sank into a crouch beside the prostrate man with Juliana clasping his shoulder. Though her touch was light, it steadied him in a way he could not explain. "Who is Emile, Bastien? And who is trying to kill him?"

"You must accept my oath," Bastien insisted into the dirt. "You must give Emile the protection you claimed you would owe me."

"I will help you if I can, whether you swear or no, but you need to explain what you need my protection for."

Bastien's head lifted from the floor. "You accept me into your pack?"

Ulric sighed. Bastien might not be manipulating him on purpose, but he could tell he was not going to get answers until he agreed. As if Juliana sensed the moment he needed it, she stroked his hair. The sensation brushed as sweetly along his nerves as it would his wolf's. Whatever her doubts about Bastien, Ulric knew her inclination was to help. His was the same, though he understood better than she the responsibility involved in adding to his pack.

I must trust my instincts, he thought, and I must trust hers. I cannot hope to make her queen if I do not.

"Sit up," he said to Bastien. "Meet my eyes and promise you will serve with honor."

Bastien dragged his sleeve across his mouth, his body shaking. "I will," he said. "You have my word."

With the declaration, a shock snapped through the air between them, a sign that the vow had taken hold. The bond was breakable, but only at the cost of extreme discomfort to the forsworn. Bastien's word was genuine.

"Good enough," Ulric said. "Now tell me what has befallen your friend."

His oath accepted, it seemed Bastien's words could not tumble out fast enough. "Emile is my brother wolf. We escaped from our pack in Burgundy when our leader began using magic to shore up his power. He was getting old with no sign of becoming an elder, while some of the younger ones were growing into their gifts. Terror was the only way he could keep them down. Some of the punishments he imposed . . . He would have done worse than kill us had we not broken our oaths and run. I hid Emile in the woods while I waited to see if I could trust you to take our side. I was hoping—"

He stopped and shook his head; whatever he had been hoping was apparently too much to share. "Maybe I should have told you sooner when I saw you were not like Hugo. Or maybe I should have moved Emile within the barrier Juliana erected around your lands. I was afraid you would smell him if he came inside it. Now it does not matter because the English soldiers have dragged him from his concealment. Their leader wants Emile to make him immortal. I fear he will kill Emile when he cannot do what he wants."

"*English* soldiers?" Juliana said, exchanging looks with Ulric.

"Yes. A troop of them with an older man at their head. Emile was crippled by our former leader. He cannot defend himself. I wanted to stop them from taking him, but they were too many for me to fight."

Ulric knuckled his forehead, trying to arrange the jumbled pieces of this explanation.

"Could it be Drake's men again?" Juliana asked even as the suspicion formed in his mind.

"I do not know," he said, "and we might not have the luxury of finding out. Wake the others, Bastien. Whoever is strong enough to change will join us in wolf form."

"Thank you," Bastien breathed as he rose to hurry off. "I will not forget this service!"

Ulric imagined the day ahead would be memorable for them all. With a frown and a shrug, he turned to shake Helewis.

Juliana knelt beside him to help, her expression considerably more perturbed than his. "If these men are Gideon Drake's, then I have brought danger to you all."

"No more than I have," Ulric said. "For that matter, no more than Bastien."

"But I—"

"No," he said firmly. "Blame is useless. Save your energy for what lies ahead."

She bit her lip and nodded. "I will," she said. "I want to help however I may."

"Good," he said. "Just try not to help so much you get in the way."

It was his good fortune that Helewis's awakening grumble cut short Juliana's sputter of offense.

———

NO matter what Ulric said, Juliana was determined to go along. This was her pack now—or nearly. If there was even a chance that she could help them combat this danger, she must try.

Of course, vowing to help was easier than keeping up with six fleet *upyr* wolves. All had woken eventually despite the hour, and none—not even Gytha—had protested being asked to fight for a stranger. They seemed eager to cross swords—or teeth, as it were—with whoever had abducted Bastien's brother wolf.

This was a side of the pack she had not seen before.

Willing though she was, Helewis was almost too wooly headed to change. Gytha solved that problem by slapping her briskly across the face. Juliana suspected the blow was not completely altruistic, but under the circumstances Ulric allowed it. Gytha also had the foresight to give Juliana a nasty-looking, forged-steel scythe. Pearls and rubies studded the handle, but the strong, curving blade was bright. Juliana could only assume Gytha had done some cave exploring of her own. Far deadlier than the knife she had brought from Bridesmere, which she had taken to wearing tucked in her purse, the scythe was the perfect size and weight for her human hand.

"For when you catch up," Gytha said with her usual derision, "because you have no proper defense."

Juliana bit back a smile as she thanked her, saying she appreciated her thoughtfulness.

"Hah," Gytha barked. "Try not to drop it on your foot."

Though no one said the words, it was obvious Gytha's shunning was suspended for the time being.

Armed now, Juliana's next challenge was following the pack's silent progress through the woods. Fortunately, their wolf forms did leave signs. Eyes sharpened by her tie to Ulric, Juliana was able to make out the trail of galloping paw prints and broken plants.

The time this took gave her plenty of chances to drink in the day. After her weeks in the cave, the sun cast a magic spell. Its beams were columns of bright green fire slanting through the leaves, dancing with golden motes, catching the colors of bird and flower. Even spiderwebs seemed like signs of a fairy realm. Never again would she take this wonderment for granted.

Once she was changed, she would have to take her wolf soul quickly. Only thus could she visit the daylight world.

Sadly, even with her improved sight to guide her, she made more of a racket than she wished battling through the trees. Branches caught at her clothes and bracken tangled her feet, but she could not slacken for fear of finding them too late. The noise was a risk she would have to take. These were humans they fought, and

Juliana might know something the pack did not. Nerves taut with determination, she was dripping sweat by the time she reached the stones that marked the border of Ulric's land.

Apart from their carvings, the menhirs seemed perfectly ordinary as she passed between them, their surfaces white with bird lime and green with moss. Noting that the paw prints she followed were now coming closely placed, she moved more cautiously. She did not wish to accidentally overtake the pack, or to interfere with their strategy. Better that she concentrate on being quiet.

As it happened, Fate cared nothing for her good intentions. Juliana found the soldiers before she suspected how close they were.

A face surprised her as she edged around a tree: a human face with a dirty linen coif beneath one of mail. The mortal's breastplate was dented steel, his leg guards worn ox hide. A crude wooden cross dangled crookedly from his neck. Juliana had a second to register his startled eyes before his dagger pricked the soft spot beneath her chin.

He seemed not to care that she was female.

"Drop it," he ordered, nodding curtly at the scythe she had unthinkingly raised before her. Feeling stupid, but not knowing what else to do, she let it fall. Her only comfort was that it did not land on her foot.

This was precisely what she had hoped to avoid.

"Captain!" the soldier called. "There is a woman. Human, I believe."

You *believe*? Juliana thought, her brows rising. She could not fathom how there could be any doubt.

But he had called for a captain, probably the same she and Ulric had encountered in Dunburn. Ulric's thrall must not have taken, thwarted perhaps by the captain's cross. Now the others were wearing them, too.

We should have killed them when we had the chance, she thought, but was not certain they would have even if they knew. Racking her mind for some way out, she clenched her hands as she

waited for a response. When the soldier got one, her worst fears
came true.

"Bring her over by the other," said a steel-cool voice Juliana
knew all too well.

Her shoulders hunched in revulsion. It was Gideon Drake, her
would-be spouse.

The merchant broke into a smile as his man dragged her into
view. Mailed like the others but dressed in silken raiment atop,
Drake's garments bore the stains and creases of hard travel. Within
them, he seemed as controlled as ever: tall and angular with long,
waving gray hair whose fullness she knew was a source of pride.
Unlike other men of his years, Gideon Drake wore no beard. He
was handsome in his way, despite his slightly bulging eyes and his
too-thin, too-small mouth.

It was not, Juliana thought, the mouth of a full-grown man.

He tapped his fingertips before it. "How convenient," he said,
"we can question them both at once."

Juliana waited for him to say her name, to berate her for rebelling against her father and him. Instead, he flicked his fingers for
his man-at-arms to take her away. She did not think he was pretending not to know her. He simply did not consider her important
enough to acknowledge.

"Tie her well," he said, "if they have begun to change her, they
might have infected her with their strength."

She struggled wildly when she saw where the soldier was leading
her. An unfamiliar *upyr*—Bastien's brother wolf, she presumed—had
been bound from shoulder to ankle to the trunk of an ancient oak.
From the way he sagged in the ropes, she concluded he was unconscious, though she saw no signs of the crippling injury Bastien had
mentioned. To her surprise, the *upyr*'s head lurched upward at her
approach. Within his hood, she spied a gaunt and shadowed face.

Juliana knew it was daytime and his strength was low, but his
skin did not glow at all. Rather, misery burned in his eyes like dun-
brown flames, the purest suffering she had ever seen. Hell on earth

took on new meaning as she met his gaze. If he were trying to send her some message, she could not read it. She did, however, stop thrashing in her captor's hold.

She could not leave this man to face the enemy alone. She might be useless, but at least she was company.

The tree they had tied him to was huge. They lashed her to it beside him, close enough that she could touch his gloved hand with her bare pinky. He jerked when she did this, then closed his eyes as if the contact hurt. Barely visible shimmers in the air around his head told her his hood was insufficient shelter. Turning those shimmers into smoke would not take much. She wondered if Drake knew he was in danger of incinerating his prize.

"You should shade him with a blanket," she said, "unless you want him to burn."

The *upyr* made a soft and indefinable noise. Drake stared at her, then snapped his fingers for his captain to comply. The captain moved off hastily, stepping between a pair of bloodhounds who had flopped tiredly to the ground. They were obviously the means by which Drake had trailed her and Ulric. Just as obviously, now that she had a chance to look around, she saw that she had stumbled into his camp. Easily two dozen soldiers guarded its perimeter. Her skin tingled with alarm to take in their demeanor. These were hardened warriors.

She did not know whether to be relieved or sorry that she did not see either of Drake's sons. If Ulric's thrall had permanently impaired his precious male issue, the man would be out for blood.

As she searched one more time for Milo and Milton, she spotted something she sincerely hoped no one else would: a single, black-pointed tail sticking out from a bank of ferns—Stephen's tail, if she did not miss her guess.

She looked away without delay, but not before a sudden knowledge flared in her mind. The pack was all around her. They had been lying in wait all along.

She wondered why they did not attack: if the soldiers were too

numerous, or the sun too great a drain on their wolfish strength.
Were they simply playing it safe? Would they move if presented
with a more immediate threat than having their friends tied up? Or
was a good distraction all they required?

*This* was why she needed to know everything—so she did not
have to guess in an emergency.

Her frustration was worse than pointless. Shoving it aside, she
tried to reach out for Ulric's mind. Her efforts gained her nothing
but a mild headache. The realization that her own judgment was
all she had to rely on impelled her to square her shoulders and lift
her chin.

Whatever came, she would meet it as well as she could.

At her movement, Drake stepped close enough for her to smell his
days' old sweat. After her time with the wolves, who never smelled
unpleasant, the scent was unnaturally rank.

"Juliana," he said, finally deigning to say her name. "My lovely,
almost-bride. I wonder if you comprehend the trouble you are in.
Your father has disowned you, you know. Told me I should not
bother to chase you down. He was trying to ingratiate himself, of
course; our partnership keeps him in slippers and venison. But I saw
such rage in that pettish old face, I am far from certain he would
care if I slit your throat."

Juliana was not certain, either. She knew how her father got
when his pride was wounded. Outwardly, she was careful not to
respond. Whatever hurt she might feel was her own concern.

Drake responded to her silence with a subtle smile.

"You know these creatures," he said.

She shrugged, as cool in manner at least as he.

"They have shared their secrets with you."

"Some of them."

Impatience tightened Drake's childish mouth an instant before
he wrapped his hand around her jaw. By chance or malice, he
pressed the spot where the soldier had pricked her skin. "I want
you to tell me how they turn humans into *upyr*."

"I am not privy to that mystery."

Giving her no warning, he backhanded her hard enough to knock her temple against the tree. White exploded behind one eye, then went away. Blood filled her mouth from accidentally biting her tongue. She spat it out and straightened. She was shaking now, shocked by his violence, though it was no more than she expected of a man like him.

To make matters worse, the other *upyr*, Emile, had turned his head slowly toward her, most likely attracted by her injury. She did not want to look at him, but somehow she could not help it. A hint of fang glinted within his hood. His breath came disquietingly harder than it had before.

Wonderful, she thought. My fellow captive wants to eat me.

Given her suspicions, he surprised her with his defense. "Leave her alone," he said in a dark, hair-raising growl.

Drake could not repress a shudder, though he recovered quickly enough. "I do not care which of you tells me, as long as one of you does." He examined a bit of soil caught beneath his nails, then offered the *upyr* a sly, man-to-man smile. "Perhaps you are in need of an incentive. She looks healthy, does she not? Living with monsters has given her a bright new bloom. Though by rights she should be mine, I would cede her to you, should you decide to cooperate."

This time the *upyr* shuddered—and not with fear. "If I . . . fed from her," he said, his voice gone thick. "My strength would be restored. I would break these bonds and kill you before you had the chance to use what you had learned. This is a bargain you cannot afford to make."

Drake's captain had finished propping up a blanket as an awning over both their heads. He shrugged at his master's inquiring glance. "It might be true. Frankly, I did not expect them to have any strength after dawn."

"Torture it is then," Drake said cheerfully. "Someone hand me a nice, sharp knife. We shall see how desperate for blood this creature gets once we let some of it out. I expect it will be willing to sell its soul for a sip or two."

Juliana's companion tensed in his bonds. She hardly liked the prospect of being a goad for his suffering, but what she sensed from him went deeper than horror. She worried whether, in his weakness, Emile might have little blood to spare. If that were true, his reluctance to harm her was all the more admirable.

Of course, what might be causing him to shrink in horror was his despair of resisting. Though she had never felt that kind of threat from Ulric, a maddened and starving *upyr* might be capable of causing death.

*Lord save us,* she prayed. *I must find a way to help us both.* She reached again for what sense of the pack she had, trying to drop whatever guards were keeping her from contact. If she discovered what they were planning, she could ensure her actions did not make their situation worse.

<hr />

ULRIC had no choice but to let Bastien lead the chase. Not only did the Frenchman know where the soldiers were, but only he, of all of them, was functioning at anything near full strength. Even in wolf form, Ulric felt as if he were half asleep. Though determination forced his feet to run, it failed to clear the fog from his brain.

*This way,* Bastien thought at him after snuffling around a recently dug-up burrow. *I can smell which way they have moved him.*

All Ulric could smell were clods of earth and pine sap.

Adding insult to injury, Bastien was skilled at mind speech, more skilled than Ulric. Between *upyr,* this was a tricky matter, depending on both parties being willing and attuned. To Ulric's chagrin, his inner hearing was as muffled as his nose, as if Bastien were speaking to him from a pit. Trying not to pant too loudly, he gathered himself to run where Bastien directed. The rest of his pack fell in behind him with wolfish sighs.

If nothing else, this experience was teaching him he had not been keeping his charges in fighting trim. From here on out, he would get them in the habit of taking a little sun—assuming, of course, that they survived this day.

They reached the camp in a shameful state of windedness.

Bastien had not exaggerated when he said there were too many soldiers for him to take, nor did their opponents display any shortage of weaponry. Ulric swore to himself as he counted swords, any one of them sharp enough to lop off their heads. If he had trusted his power to thrall, he would have lured the men out one by one. Regrettably, in his wolf form and in full daylight, he doubted the ploy would work—not when he could barely hear the thoughts of his pack. Ulric was no coward, but he had no desire to lose a single life if he could avoid it.

He signaled the wolves to stop behind a bank of blackberry brambles. He directed his thoughts to Bastien, confident that he at least would hear.

*I think we must wait till sunset unless these Englishmen force our hands. See if you can get a message to your friend not to worry if we delay.*

Bastien's head swung toward the tree where Emile was tied. *I am not certain he can hold out. Hugo put a curse on him, one that worsens progressively. Emile needs blood to stave off the growing weakness, more blood than most upyr. I am afraid I did not get the chance to feed him this morning.*

Now Ulric understood Bastien's greed and the bite marks on his throat. He cursed the mistrust that had kept him from confiding in Ulric before.

*Can you reach him at least?* he asked. *Let him know that we are here and find out how bad his condition is?*

Ulric did not think this an awful question, but Bastien sank down on his haunches and dropped his muzzle dolefully to his paws. *I have not been able to speak to his mind for days.*

From his half-pleading, half-woeful expression, Bastien clearly expected Ulric to pull some miracle out of his ear—despite Bastien being, for the moment, the strongest wolf they had.

This, Ulric thought in an ironic flash, was what came of encouraging people to obey you.

*Very well,* he said, bringing the rest of the pack into his thoughts with all the force of his concentration, trying to hold his sense of each in his head. *We will surround the camp in groups of two. If possible, we will wait for sunset. If Emile looks to be in urgent danger, I will give the signal and we will attack, bringing down whatever soldiers each of us can reach first. With luck, the confusion this causes will give us enough advantage to defeat the rest. Pairs, you are responsible for keeping each other awake.*

To his relief, everyone heard him. He kept Helewis with himself, Ingrith with Stephen, and sent Bastien off with Gytha. The two might be at odds, but together they would fight hard. Gytha's desire to show no weakness in front of her former lover would keep her sharp.

Ulric was settling in for a wait when Juliana's appearance as the soldier's captive turned his heart inside out. He had forgotten she was following and had not thought to caution her away.

*Quiet,* Helewis warned when his throat began to rumble.

Helpless to interfere and straining in every muscle, he watched them tie her to the tree. Drake's revelation about her father was cruel enough, but when the Englishman hit Juliana, Helewis had to bite his scruff to hold him back.

*She is not truly hurt,* Helewis soothed, her mind voice going in and out like a fitful wind. *Maybe, by . . . there, she . . . steady Emile.*

Ulric was more concerned that she would stir Emile's hunger. He tried to reach Juliana's mind, then fought panic when he could not. What if she thought she had been abandoned?

*She will not think . . . such a thing,* Helewis insisted. *Juliana might be human, but she is brave. It would be useful, though, . . . get a message to her.* Helewis panted quietly as she considered how to do this, her tongue lolling over her jaw. *Maybe Bastien can reach . . . not as drained by the sun.*

A wave of jealousy swept through Ulric, as blinding as a mirror's flash. For a moment, he could not breathe.

*Never,* he declared. Never would he let another man, much less Bastien, share that intimacy with Juliana. Ulric would not lose her!

*You cannot lose her,* Helewis said, *unless . . . hold on too tight.*

Coming from Helewis, this advice was unexpected, to say the least. With a crackle of undergrowth, he sat back on his hind legs. Helewis did not seem a bit intimidated by his amazement. When he agreed to improve her standing with the pack, he had not expected this end result.

*She is your queen,* Helewis said, as if this were a fact any pup should know. *I can see . . . even if you cannot. It is safe to let go.*

Ulric peeled back his lips in protest. *I am not going to let go so much that I am no longer holding on!*

Helewis grinned, both woman and wolf in the expression. *Why not?* she said. *Can you not trust . . . stay with you on her own?*

A sound of extreme mental disgust cut through their communication. *I know you are punishing me,* Gytha said, her words perfectly clear, *but must you make me this sick? We need to contact one of them. If you cannot do it, Bastien must try.*

Like it or not, Ulric knew she was right.

# Fifteen

————

JULIANA would not have guessed it, but being tied to a tree
was rather exhausting. She was grateful she had thought to
take care of her human necessities before she left. Now she was
merely tired, thirsty, and a little frightened. The hour was nearing
noon, and she had yet to see any sign of Ulric. She told herself he
was doing exactly what she would have wished: waiting for an advantage. She did not want the pack to needlessly risk their lives. She
had no real reason to believe that they had fallen asleep in the sun.

However anxious she was, her discomfort paled beside Emile's.
He was sagging ever more limply in his bonds, responding ever
more wearily to Drake's demands. He could not reveal what he did
not know, he said—though this did not save him from Drake's
knife.

For his part, Drake seemed fascinated by the way the cuts he
made slowly closed. Juliana could practically hear him measuring
this gift for himself. She did not like to think what would happen
if he obtained it. The London merchant was both ambitious and
sly. With the power of immortality added to that of his wealth,
he probably thought his aspirations would have no check. She

supposed it was just as well he was not aware that a strong *upyr* would have healed much faster. As it was, Emile was sweating with pain and weakness, his pale, smooth skin gone faintly gray.

"Do not be distressed," he whispered to her when Drake stepped away for a cup of ale. "I shall not hurt you no matter what."

He might have been trying to convince himself, but Juliana nodded as if she believed. "I shall not hurt you, either," she said, which seemed to amuse him.

This exchange would have pleased her more if the teeth he bared with his smile had not been so sharp.

Trying to act as if she had not noticed, she cursed a persistent buzzing between her eyes. All morning it had been bothering her, and naturally she could not scratch. She tried squinching her forehead, but found no relief.

Fine, she thought at the troublesome spot: Itch all you want.

With the surrender, she realized a voice was calling her name.

*Yes,* she thought as strongly as she could. *I am here.*

Someone sighed in relief. *Juliana. Raise one finger if you hear me.*

Juliana did, recognizing with some surprise that the speaker was Bastien. He must have been trying to reach her for a while.

*Just listen,* he said. *Do not react. I know, as a human, you are not used to mind speech. You must stall these soldiers. Give Drake a reason to wait until dark before doing anything dire. Then we can move on him with full strength. We will rescue you earlier if we need to, but the chance of everyone coming through the fight alive will be better when the sun has set.*

Juliana moved her hand again to indicate she understood, though her eyes focused unswervingly on Drake's return.

His lips curved gently in anticipation as he used one fingertip to test his freshly sharpened dagger. "Well," he said, "now that I am refreshed, shall we try my skill at probing more sensitive spots?"

Juliana had never seen her father's associate look this pleased. For Emile's sake, she did not want to consider what spots he meant.

"Midnight," she burst out before he could inflict a new torture.

"Midnight?" Drake repeated, his wispy gray eyebrows cocking up.

"Yes," she said, the idea forming even as she spoke. "Midnight is when the *upyr*'s power is at its height. Only then can they transform a human."

The captain had returned with his employer. "If that is true," he mused to Drake in an undertone, "it would explain why they are sometimes called the children of midnight."

"I do not care how they got their name. I want to know how they share their gifts." Drake set the point of his blade at Emile's groin, then turned coolly smiling eyes to her. "Care to elaborate, Juliana, or would you like to hear how loudly this wretch can scream?"

Hardly needing to pretend that she was scared, Juliana moistened dry lips. Selling this tale would require all her storytelling art. She sent a prayer to her mother to look down from heaven and guide her now.

"The secret is in their blood," she said, "in an exchange of vital essences. Three times they drink from your veins and three times you drink from theirs. When this mingling takes place at the sacred hour, the change is done."

Drake slitted his eyes. "It cannot be that simple. If you are leaving anything out . . ."

Emile jerked as the knife pressed deeper into his clothes.

"They might say words," Juliana gasped, feeling terrified and brilliant in equal parts. "But I do not think they matter. The blood is what conveys their power."

"Woman," Emile growled, the sound disembodied within his hood. "You have broken a sacred oath."

Juliana said a silent thanks. Emile must have figured out what she was attempting and decided to play along. She did not dare meet his glare for fear of giving the game away. Instead, she shrank away from him in her bonds.

"Tut-tut," Drake chided. "Why scold her when she breaks her

oath to spare you pain? Women can be such tenderhearted creatures. One should not trust them with important secrets. In fact,
one should not trust them at all."

For once Juliana was grateful he was right.

"Maybe," she said hesitantly, "you should refrain from spilling
more of his blood. I am not certain how much he needs for the rite
to work."

"You had better pray it works," Drake warned, "or I shall kill
you both as slowly as possible."

Sheathing his knife, he ordered his men to secure their camp
against the dusk. Juliana watched their preparations, her emotions
too numb for fear. She had done what she could. The rest was up to
the pack.

⸺⸱⸺

THE soldiers grew very quiet as the end of the day drew near. Some
crossed themselves in superstition. Some fondled the hilts of their
swords. All listened intently to the natural noises of the woods. The
raucous cry of a jay set half of them atwitch. As the light turned
from gold to blue, then from blue to smokey purple, a few exchanged laughing boasts.

"Our blades shall drink eternity," one of them joked.

Ignoring them, Juliana closed her eyes and rolled her head
against the bark of the tree. She tried to look no different than she
had during the day, but she was suddenly deeply aware of the
pack—not so much in her head as along her skin. Currents of energy ruffled each tiny hair, filling her with the wolves' pent-up urgency. The sensation was so compelling she felt as if she could
break free of her bonds and join them in wolf form. Her heart
thumped with excitement, her thoughts taking on a painful clarity.
Scents flitted distinctly past her nose: leather, steel, even one scent
she could only call eagerness.

She marveled that the soldiers did not sense the impending
threat.

A wolf in truth, Emile must have felt what she did. He touched her hand with his glove, either in caution or reassurance.

"Water," he rasped to Drake, calling the man's attention just as Ulric attacked.

Even without the distraction, the wolves were mere streaks of fur and teeth in the new twilight, nightmare shapes too blurred to discern individuals. The soldiers fell on every side, screaming, gibbering, raising their swords, and trying to fight back.

Juliana heard a wolf yelp in pain and struggled frantically against the ropes. One of the pack must have bitten partially through them, because she felt them snap. She stumbled forward and was free.

As she did, Emile teetered as well. To her horror, Drake caught him and began dragging him off, holding the *upyr* in front of him as a shield. Emile's legs appeared not to work at all. Desperate to thwart Drake, Juliana grabbed a dead man's sword.

For all its size, the weapon was surprisingly easy to lift.

"Behind you," Stephen shouted in human form.

She turned and, with what felt like the purest chance, spitted a soldier through the gut. While she stared in amazement at what she had wrought, Ingrith finished the man by ripping out his throat. This taken care of, she greeted Juliana with a bark and an incongruous wag of her tail.

Juliana was fortunate no one attacked her then, as she took a moment to shake off her daze.

"Emile is gone," she called to the dark wolf who was Bastien. "Drake dragged him away."

Bastien was circling two nervous soldiers who stood back-to-back. *I shall send Helewis to get him,* he said in a tone that reflected his distraction. *She is most ferocious when defending those who cannot defend themselves.*

Juliana agreed with this assessment but decided she ought to help as well. After all they had been through, she wanted to make certain Emile survived. Too, she seemed less likely to get in the way while searching for Emile than in the thick of the struggle. The camp was chaos as the pack fought those who had not been taken in the first assault. Ducking and weaving between combatants, four-legged and two-, she moved as fast as she was able in the direction she had seen Drake disappear into the trees.

Ulric barked at her in passing, and she sent as clear an explanation as she could. *Be careful,* he said, seeming to accept her choice.

Though she had no wish to repeat the morning's debacle, she felt much safer knowing she could call him at any time.

Gradually, as she penetrated the wood, the shouts and growls of battle began to fade. She halted and held her breath when the sound of Emile's voice drifted to her ear.

"Take it," he was taunting, "if you're man enough to dare."

She crept forward to find him on the ground with his back propped on a fallen tree trunk. Someone, perhaps Emile himself, had torn his tunic open to the waist. He looked better now that it was dark. His skin was white as marble, shining faintly except for a slowly bleeding slash high on his chest. Drake knelt beside him. He was staring at the cut as if enspelled.

"Take it," Emile repeated. "Drink. Grasp the fate you have chosen."

Though Juliana suspected Emile was not thralling the other man, Drake fell on him as avidly as if he were. Juliana covered her mouth in horror as he drank. This could not be the way humans were changed. Juliana had invented the tale herself. Surely, if it were true, Emile would not allow his tormentor to be transformed.

Before she could solve the puzzle, Drake reared back. His mouth was wet and gaping, his skin beginning to scintillate with blue sparks. "Forever," he breathed as if he were drunk. "I shall live forever."

Then, with no more than a cough, he keeled face forward across Emile. His thick gray hair fanned across them like a cape. Once the last locks settled, he did not move.

"Good Lord," said Juliana. "He cannot be dead!"

"He can," said Helewis, stepping unexpectedly out from behind a boulder. "You chose your fiction well. Our blood is poison to humans. The moment he drank, he was doomed." Bending down, she pitched Drake's body aside as if it were made of straw. Juliana winced at the sight, wondering if Helewis thought she had planned for him to die. His demise seemed not to bother her in the least. She looked down at Emile, her hands propped on her hips like a Valkyrie. "Shall I carry you?"

"If you would," Emile said politely. "My legs are not much use."

Juliana felt odd leaving Drake untended behind them but did not wish to make a fuss. Nor did she explain that she had caused the death accidentally. It seemed a foolish cavil since she could not claim to be sorry. With no more talk, the three returned to the soldiers' camp, now eerily quiet.

To Juliana's surprise and—admittedly—her relief, the soldiers were not all dead. No matter how despicable she thought their employer, she did not feel comfortable seeing them slain. The ten who remained were lined up in two rows, kneeling in the dirt with their hands laced atop their heads. Drake's much-battered captain was among them, his eyes glassy with shock.

The pack, who were guarding them in human form, had come through the fight with little more than bruises.

"We have no choice but to kill them," Bastien was saying to Ulric. "I am not any happier about it than you, but your thrall failed once before. For the future security of the pack, you dare not release them. If even one of them regained his memory, they would return, most likely in greater numbers. Immortality is too sweet a prize not to chase."

Ulric rubbed his jaw. "They did not break through the barrier Juliana raised by feeding the standing stones."

"What of it?" countered Bastien. "Do you really want to be reduced to cowering inside your lands?"

"These are hired men, Bastien," Ingrith put in before Ulric could answer, her voice soft but steady. "Good or bad, but we cannot kill them in cold blood. If we did, we would be no better than the pack you and Emile fled."

"But the risk—" said Bastien.

Juliana stepped forward, turning all eyes to her. "I think I can ensure a thrall does not fail."

"Oh, you can, can you?" Gytha scoffed. Despite her sneer, her tone was not entirely skeptical. Perhaps watching Juliana hold up under pressure had won her respect.

"Yes," said Juliana. "I can because I understand why it failed before, at least for the captain. Evidently, the memory of Drake's sons remains a blank." She gestured toward the captain's neck, where glints of light danced along his cross. "The symbol of his faith protected him. Remove it and you rob him of his resistance."

"Heathen bitch," the captain burst out. "May you roast in hell for your treachery!"

Juliana smiled. Even if her claim was false, the captain believed it. She imagined his men would as well. Their credulity would be the key to Ulric's success. As she suspected had been the case when Bastien hurt Ingrith, the men would bolster Ulric's thrall by convincing themselves.

Spying Gytha's scythe lying in the grass, she picked it up. The captain flinched when it caught the moonlight.

"In these woods," she said, " 'bitch' is a term of honor."

"Hear-hear," said Helewis and gently set Emile down.

Bastien hurried over to gather his friend in his arms. The expression on their faces told a story of profound relief and regret. Juliana had to look away when Bastien pressed Emile to his neck to feed. Had she been able, she would have shut her ears to Emile's moan. The emotion it implied was much too private. With an effort, she returned her attention to Ulric.

"You are certain about this?" he asked.

Juliana nodded. His thrall would be strongest if he had no doubts. She could, after all, tell him the truth later.

"It is decided then," he said. "We will thrall these humans and send them home."

———

ULRIC wasted no time enforcing his decision, though it was not a process he enjoyed. To push through the horrors these soldiers had just faced, to see his darkest nature through strangers' eyes was more than a little disturbing. Though the soldiers would not recall the beasts who had attacked them, Ulric would. From this night forward, he would know how he looked when he killed.

Even with Bastien's help, even with the advantage of removing the humans' last defense, Ulric was exhausted when they were done.

He sensed his influence was firm. Drake's men would know they had fought a battle, but not where it had occurred, nor precisely why. Too much drink was the explanation he and Bastien had devised, a long debauch that started the day they were hired and ended in being set upon by ruffians. Maybe they would have nightmares or dread leaving home again. Possibly they would shudder at tales of wolves. He and Bastien ordered them to cross the border to England as fast as they could. Every one of them plodded off obediently.

Relieved but weary, Ulric fell to his knees by the nearest stream and tried to wash their taste from his mouth. Again and again he cupped the water. Again and again he pushed someone else's terror from his thoughts. When he finally sat back trembling on his heels, Juliana was beside him.

He wished he had taken the opportunity to embrace her earlier. Now it seemed too far to reach.

"I am well," she said with a little smile, answering the question he did not have breath to ask, "and I can see how you are." Her hand reached up to smooth his dripping hair back from his face. "I imagine your head is full of them. Their fear, their pain. Bastien had anger to shield him, but you faced it all."

"It is the last respect," he said, the words rough in his throat. "To read what you are about to destroy. And I could not be as careful otherwise. I wanted to leave them with a memory of those who fell. Their kin deserve to know they are gone."

Her eyes shone with understanding. When he reached for her, both of them kneeling in the squelching mud, she held him as tightly as he held her.

She was warmth itself, as comforting as he had wished he could be to her. Her words stirred softly against his neck. "I am sorry I let myself get captured."

Her confession released his. "I was afraid," he said into her hair. "I did not want to lose you. I hated having to leave you there all day. When that Englishman struck you . . ."

"You did the right thing," she crooned, rubbing his back in sweeping strokes. "The wise thing. You brought everyone through the battle safe. I am grateful"—she hiccupped and caught her breath—"so grateful that you trusted me not to break."

He kissed the bruise where her cheekbone had hit the tree, tasting solace and salt. How could she break when her heart was this strong?

"I trust you with my life," he said, feeling the words in his bones, "just as you trusted me with yours."

# Sixteen

ULRIC was the last of the pack to climb the cliff, his way of ensuring all arrived safely. He found Ingrith waiting at the entrance, looking stronger and happier than he had seen her in some time.

"That was good," she said as she turned to walk with him. "Nothing pulls a pack together like a fight."

Ulric squeezed the back of her neck through her silky hair. "I am glad you are feeling yourself again."

"How can I not when your Juliana proves even a puny human is not helpless?"

"She was resourceful," Ulric agreed, watching his lover—his queen, said his heart—move down the passage beside Stephen, "and this was the longest day of my life."

Ingrith rubbed his arm with a sympathy rare in a subordinate. "Maybe we should help the others with Emile. His weakness makes them uneasy."

Ulric had noted this himself. Now leading the way with Emile between them, Bastien and Helewis had conveyed the ailing *upyr* up the cliff in a makeshift sling. Though Bastien had assuaged his hunger, Emile did not appear much improved. The pack was unaccustomed to seeing injuries that did not heal. Because of this, the atmosphere was tense as they laid him on the floor in Bastien's room.

"I will get more furs," Gytha volunteered, which would have been kind had she not seemed so eager to leave.

"My condition is not catching," Emile called after her with rueful humor. "If it were, Bastien would have succumbed long ago."

At the moment, his friend looked tired and worried.

"Are you still hungry?" Helewis asked, hovering near, no doubt prepared to offer herself as his next meal. Ulric could tell Emile called to her protective urges. He suspected she was disappointed when he shook his head.

Stephen knelt, lifting the *upyr*'s arm to check its veins. He ran his fingers along them to the elbow. "I do not think he needs blood," he said. "I think he needs energy." He turned his gaze to Ulric. "If you made him pack, we could share ours."

It was a statement, not a plea, but Stephen appeared unafraid to make it. He waited quietly for Ulric's decision. Just as quietly, Juliana slid her arm around Ulric's waist. Oddly, though Emile might end up presenting a burden, Ulric was less concerned about accepting him than he had been about Bastien. Maybe it was because Emile was not a dominant wolf, or maybe the slaughter they had left behind them made him wish to be kind.

"Is that what you want?" he asked Emile. "To join my pack?"

Emile's eyes flicked to Bastien and back. "Yes," he said, then broke into the sweetest smile Ulric had ever seen. "The quality of your queen convinces me you lead with honor. Her courage kept me from despair."

Gytha returned with the extra furs in time to sigh. A sigh, however, was an improvement over a snort.

"I am not his queen," Juliana clarified, "merely a future pack member like yourself."

"You are *my* queen," Emile said, kissing her hand.

Ulric fought a twinge of irritation. The man was not flirting, simply being gallant, and Juliana more than deserved his homage. All the same, he was not sorry when Gytha spoiled the Frenchman's gesture by dumping the furs in his lap.

⸺⸺⸺

EMILE'S oath took place with more ceremony than Bastien's, but—in Juliana's opinion—the rite was still quite plain: an exchange of promises, an odd concussion of the air to mark their acceptance, and it was done. Ulric's pack was seven instead of six.

The process of sharing power involved even less ritual. Everyone lay down close to Emile, their limbs tangled together like a pile of pups. Emile immediately closed his eyes and fell asleep. For Juliana, who had not shared a bed with anyone but Ulric since she was a child, such casual intimacy was awkward.

"Come," Ingrith urged, waving her down. "This is about giving comfort. No one will be forward."

"Speak for yourself," Stephen laughed, then winced at Helewis's buffet.

"I should wash," Juliana said, though she was not as filthy as she might have been.

"No, no," said Stephen. "To us, you smell good."

To him, she probably smelled like dinner, but she wriggled into the space between Ulric and Ingrith. She was wearier than she had realized, her muscles seeming to sigh in relief as she lay down and wrapped her arm around Ulric's ribs. His back was broad and firm, and he kissed her palm before pressing it over his slowly beating heart. Ingrith was right. There was comfort in this. For the first time since Bastien had staggered panting into the cave, she felt completely safe.

"Ooh," said Stephen as a flare of heat moved around the circle. "The human is nice and warm."

"The human has a bit of extra energy," Bastien commented blandly. "Your pack leader must be good at sharing."

"Enough," said Juliana, hiding her face against Ulric's neck.

Comforted or not, she decided she was extremely thankful for her gown. She was "sharing" enough as it was.

*Not much longer,* Ulric teased, *before you will have to relinquish your modesty.* His mind-voice happy, he took her hand and shifted it to Emile's chest. Every member of the pack was touching the *upyr's* skin, but when Juliana's palm met his bare flesh a spark leapt up. She tried to ignore the sudden prickling at her nape. The air must have been dry.

"Hmpf," was Gytha's succinct response.

"I think it is time you told us your story," Ulric said to Bastien once the general snuggling down subsided.

Bastien lay on his side at Emile's head with his hand curled loosely over his friend's neck. Stephen's cheek rested on Bastien's calf, while Helewis spooned his back. Bastien seemed comfortable with the contact but reserved. He did not, Juliana surmised, ever wholly let down his guard. He frowned slightly before he spoke.

"There is not much more to tell than I have already. Our leader, Hugo, established his pack in Burgundy. Like Ulric, he served as guardian to Auriclus's children, those humans Auriclus changed on the Continent.

"Hugo was, I believe, four or five centuries old. Four is generally when indications that one might become an elder appear, but Hugo showed no signs. That potential," he said to Juliana, "to change humans, to master the higher powers, must be inborn. All *upyr's* gifts develop as we age, but after a certain point our strengths plateau. Hugo seemed to have reached that point, which would have been fine except some of the younger members of his pack, myself included, were getting strong enough to nip at his heels.

"Rather than lose his place to a challenger, Hugo decided to use magic to keep us down."

"Where did he learn it?" Juliana asked.

"From one of Nim Wei's children, an *upyr* named Damiano who was trying to establish his own empire. The magic is based upon the science of the stars."

"Nim Wei is another elder," Ulric explained. "A rival of Auriclus. There has always been a divide among the *upyr* between her children and his—not unlike the English and the Scots. Nim Wei's broods live in the cities and cannot take animal form. They are, however, allowed to practice the darker arts. Nim Wei tends to keep a tight rein on those she begets. This Damiano might have been acting without her knowledge."

"It is true Nim Wei's children are not famed for their loyalty," Bastien agreed. "But to each his own. Damiano probably hoped Hugo would teach him the secret of turning wolf. Whether he acquired it, I do not know. I heard rumors that Damiano was killed by a human monk shortly after he left us—some other plot gone bad. Whatever his fate, Hugo took Damiano's magic and turned it on us."

As if it soothed him, Bastien combed his fingers through Emile's hair, the strands a berry-black that matched his own. A moment later, he went on. "Hugo was hardly a saint before, but his new powers seemed to warp him. Cruelty became an end in itself. He would hurt his people even when they did nothing wrong. Our queen was no better. She spurred him on. I suppose she knew the next king would discard her. She never was well liked."

"And you tried to stop the abuse," Juliana said.

"Emile and I both. We tried to convince the others that if we stood together, Hugo could not win." He swallowed hard and his hand shook against Emile's cheek. "They said I spoke from ambition, that I would be no better if I ruled. They claimed Hugo was only instilling discipline—as if the outrages he committed could possibly be called that!" His voice broke with remembered anger, causing Emile to stir in his sleep. Helewis stroked Bastien's arm.

"Our brothers and sisters betrayed us," he said more quietly. "We were trying to save them, and they chose Hugo's side. When he heard what we were planning, he cast the spell that crippled Emile. I think he feared I might be able to resist his magic, but knew I could be controlled through a threat to my friend. Hugo promised he would remove the curse if I stopped rebelling, but I knew he lied. My only choice was to watch him closely and try to recreate his spells. Alas, I never found the secret to the one he used on Emile."

Without warning, tears spilled from his bright green eyes. "I am sorry, Ingrith," he said. "I thought if I could control your pack, I could make myself king and summon all the wolves of this realm to fight Hugo. I could compel him to heal Emile. But there was no excuse for doing the same to you."

Ingrith considered him in silence. Whatever she was thinking, she was keeping it to herself. Strangely enough, Bastien calmed beneath her scrutiny.

"It is done," she said at last. "You did not know you could trust us. Now you do. You also know that as a member of this pack, you will be held to a higher standard."

Bastien drew breath to speak, but Gytha broke in. "*I* am not apologizing."

Ingrith responded with dignity. "I would not expect you to, Gytha. If I decide to forgive you, it shall be for my own benefit."

This brought a grin to Helewis's face, though she was cautious or—perhaps—kind enough to hide it.

"I am grateful to you all," Bastien said seriously, "for Emile's sake as well as my own. Even if we cannot cure him, I know that, here, the time he has will be happy."

"We will cure him," said Helewis, her chin tucked around his shoulder. "Juliana will find a spell."

Her confidence was flattering but misplaced. Juliana began to deny the possibility, then thought better of saying a word. Even if there was no magic in Lucius's books, she could pretend. At worst, she would raise false hopes. At best, the pretense would work as well as Ulric's thrall had on the soldiers whose crosses they had removed.

She decided she would try, then confess what she had done if Emile improved. Better the pack know their own power than think she was a sorceress.

The resolution inspired the last of her tension to seep away. Closing her eyes as trustingly as Emile, she gave herself to the balm of sleep.

———

SUNRISE woke Juliana, along with the alteration it brought to her companions. Huffing a bit to shift their heavy limbs, she squirmed out of their hold and stood looking down.

The pack was pale and lovely: statues twined among the furs with faces as blank as stone. Signs existed, however, that they were living beings. Her lips twitched to see that Stephen had stretched his leg across Emile and Ulric to touch Ingrith with his foot. Seeing this, seeing them all, she experienced a bit of what she would have watching children sleep.

The recognition that she was different, and maybe always would be, did not inspire loneliness. Despite the bonds they shared, the members of the pack were also individuals. They held mysteries inside their hearts that Ulric would not disturb. This morning, safe and sound, that seemed a boon. Part of her would belong only to herself even when she joined them.

Content that it should be so, she left Bastien's chamber to head for the cold fountain. A splash of icy water across her face was just what she needed. Halfway down the passage something stopped her—neither sound nor sight, but an abrupt awareness of the world outside the cave.

Though she could not say how, she knew that a fine, warm rain—almost a mist—fell on the forest. The dampness lulled the animals into a doze but brought the growing things awake. The soldiers who had died the day before were beginning to be reclaimed, as if they had always dwelled in this place. Rust would take their armor, predators their blood and flesh, until no trace of their deaths remained.

Their families will miss them, she thought, then rubbed her face. The soldiers must have known the risks they were taking when they signed on with Gideon Drake. For him she experienced no regret; no rejoicing, either, just a sense of unreality that he was gone. The man she had run from, the man her father had schemed for her to marry, was no more.

Added to the knowledge that her father had disowned her, this made her feel as if she had cut the final ties to her human life.

She could not claim she was entirely comfortable with that idea.

She started to walk again, unsettled by her vision but unable to doubt its reality. Figments of the imagination were not that detailed. She was still shaking off the effects when she reached her destination.

The chamber of the cold fountain was ringed by three mosaics: one of wolves hunting deer, one of an island breaking into pieces while being swallowed by the sea, and one of *upyr* flying against a backdrop of stars. Juliana assumed these were illustrations of events in the *upyr's* past but had no way of being sure. Stephen had mentioned Gillian often wondered at their meaning and had liked to sit here for hours on end. That had been enough to stop Juliana from making it her favorite spot.

She had no desire to feel any more haunted.

The fountain itself bubbled up from an unknown source, its waters glowing an uncanny blue that reflected off the mosaics and made them dance. Glow aside, the water was free of taint—sufficiently pure for Ulric and the rest to drink. Dirty water disagreed with them even more quickly than it did with humans.

Juliana stepped through the arched door in full expectation of having the room to herself. Instead, she came to a startled halt. An unfamiliar *upyr* sat on the fountain's rim with his legs extended and his ankles crossed. He was slim and quick-looking, even though he was motionless. His hair was closely cropped and brightly silver, his garb a rich, dark green. His hose clung to his legs like a second skin. His doublet, of equally exquisite fit, quite obviously required no padding. Atop one leanly muscled thigh he held a large, bound volume: the Aristotle she had dug out of a cache. He did not look sleepy, as most *upyr* would, but like a man who had had a nice, long walk and now savored sitting down.

His stone gray eyes met hers with the faintest smile, their sparkle the only part of him that moved.

"You must be Lucius," she said, oddly unafraid.

He conveyed a sense of stillness, inside as well as out, which precluded any sense of threat. Or perhaps his confidence was what calmed her. He would not attack because nothing could threaten him.

"I am Lucius," he conceded after a pause that seemed, to her, a few breaths too long. "I am afraid I do not know you. Sadly, I arrived too late for proper introductions."

"I am Juliana Buxton, a friend of Ulric."

This elicited another pause and then, after Lucius finished thinking whatever he thought, a slow, white smile. The smile brought an unearthly beauty to his face, making her heart beat faster for strictly feminine reasons. She did not believe this had been his aim. Unlike Stephen and Bastien, this man did not strike her as a flirt.

"I feared Ulric would be unhappy after recent events in which I played a part," he said. "Thus, I returned. I am glad to see I wasted my time."

He rose as if he meant to go, as if the idea of speaking to Ulric himself after journeying specifically to see him were now pointless. Juliana's jaw dropped in disbelief. Of all the *upyr* she had met, this was the most peculiar.

"You cannot leave," she said, finding her voice.

"No?" said the *upyr*. He tilted his head unsurely, as if he truly did not know what courtesy required.

"No," Juliana said. "Ulric might have been worried about *you*, or he might want to wish you well in your new life. If I am not mistaken, you were with the pack a long time."

"That is true," said Lucius. "It was rather long." He pursed his lips in a thoughtful frown. "I suppose the others will want to greet me as well."

"Most assuredly they will. And I"—Juliana gathered her nerve—"should very much like to ask you some questions."

Lucius lifted his elegant silver brows and assumed a receptive pose, both hands crossed and gripping the book he held against his thighs. She tried not to be distracted by the fashionable shortness of his tunic. Apparently, he expected her to ask her questions then and there.

"I need a spell," she said, the first topic that came to her mind.

"A spell?" he repeated. His manner suggested no explanation in the world could take him aback. Before she knew it, she was telling him everything that had been happening to the pack. He listened with great attention, only breaking in occasionally with comments like: "*Two* new wolves?" and "Thought you were an *upyr,* did they?"

She told him a great deal more than she intended. In fact, now and then during her recitation, she felt as if she were not speaking at all, but that he was lifting the words straight from her mind. He seemed to understand whatever she said without explanation, until it was like a dream of a conversation, rather than a conversation itself.

"Interesting," he said when she finished, then spent a good three dozen heartbeats—her sort of heartbeats—staring at the wall. During that time, Juliana neither saw him breathe nor blink. He was so motionless, he practically disappeared, like a chameleon freezing on a rock. The fountain's glow slid over him in waves.

"You should not assume," he said, reanimating without warning, "that the Christians' cross has no power over our kind beyond an individual owner's faith. Symbols become invested with the energy of many believers and can carry that energy even in the face of doubt, like a flagon carries wine. The English captain might have expected more of his cross than it could deliver—that it be an invincible weapon rather than a modest shield—but that does not mean it had no real strength.

"Too, if such entities as gods exist, I see no reason why they cannot bless their tokens. No doubt these tokens' protective powers are smaller than they would be if they spoke in the original language of the *upyr*, but the effect might well be more than a trick of the mind. Or that is what I believe. I could be completely wrong. I have seen *upyr* who wore crosses themselves, who did not bat an eye at having one shoved in their face. Maybe it is a matter of power turned to a specific purpose by belief: of latent force activated by human will. If the *upyr* knows what to defend against, his will can reign supreme."

He smiled as if bemused by the workings of his mind, a sentiment Juliana shared. She recalled Ulric mentioning that Lucius had only recently regained some of his memories, that he had forgotten he was an elder. If this were true, it might account for the eccentricities of his speech.

She rubbed the bridge of her nose. "I do not suppose you remember any spells."

"Not a one," he said cheerfully, then thought again. "No, actually, I did remember how to call a fog. Pretty little charm. Latin. But I am sure I could invent a spell to help this Emile. Perhaps in a language no one understands? I would be interested to test your theory concerning inherent power versus mere belief."

Then he yawned and she realized she had kept him long after dawn.

"No matter," he said before she could apologize. "I will seek my old room and we shall talk again after I have slept."

He offered her the Aristotle as if he had borrowed it from her, rather than the reverse. When she declined, he smiled and left by the farther doorway, leaving her to shake her head.

He was not what she imagined an elder would be.

Dazed, she turned her footsteps toward the hot spring chamber for a soak. She needed time to consider what she had learned.

LUCIUS was back.

The elder was sitting on Bastien's bed when the pack awoke, as if there could be no question that he belonged. The moment Ulric saw him, his heart sank to his gut. *Not again* was all he could think. Juliana had never felt more like a member of his pack, and now the *upyr* who had helped Ulric's last lover run away from him had returned.

Ulric had changed. For Juliana, he had stopped trying to hold on so hard. He had been gentler, less controlling. He had taken the time to learn who his beloved was, as opposed to who he wished her to be. He did not deserve to have to confront this specter from the past.

Fighting to hide these thoughts, he watched Ingrith and Helewis greet the prodigal with shrieks of pleasure. Stephen hugged him and clapped his back. Because Gytha rarely waxed sentimental, her nod of welcome did not insult.

"It is good to see you," Lucius said, seeming surprised by his own delight. "You all look very well."

Then he turned to Ulric.

"Lucius," Ulric said, unable to refrain from crossing his arms.

Lucius ran his hand down the front of his dark-green tunic, a gesture that for one strange instant reminded Ulric of a human.

I do not know this *upyr*, he thought. And maybe I never did.

Lucius blinked, went down on one knee, and inclined his head. "Forgive me, pack leader," he said gravely. "I should have asked your permission before I returned."

Ulric let out his breath, realizing how conspicuously he must be bristling if Lucius felt obliged to kneel. "You do not need permission. You did what you believed was right by helping Gillian. You will always be welcome among my pack. Not that I could stop an elder like you."

"You are an elder?" said Emile, who had been waiting along with Bastien in wary silence.

"It appears I am." Lucius turned to the newcomers as he rose. "Juliana told me you might be in need of a spell."

"You met Juliana?" Ulric demanded, an inadvertent growl darkening his voice.

Lucius smiled faintly. "I did. While you were sleeping. She was kind enough to share what has been happening in the pack. An interesting woman, and most attractive. I can see why you are more inclined to forgive me for Gillian."

"Ulric," Ingrith cautioned, catching his arm as he stepped forward. "Lucius is teasing you. He means no harm."

"No harm in the world," Lucius agreed. "In truth, I hope to pay off a debt. I enjoyed the hospitality of your pack for many years and, though I did not mean to, under false colors. Would you allow me to see if I can help Emile?"

Only a cur would have refused him, but Ulric was not given a chance.

"Oh, can you?" Helewis breathed. "That would be marvelous!"

Lucius tipped his head to the side, gazing at the sturdy *upyr* as if she were the marvel.

"What?" said Helewis, touching her throat nervously.

"I am wondering," Lucius said, "why you all seem different when I am the one who has changed."

---

JULIANA had not felt comfortable returning to Bastien's chamber after her soak. Sleeping *upyr* could be unsettling company. Instead, she spent the rest of the day reading and napping in Ulric's bed. When she rose, some time past nightfall, to see how Emile was doing, she found a scene that caused a brief stab of hurt.

Lucius had not waited for her to perform his experiment. The pack were all in Bastien's room, gathered around Emile with varying expressions of wonder. His complexion gleamed white and clean as he sat upright on the floor wiggling his toes.

"I can feel my feet," he cried, "and I can move them!"

Then he burst into tears.

"It was nothing," the elder demurred, clearly uneasy. "You would be amazed what you can find in these old books." He patted the volume he held at his side, the Aristotle, conveniently scribed in indecipherable Greek.

"How interesting," Stephen commented softly, "that Juliana found no mention of magic in her searches."

"This text is in the tongue of Alexander," Lucius said with a passable imitation of affront. "Hardly any humans read that these days."

"And maybe some people"—Stephen leaned closer—"do not want word to get out that they can heal curses by laying on their hands."

"Nonsense," Lucius began to say when Bastien engulfed him in a bone-crushing hug.

He was crying, too, and noisily slapping Lucius's back. So much, Juliana thought, for Bastien's reserve.

She was not the only one grinning at his effusiveness.

"You have saved my friend!" he declared, seeming for once thoroughly French. "If I had not sworn to Ulric, I would follow you. The good Lord bless you, *mon ami*!"

Lucius freed himself gingerly. "No, no," he said, raising his hands and backing away. "I do not wish to lead anyone."

He retreated all the way to where Juliana stood in the door, so disconcerted he jumped when she touched his arm. Elder or not, it was impossible to be intimidated by this flustered man.

"Did you cure Emile with your touch?" she asked in an undertone.

Lucius wagged his head like a worried dog. "I cannot say. I thought the made-up spell was working, but perhaps I do not know my own strength."

"You will know it. Give your memories time to come back."

He grimaced as if this prospect failed to fill him with joy. "Speaking of strength . . ." he muttered to himself. He lifted his hand to catch Ulric's eye. Ulric was helping Emile see if he could stand, but he let Helewis take his place when Lucius beckoned.

"Come with me," the elder said. "We need to speak privately."

Juliana pressed her lips together to hide her smile. For someone who did not want to lead, Lucius was not shy about giving orders.

# Seventeen

EMILE was sleeping again, with Bastien and Helewis watching over his bedside. Juliana could see their newest wolf had a gift for winning people's affections. Since Stephen and Ingrith were reluctant to leave his vicinity—in case he required more help—Juliana was working with Stephen on his letters in the hall outside Bastien's room.

This was the first chance they had gotten to fulfill her promise to teach him to read. Like all *upyr*, he was quick to learn, though it did take some doing to keep his mind on the task at hand. For Stephen, the attention of two living, breathing females meant it was time to play.

"No more 'cat' and 'hat,'" he said. "I must learn to write 'Ingrith is beautiful.'"

"Only beautiful?" Ingrith inquired. "What about clever and brave?"

His response was cut short by Ulric's appearance. The pack leader had returned from his talk with Lucius looking grim.

Juliana's eyes widened at his frown. "Is everything all right?"

"Fine," he said, not seeming it at all.

"He did not make you lose your temper?" Ingrith asked worriedly. "I know you never liked when he forgot his place."

"No." Ulric rubbed his brow with the heel of his hand. "Not that I know what his place is now."

"Did he have a message from Gillian?" Stephen asked with his usual dearth of diplomacy.

Ulric shook his head as though his thoughts needed dislodging. "He did not mention her. He wanted to speak to me about Juliana."

"About me?" Juliana set down the stick with which she had been drawing letters in the dirt.

As she did, Ingrith jumped to the worst conclusion. "He cannot be trying to prevent her from becoming pack!"

Again Ulric shook his head. "He had no objection to that." His tone implied that Lucius had objections to something else. He turned to Juliana. "Walk with me. I will share what he revealed."

Juliana rose to her feet and shook out her skirts. "It is not bad, is it?"

"No, love." Ulric petted her cheek. "It is not bad."

But he sounded as if it were. With some anxiety, Juliana accompanied him down the passage to the entry ledge. There, in privacy, they sat with their legs dangling over the rock. Juliana lifted her hair from her neck. The outside air was warmer than she expected, a true hot summer night. Crickets sent their song in waves through the sea of trees. In the distance a lone wolf howled.

Ulric smiled to hear it, but to her the smile looked sad.

He must have seen her concern because he wrapped his arm around her shoulder. "What would you think," he said, "if you did not have to be changed?"

"Not be changed? What do you mean?"

She thought he was going to withdraw his invitation to join the pack, that despite his denial to Ingrith, Lucius had given him some reason why she could not be one of them. Her throat tightened, her mind already searching for ways to argue against she knew not what.

"It is not what you fear," Ulric said, his mouth pressing briefly into a line. "Lucius tells me that changing you might not be necessary, that your transformation has already begun. He says that when a human and an *upyr* are especially well matched, the normal sharing of power becomes something more. They actually begin to blend their essences. The process is slow, but in ten or twenty years, you would be *upyr*."

A tingle of shock streaked down her spine. Was this why Drake's soldiers had wondered if she were human: because in truth she was not?

Her reaction to the possibility took her by surprise. Perversely, it was more disturbing than being refused a chance to become *upyr*. That she could have fought. This had been thrust upon her without her knowledge.

"No," she breathed. "It cannot be."

Ulric shifted on the ledge to face her, his gaze intent. "Look at the evidence, Juliana. You are stronger than you were when I met you. You woke the menhirs and can climb our cliff without aid. Emile said you broke the ropes you were tied with all by yourself. You can see in the dark almost as well as I, and I cannot remember when I last had to uncrease your clothes. Those are not things the average human can do."

Juliana pressed her hands together over her mouth, her emotions in a turmoil she could not explain. "This morning, right before I met Lucius, I had a vision in which I saw the forest, even though I was inside. I knew it was misty. I could feel the growing things."

"Maybe that is your gift, to sense the life of the land."

"My gift . . ." She laughed, the muted nature of the sound failing to hide a hint of hysteria. "I read. I cipher. I bargain well in the market. Those are my gifts."

Ulric stroked her hair behind her ear, his hand as gentle as it could be. "Those are human gifts. All *upyr* have special talents. Some excel at thralls, some at feats of physical prowess. Do your abilities really trouble you that much?"

"How can Lucius know?" she demanded, evading his question. "I thought he had forgotten his past."

"He said he remembered that kind of changing when you described the reaction of Drake's guard. He said he thought it used to be more common, but now mortal and *upyr* live too much apart. He claims you smell too much like us not to be altered."

"His memory cannot be reliable!"

"According to him, skills come back more readily than life events. He was certain, Juliana. He would not have spoken if he were not."

Too agitated to sit, Juliana pushed to her feet and began to pace across the passage. Her prints pressed deeper than the *upyr* who had trod before her. In that, at least, she was human.

Ulric watched her from where he was. "Why does this upset you? I thought you wanted to be one of us."

"I did. I do. I simply thought it would be my choice, that I would have time to prepare. I thought you would summon Auriclus and he would judge if I was worthy and only then would I be changed."

"You are worthy," Ulric said. "You should not doubt that. But perhaps you did not truly think your decision through. Perhaps you made it in a weakened moment."

She could tell he was forcing steadiness into his voice, that he was no calmer than she. Her throat squeezed out a tiny noise she did not mean to make. The panic that surrounded her made no sense. Yes, she had told him she did not need to wait until summer's end because she thought it would make him happy, because his handling of Bastien had filled her with admiration. That said, she did want to be *upyr*. She was as ready as any mortal could be. She had seen how they lived. She could accept both best and worst. She ought to be grateful to join his pack—no matter what the means.

She would have been grateful if she were not terrified. It was all she could do not to wring her hands.

"I do not suppose," Ulric said with a touch of dryness, "that I would improve matters by relaying Lucius's other offer."

Juliana commanded herself to be still. "What other offer?"

"That he could change you himself as soon as you wished. To-morrow, if you pleased. He is powerful, Juliana. Whatever his loss of memory, you could not want for a better sire. I doubt Lucius would ever force you to his will. You heard him with Bastien. He has no desire to rule. You would be indebted to someone who would probably never claim recompense."

Juliana thought this was true. So why did she feel as if she could not breathe? Why should being changed tomorrow be any different than a month from now?

Ulric rose, approaching her as carefully as he would a trembling hare. "There is another choice," he said, then exhaled heavily. "You could leave me before the change goes any further."

"No—"

"Hear me out, Juliana. You are stronger, but you are still hu-man. If you lived among your kind, in some town where no one knows you, I doubt you would ever be at anyone's mercy. You could marry or not as you chose. Lucius said you might even have a little power to thrall. You are better at mind-speech than most humans. If you decided to go into trade, as you once said you wished, you would have a definite advantage."

His face was now totally unreadable, a perfect alabaster mask. But this could not be what he wanted. She knew he cared about her. Even if he did not love her as he loved Gillian, she knew he wanted her to stay.

"Think it over," he said. "You owe it to yourself to make a care-ful choice. Forever is a long time for regrets."

She dropped her head. Her indecision shamed her, but he was right. "I will think, Ulric, because I owe it to us both."

---

ULRIC waited until Juliana had disappeared down the passage to slam his fist into the wall. Damn playing fair and damn Lucius for convincing him he had to.

"You must give her a choice," Lucius had said, "a true choice, to stay, to be your queen because her heart yearns toward yours, not because she believes she has nowhere else to go. If you love her, you must put her happiness before your own."

Ulric wanted her to be happy. He understood that if being with him did not lead to that end, he should be willing to let her go— truly willing, not just willing to say the words. He simply had not realized it would be the hardest thing he had ever done.

He had not believed she really might change her mind.

He clenched his hands on the stone, pushing it in his frustration, feeling the cold, rough surface begin to crack.

Helewis claimed he would only lose Juliana if he held on too tight, but Helewis had not seen her fear. Juliana was not as ready to be one of them as he hoped. Now that Drake was dead, maybe she felt she dared return to her own kind.

A shard of granite split off beneath his fist.

I gave up too easily, he thought. I should have fought harder. Surely he was entitled to argue for what he loved.

He pushed from the wall to seek her out, then commanded himself to stop. This was the same mistake he had made the last time. Juliana needed room to breathe, room he never gave Gillian.

A love he forced would try to escape.

<hr />

JULIANA moved through the darkened tunnels in a daze, struggling to understand the storm in her heart. Did she not trust Ulric? Had he not proved he would treat her well? Was she so set on being loved better than Gillian that she could not appreciate what the pack leader offered her? Every woman could not come first. That was simply a fact of life. Some had to settle for second best.

She stopped at the rubble-strewn entrance to another passage, this one too narrow to traverse. She shook her head at the stony floor.

Listen to her talk of "settling"—as if Ulric's love, second best or no, were not better than what thousands of women had. Compared to the dutiful misery she would have shared with Drake, it was a blessing. If she became *upyr,* she would be strong and cared for, not just by Ulric but by his pack. They would be her new family, and together they would live an adventure such as few dreamt. She would run as wolf and explore as woman, blessed by the company of a man she adored. Surely that was what mattered most. Love was about the gifts one gave, not those one got. Juliana had known that since she was young. How else could she have loved her father? That exchange had never been equal.

She pressed her palm to her heart. From its sudden ache, she realized she had stumbled onto the reason for her distress.

Ever since meeting Ulric, she had been trying to make herself as indispensable to him as she had made herself to her father, offering her body and her blood just as she had once offered Henry Buxton a nice, hot meal. Even her human learning she had placed on the altar of usefulness. How different was searching for magic spells from helping her father with his accounts, or entertaining the pack with stories from pouring her father's port?

She trusted Ulric to protect her. What she did not trust was that he would love her for herself. That gift she had never been given by any man.

With Lucius here, no one needed Juliana to seek the secrets of the *upyr.* With Stephen learning to read, no one needed her to tell tales. Helewis and Ingrith were beginning to stand up for themselves. Once, she had envied the *upyr's* beauty, but as soon as Juliana became one of them, she would lose her last distinction: her human warmth. She would be the same as every female Ulric knew. Nothing would bind him to her but whatever affection she could inspire by being who she was.

It seemed a paltry weapon when he had won all her heart. After all, as soon as she lost her usefulness for her father, he had disowned her, had told Drake not to "bother" to chase her down. Little though it surprised her, the betrayal hurt. A parent should love a child no matter what. Knowing that Ulric was a very different kind of man could not ease her dread of being cast aside.

Clenching her hand before her breast, she forced herself to walk again. Enough of this self-pity! She did not wish it said that her mother had raised a coward. Her mother, after all, was the parent who had taught her how to love.

Juliana had the chance to live out a truly extraordinary fate with a truly extraordinary man. She would not shy away because she feared Ulric would never care for her as much as he had for Gillian. If he loved Juliana, however much he loved her and for however long, it would be because his heart chose, not because she made his life comfortable. That was the sort of love she wanted, the sort she deserved.

If he asked her to be his queen, so be it. If not, she would take pride in sharing his bed. Never would he doubt she was thankful for what she had or that he had been right in asking her to be pack.

Then again, she thought with the beginning of a wolfish snarl, if he *ever* took another female—as queen or lover—that would be the last he slept with Juliana. There were limits to what even a second-best love would stand!

Despite her satisfaction with this decision, she should have known it would not smooth every obstacle from her path. Through chance or unknowing intent, she had made a circle in her wanderings, returning to a finished section of the tunnels. She recognized the rosette carvings on the door up ahead. This was one of the entrances to the Hall of Columns, most likely the shortest route back to Ulric. She heaved at the door with her shoulder to overcome the ancient hinges' tendency to stick.

Inside the hall, lights sparkled on the polished pink marble floor, reflections from the two functioning chandeliers. It was a pretty effect, like jewels strewn on a pond. Distracted, Juliana did not at first see the person curled into a ball on the tiles.

Then Gytha lifted her head.

All at once, Juliana remembered she had not seen the *upyr* since Emile was healed.

Gytha's tears dried in a twinkling, but not before Juliana saw their tracks. She suspected more than a few had been shed in rage. The pack's acceptance of Emile and Bastien—formerly Gytha's ally—must have pushed her past the limit of what she could bear, a limit Juliana did nothing to restore by walking in on her suffering.

"Come to gloat?" Gytha said, her voice darkened by defiance. "I suppose you think you have everything you want. Ulric's love. The pack's loyalty. Why, that Emile can hardly stop singing your praises. If Helewis were not so busy cosseting him, Ulric might take offense."

Unfolding her long, lean body from the floor, Gytha stalked closer to Juliana, completely unashamed of her nakedness. Truth be told, she had no reason to be ashamed. The black-haired *upyr* was as perfect a female as nature—or art, for that matter—could create.

"My intent was never to hurt you," Juliana said cautiously, aware of the weight of the purse that hung at her hip. Her knife was in it, along with Gytha's scythe. She decided now was not the time to return it.

"I believe you," Gytha said, flashing an alarmingly sharp-toothed grin. "Now ask me if I care."

Juliana could see no benefit in that. "Do not do this," she said instead, shifting position as the *upyr* began a slow and ominous circling. "If you could learn to control your temper, you would have a chance of earning back everything you lost."

"Not Ulric."

"Ulric was never yours to lose."

She had said it gently, but the *upyr* was crouched now, heart-beats from attack. Juliana's pulse pattered in her throat. She dared not assume Gytha intended anything but to kill her. Gytha had not earned her position as lead female with empty threats. The *upyr* paused long enough to gather her leg muscles for a leap. Without a moment for second thoughts, Juliana seized her chance.

She did not waste time opening her drawstring purse. She grabbed it and thrust as Gytha jumped, snapping the cord that held it to her waist with the same strength that had surprised Emile earlier. Gytha jumped back and danced away, her reflexes too quick for Juliana to take more than a glancing cut out of her belly—even with both blades splitting the chamois cloth.

Frankly, she was impressed she had managed that.

Wrenching the knives free of the purse, she took one in each hand and barreled toward the *upyr*. Juliana had no training in knife play; Gytha could have evaded her as before. Instead, she laughed, braced her feet, and stuck out her arms to halt the rush. As Juliana had hoped, the *upyr* underestimated her speed.

When Juliana hit her, Gytha lost her footing. Even so, as she fell with Juliana atop her, she was able to sweep the scythe aside. The knife was a different matter. Held in Juliana's stronger right hand, it stabbed through Gytha's palm and pinned it to the floor.

Gytha did not bother to scream. Though her lips peeled back at the pain, she was already preparing to tear free when Juliana stopped her. Thanks to Lucius, she had one more trick the *upyr* did not expect.

*Do not do this,* she said with all the force of her mind.

Gytha froze, either with shock that Juliana could speak in her thoughts without Ulric there to help, or because the order held an edge of thrall. Juliana prayed it was a bit of both.

"Think, Gytha," she said, her knees planted stubbornly on the *upyr*'s ribs, her voice surprisingly hoarse. "If you kill me, you lose. Even if you hurt me, Ulric will banish you from the pack. He will do so not because he loves me, but because as long as I am human, there can be no equal battle between us. After what you did to Ingrith, you are already on your last chance. The only way to win is to stop fighting. Maybe one day you will find a pack you like better, one where you can rule, but if you become known as someone who preys incessantly on the weak, who do you think will allow you in?"

"The weak!" Gytha laughed shakily. Blood puddled on her palm around the blade, her fingers twitching in little jerks. Juliana swallowed, striving neither to wince nor let up. Gytha's wolf instincts drove her to dominate. The slightest sign of hesitation might inspire an attack.

Juliana did not want this fight to have more consequences than either of them could survive.

"I caught you unawares," Juliana said levelly. "I doubt you will give me that chance again."

The *upyr*'s gaze locked onto hers, narrow and searching. Juliana knew her firmness was being weighed. "You could call the pack leader," Gytha said, "using your mind. You could tell him of my assault."

"I could. Whether I do is up to you."

"I could bide my time until you are *upyr* and challenge you then."

At this suggestion, Juliana flashed her own toothy grin. "Lucius has agreed to change me. I could be wrong, but I suspect he is older and more powerful than your sire. Because his strength would determine mine, you might not find me easy to subdue."

Gytha spat out a pithy curse. "I am not exactly 'subduing' you now." She rolled her eyes and shook her head, her fangs retracting as Juliana watched. The *upyr* heaved a disgusted sigh. "It is done. I acknowledge your superior rank. I would offer you my throat, but you do not have the teeth to bite it."

"That will not be necessary," Juliana said, "as my knife has already tasted your blood."

A muffled thump in the air between them startled them both. This was followed by a flash that signaled the unexpected lighting of a third chandelier. With the added illumination, the pink of the marble paving edged closer to red. Juliana fought a superstitious shiver. Grudging or not, queen or not, the outcome of this informal challenge had been accepted by whatever forces ruled the *upyr*.

"Wonderful," Gytha said sourly. "Now you can let me up."

This Juliana did, bracing her weight on Gytha's palm as she withdrew the knife. To her relief, the blade came out cleanly. Gytha immediately cradled the wound to her chest, gripping her left hand with her right until the bleeding stopped. The slash on her belly was already closed. All that marked where it had been was a line of puffy red across her muscles.

When the worst of the pain seemed past, Juliana offered her hand.

"Pull it back before I bite it off," Gytha snapped. "We are not friends."

"As you wish," Juliana said, turning away before the other saw her amusement. Shameful though it was to admit, she had enjoyed getting the better of this *upyr*.

<hr />

ULRIC waited in the entrance to his chamber, one hand propped on either side of the open door. The light shone from behind him, outlining his naked form. Ropelike muscles stood out in his arms, and his torso was taut with impatience.

As was usual, her portrait locket hung around his neck, a belonging he had never asked leave to keep. The sight of it touched her, but just as inspiring was the tapering of his chest down to his hips. Juliana bit her lip. One of his legs was cocked, the other straight, the hair on both gleaming gold. Even the hang of his sex was arrogant, his shaft a bit too substantial to be at rest.

*I am king,* said the pose, *and woe betide anyone who denies it.*

She could see he had been fuming since she left.

He truly did not want her to leave.

Though her clothes were straight, Juliana felt disheveled and breathless, heat moving through her in heavy waves. Tonight Ulric resembled the *upyr* she had met in Bridesmere, the *upyr* who pursued his desires without apology.

When he spoke, his words did nothing to contradict that impression.

"I do not care what you have decided," he said. "I will not lose you—at least, not without a fight."

Juliana bowed her head to hide her smile. "If you do not want to lose me, you should probably stop blocking the doorway and let me in."

His look was wry as he stepped aside. "This is no game, Juliana. I told you what Lucius said, that the two of us are unusually well matched."

She moved past him to the other side of his chamber, shy of letting him see her pleasure, wanting to be certain she understood. With restless fingers, she touched the seat of his unbroken stool. To its left was a new malachite-topped table, which he must have carried from one of the storerooms to hold her books. To its right— Her heart stuttered for a moment. To its right, above the level of her head, a pair of thick bronze hooks were screwed into the wall. They were also new, though less obvious in their use.

She turned her back on them hastily, embarrassed to betray the ideas they stirred. No doubt Ulric had a lamp he wanted to hang up.

As he followed her into the room, the door swinging shut behind him, she searched his solemn face.

"One match in thousands," he said, "and we found each other, not by looking but by fate. That tells me we were meant to be together."

"We are together," Juliana said.

He took her by the shoulders and gave her a little shake. "As mates, Juliana. Bonded. Like a marriage among your kind."

"Like king and queen?" she said very softly.

A subtle flush flooded his face as he crowded closer, almost close enough to kiss. "I will not deny that is what I mean. I want you to be mine. Not like Stephen and Ingrith, not like Gytha and Bastien, but mine as in my other half for as long as our lives shall last." His wonderful scent grew stronger as his body warmed. "If you insist you need more freedom, I will concede, but I will not pretend for one more night that complete possession is not my aim. It is my nature, Juliana, to hold what I love."

"Ulric, I—" She meant to assure him their wishes were in accord, but he cut her off.

"Just listen," he said, and she hushed instinctively at the authority of his tone. "I know I have made mistakes in the past, that I held too tight when I should have given freer rein. I will try not to repeat those errors. I will try to be gentler, to listen, but I will not hide who I really am."

"I would not want you to," Juliana cried, lifting her hands to caress his forearms. "Ulric, love, I think you are laboring under a misapprehension. Whatever Gillian wanted from you, I am different."

"Yes," he said. "You are." He looked into her eyes and drew a chest-swelling breath. "She was the love of my pride, Juliana. You are the love of my heart."

For a moment, she was speechless, blinking against the burn of tears. To have had what she wished for all along . . .

"I thought—" She swallowed, scarcely able to speak the words. "Everyone told me how much she meant to you. You told me yourself. I always felt I was in her shadow, that even if you wanted to, you would never let yourself love me as much as you loved her."

A smile lifted one corner of his mouth. "I did not want to love you more," he admitted, his hands sliding over her shoulders. "I simply could not help it. You were like her in too many ways, with your books and your questions. I thought I would lose you if I did not change. But I can only change what I do, not who I am."

"I love who you are! I think . . ." She wrapped her arms behind his waist. "I think some of the changes you have made are good, but I loved you before you made them." She hid her face in his shoulder. "I even love your arrogance. Helewis said something that first night when you wounded Bastien and I ran away. She asked me not to fight you. She said when the leader is strong, everyone feels safe. Maybe I am less of a follower than I believed, but part of me, an important part, only feels safe when you are in charge. I like it when you are gentle, but that is not all I like, and it has never been what I like best."

Her voice sank to a murmur at the confession. To her relief, he appeared to understand what she meant. His pulse sped up and his shaft surged strongly against her gown. She hugged him tighter rather than let it rise.

"Is that so?" he asked huskily. "In that case, I think you will like how I planned to treat you tonight."

His eyes were dark, his irises a ring of burning gold.

"Planned?" she repeated as his fingers trailed shiveringly down her spine. "You mean you did not intend to ask?"

"Not this time. Not when asking might have meant letting you slip away."

His hands caught her wrists and pulled them from behind his back, not hurting her, but not letting her refuse. With the release of her embrace, the crown of his erection brushed up her dress. She wanted to see it, to measure the starkest evidence of his need. When she began to lower her eyes, his grip turned hard.

"No," he said. "It is my turn to admire you. Remove your gown, Juliana. I cannot treat you as I wish until it is gone."

The order turned her liquid deep inside. Unable to speak, she fumbled with her laces, only with difficulty able to pull the bodice down. As she wriggled it over her hips, a vein beat noticeably in his jaw.

She felt a surge of triumph when he wet his lips.

"Chemise, too," he said, "and then stand still."

She did as he demanded, aware of the heat and throb of her body as never before. Ulric backed up to watch, his erection as hard as horn. He clucked his tongue at her disobeying his order not to look, but since his penis jumped a fraction higher, she thought he was not displeased. His gaze centered on her nipples, hard now and tight, then slid to the apex of her thighs. His perusal was like the most delicate touch, making her swell and dampen, making the bud of her pleasure push between her folds.

When Ulric saw it, his teeth slid out.

"It is almost worth letting you wear clothes," he said hoarsely, "to watch your body react when you take them off."

She could only manage to gasp his name.

"Do you want me to kiss you?" he said, seeming determined to make her speak. "Do you want me to shove my tongue in your mouth?"

Juliana shuddered. "I want you to do exactly what you please."

The air shimmered around him as a growl rumbled in his chest. She thought he was going to change, but he held on. A trickle of arousal ran down her inner thigh. His nostrils flared when he caught the scent.

"Back up and lift your arms," he rasped. "I want you to hold those hooks."

She had known what they were for as if she had read his mind, but having the guess confirmed was like stepping into a dream. Though the bronze was colder than the chiseled wall, her body felt as sultry as the night outside. With bated breath, she awaited what would come next.

Ulric did not keep her in suspense. Simply gripping the hooks was not enough for him. He bound her to them with two long strips of fur-lined hide, wrapping her wrists tightly enough that even with her enhanced strength, she was unable to break free.

She hung on them for a moment just to be sure.

"There," he said, "now I can pleasure you as I wish."

He was breathing especially hard for one of his kind, and across his belly his cock cast a shadow that pulsed and surged. The air around him seemed to vibrate, the force of his lust too great to contain.

"You are my prisoner," he said, the words as rough as sand.

She could not help wondering if he were not one as well.

# Eighteen

ULRIC had never been this aroused in his immortal life. His body was pounding so hard he felt as if he were shifting form. When Juliana moaned, he nearly did. Gone was his fear that she could not love him, leaving him elated and light of head.

She wanted to be his prisoner.

Triumph soared through his veins like heated wine. Everywhere he faced her, his skin felt tight.

"All this time," he whispered, wrapping his hands behind hers on the hooks. "All this time I wasted trying to keep my beast in check when I could have been running wild."

"I liked watching you struggle," she whispered back.

He laughed low in his throat and kissed the tip of her nose. Unnaturally hot though he was, her flush was a trembling fire. "I wanted to tie you up to show you what you would be missing if you left."

"Show me," she said, "what I have to look forward to."

He shifted his hands until his fingers twined with hers, the interpenetration a reminder of what would come. Other than this, there was no contact between them: only the mingling heat of their bodies, only the rapid brush of their breath. Their energy was so high her hair had begun to dance and his prickled on his chest. He moved his hips forward just enough for the throbbing tip of his hardness to strafe the silk of her abdomen. She jerked at the contact, then settled as he drew the crown right and left. He was damp with excitement, heating and cooling by turns.

Her lower lip whitened delectably beneath her teeth.

"There," he said on a puff of sound. "That is what you have to look forward to. My cock driving inside you, pushing, rubbing, filling you up until you want to howl."

Stirred by his own words, he tilted his head and kissed her hard, his fangs making it awkward, though neither of them seemed to mind. Her tongue curled between them, tickling and tempting until his hunger to bite her slim, smooth neck squeezed his ribs around his lungs. Panting uncontrollably, he pulled free of her mouth. The pad of his thumb drifted up her strongest vein.

She must have guessed what he longed for, because she wet her lips.

"Not yet," he said, though he reveled in the knowledge that her desire echoed his. "If I feed, my lust will drive me too fast. I want to savor teasing you first."

He palmed her breasts in both hands, smoothing the rich curves upward, squeezing her rosy nipples between his pale fingers.

Only when her head lolled back did he bend to kiss them.

"Ulric," she gasped, then murmured a broken prayer.

Suckling her was his prayer, tormenting himself with the way her blood rose sweetly beneath her skin. He moved his hold to her back to press her closer, spreading his fingers out. One breast enthralled him, then the other, her muscles tensing and relaxing under his hands.

Sighing, he sank to his knees and kissed her belly, softly at first, then hard enough to leave a mark. Her thighs trembled as he caressed them, as he pushed them gently apart. Her excitement smelled like his idea of heaven.

"Ulric," she said, trying to close her knees.

He drew his tongue up her hipbone, then kissed the crisp, warm triangle of her hair. "You do not have my permission to hide. All of you belongs to me."

"Ulric—"

"Hush, love, unless you want me to believe you have forgotten every word but my name."

He spread her secrets and kissed her tenderest bud, delighting in her rising tension, exulting in her broken gasps. She was satin and cream and hot, swollen folds of plumpness that were perfect for pulling against his tongue—now gently, now with groan-inducing force. She squirmed beneath his ministrations, his fangs a pressure he knew how to wield to excellent effect.

He heard his name moaned more than once as he coaxed her to the brink and then backed off.

When he rose, shaking slightly from his own unmet needs, the knuckles with which she gripped the hooks were white.

"Take me," she said, her frustration giving the plea an edge.

Ulric shook his head and leaned in to lick her full, red lips. "Not yet."

"You want to."

"I do, but first I want to feed."

"You could lose control from that. You could spill."

"I could," he said, knowing it was true, especially with her, especially tonight. "But I will not. You cannot be king unless you know how to rule your desires."

She craned forward to catch his mouth in a kiss. He let her, delving deep, drawing and being drawn until he could barely think. She lifted one knee to caress the side of his leg.

He knew his eyes were glowing when he pulled back.

"Ul-ric," she complained with an expression so close to a pout, it threatened to break his control. Instead, he smacked the curve of her bottom, relishing the way it shimmied beneath the blow. Caught by surprise, she squeaked and went on her toes.

"First one hunger," he said, "then the other. I want to swive you slowly tonight."

"But—"

"I will take you hard, Juliana, bruising hard . . . and slow . . . and deep until neither of us can keep from exploding."

Her eyes widened and her cheeks grew pink. He knew he had voiced her wish. Smiling softly, he cupped her mound. For a moment, he simply enjoyed her heat, then slid two fingers between her folds and curled them inside her, holding them tight to the front of her passage with an opposing pressure from his thumb. She made a broken sound as he rubbed a circle on both sides.

"That should keep you," he breathed close to her ear, "until I shove what you really want up in there."

He licked her lobe and made her shiver, then mouthed the salty skin beneath. Gradually, her neck relaxed and her hips began to rotate against his palm. She smelled like musk and felt like oiled velvet.

"Tell me when you want it," he said. "Tell me when I should bite you."

He knew from her smile that he should not have given her the power. She used his exhortation to take revenge, waiting until he had nuzzled the length of her collarbone, until he had tugged her nipples between his teeth and buried his face in her breasts. His breathing grew labored, his muscles tight, while her sexual scent curled maddeningly up from his hand.

"Now," she sighed just as he was sure he would lose his mind.

His mouth was at her neck before the word faded.

When he pierced her skin, he almost brought her to pleasure. He could feel her passage clenching around his fingers in soft spasms of greed. His peak was just as close, plucking with dangerous insistence at his nerves. His promise, or mayhap his boast, was all that kept it back.

Tightening his arms around her, he lifted her until her wrists slid off the hooks. With her bonds for bracelets, her hands plunged immediately into his hair, holding him to her as he fed.

The connection between them nearly stopped his heart. Her pulse, her very life, beat in his mouth, offered freely and with love.

He himself could hold nothing back. His soul was open, his nature bared. That he could trust her with both was a miracle. He drank her in tiny sips, wanting the closeness to last, pulling the ecstasy through her veins like golden fire.

Her thighs rose smoothly to wrap his waist. The moment his mouth released her, she slid her creamy warmth over his cock. Speechless with the sensations, he planted his legs a little wider to help her sink.

"Promise," she murmured next to his ear. "Promise it shall be hard."

She had no doubt he would oblige.

Groaning, he eased her closer, one arm like sun-warmed marble beneath her bottom. He did not move, as if he did not dare, carrying her squeezed tight against him and lowering her to the bed. He lay her crosswise in his sleeping niche with her hips positioned on the edge. He was kneeling between her thighs, hard and thick inside her, almost grinding her in his need.

She stretched her arms above her head until they touched the wall. The sound she made as she arched her back could only be called a purr. His cock quivered in response.

"You want it hard," he said.

Though it was not a question, she nodded and braced her hands on the stone.

He drew back, slowly, his expression tight. Her body clung to his hardness, as if it could not bear to let go. She sucked in a breath and held it. Then he drove in, every bit as forceful as she wished, all his frustrations in the shattering thrust. At her cry of helpless pleasure, he did it again. The blows were perfect: deft, determined, gradually gaining in speed as he built up a strong rhythm. The tautness of his muscles, the grinding of his teeth told her how badly he longed to spend. The night's first coupling was, for him, always the most intense. Sweat began to roll down his straining body, now as hot as hers.

King or not, he was not used to waiting this long.

"More," she moaned, feeling delightfully cruel.

He gripped one of her thighs and pushed it wider, opening her completely to his long, hard thrusts. She clenched around him to pull him in.

"Juliana," he said in warning, a muscle in his jaw ticking for control.

"More," she whispered, betraying herself with a grin.

The grin, or maybe the fact that she dared to give him instruction, turned him wild. He made a sound between a growl and a grunt, his motions suddenly too quick for human speed. Sensation swelled between her legs like a wailing wind, causing her to clutch at him and gasp, narrowing her awareness to the places their bodies met. In heartbeats, he cried out, bringing her with him in a spangling flood.

"Juliana," he groaned. "Lord Almighty."

Before she could catch her breath, he flipped her over and slid into her again, for once seeming even more desperate for a second ride. Glassy smooth and hot, he pumped into her from his knees, rubbing the front of her passage, taking full advantage of the slickness he had made.

His thumbs pressed the cleavage of her buttocks, stirring sensations she did not expect.

"You . . . are . . . mine," he said in time to his movements. "You shall never refuse me again."

Her nerves already primed, Juliana came twice more before he thrust one final time and held. His orgasm hit him with brutal force, his arms tightening around her while his prick gave up its burden as deep as it could reach.

Her pleasure flared like a tinder tossed on a fire.

Ulric groaned, finally relaxing, his cheek coming to rest against her sweaty back. Gently, he nuzzled her nape. From the tiny sting and the glow that even now spread through her body, she knew he had bitten her again at the end.

"Good," he said, the word coming out on a heaving breath. He had softened inside her, but not enough to slip out. "That was the way it should be."

At her wriggle, he eased back enough to allow her to turn around. With her calves crossed comfortably behind his thighs, she drew one finger down the side of his face. His hair hung toward her in a spill of lamplit gold, increasing her sense of their bond. For this moment, he was all she wanted in the world.

She knew he felt the closeness, too. He turned his head just enough to kiss her wrist where her pulse had begun to slow. His lashes fell, hiding the glow of his eyes, despite which his happiness was plain to see.

"Speak to Lucius soon," he said, his lids lifting slowly to meet her gaze. "I want you safely settled in your new life."

Juliana smiled, half to herself and half to him. Autocratic though it might be, the order suited her to the ground.

# Nineteen

A N upwardly sloping tunnel with rough-hewn walls led Juliana
and her two companions to their goal: the octagonal chamber
with the marble benches, where the natural chimney let in the sun.
Lucius had chosen this isolated spot as the setting for her transformation. As the hour was close to midnight, the light would pose no
problem for him or Ulric—assuming, of course, that Lucius could
be harmed.

Because the elder led the way, Juliana was able to observe that
his footwear left no marks, not even briefly, as if he were more
ghost than man. She could not imagine how it would feel to possess
more power than anyone you knew, much less what it would take
to hide that power even from yourself.

The passage ended at a door capped by a triangular pediment.
None of them spoke as they walked beneath it. The room seemed
ancient to Juliana—because of its parchment smell perhaps, or the
well-worn mellowness of its sand-colored stone. At the junctures
of the walls, unknown masons had carved the rock into grooved
pilasters. The eight half-columns gave the room the air of an ancient chapel, one that followed unfamiliar rites. Plain, beveled

squares incised the walls between. A single torch leaned out from each.

Once closed, the door was thick enough to block all sound.

"Privacy," Lucius explained as she and Ulric moved farther in. "We cannot have that Frenchman adding to his repertoire of tricks. You, of course," he said to Ulric, "must be included, though Auriclus would have my hide if he knew."

The pack leader pulled a dubious face. "I am no longer certain my sire could take your hide."

Lucius's smile was pure, boyish joy. "True," he said, "and how nice it is to realize that likelihood."

From this and other comments the pack had made, Juliana concluded Ulric's sire could be a bit of a prig. Maybe it was better than she knew that she was not waiting for Auriclus to change her.

She and Ulric took a seat on the bench opposite the door, while Lucius lit the ring of torches with a flint. They all burned smoothly in their metal sconces, a soft, rich blue that did not sputter or smoke. Like the chandeliers in the hall, Juliana suspected these were part of the cave's oldest furnishings. They did not work like human creations.

Her excitement rose as the strange, clean flames brightened the room. She was going to take part in a mystery.

"Atmosphere," Lucius said when he had finished his circuit. "In case, as Juliana posits, our success can be enhanced by faith—not that I have any doubts about the result."

"I am wondering what you need me for," Ulric said. "Since this process is supposed to be a secret."

"You are here to open Juliana's heart. As closely bonded as you two are, her spirit might resist me if I tried to change her on my own." Lucius rubbed one finger across his lips and turned to her. "There is a question I should ask you first. As Ulric knows, traditionally a new *upyr*'s memory of the change is erased as soon as it is complete. The elders, in their wisdom, did not think our population should increase indiscriminately. As a pack leader and his future queen, however, you might have a need to know. I thought I would leave the choice up to you."

"I want to remember," Juliana said without hesitation.

"I as well," Ulric added behind her.

Regardless of their agreement, Lucius had a caveat. "Knowing how the change is accomplished does not guarantee that either of you would be able to perform it. That gift depends on age and in-born power. Besides, it might be risky knowledge to have, should someone learn you possess it and want it for themselves."

"I want to know," she repeated, leaning earnestly over her knees. "I am sure we can be discreet."

"As you wish," Lucius said. "You have shown tolerable judgment up till now. I will leave your memories intact."

Though euphoric over his concession, Juliana tried to conceal her feelings. Responsible people did not leap about excitedly.

"Do we need to do anything special?" she asked.

"As in hop on one foot chanting prayers?" The elder smiled gently and shook his head. "I see no reason to engage in empty ritual with you. No, I think you should simply sit in the center of the floor—tailor fashion, as the humans say—and we will do the deed without more ado. Ulric, you sit behind her and put your hands on her waist. That should reassure her spirit that I do not mean to tie it to mine."

Somewhat unnerved by his talk of spirits, as if hers might be doing something behind her back, Juliana and Ulric arranged themselves as the elder wished. Lucius sat directly before her, his hose-clad knees bumping hers. At his instruction, he and Juliana grasped each other's wrists.

Her contact with the elder's skin did peculiar things to her heart, which seemed unable to decide whether to slow down or speed up. She swallowed back a touch of alarm.

"Breathe with me," Lucius said, "and relax."

Juliana did her best, though her nerves were jumping like field mice. In time with Lucius, she filled and emptied her lungs while

Ulric did the same behind her. The procedure did relax her. Soon
Lucius looked as still as all *upyr* did in sleep, more statue than living being. He was as lovely as a statue, one carved by an expert hand.
High brow. Straight nose. Lips like a Roman coin. His jaw was as
lean as a fasting saint's. She noted, too, that his glow was brighter
than before, rolling over his skin in gold-white waves.

Watching it made her eyes want to cross.

*Relax,* said Lucius in her mind, reassuring her he was awake.
She only wished she did not have an itch on her nose.

Thankfully, Ulric rubbed it for her.

*Maybe you should close your eyes,* he suggested with a hint of
acerbity. He must have sensed her admiration for the elder's looks.
She would have been glad to allay his concern, but feared she
would miss the most exciting part.

Then, as if to justify her desire to watch, Lucius's glow began to
flow down his arms like smoke. Over his wrists it curled and up
and through her sleeves. As soon as the smoke-glow reached her
neck, her skin went numb. The feeling was unexpectedly pleasant,
similar to being about to drop off to sleep. Her eyelids grew so
heavy she had to struggle to keep them up.

A moment later, she was glad she had. A body formed of light—
this one supremely naked—detached itself from Lucius's solid form.
As sinuous as a cat stretching its spine, the figure rocked forward
on its hands and knees. Then, before she had a chance to be
shocked, the light-body slid effortlessly into hers.

The invasion was accompanied by a ferocious tingling and the
very odd impression of being stretched.

Heavens, she thought. He is inside me.

She had only an instant to comprehend this. Her heart gave one
great jolt as the edges she had always known herself to live within
disappeared. The floor of the chamber, the soft blue light of the
torches, Ulric's hold on her waist—all dissolved to black. On every
side, even under her now-invisible feet, stars whirled and bobbled
like drunken moths. She felt as if she floated high in the air, both

immense and inconsequential, the forest and the beings who lived within it beating far beneath.

Though she was afraid, it was the kind of terror that brings delight. Somehow, beyond any promise, she knew she would be safe.

*Where is this?* she thought, the question echoing in the spaces that were her head. *How did I get here?*

*This is the nothing place,* answered someone who was not quite Lucius, the voice so close it seemed to resound inside her, as if she spoke and listened at the same time. *This is where everything comes to change and where everything remains the same. The void gives birth to the spark.*

*Are you Lucius?* she asked.

*I am*—the other trembled on a hesitation—*the Lucius at the heart, the Lucius who remembers the beginning.*

This pricked up Juliana's ears.

*Tell me where you are from,* she asked eagerly. *Tell me how the* upyr *came to be.*

The stars swelled hugely, swallowing the velvet sky, then dwindled to pinpricks. *I can,* he said, *only show you a piece.*

※

**THROUGH** the heavens a ship was sailing, silver sleek and arrow light. It had no mast or oars, no portholes, and no deck. The only reason Juliana called it a ship was because that was how Lucius thought of it. He rode in a tiny compartment shared with two other men, deep within the needle-shaped hull. He was young—no king, no elder, but a cleaner and fixer of broken things. He barely understood the voyage he had been conscripted to embark upon.

The ship, such as it was, circled ever closer to a planet of deep-blue waters and swirling clouds. Though she had never seen it from this perspective, Juliana knew the planet was Earth.

As the vessel approached the surface, flames danced along its skin, creating a beautiful, white-pink glow. Juliana was afraid, but the fire did not burn. Still cool as snow, the ship landed like a feather on an island in an unnaturally placid sea. With wonder and fear, humans rushed out to greet the intruders. Many in the ship were carrying weapons, but not Lucius. He was not sufficiently important. Despite his defenseless state, his mind buzzed with interest as he descended a sloping, silvery ramp in the midst of a murmurous crowd.

His surroundings came as a surprise.

The sun was brighter than he was used to, and peculiar on top of that, creeping like spider silk along his arms. Nearly blind, he had to shield his eyes to see where he and his shipmates had ended up.

To his astonishment, once his vision cleared, the natives' city appeared as marvelous as the ones he had left behind—spires of stone and glass rising from a shimmering net of canals. The architecture was unfamiliar but pleasing, and the scent of many gardens perfumed the air.

"Greetings," said Lucius's captain in a gentle but carrying tone. "We are the *upyr*. We come in peace to trade knowledge with your people. If you allow it, we hope to live among you for a time."

Though little more than a serf, Lucius knew the captain lied. He hoped to live here forever. He was an exiled prince who had headed a failed rebellion. He and his crew could never go home.

He is desperate, Lucius thought. We do not even know if this place is safe.

As if to underscore his fears, the bright-yellow sun seemed to glare at him from the sky, glinting off the glassy towers, burning balefully from the sea. Lucius could feel the alien light bouncing all around him, poking here, prodding there, like a living being who was not sure it liked this planet's new guests.

The light felt as if it wanted to change them, to warp the very particles that made them up.

He shivered strongly at the foreboding, then just as strongly shoved it aside.

I do not care, he thought with the rebellious optimism of his youth. Here all started fresh. Whatever came, he would make the best of it that he could.

———

A roaring like the ocean filled Juliana's ears, shaking her from the dream.

"You had no special powers," she breathed, the sound of her voice an oddity. "The *upyr* were like humans when you first came."

Whatever had just happened, she was back in the eight-walled chamber, back in her body and her mind. She was not, however, satisfied. "Where was that city?" she demanded. "And how long ago did you arrive? I am sure I never heard of a place like that, not even from merchants' tales!"

Before Lucius could answer, she covered her mouth with both hands. "Oh! Those people who were in the flying ship with you must have been the first elders. The sun must have changed them just as you feared. How horrified you must have been when you had to start drinking blood . . . unless you did that before?"

Lucius gaped at her as if her face had grown a second nose. "Flying ship?" he said weakly.

Still behind her, Ulric chafed her arms. "You are babbling, love. Are you all right?"

"Of course I am all right. I saw one of Lucius's memories." She turned to the elder for confirmation and met a blank. "You do not remember, do you? Oh, Lucius, I am sorry, but I would be happy to share what I saw."

"No," he said, putting out a forestalling hand. "I . . . lost my awareness when I slipped inside you. If you told me what you saw, it would be meaningless."

"I cannot believe you do not want to know."

The elder's arm fell to his side. "If I were ready, my past would come back to me on its own."

"Hush," said Ulric when she drew breath to speak again.

"Everyone is not as curious as yourself. What matters is that you came through the change with no ill effects."

"Came through—" Struck speechless, Juliana turned on her hip to face him. "Do you mean to say that was it?"

Behind her, Lucius snorted out a chuckle. "Loss of memory notwithstanding," he said, "I wager you are the first *upyr* not to realize she was changed. But I am certain you two have many things to discuss. I shall leave you to it and wish you well."

Before she could open her mouth to protest, Lucius bowed and withdrew.

"Well," said Juliana. "I wager I am the first *upyr* to frighten off her sire. He might have stayed to say 'congratulations.' "

Ulric hugged away the sting of the elder's hasty departure. "Lucius has always been very private. No doubt the closeness involved in the change was a bit too much. And better you frighten him than the reverse."

"Did you understand what he did?" she asked. "Because I am convinced I could never tell anyone what it was."

"I believe I understand, in principle at least. Lucius let go of his physical form, somewhat as we do when we turn wolf, but instead of altering his body, he left it behind. Then he merged his spirit form with yours. I suppose he must have left an essence of himself inside you when he drew out, and that was what allowed you to become *upyr*." Ulric buried his nose in her hair. "You do smell a bit like him now, like snow that is about to fall. Auriclus's children tend to smell like the forest."

Remembering Ingrith and Stephen's argument about whether Lucius had a scent, Juliana smiled. How long ago that seemed, and how unimportant. Tonight, she was content to let Ulric hold her as she tried to decide if she felt different. More sensitive perhaps, and quieter deep inside. The effect of Ulric's hand stroking her hair was like a drug.

"The light has more colors," she said as Ulric pressed his lips to her cheek.

He was warmer than she remembered—unless he merely seemed warmer because she was cool, like a basin of tepid water that feels hot when one's hands are cold . . .

Before she could reason her way through the puzzle, a hot, thick flush uncurled from her core. She would have thought it an aftereffect of the change, except for it centering unmistakably between her legs. In instants, her flesh was pulsing. Had it been possible to get any warmer, she would have blushed.

Embarrassed, she fanned her face.

"That is normal," Ulric said, his amusement clear as he hugged her closer. "Your new body is eager to be tried. Shall we slip into the hot spring chamber where we can see to its needs comfortably?"

She wanted to say something witty, but the strength of her arousal robbed her of speech. The best she could manage was a definite nod.

They made it through the door before she tore her clothes over her head, pushed Ulric to the floor, and fell on him like a madwoman. Touching him, kissing him, and most of all, taking him inside her seemed like a matter of life and death. Happily, he let her do it, only rolling her beneath him once she had accomplished her first climax. Its spine-wrenching nature banished all doubts that she was more sensitive, not to mention more greedy. She had not caught her breath before his quick recovery made her writhe again.

To her relief, Ulric did not need to be told to pound her with all his might.

Once this second struggle was satisfactorily concluded, he managed to coax her into the steaming pool. There, face to face, with the hot mineral water seething all around them, they experienced their first truly equal coupling.

To know one's partner could withstand whatever one asked was wonderfully freeing, but to know one could do the same was utter bliss. Juliana hardly recognized the woman who met her lover with such abandon, who clutched his buttocks and nipped his shoulder and murmured hoarse encouragements in his ear. Similarly inspired,

Ulric wedged her against the side of the pool for his lightning thrusts, right where the spring gushed out from its narrow channel. The combination of pressures rocked her body with ecstasy.

It seemed natural to bite him at the final moment, to feel the spicy richness of his life overflow her tongue.

He groaned and shook and she knew that this, as much as anything, had pushed him over the edge.

"Juliana," he said on a sigh. "Juliana, I love you so much."

For long, panting minutes, she could only stroke his water-slicked back. Her body was sated, her spirit peaceful, her intuition—or perhaps her new *upyr* senses—telling her he felt the same.

"I thought you did what you wanted last night," she said when she found her voice, "but you must have been holding back."

Against her neck, Ulric's lips curved in a smile. "A little. Now that you can keep up with me, I think you had better be on your guard."

"Mm," she hummed, not worried at all. From under heavy lids, she gazed idly around the chamber. While she had enjoyed its amenities before, tonight she saw it through different eyes. The grotto had been left rough by whoever found it, but it was naturally beautiful. Above her, a bank of black and yellow crystals twinkled and zinged in the dark, now colorful and defined. Her ears were also sharper. The rushing, bubbling water cocooned them in sound, making them seem the only *upyr* in the world.

"Ulric?" she said as something occurred to her. "Please do not tell the others I did not realize I was changed. They would never let me live it down."

"Your secrets are safe with me—until I need to hold them over your head." When she punched him at his joke, he rubbed his ribs. "Take care," he teased. "You would not want to injure your new king—although, strictly speaking, you have not accepted the post as queen."

"Strictly speaking, you have not asked."

"Most certainly I have."

"You demanded. That is not the same thing."

"Very well." He gathered her in his arms until her front floated against his. "Juliana Buxton, heart of my heart and light of my soul, keeper and sharer of important secrets, would you do me the honor of being my queen?"

"I would," she said, "gladly."

She expected the same sort of thump that had greeted Gytha's surrender and Bastien's oath. Instead, a bouquet of green and golden sparks sprang into being around their heads. Startled, Juliana gave a little shriek. Ulric laughed and batted them as if they were gnats. "Really, Juliana, I know you are happy to rule at my side, but there is no need for such fireworks."

She twined her arms around his neck, his chest and hands supporting her easily. "You started a few yourself a little earlier."

"Just a few?" His mouth whispered over hers.

"An excellent beginning," she assured him and kissed him for sheer pleasure. When she released him, it was only to trade that pleasure for snuggling close.

"Thank you for letting Lucius change me," she said, her body as limp as if it had been steamed. "I imagine it must have been difficult being left behind while he and I, er, while we did whatever in the world that was."

"As to that," Ulric said, sounding vaguely uncomfortable, "I saw a snippet of his mind myself."

"You did?" Juliana pushed back to see his face. "Tell me what you saw."

"Well, not a flying ship. I saw him here, in this cave in the hall of columns, dancing with a dark-haired woman."

"Really?" Juliana's brows shot up with interest. "Did it seem as if it was a long time ago?"

"I think it must have been. The cave was . . . shiny. Not like it is now, half preserved and half gone to ruin. I got the impression that many *upyr* lived here, that the rock was riddled with sleeping rooms."

His gaze was distant as he remembered what he had seen.

"Tell me," she prodded. "If he was dancing, was it a ball?"

"I think so. A formal one, with simple, elegant gowns and some sort of uniform. The oddest thing is that more than half the guests were human. None of the *upyr* acted as if that was strange. The woman Lucius danced with was a human. She was . . ." He searched for a word. "She was a diplomatic liaison, appointed to ease tensions between the races. I think by then our kind must have been what they are today. Blood drinkers. And maybe wolves, as well."

Ulric wrinkled his forehead before going on. "I think Lucius was in love with the woman. At least, she felt very dear to his heart. She was sick, though, and refused to let the *upyr* change her. He did not have the power he has now. Every moment he had with her seemed precious. It made me realize how fortunate we are."

He clasped her face in his hands. "We should live like that, Juliana, like the humans, as if every night were a gift. We should not take for granted what we have been lucky enough to find."

"All humans do not live that way. Only the wise ones."

"Then let us be wise."

His seriousness made her smile. Despite his years, at that moment, he seemed achingly young. She prayed she would never disappoint him.

"I shall make you a bargain," she said lightly, one hand lifting to smooth his golden hair. The locks slid through her fingers like the finest silk. "Whenever you please, you may remind me how lucky I am—preferably in more than words."

Undistracted by her wagging brows, he saw the tears that burned in her eyes. His own glittered dangerously in response.

"I shall remind you any way you wish," he vowed. "From now until the last midnight."

# After the end

THE new queen had a way about her that Emile liked.

He and Bastien stood among the encircling trees, watching the packs approach the clearing. From Juliana's bemused expression, she had not expected to be made queen of quite so many. Nonetheless, she stood calmly beside her king, the moon a hammered coin above her, the upyr slowly filling the open ground—hundreds, all told, every one of them wondering what her accession would mean to them. It had been the wolf called Stephen's idea to channel her subjects to her between the standing stones—for drama's sake and to at once establish her credentials.

Emile considered it a stroke of genius.

No *upyr* who felt that wall of force break prickling across his skin, who sensed the new queen's personal blood magic twined within it, could doubt this female was born to lead. Emile saw more than one hand rub the back of a neck where tiny hairs were standing on end.

By the time the crowd had gathered, Ulric's formal introduction was somewhat moot.

"Thank you for coming," she said, her hand locked tight in his.

Her voice was soft but steady, both richer and sweeter now that she was *upyr*. "You honor us by joining our celebration. I only hope that, with Ulric's guidance, I shall be able to contribute to the future well-being of the packs."

Emile smiled to himself, having heard a few of her plans. Their guests had a treat in store if they thought this pretty queen was just for show. She had learned to trust her strength as a human. By becoming *upyr*, that strength won a wider scope.

"Tomorrow we discuss mutual interests," Ulric said, the warmth he felt for his mate spilling over to touch them all. "In addition to our own concerns, a situation exists in France which, together, we might see a way to address. For tonight, I ask only that you enjoy. Once the ceremonies are dispensed with, we shall hunt and dance and be happy that we are pack. Each of you please come greet my queen. She is beautiful, as you can see, and very gracious. When you know more of her, you will realize how much we have to celebrate."

Because everyone knew this was an order and not a request, there were no complaints at what was sure to be a lengthy business. One by one, the crowd began filing forward. Though they tried to hide it, they seemed impressed by the small green sparklers that met their oaths.

"She looks well," Emile commented to his companion. "Regal."

"Anyone would in that cloak," Bastien scoffed, crushing an old, dry pinecone in his fist. "I am surprised Ulric let her wear it."

Emile considered the sweep of scarlet velvet draping Juliana's back. It was trimmed—appropriately enough—in spotted ermine that Ulric himself had caught. "He wanted her to be comfortable, I expect, and to signal the old ways are passing."

Not passing entirely, of course. Beneath her sop to modesty, Juliana was gloriously bare. She had been a pretty human; now she was a goddess: her figure strong, her carriage confident. Emile felt a flush of pride at their queen's good looks—though he suspected they were in part responsible for Bastien's sourness.

Bastien had been born to rule himself. His nature dictated that he desire the lead female.

"Her eyes are twinkling too much," he groused now. "She looks as though she would rather laugh than fight."

"Would that more queens embraced that attitude," Emile muttered under his breath, then caught himself when Bastien's head snapped around. "I said you should laugh more, old friend. We are safe here, and our pack stands first among them all."

"There is that," Bastien admitted, letting his shoulders sag on a sigh. "And I suppose she cannot be too pacific, or Gytha would not be serving as her right hand."

In tandem, their gaze went to the scowling, black-haired *upyr* who stood next to their queen, radiating every ounce of intimidation Juliana did not. Emile, who was surprised by little, had been stunned by Gytha's determination to hold that job. Not even Juliana's demand that she give Ingrith an overdue apology had put her off.

People can change, he thought, then smiled as Gytha insisted the pack leader from Skye bow a little lower. Thankfully, they did not change too much.

"She would take you back," he said to Bastien, eyeing his brother wolf at a slant. "You only need to smooth her hackles."

Bastien grimaced and waved his hand. "That female is too much trouble. A man hardly dares close his eyes with her in his furs."

"Then you would not mind if I pursued her?"

"You? And *Gytha*?"

Emile grinned at Bastien's open mouth. "She appeals to me. I understand how she feels, always standing just a little on the outside."

Bastien shook his head, though not in refusal. "It is your back that will feel her claws. But you have my blessing if that is what you wish."

Emile confirmed this, pleased he could proceed without offending his friend. Gytha did not know it yet, but she was about to discover how irresistible a brown-eyed Frenchman could be. As for

Bastien . . . Emile paused to study his companion's habitually cool, stern face. Despite their acceptance into the pack, Bastien remained on guard. Emile dreaded what might happen if Ulric discovered he had spied on their queen's transformation, literally pressing his ear to the ground beside the opening for the sun.

"Knowledge is power," Bastien had said when Emile expressed dismay. "If nothing else, Hugo taught me that."

But Emile refused to worry tonight. He doubted Ulric would give Bastien cause to move against him. His rule was too fair and his power too firmly established. It might be centuries before Bastien had the strength to use what he learned. Until such time, he would be more than careful to hide his ambitions—especially with Emile keeping Gytha out of his hair.

Bastien would be better off, for now, with Helewis. That the mothering redhead would approach him seemed assured. She had lost interest in Emile as soon as he was hale. Bastien, on the other hand, still had healing to do.

His world arranged to his liking, at least in his own mind, Emile turned his attention to the dancing that had begun in the trampled dirt. The patterns were dizzyingly intricate, involving wolf form and man and great bursts of *upyr* laughter when the inexperienced missed their steps. Ingrith and Stephen added to the merriment by trying to redirect those who got lost.

In the center Juliana and Ulric spun, part and apart as lovers are wont to be, their cheeks aglow with humor, their eyes as dazzling as the sun. Juliana's cloak whirled with their movements in blood-red arcs. On the other side of the clearing, the elder, Lucius, clapped. He and Helewis sang the instructions that led the dance, their voices twining melodiously. The elder almost looked normal with his face split into a big, wide grin.

This is good, Emile thought, feeling the waves of enjoyment flow through the crowd. This is what our kind was meant to be.

"Come." He nudged Bastien's arm. "Everyone is at peace here. Let us join the fun."

Bastien hesitated, his muscles stiff.

"We need to celebrate," Emile insisted, "because we survived."

He smiled at his too-serious friend, putting his understanding into his eyes. *Your turn will come,* he promised Bastien silently. *Someday, when you are ready to admit you want it, you will have your own pack.*

"Plenty of pretty *upyr* out there tonight," he coaxed aloud. "If you do not claim them, your rivals will."

"Oh, very well," Bastien surrendered, answering his friend with a flash of sharp, white teeth. "I suppose I could manage a dance or two."

# The Night Owl

*To Suzanne Powell,*
*animal-lover extraordinaire*

# One

THE naked man stood at the edge of the forest, looking back over one broad shoulder at Mariann. His hands were braced on a tree trunk and he was leaning forward, as if he were a runner she'd caught stretching out his calves. Partly obscuring her view, his long, dark hair spilled over rugged musculature to his waist.

It was night. She should not have been able to see him, but light shone from him in the darkness, a scintillation of moonlike shine. Whatever the source of the glow, it made his beautiful form even more distinct. His hips were narrow, his buttocks a tight, lip-licking curve. One of his statue-perfect legs was bent. In the space between his thighs, she could just make out the hang of his scrotum.

Watching him, wanting him, Mariann's body tightened with awareness. Fingers curled against her urge to touch, she swallowed and took a step. She knew there had to be a reason she could not see the rest.

The man knew the reason. He smiled with wicked self-assurance. "I've been waiting for you," he said. "Don't you want to come with me?"

---

"CRAP," sighed Mariann O'Faolain as her old-fashioned, windup alarm clock started jangling at 3 A.M.

Her body pulsed with frustration. The last thing she wanted was to shake off her dream. It was, after all, the closest she'd come to getting lucky in the last six months. But that was no reason to hug the pillow. Rolling over, she slapped the ringing silent with a single blow, then blinked into the country dark.

I'm a vampire, she thought, breaking into a crooked grin. Up with the moon and down with the sun.

Her mood improved, she threw the sheets off with a flourish no one was there to see. She had half an hour to shower, dress, suck down a mug of espresso and feed her cat. Then it was off to O'Faolain's, to get in a few uninterrupted hours of baking before the first of the muffin-and-coffee crowd stumbled in. Mariann enjoyed her customers, but she loved baking even more. How could she not? For nearly forty years O'Faolain's had been her second home—more of a home, in fact, than the suburban rambler she'd grown up in. As to that, her current residence, a drafty, nineteenth-century clapboard farmhouse inherited from her grandparents, was much closer to her heart. Fake wood paneling and two-car garages would never be Mariann's style.

Her mind ticking away at her to-do lists, she barely noticed she'd been in and out of the bathroom until she unwound the sopping towel from her mop of tight black curls. A fresh white T-shirt, courtesy of Maynard's Laundry, no-iron chinos, and a pair of sky-blue Keds comprised her uniform for the day—for every day, actually, but Mariann couldn't be bothered to dress like some freaking beanpole out of *Vogue*.

She was a working girl, thank you very much. Comfortable and clean was good enough for her, and naked was strictly for dreams!

Her body still buzzed in memory as she clattered down the creaky stairs. The stove light from the kitchen provided just enough light to see, and she promised herself for the umpteenth time that she'd hire a carpenter to fix the missing spindles on the railing. Her mind skimmed over the vow without a ripple. The peaches had been fantastic this week: juicy, firm, their flesh a rich, ripe yellow that made her mouth water by itself. She'd bake tartlets for the chamber of commerce supper, and maybe whip up a batch of peach caramel ice cream.

Ginger, she thought, pausing on the final tread to have a reverie. Ginger would add the perfect bite.

Coming back to herself with a snap, she skidded across the kitchen's cracked green linoleum and began to hum. With quick, economical movements, she arranged a few chunks of bittersweet Sharffen Berger chocolate onto a heel of crusty French bread, then popped her idea of breakfast into the microwave. Even as she punched the buttons with her left hand, her right lit the burner beneath her shining Italian pot. Grabbing a mug from its hook, she twirled the handle around her finger like a gunslinger, slammed it on the counter and poured a one-ounce blurp of Vermont cream into its maw. Pirate Vic's bowl and kibble became her next partners in the dance, one she'd performed—at first with forced cheer, but now with real—ever since her husband became her ex.

Five years of her life she'd given to that man, four-and-a-half more than he deserved. She should have known not to trust a broker.

"No more stinking, store-bought granola," she sang to the fading daisy print walls. "No more *Wall Street Journal* and God-darned low-fat milk."

"*Gosh*-darned," she corrected as she finished shaking cat food into the bowl.

She'd been trying to cut back on her cursing. With Tom gone, she thought she shouldn't feel the need.

"Here kitty, kitty," she called as she set the kibble on the dark back porch. Pirate Vic, her black-and-white, one-eyed tom (whom Tom had hated, she reminded herself with satisfaction) usually interrupted his nocturnal rambling long enough to let her feed him.

This morning he was either too far away or too entertained by his adventures to heed her call.

She sighed, missing him a little, then decided to eat her breakfast outside. The back steps needed a carpenter's attention as much as her stair rail, but she sat on them all the same. The air was cool and soft, a pleasant start to an August day. Familiar rustles filled the woods that surrounded her scraggly lawn. She owned ten acres, all told, on the southern tail of the Green Mountain spine.

Tom had wanted her to cut down the trees and sell them.

"God bless you, Gramps," she murmured, morning prayers more her style than evening. "Give Grams a kiss for me and, uh, do your bit for world peace."

She was about to try calling Vic again when a shadow slinking through the brambles brought her alert.

"There you are," she cooed, before she realized the intruder could not possibly be a cat.

The shape froze at the sound of her voice, the forward-canted ears obviously canine. It had to be a neighbor's dog. Plenty of folks in Maple Notch let their pets run loose. She expected the dog to flee but, after a pause, it crept foot by silent foot into her yard.

Her first clear sight of it made her pulse patter in her throat.

Her visitor was not dog but wolf, a big, glacial-eyed, gape-jawed beast. Its markings were black, its undercoat a lighter shade she could not make out. Its upcurved tail waved slowly from side to side. It had locked its gaze on hers as if gauging what sort of welcome it would receive. Perhaps unable to decide, it halted midway between the forest and her porch.

It was the wildest, most breathtaking creature she had ever seen. In watching it, she completely forgot her loneliness.

"Omigosh," she whispered, the hair at the nape of her neck prickling like a sunburn. She wasn't sure if she was frightened or simply thrilled. Vermont didn't have wolves. At least, she didn't think they did.

Wherever this one came from, she hoped it hadn't eaten her cat.

The wolf woofed at her as if to object.

"Would you like some kibble?" she offered, thinking the smell of food might have been what drew it. "Or maybe you'd rather try my chocolate?"

The wolf whined at this and resumed its careful forward advance. Maybe it was a crossbreed, or had been raised by humans in a preserve. It certainly didn't appear to be afraid of her. In fact, it was acting like it didn't want to startle her.

The intelligence in its pale, bright eyes made this theory seem less outlandish. At that moment, she wouldn't have been surprised to discover the creature could read her mind.

Trembling, she held her half-eaten bread as far as her arm could reach. When the wolf was close enough to sniff her offering, it sneezed, licked a drip of 62-percent-pure dark chocolate, then delicately took the crust in its teeth. Mariann was almost too shocked to let go, reminded only by a gentle tug. A toss of the wolf's head and a snap of its powerful jaws made the treat disappear.

For a moment, the animal's eyes glowed like hot, green stones. Then, as if all that had gone before hadn't been amazing enough, it crouched down on its forelegs, groveled the tiny distance toward her across the grass, and gave the very tip of her fingers a pink-tongued kiss.

Mariann gasped and snatched back her hand. Immediately the wolf sprang away, trotting toward the trees with its head turned over its shoulder to her. Her imagination lent it a look of regret.

It vanished into the bracken without a sound.

"Wow," she breathed, her hand pressed flat to her pounding chest. Forget sex dreams with naked strangers. This had to be the most exciting morning she'd ever had.

⸺⸻⸺

UNDERSTANDABLY, Mariann's quarter-mile bike ride to the bakery passed in a daze. The winding back road she lived on led pretty much nowhere. She didn't see a single car, parked or otherwise, until

she hit Maple Notch's main street. City people might have been
nervous at the isolation, but Mariann loved it through and through.
Because of a promise to her father, she had her cell phone and her
pepper spray tucked into her fanny pack. Truth be told, though, in
all her time here she'd never come close to needing either one to
protect herself—not even in the height of tourist season. No matter
her upbringing in the burbs, she'd been born to be a small-town
girl.

With an absentminded glow of gratification, she pedaled past
the country store and the post office, then turned left at the one
stoplight.

O'Faolain's wasn't much farther. Formerly a carriage house,
since her grandfather's time the bakery had been an adjunct to the
Night Owl Inn—and one of its prime draws. Guests raved about
the breakfast baskets left at their doors, often coming back just for
them. The current proprietors, who owned the land on which her
bakery sat, were continuing the partnership.

The Luces had caused a stir upon their arrival in Maple Notch.
With their flowing hair and incredibly fit physiques, either of the
tall, dark, handsome cousins could have stepped out of the pages
of a magazine. The older one, in particular, dressed like a front
man for Armani—perpetually on the verge of looking too cool for
the town.

Familial relationship aside, rumors that the Luces were a couple
seemed inevitable. Once raised, however, they were quashed with
surprising speed. No gay man, common female wisdom decided,
could look at a woman like those two did. After encountering the
younger Luce on his nightly run, the owner of the Clip 'n' Curl declared rather breathlessly that she thought he had "wanted to eat
her up."

That she would willingly have been devoured was understood.

If this influx of testosterone weren't sufficient to set tongues
wagging, the cousins were, apparently, filthy rich. Workers were
hired at ungodly wages: architects, plasterers, even a sommelier.

The neighboring antique shops were beside themselves trying to supply the inn with period furnishings. No one doubted the Night Owl would be a Victorian showpiece when it was done. Previously a bastion of shabby kitsch, soon it would be a gem to swell the breasts of all and sundry with local pride.

If the Luces sometimes acted as peculiar as they were rich, that was dismissed as "furrin" eccentricity. They were Frenchmen, after all, and to a native Vermonter that was strange indeed. So what if they had never heard of Ben & Jerry's? So what if they slept all day and had some bizarre allergy that kept them out of the sun? The Luces were giving Maple Notch an unexpected shot in the arm. As long as their checks kept clearing, no one gave a darn what they did.

Mariann herself viewed them warily, though the younger of the two, Emile, was extremely charming. Despite her doubts, she helped them redesign their kitchen and promised to continue supplying them with baked goods. O'Faolain's, they assured her, would always be a valued friend to the Night Owl Inn.

Sometimes she thought she'd have trusted them more if they'd been plain. Her ex had been handsome, a golden boy with a heart of brass. After a brief, six-month honeymoon, during which he'd treated her like a queen, he seemed to view cheating on her as his right: life, liberty and the pursuit of secretaries in short skirts. When Mariann looked at Emile and Bastien, she couldn't help thinking: been there, done that.

If she thought it a little more when she looked at Bastien, that was no one's business but hers. It wasn't his fault he'd been creeping into her dreams.

Shaking off the prejudice—which she admitted had no real cause—she noted the removal of the scaffolding that had obscured the inn's facade for the last few months. Built in the 1840s, the Night Owl resembled a castle more than a house, its granite facade and Gothic windows bringing a touch of olde England to their humble burg. The sward of grass it sat on, smooth enough for a round of golf, put her patchy yard to shame.

She had to admit she was impressed. She'd never seen a reno-
vation move so fast. Then again, maybe the heaps of cash the
Luces tossed around encouraged even the laid-back locals to get in
gear.

Swinging off her old brown Schwinn, Mariann wheeled the bike
the last few feet up the gravel drive. Above her head, the O'Faolain's
sign clanked on its chains. A second plank hung beneath the first.
"Family recipes since 1940," it said, "no matter what anybody
claims."

She nodded approvingly at the addendum and leaned her bike
beneath the front window. O'Faolain's had a small seating area, a
diner-style counter and a kitchen behind that. Since the lights were
on, she knew her assistant must have managed to roll out of bed.
Heather was just eighteen and had a boyfriend. To Heather's credit,
she always showed up . . . just not always on time.

Smiling to herself, Mariann entered and called hello.

"In the kitchen," Heather called back, sounding suspiciously
teary.

Mariann found her glaring at six just-baked trays of mini pie
shells.

"They're not flaky," Heather moaned with all the drama of her
youth. "It looked so easy when you showed me, but no matter what
I did, they turned out flat."

Mariann pinched her lower lip and wondered if she should
scold. It was good of Heather to anticipate her wanting to make
tartlets, but now they'd have to clean up and start from scratch.

"Did you remember to feed the bread starter like I wrote on the
prep board?"

"Yes," Heather quavered, her arms crossed protectively at her
waist, "and I didn't make a mess."

Mariann had already noticed the counters' gleam. Her admoni-
tions for Heather to tidy behind herself were sinking in. What
wasn't sinking in were her reminders not to run before she could
walk. A cooking school dropout whose parents played bridge with

Mariann's, Heather had been a pity hire. At the time, the teenager could barely be trusted to boil eggs.

As if she knew what her boss was thinking, Heather's chin quivered like a child's.

"Oh, honey," Mariann relented, squeezing the girl's shoulder. The kindness made a tear roll down Heather's cheek. With her shining wheat-brown hair and her peachy skin, she was blooming even more than usual. In truth, she looked like an actress crying for the camera. Appearances notwithstanding, Mariann knew the girl's emotions were as real as a summer storm. She was a babe in the woods, and Mariann hadn't the heart to toughen her up.

Business was slow with the inn shut down for renovations. Heather's trial by fire could wait.

"It's just experience," Mariann said. "And my cold Irish hands. They keep the butter from melting in the flour. When I worked in Boston, I knew an Italian who'd plunge his hands in ice water for two whole minutes before he'd look at a ball of dough."

"Yeah, yeah," said Heather, swiping her sleeve across her eyes. "The few, the proud, the pastry chefs."

Mariann laughed, knowing Heather was all right if she was cracking jokes. Heather smiled shyly back.

"You're late," she pointed out with a sly glance toward the clock. Apparently, this unheard-of occurrence improved her mood.

"Hair emergency," Mariann explained to her own surprise. When she left the house, she'd have sworn her *Wild Kingdom* encounter would have been the first thing out of her mouth. Now—though Heather eyed her curls skeptically—she did not retract the lie.

For reasons she didn't care to examine, Mariann wanted to keep her morning visitor to herself.

# Two

BASTIEN Luce stood in the shadows outside the bakery, looking in at its lights. Perfectly still, with a heart that could beat as seldom as once an hour, he opened his senses to search for threats. Few were great enough to harm him. The night was his dominion, the sun his enemy. Humans—had they known of his existence—would have called him vampire. Among his own kind he was *upyr*.

Theirs was a race of shape-shifting immortal beings, part wolf, part blood-drinker, with a power and beauty no other creature could match. Both power and beauty had to be hidden when *upyr* traveled the mortal realm. These days, few could survive without a knack for glamour and thrall, the gifts that allowed them to look like humans and, when that proved impossible, to convince the humans they had not seen what they thought they had. Sadly, there weren't enough wild places left for them to live wholly apart.

Like their four-footed brethren, *upyr* fought to survive. Immortal did not mean indestructible, especially when modern life held so many dangers. Cameras could watch them without their knowledge, doctors could probe their unique genetics, and swordsmen were hardly necessary when any idiot with a buzz saw could lop off their heads. Even broken hearts could drive his kind to their doom.

Bastien didn't think he was in danger of facing that, but he'd definitely had happier times. Not six months ago, he'd been kicked out of his pack.

For the second time in his life, he'd been forced to leave a country he called home—first by a tyrant, now by a friend.

At least his second exile, from Scotland this time, had been kindly done, complete with murmurings of "time you stretched your legs" and "we could really use your help establishing a power base across the pond." No matter what his pack leader, Ulric, said, Bastien knew the truth in his bones.

He was getting too powerful to keep around, powerful enough to be an elder: one of few who could change human into *upyr*. Bastien couldn't be an underling in someone else's pack when his nature drove him to rule his own. Indeed, as the years went by, it seemed inevitable that he would challenge Ulric for rule of his. Bastien's pack leader was much beloved. Even if Bastien could defeat him, the pack wouldn't want him to. They didn't trust him to rule as well.

For that matter, Bastien didn't trust himself.

This, he thought, was why he'd been drawn so strongly to the bakery. Its warmth, its wonderful, comforting scents, the history that clung to it like a spice, pulled him inexorably. He'd already been thinking he'd buy the Night Owl. The inn had the atmosphere he wanted, and ample surrounding land. He'd believed it would repay his investment and hoped it would tempt visits from his friends. It was the sight of O'Faolain's, however, that sealed the deal.

He only wished the sight of its owner hadn't sealed his fate.

Mariann O'Faolain was as tart as one of her pies—a scrappy little woman with wiry muscles and subtle curves. Though her looks were striking, she appeared to have no vanity. Her unstyled mop of hair was as dark as her favorite drink, her eyes like an April sky. She slaved at her business like no one but humans could, twelve hours at a stretch, as if she feared her life would end too soon for her to work herself into the ground. She had no husband—at the moment, anyway—no child, just a town full of admirers and a chewed-looking cat whose spirit was as fierce as hers.

Bastien wanted her with an intensity that set his blood ablaze: to love with, to hunt with, to make her queen to the king he did not dare be. Centuries would not suffice to slake his thirst for her sweetness.

Unfortunately, it looked like centuries would be required for him to muster the nerve to court her. Since meeting her, he hadn't been able to say two words without tripping over his tongue. The closest he'd come to flirting had been his wolf eating from her hand. He hadn't intended to surprise her. He'd simply been unable to resist going to her house.

The Frenchman in him found his clumsiness pathetic. The man in him just felt lost. As the Americans so colorfully put it, falling in love was a bitch.

His friend, Emile, his sole companion in exile, chose then to appear at his side, probably not by his accident. He wore his usual jeans and polo shirt, and tiny lights blinked in the soles of his running shoes. This was an activity he had taken to with a vengeance. Long ago, Emile had nearly lost his legs. The length to which Bastien had gone to save him was something neither of them spoke about. Brothers at heart, they'd always resembled each other, which had led to the fiction that they were kin. Ironically, almost dying had given Emile a more humorous view of life than his supposed cousin. He took things as they came, and gave thanks for what he had.

For a moment, he was content to stand drinking in the night. Sadly, for Emile peace was never as good as the chance to tease.

"You know," he said, a smile in his voice, "Mariann won't bite you if we go in—unless that is what you are hoping for."

Bastien blushed, no easy feat for his kind. He was glad Emile had not witnessed his ridiculous morning tryst.

"Eff you," he said and, as he'd intended, Emile laughed.

"Very good, *mon ami*. Keep that up and soon no one will guess you were born anywhere but here."

With Emile there watching, it was impossible to hang back. Emile might have been Bastien's best friend for hundreds of years, might have seen him at his very worst, but that didn't mean Bastien wanted to be thought a coward.

He had taken a single step when Emile gave the back of Bastien's suit a shake.

"Hold it," he said. "Leave this off, old friend, and loosen that starchy collar. For once you need to quit pretending you are here on business. No woman wants to be wooed by a stick."

"Fine." Bastien removed his jacket, tossed it into the bushes and attacked the small white button that trapped his neck. Then, to prove he would not do this halfway, he rolled up his sleeves as well.

"*C' est bien*," said Emile. "Now you are casual."

Gritting his teeth to hide his agitation, Bastien pushed through the bakery door. From previous visits, he knew the CLOSED sign did not mean locked. The people of this town were alarmingly unparanoid. Inside, the decor was that of a fifties diner—not re-created but preserved, with all the cracks and worn spots left intact. Bastien had enjoyed the decade as he recalled: the films of Gary Cooper, rock and roll, the smell of cheeseburgers on a grill.

It was odd to think Mariann hadn't been born yet.

He'd been more alone than he knew.

Shivering, he trailed his hand along the counter's silvery trim, his heart thumping faster at the prospect of seeing the object of his dreams. The things he longed to do to her would have made her hair curl even more; his need to possess her was quite savage. Awkward or not, her company had become as necessary to him as food.

"*Bon soir*," Emile called toward the kitchen door. "We have come to keep you lovely ladies company."

"Emile!" Heather exclaimed as she bounded out, her floppy chef's hat nearly falling off. "You're just in time to get me out of the doghouse."

Unlike himself and Mariann, Heather and Emile had become fast friends within instants of their meeting, as evidenced by the laughing kisses they gave each other's cheeks. As far as Bastien could tell, the girl didn't have a suspicious bone in her body. Emile barely had to use his glamour to trick her into thinking he looked human. Perhaps, young and pretty as she was, she was blasé about handsome men. At the least, Bastien knew she was not cowed by him.

"Late night?" she joked, cocking one brow at him.

"Planning," he said as he tried not to peer too obviously behind her shoulder. "For the leaf peepers in the fall. We're thinking of having a grand opening in time to take advantage of the tourists who come to see the colors change. When we finished brainstorming, we decided to stop by for a cup of joe."

"Sur-re," Heather said in her teenage drawl. "Cuz coffee is what everyone wants before they toddle off to bed."

Bastien wasn't certain, but he thought he saw her exchanging winks with Emile.

"Relax," she said at his frown. "Cinderella has pots to scrub, but I'll get the boss to set you up."

His palms immediately went damp. "Only if she's not too busy."

"We're always busy," Heather teased, "but never too busy to make time for you."

With his keen *upyr* hearing, Bastien couldn't miss the whispered argument that ensued behind the kitchen wall. The words "pretty boy" and "weirdo" were particularly clear. Apparently, Mariann didn't want to see him. His ears grew hot with a shame he hadn't felt since he was human.

"Get out there," the teenager hissed at the last, "and for God's sake get a life!"

When Mariann emerged, Bastien prayed his face was not as pink as hers. He didn't know why, but he found her completely adorable in her buttoned-up baking jacket—not the most opportune reaction, considering her response to him.

"The usual?" she asked, immediately busying herself at the elaborate coffee-making machine.

"Please," he said, then cleared his throat. "With a cup of water."

Emile's interjection was too soft for anyone but him to hear. "Very smooth," he said. "I'm sure you've almost got her now."

Bastien had to admit his friend was right to mock. At this rate, Bastien would be dust before he and Mariann held hands.

"You look pretty today," he blurted out desperately, his eyes honing helplessly on her nape, so slim and bitable. Cursing to himself, he tried to quash his arousal. The last thing he needed was to flash his fangs. "Your hair, um, looks very free."

The sound Mariann made was more snort than laugh. " 'Free' is what my hair does best."

To his relief, when she turned to set his coffee and water on the counter, she was smiling. For the first time in what seemed like ages, she met his eyes. Hers were so warm and soft he could have drowned. "You know, Mr. Luce, if the espresso is too strong for you, I can make drip."

"No," he said, his voice gone dark, his hand moving impulsively to cover hers. "I like the way your espresso tastes."

In all their meetings, he had been careful not to thrall her, wanting her to fall for him on her own. Despite his restraint, she went as still at his touch as if he had. Her pupils swelled, her delicate, rosy lips parting for breath. She wore no lipstick. All her colors were her own, from the flush on her cheeks to the tiny freckles on her nose.

I love you, he thought, force of will all that kept the sentiment inside his head. I would do anything to make you mine.

"It's Bastien," he corrected, some scrap of his brain still functioning. "Not Mr. Luce."

"Bastien," she said dazedly.

A smile spread across his face. She might think he was a weirdo, but she was warming to him all the same. He could hear it in her voice. He felt himself all of a sudden confident and masculine.

"Mariann," he said, letting his accent soften her name. "Would you like to—"

He would never know if his invitation to dinner would have been accepted. The outside door slammed open and a tall blonde bombshell stalked inside. Shaped like an expensive hourglass from bust to hip, she wore a snug-fitting, ash-gray suit, her debt to Marilyn obvious. A diamond as big as a blueberry sparkled on her left hand. Despite her bursting in like a squall, not a hair on her head was mussed. She was just as fresh as if it were ten in the morning instead of five. Whoever she was, either she got up early herself, or she'd put some planning into this entrance.

At her appearance, Mariann yanked her hand from his.

With one frosted pink nail, the woman pointed at his beloved. "You," she said, "had better stop spreading lies."

Mariann lifted her sharp little chin. "Which lies would those be? That you stole my grandfather's recipes or that you ran off with my husband? You're welcome to him, by the way, with my thanks."

Bastien had tensed in preparation to protect her, but Mariann's quick retort assured him there was no need. The other woman might have been grateful if he'd interfered. An unhealthy shade of brick washed her sculpted cheeks.

"You were always jealous of me," she said. "Always hoarding your little secrets, pretending I wasn't good enough to bake your precious grandfather's pies. But the whole world knows I'm good enough now. If you keep trying to smear my name, the studio's lawyers will sue your stupid, no-iron pants off."

"Really? Even if I can prove every word I say?"

"You can't." The woman's confidence was clear as she tossed her head. "It's your word against mine."

"Not exactly." With a smile that would have done a Borgia proud, Mariann brought a stained leather journal from beneath the counter. She set it on the clean glass top of the display case next to the register. "This is my grandfather's recipe book, which tracks the development of every signature dessert he made, from 1940 on. I had the paper, the handwriting and the ink authenticated by a lab. So you see, Arabella, when I spoke to that reporter at the *Boston Globe*, I had evidence to back up my claims."

Her breath hissing through her nose, the woman grabbed for the book. Bastien slapped his hand on top of it before she could. She gaped at him as if he were mad, then turned dismissively back to Mariann.

"You're nothing," she said. "Just a small-town Betty Crocker who hasn't the sense to hold on to anything she has. I proved it eighteen months ago when we split and, believe me, I will again."

She swept out as regally as she'd swept in, leaving the grounds with a squeal of tires. Bastien broke the silence by sneezing at her perfume. Heather's response was more deliberate.

"So," she said, "that was the famous Arabella Armand. Can't say I'm terribly impressed."

"She's usually more charming," Mariann said tightly. "She saves the Hyde side of her personality for her friends."

Heather laughed, but Mariann made a sound like a hiccup and ran into the kitchen.

"Stay," Bastien said when Heather would have followed. "I'll make certain she is all right."

He put a touch of thrall into the command. The girl fell back like a doll.

"Careful," Emile said as he caught her shoulders.

Bastien knew the warning was meant for him.

He would listen, just not right then.

---

MARIANN'S kitchen was bigger than her café, with stainless-steel cabinets and a terra-cotta floor sloping to a drain. Everything about it was oversized: the overhead lights, the counters, the convection ovens and range. The refrigerated walk-in required a stepladder, and was stocked with hunks of chocolate and butter better fit for giants. That such a tiny female ruled this domain filled him with amusement—not that Mariann ever seemed less than up to the task.

He found her at the butcher-block island, splitting what had to be a real vanilla bean with a knife. As she scraped the seeds the smell overwhelmed his senses: a pungent sweetness that managed to combine homey kitchen and jungle. His body hardened as only an *upyr*'s could, in the space between mortal heartbeats, with a gut-punching thoroughness that nearly buckled his knees. His formerly modest Italian trousers lost their perfect drape, while the itching in his gums warned him his fangs were very close to shooting out.

"I'm fine," she said curtly before he could speak, lifting her elbow high enough to blot her eyes. "I have work to do."

Standing behind her, seeing the prideful stiffness of her spine, he felt as he had been creeping toward her across her yard, desiring contact so badly he would risk frightening her away.

He put his arms around her, gently, slowly, stilling her wrists with his hands. Her fingers were scarred from years of kitchen work: cut, dinged, callused, burned, dried from constant washing and cracked along the seams. He knew she was proud of every imperfection. Many times, when she did not know he watched, he would see her turn them back and forth and smile.

"You're not fine," he said, his nose nudging softly behind her ear. This close to her, with their auras mingling, he could not help but sense her troubled emotions. He had always respected her privacy, but he was too good a mind reader not to catch a wisp of her feelings now. "That woman upset you."

Mariann sniffed out a laugh. "Arabella would be terribly insulted to know you didn't recognize the Cooking Channel's newest darling."

Bastien acknowledged no darling but her. Humming at the pleasure of finally having her in his arms, he drew his lips across the silken skin where his nose had been.

Mariann began to tremble. "You shouldn't be doing this. You're my landlord."

He didn't see what that had to do with anything, but humans did sometimes have strange rules. He slipped his fingertips between the knuckles of her battered hands, which caused her little knife to clatter to the floor. Her head sagged back against his shoulder, baring the line of her throat. Among his kind, this was a gesture of surrender, sexual and otherwise.

His voice sank unavoidably to a growl. "I've been wanting to get close to you since we met."

Her answer was a broken sigh. "You're making it worse."

"How can my holding you cause any harm?"

He kept his tone as soothing as he could, but her neck snapped up again. "The harm is that I don't want to cry!"

He let her turn in his arms, but did not release her from the cage they formed. True to her words, her face was streaked by fresh tears. In spite of this, or possibly because of it, her soft blue eyes blazed with defiance, her passion an aphrodisiac to one like him.

Only her vulnerability called to him more.

"You haven't been held in a while," he said, his blood surging at the thought of everything else she might not have done. "That's why my touch makes you weep."

Sheepish, she ducked her head. "Tom never was much of a hugger."

"An unfortunate trait in a husband."

"I thought so. I mean, I wasn't asking him to hug the world. Only me." She had been gaining in composure, trying to joke, but her voice cracked on the last and she made a face. "Honestly, I don't care. He's a jerk, and I'm better off without him."

"You are," Bastien agreed. "By a thousand times."

"What she did was worse," Mariann said, and Bastien knew she meant Arabella. "We survived the restaurant scene in Boston, two women turning out hundreds of plates a night with those stupid, ass-grabbing line cooks. She convinced me to bring her here as my partner after Grandfather died. We were friends. I thought she liked me. And then she pretends my grandfather's work is her own. 'A little

something I came up with,' she says on her show. The first time I
heard it, I thought my head would explode.

"In all the time I worked with her, she never came up with anything. She could cook, but she was lazy. Her first question was always, 'What's the shortcut?' But good baking comes from love,
from the desire to create something your customers will really and
truly enjoy. You can't take shortcuts with that!"

Disgusted by the memory, Mariann rubbed her nose. When she
went on, her tone was resigned. "I never did want to share his
recipes with her, but I thought, 'Well, she's not just my partner,
she's my friend. I should learn to be more trusting.' Hah. All I did
was hand her everything I had."

"Everything you have is here," he said, one hand reaching up to
tap her heart. "At least everything that counts."

"Thank you, Zen Master Luce. I'm sure I'd agree with you if I
were equally evolved."

"All right," he laughed, enjoying her acerbity. "You have a reason to be mad."

She blinked at him. "Why are you being so nice? You barely
said 'boo' to me before today."

Her eyes were wide, her expression willing to hear. Sensing she
would allow it, he stroked his fingers through her curls. Though his
power undid the tangles, the little twists clung to his hand as if they
liked the touch. "Maybe I was waiting for you to think of me as
more than a pretty weirdo."

"Yeesh. I'm sorry you heard that. I—"

"No." He touched her lips to hush her apology. "I'm sure I do
seem strange. I only hope you'll give me the chance to show you
what else I am, what else I'd like to be to you."

"Be?" she repeated. "To me?"

This time he could not miss her breathlessness. Arousal barreled
through him in a roaring wave. It was all he could do not to moan.

*Oh, Mariann,* he thought. *I'm going to kiss you to kingdom
come.*

# Three

———◦———

S HE knew he was going to kiss her. Worse, she knew she was going to let him. Never mind she'd sworn off unfairly good-looking men. Never mind her schedule barely had room for her schedule. When his hands surrounded her face and his dark, silky hair fell forward, her temperature sizzled like butter set to sauté.

Close as he was, his scent shot up her nose, sending her already buzzing hormones into overdrive. His skin smelled of wood and earth, of mossy water and Beaujolais. He had rolled up his shirt-sleeves and opened his collar. She didn't think she'd ever seen him without a jacket. For some reason, she found the sight of his mus-cled forearms sexier than another man completely bare—not that she hadn't entertained the thought of him that way as well.

To her dismay, he was giving her the laser-beam look he shared with his cousin, like she was the only woman left on the planet and he would give his life to have her. Mariann didn't anticipate that kind of sacrifice being required. She was going to topple quite easily.

"Your hands are cold," she said in a nervous bid for delay. "I should teach *you* to make pie."

"My hands will warm."

He said this with such sensual promise she doubted he'd understood. Up close, his eyes were a pale peridot green, their brilliance heightened by their half-lowered frame of black. Their steadiness unnerved her, the way they seemed to pierce her soul. It was probably her sex-starved imagination, but his gaze looked sad, as if he longed for something he feared he would never find. Without intending to, she held her breath as the look drew out.

He broke the tension before she could.

"Ah, Mariann," he said with an embarrassed laugh. "I've been dreaming of kissing you for so long, I'm almost afraid to do it."

"You better get over that. 'Cause I swear, if you leave me hanging, I'll never give you another chance."

His grin was a blinding flash. "I love your fight," he whispered, "most of all."

She didn't have time to wonder what this meant, because he tipped her head up and lowered his. His mouth molded over her lips, a gentle, testing intimacy. Whatever the test was, she passed it. He moaned low in his chest, the loveliest sound she'd ever heard a person make. His arms slid down her back and tightened as his tongue went deep.

He tasted as good as he smelled. In moments, her head was spinning with the erotic rush. As if he knew, he savored his victory, refusing to hurry a lick or pull, enticing her to respond in kind. She sighed with pleasure as she accepted. To her mind, nothing was better than a man who loved to kiss, and every indication said Bastien did.

She couldn't suppress a whimper when he stopped.

"Touch me," he said, the merest breath against her trembling mouth. "Put your hands on my skin."

"Heather might—"

"Heather is perfectly safe with Emile." His gaze burned into her from inches away, mesmerizing, penetrating, trying to convey some message she could not quite read. "Your touch is what I want most. It's what I crave."

If she'd ever doubted he was strange, this would have capped it. What sort of man talked this way? But his strangeness didn't matter. Directed by cravings of their own, her fingers found the finely woven cotton of his business shirt, smoothing it up his chest. His pecs were steely, his shoulders broad enough to ride. He wore no tie, and at his throat one strong, blue vein pulsed out a wild rhythm.

"Do it," he said, then swallowed hard.

Gripping his shirt at the back, she tugged its tails out from his trousers. For a moment, she thought of ripping it another seam. With shaking hands, she slid her arms beneath.

Whatever she was expecting, it was not this. His back felt like moon-cooled marble under her palms, impossibly smooth, invitingly firm and strong.

He jerked as if her touch had burned him, then closed his eyes. "Yes-s," he hissed, a sound of rapture. "I love your heat."

"You're freezing!" she exclaimed, chafing her hands up his spine.

Swearing softly, he lifted her off her feet.

His next kiss silenced what was left of her yammering brain. It had been ages since anyone had kissed her and, in truth, no one had ever done it with such concentrated, pent-up need. Skill aside, his enthusiasm was flattering: probing, sucking, tilting his head or hers to find new variations of their perfect fit.

When he nipped her lower lip and tugged it, she felt devoured, just as Linda at the Clip 'n' Curl had longed to be. She was glad her nails were short because her fingers dug into his skin. Groaning, he set her on the cutting block, pulled her legs apart and stepped between.

*Whoa*, thought Mariann, her eyes going wide as she registered the length and breadth of what he was beginning to grind against her, slowly, fiercely, with a gasp that sounded like relief. Her hands clutched his back in amazement. Who'd have expected a man so meticulously put together would sport an erection this rude? The surprise of it aroused her, the thrill as undeniable as it was cheap.

Not only was he harder than the eighteen-year-old boys she'd nearly forgotten, Bastien Luce was seriously hung.

Like some dewy-eyed ingenue, she found herself wondering if he would fit.

To hell with that, she decided. She'd make him fit . . . and enjoy every rock-hard inch.

With a curse, he moved his mouth to her neck. "I won't hurt you," he said, panting like a runner against her pulse. "Please do not think it."

"No," she assured him just as heavily. "Never crossed my mind."

This was true, though he was uncannily quick with his hands. She wasn't sure when he had removed it, but her chef's jacket, the one they all called whites, was gone. Now he was pushing her T-shirt up her belly, stroking the skin he uncovered bit by bit. A tingle spread from beneath his fingers, as if he were infused with electricity. She half expected to see sparks.

The effect he had on her was disconcerting. She was no slave to her needs, no silly romantic to go spineless at holding hands. But she squirmed at the sensations, her body growing hotter with every touch. She fought a groan as his palms smoothed around her ribs to pop the clasp of her plain beige bra.

Since Mariann was no centerfold, normally this was the point where she got self-conscious. Bastien didn't give her a chance.

"Look at you," he breathed, both thumbs sweeping arcs across her now bare breasts. Caught at their edges, her areolae swelled and itched. She held her breath as he bent his head.

Even though she was expecting it, her back arched uncontrollably as his mouth fastened on one peak. She barely noticed the caresses of his second hand. His tongue was clearly cleverer than the common run, finding nerves she hadn't known she had. As her muscles threatened to turn to water, he laid her back against the knife-scored wood of her worktable. He was suckling strongly, making small, hungry noises as if he liked what he was doing as much as she did.

The vanilla bean she'd been splitting crushed beneath her back.

On top of everything else, the scent was more than she could take, the sense that he had pushed into a sphere no other lover had been a part of. The kitchen was her fortress against the world. Suddenly her heels were locked in the small of his back and she was grinding against him. She'd never been so desperate for a climax, so hot and needy and tight.

"God," he choked, breaking free of her breast and breathing hard. His palm slid smoothly up her hip. "Please. Allow me."

Beyond inhibitions, she ripped her zipper down herself, inviting his hand to slip over her mound and between her folds. He sucked in air as he found her wetness. She was more than slick; she was drowning. Without resistance, two of his fingers slipped inside. His thumb rubbed slow, firm circles against her clit.

"Go ahead," he rasped, reading the way her muscles tensed. "Squeeze your thighs around my wrist."

She obeyed his coaxing without hesitation. What he was doing felt better than she could believe, better than anyone had ever done for her, better—she thought with astonishment—than she could do for herself.

Maybe she should have tried a Frenchman long ago.

A particularly sharp ache of pleasure dragged his name from her throat. His eyes came up, shocking her with their fire. His face was strained, his lips pressed whitely over his teeth. The sight told her how selfish she was being.

"You don't have to do this," she said.

He laughed and she realized with something like awe that he was shaking. "You don't know me very well if you think that."

"But you—"

"*I* want to watch you come."

She had an orgasm as he said it, a sweet, unexpected burst that seemed to swell just from the husky growl of his voice.

When it ended, his tongue curled out to wet his upper lip.

"There's a start," he said with a humor that robbed her embarrassment of its sting. "In case you haven't guessed, however, I'm a bit more orally fixated."

Any question about what he meant vanished when he yanked her sweaty chinos down to her knees. His hands slid up to caress her legs, kneading deeply where they met her torso. She fought an urge to close her knees, unable to doubt he liked what he saw. His eyes were glittering with admiration. With a salacious grin, he squeezed her admittedly well-formed thighs.

"Must be the bike," he said. "Bet you'll wrap me good."

"Bastien—" Her protest was lost as he dropped down on his knees. Abruptly off balance, she grabbed his hair. He had swooped onto her without warning, but any thought of objection dissolved into a soundless *wow*. Everything he'd put into his kisses, he brought to this. And this was a man who could tie cherry stems in double time.

She gasped as he found her favorite spot and teased it with his tongue, faster and faster, one hand massaging her sheath while his second formed a V pointing downward from above his mouth. Those fingers pressed broader, subtler nerves, spreading sensation throughout her groin. The pleasure was almost frightening. Her skin was humming, her toes curled hard. She tried to keep quiet but could not, mewling and twitching until her hips bucked upward and her body seized deliciously from head to toe.

He gave her a second to gulp for air, then pushed her over again. This climax was even sweeter, more than her greediest hunger could have asked. She was helpless beneath the spasms, gripped by ripples of joyous surfeit for long minutes. Her muscles were as warm as cinnamon when she relaxed.

"Wow," she sighed, the word coming out at last.

He was quiet, but she felt him smile, his cheek resting on her pubis, his hand spread across her abdomen.

To her surprise, she was stroking his decadently lengthy hair. She didn't know when she'd started and wasn't sure she could stop, though it seemed—perversely, perhaps, given their recent actions—a too-intimate thing to do. His hair was thicker than she expected but just as silky. The strands felt strong when she combed them up off his back, more like a cat's than a human being's. She smiled to herself, thinking she'd better not let Pirate Vic suspect he had competition.

"Thank you," Bastien said in a sleepy tone.

Mariann had to laugh. "You know, I'm pretty sure that's my line."

When his head came up, a trick of the light set his eyes aglow. "I wish I could stay, but dawn is coming, and I know you still have to work."

Mariann's hands clapped against her cheeks. How could she have forgotten so completely who and where she was?

"Don't worry," he said, helping her slide off the table and into her clothes. "Emile will have made certain Heather didn't hear. No one will gossip about what we did."

"Nice friend you have." She fought a wisp of unease as he turned her gently to do up her bra.

"The best," he reassured her. Momentarily shy, she tucked her T-shirt in by herself. When she faced him again, he cupped her face in his big, smooth hand. His skin was warm now, just as he'd vowed. "I meant it when I said thank you. I know you don't trust lightly."

"I feel bad. You didn't . . . I mean, it's not like I think we ought to be going at it in my kitchen, or that you should risk, uh, aggravating your allergy, but—"

He stopped her nattering by taking her hand and placing it squarely over his crotch. He didn't have to encourage her more than that. Her fingers curled around his huge erection of their own accord, surrounding his balls and shaft in summer-thin Italian wool. There was, she realized, nothing under that cloth but him. She remembered her dream, where she'd seen the furry hang of him from behind. He was just as hard as she'd imagined then, though she hadn't imagined quite so much of him. Within her hold, his blood pulsed with enthralling steadiness and force.

It would have taken a stronger woman than her to resist the chance to explore.

He didn't wince when she squeezed him, though his normally ivory face turned a dusky rose. Mariann's throat tightened with excitement. She sensed he'd let her do anything, try anything, and never utter a complaint.

"Don't you wrinkle?" she asked, suddenly noting the state of his shirt.

Eyes dancing with laughter, he shook his head. "I'm preternaturally tidy."

"Preternaturally, huh?" The catch in his breath delighted her as her nails dragged back along his trouser's seam. "You know that makes me want to muss you more."

He caught her hand before she could. "I should warn you," he said with a hint of roughness. "If you were touching me this way, skin to skin, with your bare palm against my cock, I wouldn't care where we were or what work you had left to do. I'd throw you down and fuck you on the village green."

His slurred Parisian accent made the words sound like poetry. She had a feeling he meant every one.

"Boy, oh, boy," she said once she caught her breath, "do you make a girl want to play hooky!"

His smile could only be described as wolfish, his eyes once again catching some stray gleam. He lifted her hand from between his legs, making an oddly sexy gesture of licking her palm. "I look forward to you making this up to me," he said, "when your schedule allows."

He was smart to leave the timing up to her. If he'd been pushy, she might have balked. Now she wasn't sure how long she could wait. Right then, a minute sounded like an eternity.

"I could maybe leave a little early—"

"No," he said, caressing the side of her neck as he kissed her brow. "Don't regret leaving me this way. You've satisfied at least one of my appetites. In fact"—his lips curled against her forehead—"you're the best breakfast I ever had."

She wasn't used to men being this nice. Flustered but secretly pleased, she searched for a joke. "Just don't expect me to be serving this to your guests."

To her pleasure, he left on a laugh.

---

AS Bastien neared the hidden entrance to his and Emile's quarters, the sun was trembling behind the trees, declaring its approach by adding heaviness to his limbs. Contrary to current fictional belief, the first few rays would not kill him, merely make him drunk and rob him of the sense it took to know when he'd had enough. Thirty minutes of full exposure would probably prove sufficient to set him alight, and less for serious burns. The more power an *upyr* had, the more sunlight he could withstand. The danger lay in growing addicted. *Upyr* who did that tended to die young.

Despite the risk, Bastien felt the lure of oblivion now.

Being in love was a powerful lot of work. His emotions were rocketing up and down like a roller coaster. Yes, he was happy he and Mariann had finally connected, but he couldn't fight his sense of waiting for the other shoe to drop. Would the gods grow jealous and yank her away? Could someone like him deserve to be content?

Screw deserving it, he thought. He'd take what he wanted and be damned.

Emile broke into his distraction. "Bastien," he called. "It's time to get underground."

He waited by the entrance to their retreat, a cleverly fashioned boulder that swung around on a pivot to reveal a flight of black granite stairs. In case this camouflage was not enough, magic also hid the opening from human eyes, runes so old their origins were lost in myth. Bastien had inscribed them reluctantly. Experience had taught him to be mistrustful of magic's power.

"I'm coming," he said and descended behind his friend. He gave his shoulders a shake. No doubt the dawn was aggravating his moodiness.

As soon as his head was clear of the door, an electric eye instructed it to swing shut. Just as convenient were the tiny lights set into the stairway's arched ceiling. Arranged to resemble the constellations, their low illumination was perfect for *upyr* eyes. The electricians had done a marvelous job, as had all his builders. Bastien regretted that he had to thrall their memories when they were done. Proficiency like theirs deserved to be recalled.

Then again, it was Bastien's power—and Bastien's bite—that had spurred them to their best. Nothing like a dose of blood-enhanced *upyr* mind power to keep your hired hands in line.

Once they stepped off the long stairs, a handsome Indian carpet lined the tunnel's heart-of-pine floor. Despite the obligatory lack of windows, the twelve-foot ceilings made the passage appear spacious. With the ease of long acquaintance, Emile and Bastien's footsteps fell into synchrony.

"This place is great," Emile crowed as he often did upon coming home. "Much more comfortable than Ulric's cave."

Though true, the reminder of Bastien's exile increased the leadenness in his gut. His legs temporarily refused to go on.

"She's the one," he announced hollowly.

Emile stopped a second after he did. "The one what?"

"My queen. Mariann is my queen. She makes me want to claim my destiny."

Emile snorted and resumed walking.

Bastien hastened to catch up. "You think I'm delusional."

"I think you're the slowest *upyr* I ever met. You should have claimed your kingship centuries ago."

"You of all people know why I can't."

"I know why you believe you can't. My opinion diverges."

Emile was probably the only *upyr* alive who could contradict him with impunity. Even with their long friendship, Bastien's hands balled into angry fists. "If I can't win her—"

"Yes, I know," Emile sighed, "you'll throw yourself off a cliff."

His condescension made Bastien grab his arm. To his annoyance, Emile's eyes were laughing when he spun around. "How can I win her when I can't tell her who I am?"

"Today you can't tell her. Next month or next year may be a different story." Emile rubbed his arm as Bastien released it. "Leave it to time and nature. Be satisfied you made a start."

"She does like me," Bastien said, his memory of her smile making him bounce on his toes. "More than I thought. But maybe I rushed her. She hasn't been divorced very long. Maybe I took advantage of her loneliness."

"*Mon Dieu!*" Emile exclaimed, forking his hands through his hair. "All's fair, you idiot. How do you think people fall in love?"

"I don't know," Bastien said, taken aback by Emile's ire. "I've never tried to do it before."

"Pah. You are a shame to your countrymen. I don't know why I stay friends with you."

This time Bastien knew Emile was teasing. He slung his arm around the other's shoulder. "You stay friends with me because you love me . . . almost as much as I love the fair Mariann."

"Oh, no." Emile shook his head. "The good Lord save me from that!"

# Four

———

ROUND about two in the afternoon, once Heather's tattooed boyfriend had loaded their last delivery into his van, Mariann was ready to call it a day.

Heather and Eric had been full of giggles, chasing each other around the lot like kids. Their antics made her smile in spite of her fatigue. She'd gotten through her work on automatic pilot, luck and experience all that kept her from culinary catastrophe. Her thoughts had been too occupied with Bastien to try for more.

She could still feel his hands smoothing up her thrumming body, still taste his kiss in her mouth. What she couldn't decide was whether giving in to him had been wise. He had been considerate, even endearing in his pursuit. Since when, after all, could a woman like her make a man like that so shy? But was it instinct that urged her to trust him, or should she chalk the inclination up to lust?

If she were honest, the answer would probably have little to do with what happened next. With a philosophic shrug for her libido, Mariann tipped two fingers to Harv, their senior citizen counter guy.

The bakery's tables were mostly full, and a family of rumpled tourists had their noses pressed with complete enchantment to the display case. Standing slightly behind her brood, the harried mother smiled. She looked as if she could identify with Mariann's long day.

"Lemon meringue pie," Mariann suggested, grinning back with equal fellowship. "Loaded with vitamins. Hardly any calories at all."

When the woman laughed, Mariann knew she'd pleased her.

"Ice cream's sellin' good," Harv called as she slipped out. "Better make another batch tonight."

"Will do," Mariann agreed.

Outside, her momentary cheeriness drained away. Her weight was barely enough to depress the pedals of her bike. Luckily, the ride home was mostly downhill. Too tired to cook just for herself, she made a meal of soup straight out of the can, peeled off her clothes and fell into bed.

To her disappointment, she didn't dream of Bastien. Instead, sometime past ten her eyelids flew up.

"Crap," she said to the ceiling. "Crap, crap, crap."

Pirate Vic, who must have curled up at her feet while she was sleeping, mewed politely in inquiry.

She'd left her grandfather's recipe book at the bakery, right under the counter where Arabella had watched her take it out. Groaning, Mariann shoved off the covers and got dressed, too annoyed with herself to laugh at Vic's attempts to steal her socks. She pulled them on, cat spit and all, then stroked his scruffy head in consolation. It was too much to hope that the journal would be safe where it was. As far as Mariann knew, her former partner still had her key.

She'd been meaning to change the locks, in a vague sort of I-should-get-to-that way. Other things had always seemed more important and then, as month after month went by without incident, it seemed silly to bother. In the end, she'd forgotten the whole idea.

Unfortunately, with her new career at stake, and her dubious sense of honor, Arabella was sure to heed temptation's call.

She biked to the bakery in a sweat, only to find the journal exactly where she'd left it. Relieved, she hugged the book to her breast.

"Thank you," she breathed to whatever guardian angel was watching over her. She didn't think she could bear to let Arabella steal any more than she had.

Tucking the journal safely in her basket, she reversed direction, pedaling slowly to enjoy the ride. Since Maple Notch wasn't known for its nightlife, she had the two-lane road to herself. She patted her fanny pack to check the presence of her cell phone, then just relaxed. Tourist season was good, but so was this emptiness. More at peace than she'd been in months, she filled her lungs with sweet rural air. The temperature was balmy, the stars like gems in the ribbon of black the treetops left. She was young—more or less—and healthy and quite possibly about to embark on a hot affair. Small-town Betty Crocker or not, she doubted life got much better.

The approach of a car behind her seemed no cause for fear. Her bike had reflectors, and her shirt was white. Certain she could be seen, she shifted onto the shoulder without bothering to look around.

Only when the car revved its engine did her adrenaline begin to spurt.

---

BASTIEN'S muzzle came up as his wolf-nose caught Mariann's scent. Appetite sated by a fat raccoon, he and Emile had been chasing rabbits playfully through the woods, racing back and forth, and generally having fun. He'd welcomed the distraction, but now the hope of seeing the source of his romantic worries seemed fortuitous.

*Chocolate!* thought the part of him that was not man, and, *Get a scratch behind the ear!*

Heedless of whose land he ran on, he galloped eagerly toward the smell.

He found it just in time to see the car roar around the bend.

It was a big, black Mercedes, running fast without its lights, nearly invisible on the mountain road. If that weren't alarming enough, its wheels suddenly swerved toward Mariann. An instant of denial paralyzed him in his tracks. Why was the driver going so fast? Surely whoever it was had to see her! But the bike fender twanged as it was clipped. Mariann went flying into the trees, farther than he would have thought she could, too shocked to cry out.

His world dimmed sickeningly at the sound of her skull hitting a rock, knowing at once that it wasn't a mild injury. Back on the road, brakes whined to a stop.

No, he thought. *No, no, no.*

A car door opened. A woman's heels clacked hurriedly.

"Jesus," muttered Emile. "She isn't calling 911. She's rummaging through the bike."

The words meant nothing. Though Bastien had no memory of changing, he knelt in human form beside Mariann. He was lucky he was in the habit of using his glamour. Otherwise, he would have lit up the road. Mariann lay sprawled and awkward behind a screen of weeds, a broken marionette smeared with blood and dirt. This couldn't be happening, not when he'd finally found her.

"Yes!" hissed a voice that seemed familiar. A car door slammed. Tires spun. The Mercedes scattered gravel as it left.

Bastien tried to breathe.

"She's gone," Emile said, appearing beside him. "She took Mariann's book. Is Mariann still alive?"

Her pulse beat so feebly in her throat that even with his *upyr* senses, Emile had to ask.

"Yes." Bastien's voice was a croak. He didn't dare touch her pallid cheek. "Barely."

Emile sank to his knees and gripped Bastien's shoulder. "Do it," he said. "Change her. If you wait any longer, there won't be time."

"I can't." Cold tears trickled down his face. "She's unconscious. She can't say yes or no. The *Upyr* Code—"

"Fuck the Code. In all the time I've known you, she's the only woman you've ever loved. If she wants a choice, she can have it after you save her."

Bastien lifted her limp, curled hand as if it were glass. For once, her skin was chillier than his. She did not move as he pressed her fingers to his heart. "I've never transformed a mortal. I've only watched others do it. If my power isn't up to it—"

"Your power is fine. All you need is the will."

Emile coaxed the hand that cradled Mariann's up to Bastien's mouth. Cold though it was, the scent of her flesh made him tense with longing. "Drink, Bastien. Just a little. It will make changing her easier."

This, too, was forbidden to Bastien's kind: to feed from humans when they had no chance to resist. He discovered he did not care. Whatever happened, he would carry a part of her within his being.

He moaned in anguish as his fangs slid free, praying to he knew not what. Let her live, he thought. *Let her live.* Within his gentle hold, her wrist bone was as delicate as a bird's. He pierced the vein and took a single swallow. She tasted of joy and sorrow, sweet beyond his wildest dreams. Despite everything, there was pleasure in the act of feeding, a quickening of sense and flesh. He had to force himself to release her. Her strength was too slight to risk taking more.

Emile's eyes glowed in sympathy. "She is inside you," he said huskily. "Use the bond of blood to make that of flesh."

Bastien thought her eyelids fluttered, but could not say for sure. Death was close to her, that he knew, like smoke clinging to his tongue.

He had no more hesitation, only the certainty one feels in dreams. With a slow exhalation, he let his physical form dissolve into light, the way all *upyr* did before turning wolf. Then, rather than reach for his beast, he sent his spirit flowing into Mariann, into the spaces between the molecules that made her up. By uniting their energies, he would leave behind the essence that made him immortal—like a yeast, Mariann would have said, that causes a bread to rise. The melding was unexpectedly sensual, a penetration beyond what solid bodies could achieve.

He expected to see visions of angels or stars such as other *upyr* had reported—though no one knew if these images were real. Whether they were or not, no visions came to Bastien. What he registered most was her: her broken body, her struggling mind blurring with his strong one. The ground was hard beneath them, the leaves a thin, damp mat. Without his presence she would not have felt anything at all. He had to fight not to lose himself in the link.

*I love you,* he thought at her with all his might. *Let me heal you. Let me bring you back.*

*Gramps?* said the tiny spark of her consciousness.

*I love you,* he said again, uncertain how to respond. If her grandfather could call her back, that's who he'd be.

She made a sound no mortal could have heard, a broken whimper that felt as if it issued from his own throat. Her pain ripped at his heart. Bonded with her as he was, he could not doubt she was his mate, the woman who could be his queen. Every instinct he had screamed out that truth. He couldn't lose her. He'd rather follow her into the dark. Had he been certain they'd be together . . . but he was not. Death, and the rules by which it worked, was as much a mystery to him as to anyone.

His words came from the deepest recess of his soul.

*I've been waiting for you*, he pleaded. *Don't you want to stay with me?*

⚮

SOMEONE held Mariann, someone with a strong, warm chest and a deep, male voice. Another man was answering, a gentle murmur above her head. Pine needles muffled the tread of their feet. She was being carried through the woods. A fired burned in her ribs and along one arm, her bones crackling oddly like Rice Krispies in milk.

They're broken, she thought, the pain as distant as a dream.

She didn't have the energy to open her eyes. She tried to remember if she had rescued her grandfather's book, if she'd gotten to the bakery on time.

In the jumble that was her mind, she kept seeing a running wolf. The funny thing was, as soon as she thought it, she knew who her rescuer was. She couldn't understand why that felt so right.

"You're fine," said Bastien Luce, pressing his lips to her hair. "Even now your injuries heal."

Her temple rested on his shoulder, barely jogged by his tireless steps. When she listened for his heart it beat very slowly, though his body had none of the coolness it had shown before. Maybe he was a yogi to control such things. Maybe he slept on a bed of nails. She smiled at the silly thought. The way he carried her made her feel as safe as a child.

"Always," he said. "You'll always be safe with me."

She knew she was dreaming then. No one could be safe always.

<hr />

WHEN she woke, Mariann could not for the life of her think where she was. She felt really good—which didn't seem right—as if she'd been to an expensive spa. Wherever she was, the room she'd slept in was completely dark, and the bed definitely wasn't hers. The sheets were silk: impractical, heavy silk, their weight like sun-warmed water on her naked skin. Aroused by their slippery clasp, she had a powerful urge to pull them closer and roll around.

Instead, she forced herself to be still, her nipples sharp, her belly and knees tingling with unusual sensitivity. As she lay there, listening, she couldn't shake the sensation of being watched.

This, strangely enough, was the most erotic awareness of all.

The rasp and flare of a match confirmed her suspicion. Bastien Luce stood by what turned out to be a low platform bed, as gloriously naked as any daydream she'd ever had. One shade paler than his sheets, his skin was a pure, rich ivory, his eyes like jewels cut out from a Caribbean sea. His long, glossy hair shone black with garnet undertones, a cape around his broad shoulders. She felt ashamed for calling him pretty. In this light, on this night, he was heart-breakingly beautiful.

As if his appearance—and never mind his presence—were natural, he touched the match to a beeswax candle, which he set into a sconce that curled from the wall.

Despite her curiosity at her surroundings, her gaze couldn't stray long from him.

She noticed her eyes weren't working the way they should. Colors danced around him sheer as veils, the likes of which she hadn't seen since one of her more adventurous boyfriends had convinced her to try a funny mushroom. She felt a bit like she had then, just a heck of a lot less queasy and a hell of a lot more turned on.

"Don't be afraid," he said. "You're perfectly safe where you are."

Maybe she should have been afraid. Maybe she would be once whatever this was wore off. For the moment, she could only feel ebullient. She looked at his shapely arms and hands, at the cloud of hair on his chest and the mouthwatering six-pack to which it led. His navel caught a pool of shadow that made her throat too tight to speak. Whatever mickey Bastien had slipped her, he had gotten his money's worth. As her gaze trailed irresistibly down the furry line to his sex, she imagined she could actually see his veins expand. When he noticed her attention, she definitely saw him swell and lift.

And lift and lift, she thought, her teeth catching her lip until it bled.

The wound inspired a breathless laugh from him.

"Ah," he said, "I see you are experiencing some side effects of the change." He swung one knee onto the silk-sheeted bed, his erection bobbing at the move. Its head was shiny and taut. Obscuring her fascinated view, he propped one arm beside her and bent to drag his tongue across her bleeding lip. The action made her shiver violently. "Perhaps I could help you get through them."

She had no idea what he meant, nor did she care. She grabbed the arm on which he was braced, yanking it toward her as she rolled his torso under hers. She wanted to crow as she straddled him. For a man of his size, he'd proved surprisingly easy to pin.

Happily, his arousal didn't fade at all. His penis thrust straight as an arrow up from his groin, hard enough that it didn't lay on his belly but hung an inch above, vibrating like a tuning fork. Mariann wanted to taste it so badly, her mouth watered.

"I'm going to give you what I owe you," she warned, her voice gone thick with lust. "And after that . . ." Unable to resist, she bent to nip his neck. "After that I'm going to ride you till you hobble like a cowboy at a rodeo."

"Ah," he said even more breathlessly than before, "I guess the answer to that is 'yee-hah.' "

---

CONSIDERING her fangs were already a trifle sharp, what Mariann proposed to do was on the daring side. Bastien could not have cared less. When her greedy mouth plunged over his aching cock, he simply arched his back and groaned. Her tongue was a touch of heaven on his throbbing shaft.

"God," she said, drawing back from the first tight pull. "You taste like ambrosia."

He probably tasted slightly of blood, that fluid a part of everything they were. Since she immediately sank down again, he decided he should be glad.

She had him trembling at the dozenth stroke, had him grabbing fistfuls of the sheets and holding his breath. She was deep-throating him without an effort, her newly tamed head of curls a silky tease against his abdomen. He could tell she'd been good at this as a human. As an *upyr,* she was sublime. Not satisfied with her amazing oral gymnastics, she cupped his balls, pressing them gently but firmly between his legs. That pressure increased the one inside him until, pushed to the shuddering edge of bliss, he started to relax and let go.

To his dismay, she took this as a signal to call a halt.

He cursed as his glans popped free of her clinging lips.

"I want you to last," she growled, crawling over him on all fours. "I want you to go all night."

He didn't have the breath to tell her he would no matter what she did.

"Wait," he gasped as she poised herself.

Her eyebrows rose until they disappeared behind the tendrils of her hair. "If you're about to say you're 'almost afraid' to make love to me, you're going to be on my sh—, uh, bad-person list."

He laughed at her determination not to curse, running his hands in admiring circles around her hips. She made a beautiful *upyr,* a bit more rounded but just as strong, the white glow of her skin faintly touched by peach. "I know you're eager," he said, "and, believe me, I am grateful. My only request is that you come down slowly for that first thrust."

Her grin was crooked. "Scared I'll hurt you?"

Happiness swelled inside him at her teasing, beyond any emotion he thought he'd know. "I think I'm up for whatever you can dish out. I just want to savor this. No lovers have more than one first time."

Her eyes filled unexpectedly, her pupils shining within their newly crystalline blue. "You know, you're pretty sweet for a weirdo."

"Honey, you haven't begun to taste how sweet I am."

She shivered at the roughness of his voice, her delicate fangs making dents in her lower lip. The evidence of her lust sent his sex surging painfully. He could hardly wait for her to discover the rest of her powers.

Her teeth bit a little deeper as she took him into her palm. The clasp had him quivering exuberantly.

"Can you hang on?" she asked, her forehead pinched with a crease of doubt. "If you need a break—"

He pulled her down and kissed away her breath, careful to lick the sensitive spots behind each eyetooth. More than a little affected himself, he broke free with a gasp. "No breaks, Mariann. Take me slowly, then ride me hard."

"All right," she said, "since you asked for it."

When she put his tip against her entrance, both of them jerked. She was ready for him, hot and generously wet. His fingers tightened on her hips as he watched her thigh muscles tense. Her eyelids fluttered when she pushed down.

True to her promise, she took him languorously.

"Oh," she said at the reach and stretch of him deep inside. Her head dropped back and rolled. "Oh, boy."

"A little more," he whispered, devastated by her clasp, by the tempting arch of her neck. "Push all the way."

She planted her hands on his shoulders and did as he asked. For just an instant, he had a sense of how he felt to her: her instinctive caution at his male invasion, her more modern shame at her delight. His size seemed too much for her—too thick, too hard—and at the same time just enough. Her eyes went round, her fingers kneading fretfully by his neck.

"Wow," she said. "I think—" She stopped to give her hips a delicious grind. "I think whatever you slipped me made me grow a few extra nerves. I can feel you up to my throat."

He laughed. "I didn't slip you anything but this, love." The upward swivel he used to illustrate made her groan. "What you're feeling is who you are."

Her head was shaking from side to side, her distress obvious to see. Her nipples stood out like pale pink cherries against her breasts. "I've got to take you," she said almost fearfully. "Now. And I've got to take you really hard."

"I wouldn't stop you if I could."

He slid his hands up in encouragement, over her new and slightly lusher curves. The moment he brushed her nipples, she went wild. She didn't even wait for him to pluck them. She bucked on him like the rodeo cowboy she'd threatened to make him earlier: hard, merciless thrusts that had his body screaming with pleasure and his teeth gritting for control.

He clung to that control with all his will. After her talk of needing a break, he was damned if he would come first.

She went over with a muffled scream, her body stiffening with her head thrown back, her nails breaking his skin. Not yet knowing why it excited her, she licked her lips at the scent of blood. "More," she said, her hips going even faster. "I can't—I have to have more."

Snarling with a response he could not control, he rolled her under him and began to pump. He had more strength than her, more speed. He shoved an arm beneath her waist to tilt her for the best angle, the one that let him bury all his length. Thankfully, her hands braced on the wall to help. The arch of her back lifted her breasts. She shuddered when her nipples scraped against his chest hair. His fangs were so sharp he could not have hid them if she chose to look.

"Harder?" he said because he wanted to hear the hunger in her response.

"Yes," she gasped. "Oh, yes."

Their madness could not have been more in tune. She came again and it made him crazy, the shudder of her belly, the way she moaned and pulled him in for more. He'd never felt anything like this, not even with his own kind. His body ruled him. He literally could not have stopped what he was doing. He couldn't bring himself to want to. This leap into the void was pure, carnal joy, especially knowing she needed it as much as he did. Her heels dug into the mattress, one hand clamping on to his buttock for leverage. He grabbed the bedframe and prayed it wouldn't break. He was slamming into her with all his strength, his orgasm swelling with tsunami force.

"Feed," he said, the order harsh. "Sink your teeth in my neck and drink."

He had so little control he'd thralled her without meaning to, and she was still young enough to go under. Her head snapped up and her fangs broke through his *upyr* skin. Fire burst in his body, a long, hard groan burning his throat. He hung on the edge of jubilation.

"Drink," he rasped and she did.

He came like the world was ending, one cock-wrenching spasm after another as she took his lifeblood into her veins. His pleasure was a spur to hers. He felt her quiver and heard her moan. The grip of her luscious, climaxing flesh returned him to full erection before he could fade.

*Upyr* weren't known for being swiftly sated, but this surprised even him.

Her mouth fell away as she collapsed beneath him, her lips reddened by his blood. She licked them and blinked in wonderment, the blue of her eyes turned to flame.

"What," she said, "did we just do?"

He kissed her before her wonder could turn to fear, discovering he couldn't quite stop thrusting. Slower was the best he could manage, and hopefully with more finesse. When her arms came hesitantly around his back, he moved his kiss to her neck. His beast panted in approval. This was what he needed: to put his mark on her, to drink in her vibrancy.

She turned her head to give him access, wanting his bite even if she didn't realize what that meant. He dragged his tongue along her tendon, tracing a delicate line of blue. Her calves tightened invitingly behind his hips.

"Ooh," she said, unable to put into words how nice what he was doing felt.

"You promised I'd hobble," he murmured against her pulse. "Why don't we see how long that will take?"

He sucked her skin, hard, lingering over the anticipation. She was his now, after all the centuries of loneliness. A heartbeat longer

was all he could bear. With a groan of triumph, he claimed his
prize. To his relief, her sigh at his bite was long, her fingers twining
in his hair. As he fed, he tasted a hint of himself. Most of all,
though, and most arousing, he tasted her surrender.

# Five

THE outraged female shriek dragged Bastien from his rest. It came from his simply appointed bathroom, a match for his spare, Japanese-style room. Bastien enjoyed the massaging shower jets, but didn't have much use for plumbing aside from that. Whatever he consumed, in either of his forms, his body converted to energy.

Thinking Mariann must have seen her reflection in his full-length mirror—a myth he enjoyed debunking—he rubbed his face and sat up. His room was shaped like a dome, with recessed golden lighting that mimicked the rays of the sun. Thus lit, Mariann looked quite fetching when she stomped back in.

"Eight pounds," she huffed, fists planted firmly on her naked waist. "How can a person gain eight pounds overnight?"

He'd forgotten about the digital scale, acquired for an experiment to see if he could gain weight. He couldn't, as it turned out, but he'd thought the device so clever he'd kept it around. Both he and Emile loved technology.

"Surely you don't think you're fat," he said reasonably.

"That's not the point. I never gain weight. Never. It drives everyone who knows me mad."

"I expect they'd be interested to hear you enjoy it."

"Well, of course I enjoy it. I'm a woman!"

He could see this discussion was veering off track. He patted the futon beside his hip. "We should talk. Come sit down."

"I don't think it's nice of you to hide your toilet," she added as she complied. "Plus, I couldn't find a comb or brush. My hair came out all funny this morning. I look like a poodle."

He pulled her hand from where it was tugging her glossy curls, which were transformed just like the rest of her. When humans changed, they became the ideal expression of their genetics. Height, weight, even age shifted to conform to rules for beauty that transcended culture and time. That being the case, it amazed him that she could complain. Women were stranger creatures than he had guessed.

"You look wonderful," he said, kissing her knuckles. "Absolutely flawless. And you obviously needed those extra pounds or you wouldn't have them. I promise you, though, you'll never have to worry about gaining another."

She stared at him. "No man can promise a woman that. What if my metabolism is getting slower? This could be the start of my downhill slide. Pretty soon I'll be as roly-poly as people expect."

He didn't know whether to sigh or laugh. Of a certainty, the next few minutes were going to be more difficult than he thought. He put his hand on her perfectly rounded thigh. "Mariann, what do you remember about last night . . . before we burned up the sheets?"

"I remember you must have slipped something into my drink."

"You remember drinking?"

"No, but—" A strange expression crossed her face, her brain trying to remind her of the seemingly impossible. Grimacing, she pushed the prodding away. "It has to be that. I never act the way I did with you—not that it wasn't fun."

Her faint peach blush charmed him to his toes. He patted her leg in thanks. "I appreciate the compliment. Now think back, don't you remember riding your bike home from O'Faolain's? Don't you remember being struck by a car?"

"Of course I don't. I . . . oh, my God. Arabella. She ran me down." Her mouth dropped open and her hands went to her breast. "Please tell me she didn't get my grandfather's book. Damn it. I'm going to wring her stupid, lying neck!"

"Mariann! There's a bit more going on here than your vendetta against your ex-partner. The injuries you took were fatal. If I hadn't changed you, you would be dead."

"Don't be ridiculous. If I'd been that badly injured, I'd be in a hospital."

Even when he explained, she fought belief. He had to take her through the proof step-by-step: how she felt, how she looked, how thoroughly she had enjoyed biting his neck. Judging it too much to absorb, he refrained from telling her about his wolf. The omission didn't seem to help. Finally, he pricked his forefinger and waved it beneath her nose.

She shrieked as her fangs shot out.

"I can't be a vampire," she wailed behind her hand. "Who's going to feed my cat?"

He would have laughed except she began to weep. Feeling helpless, he pulled her against him and rubbed her back.

"How can I run O'Faolain's?" she sobbed, her tears running down his chest. "You can't be a pastry chef if you can't eat. That bakery is my life!"

"You'll have a new life, I promise. You can't begin to imagine how much fun you'll have. Please stop crying, love. I don't think I can bear it."

"You don't understand."

"Tell me then," he said.

She sat back and frowned at him, clearly deciding how to explain. "When I was eight," she said, her palms rubbing at her knees, "I baked my first dessert for my parents. It was a caramel apple tarte tatin—a fancy apple pie, I guess you'd say, though the presentation was tricky. I practiced for weeks with my grandfather.

I was convinced it had to be perfect. Only then would my parents understand why I had to spend summers in Maple Notch. Only then would they realize there wasn't any point in sending me to camp. I didn't *want* to be like other kids."

"And was it perfect?"

"It seemed that way to me. Slid right out of the mold with every apple slice standing straight. I can remember my mother's reaction like it was yesterday. 'Why, that's pretty enough for a restaurant,' she said like I'd performed a miracle. My dad—who was a big, tough factory foreman—took a bite, set down his fork and teared up. He said he was honored I would bake for him.

"That's when I understood about cooking coming out of love. My parents and I were very different people. My mom thought baking was something you did with a mix, and only because you *had* to. When I made that dessert for them, that was the first time I could share my heart."

By now, the evidence of her tears was gone. Unfortunately, forgiveness had not replaced them.

"You did this," she said, in a frighteningly level tone. "Without my permission. Knowing full well I'd be forced to give up everything I care about."

He didn't want to feel defensive, didn't want to acknowledge she might be right. Instead, he folded his arms across his chest. "Call me crazy, Mariann, but I thought you cared about your life."

"You had a thing for me. You said it yourself. You'd been thinking about kissing me since we met. You . . . you . . . ."

"Changed you?"

"You changed me because you wanted me to be your sex slave!"

She bit her lip as if this sounded silly even to her. Bastien might not have handled this situation as well as he could, but he knew enough not to laugh.

"You aren't my sex slave," he said. "What happened last night happened because you are *upyr*. All your appetites will be stronger.

You'll control them better as you go along." He laid what he hoped was a calming hand on her upper arm. "Until that happens, I assure you, I'd be happy to help you out."

Unamused, she swatted away his touch.

"I'm going home," she said, rising to gather her discarded clothes. "I need to think."

A panic he tried to subdue welled in his throat. "You'll have to return by sunrise. We're twenty meters underground here. Your house isn't shielded. It will be years before you can risk more than a few minutes out."

She stopped with her T-shirt half pulled down. In her expression, he could see the truth hitting her again. "Will sunlight kill me?" she asked. "Is that part of the stories true?"

He turned away to hide the agitation her question stirred. When Emile spoke of giving Mariann a choice after Bastien changed her, he hadn't thought she'd truly want one. He'd thought he could make her happy. He'd thought she would fall in love. He saw now how naive he'd been.

Pressing his fist to his breastbone, he released a breath. "Yes," he said as steadily as he could. "Emile and I have some resistance, but young as you are, you could burn completely within ten minutes. Immolation is painful, to say the least, but if you were determined, you could succeed."

She said nothing, as if the answer sobered the last of her rage. After a pause, he heard her pulling on her pants. The sound of her zipper preceded her voice.

"Is it nighttime now?"

"Yes," he said. "You slept through the day. When the morning gets close again, you'll feel sleepy. You'll have more than enough warning."

"Even if I can't see the sun?"

"Even then."

He didn't know the words to stop her, and wasn't sure he ought to say them if he had. Instead, he watched her walk to the door. She paused on the threshold, one pale, perfect hand curled around the frame. Every one of the dings and cuts she'd been so proud of had disappeared.

"I understand why you saved me," she said quietly. "I might not approve of the way you did it, but I understand."

He had no response for that. Grateful though he was, her understanding was a million light-years from what he craved.

———

MARIANN found her way out of Bastien and Emile's outrageously elegant subterranean residence without consciously knowing how. The bunker was, she gathered, a series of domes connected by tunnels. The various halls bent like a maze, the dozens of doors suggesting the prospect of future residents.

During the course of his explanations, Bastien had said they "weren't very many." She hadn't had the presence of mind to ask what he meant. Were there hundreds of *upyr* in the world? Thousands? Intuition told her there couldn't be more than thousands or people would have noticed. Not sure she wanted to dwell on that, she let her body lead her, her nose sensing the dew-soaked night beyond the earth and rock.

The secret door moved at the touch of her hand. She suspected it wouldn't have if Bastien hadn't allowed it.

Once outside, she followed a slightly overgrown walking trail through the woods. Her sensitivity to sound was eerie. Every creak and crackle registered. This was not, however, the only change in her perceptions.

Her brain itself seemed sharper than before.

The accident—if Arabella's actions could be called that—was coming back in vivid detail. Despite the technicolor memory, she was having trouble believing it had occurred.

*A vampire.* Bastien Luce had made her a vampire.

*Upyr,* she corrected herself, wishing mere semantics could ease her mind. Though she tried, she could not imagine how she would cope with being one. Every turn of her thoughts brought another obstacle into view.

She reached the back of her house much sooner than she expected, her new and improved legs having eaten up the distance in record time—yet another trait she'd have to learn to hide from her friends.

The mere idea overwhelmed her. How on earth was she going to face people she knew? Her friends weren't stupid. Linda at the Clip 'n' Curl noticed if Mariann even thought of cutting her own bangs.

A rising and falling growl of feline discontentment snapped her gaze to the porch. To say Pirate Vic was bristling was like saying the Sahara was dry. Her poor cat looked like someone had stuck his tail in a socket. The last time he'd puffed up like this, he'd been the sorriest abandoned kitten she'd ever seen, spitting behind her Dumpster at the bakery.

Obviously horrified by her appearance, he'd backed up all the way to his kitty door.

With a lump in her throat, she hunkered down before the steps. "It's me," she cooed. "Mariann. The one who feeds you kibble when you're worn out from chasing mice."

At her voice, the low yowling stopped. Though his tail still twitched, his fur went down to half-mast.

"That's right," she said encouragingly, "come sniff my fingers and see it's me."

After a few false starts, he came, giving her one aggravated nip before butting her knee and breaking into a noisy purr. She hadn't realized how much he meant to her until she hefted him in her arms. She refused to acknowledge the fact that he smelled sort of yummy. Vic was her pet and she'd protect him no matter what. It wasn't like she'd ever felt the need to eat everything in sight. Vampire or not, there were rules.

"You still feel heavy," she said tearfully into his ruff. "I guess my vampire strength's not all that."

She carried him into the kitchen and fed him with extra

scratches and praise. She left him crunching happily while she went upstairs. Her bedroom mirror was not full-length, merely a waist-up square above her chest of drawers. She figured this would be less intimidating than the tall one in Bastien's bath.

Even so, she gritted her teeth to brace herself once she pulled off her clothes. Her eyes went wide as she took in the view.

She was hot. More than hot. She was curvy, something she'd never been in her life. Stepping back, she turned to the side to check out her breasts and butt. J Lo's rep was safe but, honestly, she was fine! She slid one hand over her stomach, which—to her relief—she didn't have to suck in. She had to admit she didn't hate the hint of voluptuousness. She did notice she wasn't creating a light show the way Bastien had last night, but maybe that was because she was new.

No doubt about it, though: her skin was seriously pale, more cream than white but close enough. Then again, for all she knew she would look snowy to human eyes.

I'm not a human, she thought, her knees giving out so that she had to sit on the bed. I'm not a human and if I were I would be dead.

She pressed her hand over her heart. Despite being upset, it beat slow and steady behind her ribs. Curious, she stretched her legs off the floor. Those were nice legs: hairless legs, so she guessed vampires didn't shave. She supposed she'd figure out the rules for why as she went along.

"You need to do that," she said to herself aloud, then rose to put on a fresh outfit. Her clothes were tighter than she was used to but they looked all right—sexy, if she told the truth.

Arabella would die of envy to see her looking this good.

She wrinkled her nose at the reminder of their enmity. Right now getting back at Arabella didn't seem important, no matter what she'd tried to do. Mariann had a date with her refrigerator. Bastien could drink espresso . . . and wine, as she recalled. Before she gave up her old life she was going to see just how much of it was ruined.

As Gramps liked to say, "If the third time's not the charm, go ahead and try the fourth." That philosophy had made him a patient teacher. She was counting on it to keep her from despair tonight.

THE Night Owl's reception area was Bastien's favorite part of the inn. The first section to be refurbished, it was a cozy Gothic hall with star-shaped ribbing on the ceiling and a carved oak desk like something out of a rectory. Though it was a romanticized Victorian version of the Middle Ages, Bastien took no offense at inaccuracies. For him, the style was a bridge between the modern day and his birth, a place he could feel at home but not out of step.

Behind the desk, fifteen cubbyholes waited for messages; before it, a Persian rug would welcome weary feet. Bastien didn't mind that he would never gaze out the mullioned windows during the day, or that he would have to turn much of the business's running over to others.

He had conceived this, had made this bed and breakfast a place where humans could step out of the humdrum and into another time. If it never made a penny, he'd still be proud of the accomplishment. To his mind, its greatest value was not as a potential profit center, but as a window on the mortal world. Humans and *upyr* shared the planet. In order for his kind to thrive, more of them needed to understand their fellow travelers. For those *upyr* who agreed with him, his door would remain open.

The ambition of the project occasionally took his breath away— his first taste of running anything in a thousand years. He had enjoyed being in charge more than he should. Whatever denials he'd given Emile, he had been born to rule. He could not doubt it standing in this tiny kingdom that he had made, certainly not with Mariann's accusations ringing in his ears.

*You did this. Without my permission. Knowing full well I'd be forced to give up everything I care about.*

She'd hit the target truer than she'd known. He'd thought himself beyond such dictatorial behavior, but he'd been wrong.

Regrettably, being born to rule didn't mean being born to rule well.

Impatient with his mood, he dropped into the reception desk's swiveling chair, rolling back and forth on its bronze casters. Despite his regret, he didn't see what else he could have done. Did it make him a horrible person to admit he preferred Mariann's resentment to her demise? That regardless of what she wanted, he'd do everything in his power to keep her alive? He couldn't bring himself to alter his decision, even knowing it might be wrong. In truth, what he wanted more than anything was to grab the scruff of her neck and drag her safely home.

She *was* his pack, he thought stubbornly, just like Emile. Never mind the *Upyr* Council had not approved his elevation to the rank of leader. Never mind he didn't entirely approve of it himself. Nature was nature. If it wasn't a higher law, at the least it was a law that shouldn't be ignored.

He stood abruptly with his resolve, his hands spread across their as-yet-empty reservation book. He would go to her. It was madness to leave her alone in her current disheartened state. Now was the time to press his case. She might have been a vulnerable human before, but tonight she was strong enough to fight.

As far as he was concerned, that was all the fairness she would get.

---

BASTIEN had never been in her home before, though he'd spent a night or two staring longingly at the windows. Considering his intent, he didn't wait for an invitation to poke his head into her bright kitchen. Its simplicity surprised him. Apart from a serious-looking stove, everything in it could have been found in any aging farmhouse.

He was disconcerted to find her sitting cross-legged on the linoleum with an array of dishes scattered around her. She looked up at his appearance, then shoved back her curls and sighed. Seeing how weary she was threw a wrench in his plans to bully her into his arms. Quite obviously, she wasn't up for that.

He could, however, take comfort in that fact she didn't appear annoyed to see him.

"I thought you might be thirsty," he said, lifting the bottle that swung in his hand.

Mariann eyed it suspiciously. "Wine?"

"Better," he said and popped the cork with his thumb.

The blood was dark as he poured it into a clean jelly glass. He had bought it—like the rest of his stash—from a local blood bank employee, one he'd thralled into believing he had a strange fetish. Bastien didn't bother feeling guilty at taking advantage of this convenience. It wasn't always practical to feed directly from humans. Besides, with what he paid for a single pint, the bank could purchase three more. Blissfully ignorant of these considerations, Mariann accepted his offering. She sniffed the drink, grimaced, then downed it in a single toss. A delicate flush rose to her cheeks.

"Jesus," she said against the back of her wrist. "It's totally disgusting how good that tastes. I think my mouth just had an orgasm."

He smiled, glad she was comfortable enough to speak that way to him. He poured himself a glass, this one decorated with a creature named Porky Pig. That done, he crouched down to refill hers.

"You know," he said, remaining where he was as she took a more moderate sip. "I could tell you which human food is edible. Save you the trouble of trial and error."

"Nah," She shook her head. "I'm kind of enjoying figuring it out for myself. So far I've got watered-down coffee, consommé, pulpless orange juice, and unsweetened Kool-Aid, weirdly enough. Apparently, anything with milk is totally repellent. I haven't figured out chocolate yet, but I'm thinking the pure cocoa liquor without the fat might be doable."

"That could be," he said. "I never met an *upyr* who tried."

"That's because you've never met an *upyr* pastry chef."

Despite her attempt at humor, he heard the fear and bitterness in her tone, the unspoken implication that *former* pastry chef might be a more accurate term. With a gentleness he hoped would convey his sympathy, he drew one knuckle along the side of her down-turned face. Mariann closed her eyes.

"I didn't mention this before," he said, "because it seemed too much to explain right away, but my line of *upyr* are shape-changers. We need to, er, form a connection with a real animal before we can do it, but once you take your wolf soul, you'll be able to eat what you like."

At this her head came up, her wide blue gaze zinging into his. "Take my . . . ? You mean, *you're* the wolf who ate from my hand? I should have guessed. You both have the same green eyes."

Emile would have laughed to know how flattered he was that she noticed.

"That was me," he agreed, trying to hide his pleasure by being businesslike. "So, conceivably, you could cook in your human form, then change into your wolf to taste what you'd done."

"Well, that shouldn't cause any comment!" She laughed but not happily. " 'Could you turn your back for a moment, Heather? My wolf has to see if this batter needs more salt.' "

"I didn't say it was a perfect solution—"

She stopped him by touching his arm. "No," she said softly. "It's a great deal more than I had when I was vomiting ice cream into that sink. Thank you for letting me know."

Her sincerity embarrassed him. His shoulders lifted in a shrug. "We'll probably have to go to Canada to find your familiar. There isn't much open wolf territory in the States."

"That's all right." She ventured an awkward smile. "I hear Canada is nice. And, hey, you already speak French."

"Mariann." He wasn't sure what he meant to say, but found he couldn't go beyond her name. This stilted conversation, while nowhere near as bad as it might have been, was hardly what he'd had in mind.

She must have sensed his frustration. "I'm sorry," she said. "I didn't mean to sound flip. You saved my life. I should be grateful."

"No." He dropped from his crouch onto his knees, wanting with all his heart to touch her again. "I'm the one who's sorry. Not that I saved you, but that I can't give you back what you lost."

"I'm stuck," she said with the sheepish air of someone making a confession.

"Stuck?"

"In the past." She spread her hands to indicate her surroundings, from the dated cabinets to the noisy old Frigidaire. "This is my safety blanket, this house and the bakery. All I ever wanted was to be like my Gramps. Daniel O'Faolain was a great guy, Bastien. The greatest. Give you the shirt off his back and the last brownie on the plate. Listen to you talk till his ears fell off. My parents were good people, but from the time that I could toddle, Gramps was my best friend. Grams used to say we must have been siblings in another life. Every year, I'd cross off the days until I'd come back here. If I lost the bakery . . ."

Fighting tears, she pressed her fist to her teeth. "If I lost the bakery, it'd be like losing him again. Everything I do, he's with me. Everything I know, he taught."

In spite of her best efforts, her tears spilled over and her voice wobbled. Without an instant's hesitation, Bastien pulled her against his chest.

"Crap," she said, "I'm sorry for being so weepy."

"Don't worry about that. *Upyr* shoulders dry very fast."

"So I noticed." Her laugh was muffled in his shirt. "Kind of handy."

He felt such complete devotion as he kissed her hair, he could have wept himself. "You'll find new things to love. I know it doesn't seem that way right now, but you will. And in the meantime, I'll do everything in my power to make sure you keep as much of your old life as you can."

She pushed gently back from him, her eyes glistening like rain-kissed aquamarines. "You're being really good to me," she said as if afraid of making it a question.

"It isn't hard," he assured her, coaxing her back.

He was, after all, only following his heart.

# Six

MARIANN let herself rest against him, not crying anymore, but enjoying the way his shoulder seemed specifically formed to cradle her cheek.

Though her nose was sharper than before, he smelled better: not just like a forest, but like a man—a slightly salty, slightly musky scent. Just as nice was the strong but easy circle of his arms. With a soft, satisfied sigh, he tilted his head against her hair. If she'd ever felt this comforted by her ex, she couldn't recall it now.

Though the contentment she felt might be an illusion, she was reluctant to let him go.

"This place is a mess," she said with no particular compunction to clean it up. "If someone came in now, they'd think I'd been attacked by hungry thieves."

"I'll help you straighten it," he said.

She smiled to herself when he didn't move either. Then her gaze fell on the oven clock.

"Shoot," she said, sitting back. "It's four A.M. I should be at the bakery. Heather will think I slipped a gear."

"I can call her like I did last night. Tell her you haven't fully recovered from your accident."

"I can't do that. Heather's never done all the baking by— Oh, no." She hit the center of her forehead. "Last night. I slept through my shift."

"I'm sure she managed," Bastien said, but she was already stuffing trash into a Hefty bag. "At least let me go with you. You'll need my help to look human."

"Damn it," she said, annoyed afresh by the reminder, then quickly apologized. She wasn't used to depending on other people for things like this, important things, things she couldn't do without. Her nerves didn't settle until they were walking side by side on the road, and his hand reached to clasp hers.

"You can count on me," he said, but that wasn't the problem.

Allowing him to comfort her was way too easy, way too pleasurable. Power flowed across the link between their fingers in smooth, warm waves. She'd felt the tingling before, but her perception of it was stronger. She wondered if he was trying to calm her, if that was among his gifts.

"Just how old are you?" she asked, looking up at his starlit profile. His features could have been cut from marble; they were that motionless and serene. Seeing him this way, she realized how much of his nature he'd hidden up until now.

"I was born around eleven hundred or so," he said. "Anno Domini. I was a forester—a gamekeeper, you'd call it—to a large estate in Burgundy." His mouth twisted wryly within his otherwise unmoving face. "I was not a popular figure, since my job was to prevent the starving rabble from poaching my lord's *lapins,* sometimes by rather Draconian means.

"One day, I caught a wolf who was not a wolf in one of my traps. The jaws of the trap were iron, a weakness of ours, which sapped his *upyr* strength. Unfortunately for me, as soon as I opened it to remove what I thought was a carcass, the wolf sprang up and changed into a man. Because I had more stubbornness than sense, I fought him . . . nearly to my death.

"I suppose my ferocity impressed my opponent. Auriclus decided to change me rather than let me die of my wounds."

"That was his name, Auriclus?"

He shook himself from the past and met her gaze. Watching him, she couldn't tell what he thought of his sire. "Yes. We do not have many elders, but he is one. Only an elder can change a human to what we are."

"So you're an elder."

"Not officially, but yes."

She knew this answer only told part of the story. His fingers were noticeably stiffer within her own. "Could you get into trouble for saving me?"

"That is conceivable, but not likely. Many of the *upyr* on the Council are my friends. I suppose I must pray they trust me to know what I was doing."

A gravity she didn't understand shadowed his words. "Well," she said, hesitant to pry, "I suppose I should be extra grateful you stretched the rules."

He stopped and turned to her, his back to the darkened road, his hand closing tight on hers. The glow she had seen the other night flared in his eyes. "It was my choice to do what I did. I couldn't have let you die. I love you, Mariann. In all my years, I've never felt anything like this."

The passion in his voice struck her speechless. He sounded like a crusader before a war. At that moment, she could imagine him living a millennium ago.

He loves me, she thought, the truth of it sinking home. Her happiness at hearing the declaration, her need to believe it, put a knot of wariness in her neck. Who fell in love like this? And with her?

"That's . . . quite . . . flattering," she said, the words coming out on separate puffs of air. "Considering you've been around since way back when."

She didn't see his expression shift, but between eye blinks it turned sad. His right hand rose to brush a curl the breeze had blown across her cheek. "My words weren't meant to flatter."

"Bastien," she said.

Maybe he sensed she intended to warn him he was going too fast. She wasn't ready to give him the trust a good relationship required. If this was what he expected, he didn't want to hear. He waved toward the intersection that marked the edge of town.

"We should not dally," he said. "Heather will be concerned."

<hr />

SOME *upyr* were born with a knack for glamour, but Mariann wasn't one of them. Bastien suspected she was going to have to learn the hard way, by experimenting over time. While he could cast the illusion of normalcy over her himself, he had to be touching her to maintain it, a requirement that would make working with her assistant impractical.

"No kidding," Mariann burst out once he'd explained. "Why did you even bother to let me come?"

They stood outside the bakery door, speaking in tones no human could have heard.

"I could thrall her," he said. "That lasts longer than a glamour."

"Thrall her?"

"It's a form of hypnosis, of brainwashing. It changes what people believe, as opposed to just what they see."

Mariann wrinkled her nose.

"It requires that I bite her first," Bastien added, wanting to be clear. "A blood-bond helps cement my power." She opened her mouth, then shut it when he laid a hand along her jaw. "There's something else you should know. Your friend is pregnant. From the looks of her aura, the father is the boy with the tattoo."

"Pregnant." Mariann's voice was so breathy even he had trouble hearing her response. "And you can see that? Wow." She rubbed her arms as if they were cold. "She'll want to have it. She's crazy about Eric, and she loves kids. But she'll need her job more than ever. She has no other experience. If I can't keep the bakery going, I don't know what else she can do."

"Emile and I could hire the boyfriend as our handyman. Make sure he gets a good, steady paycheck."

"That's very kind, but not as good as Heather being able to support herself. Frankly, I can't imagine her swinging a hammer."

Bastien smiled, wondering if she realized how modern such sentiments were to him.

Mariann looked up, her brows drawn together above her nose. "Would biting Heather hurt the baby?"

"Not physically. After a brief period of weakness, being bitten strengthens the human immune system. The baby would benefit as well. Chances are good, though, that the child would be born with a predisposition to my influence. Among our kind, in part because of my age, I'm a skillful shaper of minds. The question is, do you trust me not to abuse my power?"

He shoved his hands in his pockets to keep her from seeing them shake. Though he hadn't tried to read her, her doubts—about him, about men in general—were obvious.

She stared at him, her gaze as sharp as a knife. That was one trait she'd kept from her human days.

"Heather is yours," he said, "just as Emile is mine. I wouldn't do this without your approval."

"Mine to protect, you mean."

"Yes."

She paced away from him and stopped, head bent, arms crossed, the toe of her silly blue sneaker tapping the grass. "You've never thralled me," she said without turning around.

"I wanted to win your love, not compel it."

She sighed and faced him again. "I want that, too. I want Heather to interact with me just as she would have before, even if she sees me as human. I don't want her free will diminished in any way. If you can promise it won't be, my answer is yes."

He released his breath gustily. "I can promise. I'm very, very good at what I do."

She laughed, though he hadn't meant to be funny. "Modest, too."

He discovered her gift then, the particular *upyr* talent that expressed itself most strongly in her. She came to him with a swiftness that was little more than a blur, a movement that to humans would have seemed instantaneous. Putting her hands on his shoulders, she rose on tiptoe to kiss his cheek.

"I trust you to keep your word," she said, "which is more than I'd say about most of the world."

He pulled her to him and held her tight, thinking she'd never know what a gift she'd just given him.

───────────

HE had tears in his eyes when he pulled back. Mariann could hardly believe it. Apparently, her approval meant a good deal.

"Do you want to come in with me?" he asked.

She shook her head. "I said I trust you. Plus"—she rubbed one finger across her lips—"I, uh, don't think I'm up for watching you enjoy it. If my experience with a cold glass of the stuff is anything to go by, it's pretty much impossible to take blood without pleasure. But don't worry. I'm not the kind of girlfriend who freaks out over every smile. I'm a mature modern woman. You go do your thing."

Amusement had been playing around his lips. Now it broke into a grin. " 'Girlfriend,' " he repeated. "I can live with that. But don't *you* worry." He leaned close enough to whisper in her ear. "I fully expect, even hope, that you shall come to be possessive."

His shift to teasing rattled her. She could only watch as he stepped jauntily into her bakery. Remaining outside while he went in might have been her most surreal experience yet.

"Mature," she said to the swinging O'Faolain's sign. "I am entirely grown up."

She let five minutes pass, then ten, before her curiosity drove her in. The front room was clean and quiet, the floor recently swept. In spite of being left to her own devices, Heather had managed to stock the displays. Mariann saw an awful lot of cookie bars, but they seemed to have sold well enough.

"Checking up on my goods?" Heather said from the kitchen door. Mariann wasn't sure what she'd been expecting, but Heather's grin was the same as always: wide and full of sass. She looked her employer up and down. "You look good, boss. Playing hooky must agree with you."

"I . . . I didn't—"

Before she could stammer out an explanation, Heather squeezed her into a hug. Behind the girl's back, Bastien smiled at her and shrugged. He looked, Mariann thought, extremely pleased with himself.

"I'm glad you're all right," Heather said. "Not that I begrudge you your night of fun. You and Bastien are made for each other. It's just that working on my own was, like, totally horrible. I miss it when you don't teach me the baking stuff. Those jerk-offs at the cooking school were way too stick-up-the-butt, expecting me to be, like, Ms. Cordon Bleu before I even got there. You made me believe I could learn."

The compliment affected Mariann more than she expected. Blinking hard, she patted Heather's back. "I won't leave you alone again," she promised. "At least not for a while. You don't need to be overstressed."

Heather fell back from her, mouth agape, then turned accusingly to Bastien. "You told her! It was bad enough that you guessed. I wanted to break the news myself."

Bastien pressed his hand to his heart. "My heartfelt apologies, Mistress Heather. How may I make amends?"

"You can't," Heather said. "And don't call me that goofy name. Man. Old people think they don't have to ask permission for anything."

Ignoring the jibe at Bastien's age—more appropriate than

Heather knew—Mariann assured her she was happy if Heather was. Heather turned pink and mumbled a response, something about Eric and her not getting married yet, but being prepared to "act like a team." Whatever Bastien had done to impose his thrall, he hadn't changed the real her.

"I'm proud of you, kiddo," Mariann said, "keeping this place together by yourself. A lot of employees would have thrown in the towel. That tells me you and Eric should do fine. Why don't we—" She paused to take a breath. "Why don't we go back in the kitchen and I'll show how to make my grandfather's famous Vermont Mountain Fudge Cake."

"Really?" Heather cocked her head. "Your Gramps's recipe? Like, can I copy it down and all?"

"You bet," she said, feeling strangely light. "You're part of my team, too. It's time I treated you that way."

"Wow," said Heather. "Cool."

<hr />

"SHE thinks I'm a good teacher," Mariann said, still hugging the memory to her. "And she didn't seem to find it odd that I made her do all the tasting. I know it's early yet, but maybe this will work out."

Bastien squeezed her hand, then let it swing between their hips. He didn't have to say a word. She knew he guessed how sweet her optimism felt, as sweet as knowing their thoughts were in harmony. Every time their fingers twined, the contact felt more natural—until she gave up on trying to fight her pleasure. Now they were climbing the grand main staircase at the inn, following the curve of mahogany risers to the second floor. The Night Owl was dark, but Mariann could see everything perfectly, down to the muted greens and browns of the wallpaper.

She had to admit she liked her new hypersenses. Her nose had told her the state of her cooking almost as well as Heather's tastebuds.

At the top, they stopped to admire the black-and-white diamond patterns in the marble floor below. Apart from a few empty
spots in the decor, the renovations looked done. Seeming nervous,
Bastien released her hand. Mariann pretended she didn't mind.

"So," he said, "how does the place strike you?"

"Quiet. Plush. Even though a lot of this stuff is new, it looks like
the real McCoy. I feel like I'm time traveling."

"Good," he said. "That's what I wanted."

"Figure you'd get the humans to meet you halfway?"

"Perhaps. Of course, halfway for me would be more like the
Renaissance."

"I'm afraid I never was much for counting if it didn't involve
spoons and cups."

"Ah," he said, a sound that came out as awkward as it was
pleased. She suspected he was leery of putting a foot wrong. Their
new rapport must have seemed as delicate to him as it did to her.

"Bastien," she said, hoping to make him relax. "Why do you
want an inn? It seems a peculiar business for a . . . an *upyr* to
have."

"Do you want the easy answer or the hard?"

"Both."

She turned to him, resting her side on the banister. He was gripping the rail with both hands. A human's knuckles would have
been white. "The easy answer is that I wanted a window on the human world, a place where my friends and I could learn to pass un-
noticed among mortals. As the years go by, we tend to lose touch
with what we used to be."

"And the hard answer?"

He let out a rueful laugh. "The hard answer is that I wanted a
little kingdom. I need to rule, Mariann. That drive is as strong in
me as the one for survival."

"You say that like it's bad."

He pushed off the banister to scrub his face. "Neither Emile or I
like to talk about it, but once upon a time, during a struggle for

dominance, our pack leader in France put a curse on Emile that weakened him bit by bit until it threatened to end his life. To die quickly is one thing. To die slowly we find particularly gruesome. For us, pain truly can last an eternity. Hugo chose this form of torture to intimidate me and anyone else he viewed as a rival. Emile and I escaped to Scotland, but getting away proved no cure.

"Because I was desperate, I tried to take over an established pack. I intended to use its members as soldiers to defeat the man who had cursed my friend. I employed magic and force and any trickery I could think of to get my way. In the end, I showed myself no better than my enemy."

"You used magic?" The word had rolled more easily off his tongue. "Isn't being a vampire magic enough?"

"There are spells we can do," he said, his eyes showing his awareness of her discomfort, "to increase our natural powers: our thralls, our glamours, all our inborn abilities. Most are forbidden, but people do break the rules."

"And you used these forbidden spells."

"I would have committed any act short of murder to save Emile." He signed. "I started my own little reign of terror, against people who had done me no wrong. I hope I've changed since then, but I can't say for certain how much."

Mariann pressed her thumbnail against her teeth. "What happened to the *upyr* you hurt?"

"They forgave me, even the man whose pack I tried to steal. They welcomed Emile and me to their home and found a way to heal his injuries. It was a miracle, for both of us, one I doubt I'll ever repay. Unfortunately, the years have made me too powerful to share our new pack leader's territory. Inevitably, we would clash. That is why Ulric banished me to America."

Sorrow roughened his voice, a regret that held the weight of all his years. Whoever this pack leader was, Bastien admired him. She suspected being exiled had cracked his heart.

She was beginning to understand just how big a heart he had.

"I don't know," she said, striving for lightness. "It sounds as if Ulric might have meant you well. Maybe he didn't want to fight you any more than you want to fight him. Maybe he sent you here because he thinks you'd make a good leader. It might have been his version of a friendly kick in the pants."

Bastien wagged his head. "I wish I could believe that."

"Please forgive me if this offends, Bastien, but I haven't met anyone who's terrified of you now. You treat Emile like a valued partner. You thralled Heather, and she's still not afraid to yank your chain. On top of which, there's me. I may be a pipsqueak compared to your pack leader but, trust me, I'm no patsy."

"No, you're not. You're the most wonderful woman I've ever met. I wish—" He stopped himself, his expression turning serious.

"I know what you wish," she said, her voice as soft as she could make it. "And I can hardly express how gratifying I find that. All I can say is, give me a chance to catch up with you. I've only known you liked me for two days."

"Do you think you can catch up?"

For all his beauty, for all his power, he was as bashful as a French schoolboy. Smiling, Mariann laid her hand on his cheek.

"Oh, I'm pretty sure of it," she said, "almost sure enough to promise."

He caught her up and laughed exultantly, swinging her around on the broad landing. Midspin he started to kiss her, adding a light-headedness of another sort. The instant she kissed him back, she was slammed against the wainscoting.

"You'll break something," she protested breathlessly.

His hips undulated between her thighs. Somehow he'd managed to work his hand under her waistband, and was cupping her bottom beneath her pants. The seam wasn't up to the added strain. Stitches tore as she licked him behind the ear.

"Never break things," he gasped when she added the scrape of her teeth. "I'm very careful of my strength. Lord. Help me get you out of these clothes."

Released from his hold, she peeled out of them, then stared pointedly at his crotch. His erection stretched his trousers impressively. He rubbed his palms along either side, the muscle and hair of his forearms exposed by his rolled-up cuffs. She could learn to love this look: half lusty businessman, half sex god.

Not that he needed those business clothes now.

"You, too," she reminded.

"What? Oh. Right."

His zipper whined down and parted, allowing his shaft to bulge from the opening. Before he could release himself completely and charge ahead, she put her hand on the throbbing arch. "Take everything off, Bastien. Including socks."

"What socks?" he muttered, then wrenched and shoved and hopped on one foot until he was bare.

She had barely drawn breath to comment on his magnificent naked state when she was kissed and lifted, her thighs pressed smoothly to either side of his hips. The tip of his penis nudged her, shifted to find its aim, then pressed thickly inside.

Groaning with gratitude, Bastien ground her against the wall. She had a second to savor the penetration before he began surging in and out. Then she could have groaned herself. The sensitivity she'd thought she must have imagined the other night had her shuddering on the brink by the fourth forceful stroke. Her whole sheath was as responsive as only a tiny part of her had been before. The effect was maddeningly sensual.

It did nothing for her control to think his nerves must be similarly multiplied.

"Don't crack the plaster," she said as her hands clutched his back and neck. To her dismay, half the words were wailed.

"Paper . . . covers it," he huffed, but he cursed and dropped with her to the floor.

There the only danger was carpet burn.

"Wider," he demanded, his hair falling around them, his grip already stretching her thighs.

"Yes." She gulped for air as he slammed in deeper, the head of him pummeling some secret pleasure spot. When her neck arched up uncontrollably, his mouth immediately nuzzled her pulse.

"Should warn you," he said against its frantic drumming. "The first time of the night can be very fast for *upyr*."

"The first time?" Her heels climbed to midspine.

"Believe me, once is never enough."

The warning was hardly unwelcome, especially when his hand slipped between them to find her clit. She groaned at the help she didn't even need. "How many . . . times . . . do you think you'll want?"

His kiss shut her up, his fangs sliding longer around her tongue. "Can't talk," he said. "Really . . . need to fuck."

He suited his actions to his words, his thrusting growing more urgent, his breath beginning to break in swallowed grunts. As if his life depended on more access, he grabbed one of her knees and shoved it higher still. Both of them moaned at the new angle. Supernaturally strong or not, she knew mere seconds lay between them and a genuinely explosive climax.

When he screwed his eyes shut and sucked a breath, she had to grab her chance.

"Wait," she said on her very last burst of air.

"Wait?" His disbelieving gaze burned into hers. His movements slowed but did not halt. "Mariann, this is not a good time to be testing me."

She flinched at his intensity, but didn't withdraw her demand. Tom had never let her try new things. If she couldn't claim more freedom as an *upyr,* when would she ever? At her silent insistence, Bastien's hips slowed to a stop.

"Suck my finger," she said, a little breathless for an order.

His brows went up. Then he nipped it instead.

Yelping, she yanked her finger back trickling blood. Her sex contracted hotly at the tiny pain. That was unexpected but interesting. Apparently, she was going to have all sorts of new tastes.

"I can heal it," Bastien suggested hoarsely, unable to resist probing in and out of her flickering sheath. "It wouldn't take but a minute."

Mariann pursed her lips in refusal. "That's very kind of you, I'm sure, but I have other uses for this."

"Other—ah!" He jerked as she found the tiny opening between his buttocks, the instinctive clenching of his cheeks unable to keep her completely out. "Ah, okay. Other uses." He laughed at her when she stopped. "Now, now, don't lose your nerve, love. I think you must have figured out I'm rather hard to shock."

"I don't want to hurt you."

"Can't," he said with a telling squirm. "Not like this."

Still she hesitated.

"Need a road map then? Or do you have a fair idea where you're going?"

"I know," she snapped. "Theoretically."

This made him laugh again, a reaction she silenced by forging determinedly ahead. From the sound of his gasps, he was far from minding. His muscles were trembling.

"You can feel everything, can't you?" she said, her voice dark with lust. "Every inch of you is sensitive."

"Yes . . . oh, God. We're all like this. We love being touched."

His passage was satiny and tight, twitching around her intrusion as if it were hungry for every stroke. The cut on her finger was as good as oil.

"Uh, Mariann . . ." He ground himself deeper into her body. "Would now be the time to mention that the presence of blood makes everything more intense?"

"Shh," she said, hiding a grin. "I'm trying to concentrate."

He was panting for air by the time the pad of her longest finger found the firm, almond-shaped gland. She stroked his prostate very gently, delighted by the way his cock thumped heavily in response.

"Well," she whispered. "Vampire or not, I'm glad to see you've got all your parts."

"Mari-ann." Her name was a groaning plea.

"Do you like it?" she asked more shyly.

Despite his obvious frustration, he smiled beatifically, fangs and all. "I adore it, love. And I'm thinking . . ." He slid slowly out of her and back in, his girth notably increased. "I'm thinking if I like it, maybe you will, too."

She squeaked as he made good on his threat—very good, as it happened, his wriggling finger clearly more experienced than hers. Sensation spread through her like clove-spiced wine. When he withdrew his hardness and thrust again, she thought her spine would melt at all the pleasure bombarding it. It was quite impossible to restrain a moan.

"Tit for tat," he murmured against her neck. "And please do keep rubbing me."

"My toes are going to come," she warned, feeling them curl into the back of his calves.

"Be my guest, because I'm not stopping again."

Despite his threat, he stroked into her with a fond half-smile, balanced on one elbow, not quite pumping but getting there. His gaze held hers captive, his muscles tense beneath their shimmer of faint pink sweat. She licked his shoulder to see how it would taste and nearly climaxed just from that. Sensing her reaction, his pupils expanded over his irises.

When she squeezed herself around his penis, they went startlingly black.

"Bite me," she said, knowing only this could make the act complete.

For a moment, she thought he would tease her for her choice of words. Instead, his face abruptly changed: darkening, tightening, his lips pulling back in a feral snarl. He seemed more inhuman than she'd ever seen him, and she seriously doubted any force on earth could stop him now.

The realization was more thrilling than she would have guessed. She wanted to be claimed, to be ravished in the fullest sense of the word. She threw her head back in invitation. Bastien muttered a curse and struck.

Like white-hot lightning his fangs pierced her skin while his lower body worked furiously. The first suckling pull threw her into bliss. The second had her crying out. He groaned in answer and shoved so deep they both slid along the carpet. He was gone then, over the edge, coming in time with his swallows in bursts so long and hard she could count each one. The knowledge that he was taking his pleasure set her off again. She clung to him as if her orgasm were an ocean she could drown in, the waves rolling over each other in crashing spumes.

When she cried his name, he shuddered and collapsed. Silence reigned for long minutes. His head came up weakly at last.

"Whew," he breathed, sounding amusingly American.

"I'll see your 'whew,'" she said, "and raise you a 'holy cow.' I thought vampires couldn't sweat."

He laughed and rolled her atop him, his hands already sliding into new mischief.

"We can sweat," he said. "We just need a good reason."

# Seven

GIVEN their recent sexual olympics, sleeping through dawn was no great surprise. The first dusty rays were creeping across the foyer when Bastien roused. Though he gave it his best attempt, the stupor that came with daylight could not be cursed away.

Fortunately, no windows overlooked the balcony where they lay. Unfortunately, if they didn't leave the Night Owl soon, they'd be forced to spend the day in the basement.

Bastien looked down at Mariann, now metaphorically dead to the world. He doubted she'd enjoy waking up covered in cobwebs . . . or being spotted by a contractor.

His bleary mind saw only one solution. As quickly as he could, he rolled her in an area rug, yanked on his clothes and tossed a blanket over his head. Carrying her fireman style, he ran across the grounds and through the woods to his residence.

This would have gone smoothly except for the fact that, midway through his mad dash, Mariann woke and began to scream. He had to use his mind-voice to keep her from alerting any early dog walkers who might be out.

When he unrolled her at the bottom of the hidden steps, she stumbled like a drunkard. She wagged a finger unsteadily.

"A secret passage," she said, "connecting the inn to here, might not be out of place."

Bastien caught her elbow as she swayed. "Emile and I are still debating that. We're not sure we want to risk the possibility of a human guest accidentally finding the door. A single entrance is easier to guard."

"Fine," she said, bending to collect his blanket. "Let your girlfriend burn up."

Her irritation pleased him. They were squabbling like a real couple. He had to wipe off his smile when she snapped around. This time her accusing finger was completely straight.

"You spoke in my head."

"That I did."

Her eyes narrowed as she tucked the blanket beneath her arms. "Next time you do it, try saying something nicer than 'shut up.' "

"I will, love," he promised. "Any time you like."

He steered her toward the great room, hoping to grab a glass of sustenance before bed. They'd both wake happier if they weren't starved.

"Wait till you see this," he said, looking forward to her response. "I think it will reassure you we aren't stuck in the Victorian age."

Apart from its dome construction, the design of their largest room was classic Frank Lloyd Wright: stone floors, substantial leather furniture, lots of simply finished solid wood. Lush potted palms made up for the lack of windows. Discreetly screened, the refrigerated walk-in could store a year's supply of blood. The true pièce de résistance, however, was the wide screen, wafer-thin plasma TV.

Like their human counterparts, Bastien and Emile had been helpless before its siren call.

From the sound of things, Bastien assumed Emile had forgotten to shut it off.

This turned out not to be the case.

"Perfect timing," Emile exclaimed, surprising them both as they walked in. "I've got something you'll want to watch."

———✦———

BASTIEN'S friend sprawled in the corner of a cavernous leather sofa, shirtless but clad in his usual faded jeans. In the light from the nearest Tiffany lamp, he looked as fresh as a daisy—not what Mariann expected in a subordinate vampire after sunrise. Seeing him so casual and assured, the thought came to her that he might not be Bastien's junior in power by much. Maybe he deferred to Bastien because he would rather his friend be in charge.

By contrast, Bastien looked slightly haggard as he plopped beside him. "You're sure whatever this is can't wait?"

Emile's grin was devilish. "If you don't watch now, you'll miss it. You see, while you two lovebirds have been shagging each other senseless—congratulations, by the way—yours truly has been a busy boy. *En voilà.*" He pushed a button on the remote. "It's time to see my work bear fruit."

The opening credits to *Cooking with Arabella* appeared on the screen: Arabella dazzling her numerous male guests, Arabella making sultry faces while she licked her finger, Arabella wiggling her curvy butt as she served a gooey slice of Vermont Mountain Fudge Cake.

The reminder of her perfidy was more than Mariann could stand.

"Crap," she said and turned to walk out the door.

Emile caught her wrist before she could. "No, no," he said. "Trust me. You're going to enjoy this show. It's very special and very 'live.' "

"What did you do?" Bastien demanded as Mariann allowed herself to be coaxed onto the couch between them. Big as it was, both men contrived to bump her knees.

"Do? Well . . ." Emile laid one finger along his cheek. "I might have paid the divine Arabella a visit after I traced her licence by hacking into the DMV. I might have bitten her and, yes, it's possible that, in passing, I could have mentioned it would be nice if she confessed her thefts and—just in general—told the truth."

"You thralled a human to tell the truth." Bastien's tone was a mix of incredulity and awe.

"Well . . . yes, but I mentioned the part about confessing to stealing recipes first. She didn't know she'd nearly killed you, by the way," he said to Mariann, the twinkle bright in his eyes. "She thought the worst she'd done is knock you out. Eaten up with envy, if you're interested. Evidently, her subconscious considers you to be indestructible."

"Well," Mariann said at this irony, her hand spread across her chest. Because Arabella had been so hell-bent on protecting her lie, Mariann practically was indestructible now.

The commercials over, the show was everything she could have hoped in her wildest dreams of revenge. Not only did Arabella confess to taking credit for Daniel O'Faolain's work, she also felt compelled to share her not very flattering opinions of her producers, her assistant, and her goggle-eyed audience. When she began to describe her fiancé's unfortunate shortcomings in bed, the station developed mysterious technical difficulties and went to black. When it returned, a repeat of *Emeril* was shouting "Bam!"

Emile quickly switched it off.

"Wow," said Mariann, "I almost feel sorry for her. She'll have a heck of a time digging out from this."

"Not to worry," Emile dismissed breezily. "I am not the strongest spinner of thralls. The effect should wear off within a month."

"A month!" Mariann couldn't help it. She covered her mouth and laughed. "Thank you, Emile. That's the second-nicest present I ever got."

"I have your book, too, if you want it." He flashed his teeth at her gasp of delight. "You may kiss me, if you like. Here, on the cheek."

She felt Bastien relax when Emile specified the spot, but a kiss was not enough for her. She hugged his friend as well, with all her rib-cracking *upyr* strength. As she did, a peculiarly vivid image flashed through her mind, of herself handing the recipe journal to Heather. The idea made her happier than she would have thought.

Maybe it was time to share her legacy.

"Oof," Emile complained laughingly. "And welcome, sweet Mariann, to Bastien's pack."

"My unofficial pack," Bastien corrected.

"That's what you think, old friend. Ulric—our previous pack leader—and I had a little talk before we left Scotland. Then Ulric had a little talk with the Council. You have been approved to act in your full elder capacity. They sent word by e-mail last night."

Bastien looked completely stunned. "You did that? For me?"

"Of course I did. You think I want someone else bossing me around?"

Bastien rubbed the side of his head. "I'm an elder. Me. I'm approved to run my own pack."

"You could have run one at any time," Emile pointed out, "with or without their approval. You only needed to trust yourself. Then again, maybe you settled that when you decided to change Mariann."

"Surely you didn't tell them I did that."

Emile reassured him with a shake of his head. "I'm not crazy. Better the Council think they had the power to say 'yea' or 'nay.' You were born today," he added to Mariann, "in case anybody asks."

"Is it just me," Mariann asked, "or is our pack really small?"

Bastien laughed and kissed her noisily on the mouth. "What an ambitious *upyr* you are. Already thinking like my queen."

"Wait a second," she protested. "I didn't say I wanted to be anybody's—"

He picked her up and kissed her more soundly. Even with Emile watching, even with the sun high in the sky, her insides began to melt. By the time he'd released her, her legs were firmly wrapped around his waist and the blanket had drooped dangerously. She suspected more than daylight had made her dizzy.

For one thing, his excitement was prodding her pointedly. He hitched her higher to improve the fit.

"I love to work," she warned, gasping just a bit. "My ex didn't like that at all."

"You'll get your work done faster than you ever did," he countered. "And I fully expect to provide you with good incentives for coming home."

The gleam in his eye made the hottest part of her squirm.

"All right," she surrendered. "I'll be your queen, but only if you dig that tunnel and make a room for my cat."

Bastien's grin was as broad as his friend's. "You'll be my queen because you almost love me, because you're nearly positive you will soon."

"You're a bully," she said, but she could see he didn't believe her. His arms tightened teasingly beneath her rump.

"I'm the man who will love you till the end of time."

This was an awful lot to take on faith but, as she laid her cheek in her favorite spot on his shoulder, Mariann thought she might manage.